The Strongman

The Strongman

Devon Layne

ELDER ROAD BOOKS
LYNNWOOD WA

CONTENTS

1

68-POUND WEAKLING

MY LOCKER STUNK. It was the smell of a forgotten ham sandwich, sweat socks, and a particularly pungent fart. Still, I disciplined myself to wait until I'd counted to one hundred, like Mikey had warned me to. I heard the class bell ring, but no one suddenly appeared to let me out of my locker.

Ninety-nine. One hundred. I was just thankful she hadn't told me to count any higher. I took hold of the string with a magnet attaching it to the inside of the locker door and gently pulled through the vent. The latch caught and I thought I'd still have to pound on the door to get someone to let me out, but then it popped up and released. The door swung open and I could breathe the fresh air of the school hall.

Fresher than the inside of my locker, anyway.

I was going to crush the guys who shoved me in my locker. Except they'd crush me before I even got hold of them. Stupid dumb jocks. My sister, Mikey, had foreseen something like that happening. She'd warned me. Before school ever started, she'd fixed the emergency release on my locker. As long as they didn't padlock it, I could pull the string through the vent and it would trip the latch.

Not that it's changed at all, but I wasn't a particularly brilliant kid. Not stupid, but just a little slow. My sister was the smart one. A year younger, she was already in seventh grade with me, and three inches taller. She had her whole life planned out and she was only eleven.

It didn't help that I was not only a little slow, I was a shrimp. Four-five and sixty-eight pounds. A sixty-eight-pound weakling. I thought that was funny. Dad said I'd continue to grow, but I doubted it. I seemed to have stalled in the past year. Maybe I'd grow a little *some*day.

I might have some kind of learning disability. Mom and Dad didn't want to get me tested because the stigma of being a special ed kid sticks with you forever. And I wasn't that bad—just slower. I had trouble paying attention and keeping up in class. I still have that problem sometimes, like keeping things in order when I'm telling about them. Mikey says my brain is just a wired differently.

Like this whole story about getting shoved into my locker in seventh grade happened a long time ago. But every time I walk into a gym, the smell reminds me of it and I automatically look around to see if those jerks are going to attack me again. Not that they'd get very far shoving me into a locker anymore. I'd like to see them try. I still had fantasies of stuffing one of the muscle-bound assholes into his own locker.

Of course, there were no threats to me in the locker room anymore. Especially not here at the gymnasium. I just always thought about it.

YOU MIGHT HAVE heard of me if you follow sports. I'm an elite gymnast. And I have to say, I've got good prospects. They might not be what I thought they would be, but they're still good. I have a few surprises cooked up for my next competition.

I know that doesn't sound like where I started. That Paul was the Paul I used to be.

My family wasn't poor or stupid. Just me. Dad was a campus engineer at the University. Mom was Human Resources Director at a big manufacturer down in Bloomington that made outdoor equipment for home and sports. Like golf carts and lawn mowers. We lived in a nice house that overlooked the lake near Uptown.

My parents suggested several times that I invite friends over. They were sure just having a lakeside house and game equipment and a home theatre would attract people. Yeah, Mikey's friends. Not mine. I didn't have any. And I didn't much care. My classmates were even stupider than I was. What was I going to do? Invite the dumb jocks who stuffed me in a locker over so they could beat my ass at Xbox?

Mikey is my sister Michelle. She didn't really have that many friends, either, I guess. She was younger than all the girls in our class and smarter than all the girls her own age. She just came home and studied after school. And sometimes helped me with my studies. She had her life all pretty-well planned out. Knew what she was going to study in college and where and how soon.

She's also my best friend. She's the one who started me on the path to change.

"WHAT ARE YOU going to do, Paul?" Mikey asked me after the locker incident. It was looking like seventh grade was going to be a long year... or two.

"I don't know. Wait in a dark alley after school and club 'em with a baseball bat?"

"Good grief! A baseball bat would just bounce off them, hit you in the head, and leave you with no memory of who beat you up."

"You have a way with words," I snorted. She laughed at me. I didn't mind that because Mikey laughing at me wasn't mean. She just had a way of seeing the humor in about any situation.

"Why don't you change?"

"What? Presto-change-o; I'm a football hero. Oops! That didn't work. Abra-cadabra; I'm an honor roll student. Damn! That didn't work either. If I went out for a sport, I'd spend practice locked in a stinking gym locker. And nothing on God's green earth is going to make me smarter or better looking or interesting to any girls."

"You're not that bad looking. The girls in our class are all too hung up on how *they* look to be concerned about how you look. They can't see beyond their own budding breasts."

"Neither can I," I groused.

I'd started noticing girls, but none would even waste her time talking to me. I wasn't *that* rich. It's funny. Even now, girls kind of shrink away when I talk to them. I try not to be scary. Tough luck.

I didn't need to worry about that with Mikey. She was a year younger than me and a year behind the budding breasts in our class. Besides, she was my sister. I was just thankful she helped me pass my tests. Barely, but I passed.

"Why not get stronger? That's something you can control. There's no medical reason for you to be a wimp."

Good old Mikey. She didn't mince any words. Not when she was talking to me. I could always depend on her to point out how stupid or wimpy I was.

"How am I supposed to do that?"

If I went out for a sport at school, I'd be dead before I could get strong. Besides, sports didn't really interest me.

"You could start lifting weights," Mikey suggested. "Dad has an old set in the garage. You could do that and no one would ever know."

"I thought the idea was that people *would* know." Sometimes my sister was too complex for me to follow.

"You want them to see the result, not the work it takes to get that result," Mikey said. "Remember the old saying, never let them see you sweat."

"I thought that was about fear."

"What's the difference? You've got a computer. Look up what exercises you should do and what you should eat to gain muscle. You don't need to be a rocket surgeon to follow the instructions on YouTube."

I guess what she said made sense to my underdeveloped brain. I went to the garage after school the next day and found my dad's old set of weights. What the heck? I might as well start lifting them. Then I'd shove a couple of jocks in their lockers and see if *they* could find a way out.

I KNOW THIS is out of order and all if you're trying to make this into a sensible narrative, but it reminded me of the first time I walked into the high school gym my junior year—after the change. I walked over to where the team was meeting and sat down with them. They all kind of edged away from me.

"Ladies, I'd like you to meet Paul Bradley. He's joining our squad this year," Mrs. Cook announced.

The girls all stared at me with big eyes and open mouths.

"Did he, like, even try out?" one asked. Funny. I didn't know any of their names.

"No," Mrs. Cook said. "I selected him."

I kind of thought she was just inviting the cheerleaders to object. One—a little girl I couldn't believe was in high school—stood up and came to stand in front of me. I don't think she was quite four-and-a-half feet tall. Well, I was still only a foot taller than I was at twelve.

"Lift me," she demanded. Like a toddler with her arms outstretched.

"How?" I asked.

"By the waist, straight up over your head, then hold me there."

"Okay."

She turned away from me and I stood up and put my hands on her waist. It was tiny. She bounced once and then I lifted her straight up. Her legs were kind of dangling in my face, but I just held her there as she spread them until she was in the splits over my head.

"Put me down now," she said. I lowered her to the floor and she turned to face me. She held out her hand. "I'm Penny Layne. I'm a flyer and you just became my base," she said as I shook her hand.

"Pleased to meet you, Penny. I won't let you down."

"At least not until I ask," she giggled. We sat down and Mrs. Cook started explaining what we'd be doing to compete in cheer. I hadn't known cheerleading was a competitive sport until my gymnastics coach had introduced me to Mrs. Cook. I always thought they just jumped up and down at ballgames with their boobs bouncing, and slept with jocks. I was about to find out very different.

Like, all the beautiful cheerleaders I imagined in my fantasies were sitting right there and I was stuck part-nering with a little girl.

Yeah, I'll go back and pick up where I left off. Or near then if I think of it. But I have to warn you that if you're expecting me to suddenly have a girlfriend and get to the sex part of my story right away, you're shit out of luck. Because I sure was.

It's not that I didn't *like* girls. I really did. I thought about them all the time. The pile of stiff socks in my laundry hamper was ample evidence of that. But at seventeen, I'd still never had a girlfriend, or even been on a date. And that wasn't likely to change in the near future. I'd been too busy, really, to be concerned about it. And I was still a bit backward. I'd grown physically, but my emotional maturity was still a zero. Mikey was sixteen and had a date every weekend. She'd graduate in the spring and be off to college. Those poor college guys were in for a rough time if they got involved with her. I was sure she'd take the university by storm next fall. I'd be a senior in high school and my year-younger sister would be a freshman in college. How ironic.

Anyway, what Mikey told me back when I was twelve sort-of made sense. I went to the garage after school and found my dad's old set of weights. I had to unload the plastic storage bin one weight at a time before I could move the bin to where I could easily get to them. I wasn't sure I'd ever need more than the two-pound dumbbells I took out of the bin, but what the heck? I might as well start lifting them. Then, one day, I'd shove a couple of jocks in their lockers and see if they could find a way out. Yeah. I guess I said that before.

After about two weeks, I noticed the weights didn't feel quite so impossibly heavy. I actually managed ten reps instead of five dumbbell curls and presses.

Dad surprised me by getting home early one night while I was doing my little routine. The whole thing took me about fifteen minutes.

"What's up, son? You've never been interested in weights before."

"Damn stupid jocks," I muttered. Then I was dumb enough to tell him about the locker incident and Mikey's advice. "One day, I'll be strong enough to shove 'em in their own lockers. See how they like that. Maybe I'll even get a girlfriend."

"That's a kind of vengeance. Can't say I blame you for wanting to build up your strength, though I hope you never have to fight them, and that you don't turn into a bully yourself. There's more to life than the physical. Being strong carries a responsibility to help and protect the weak. It's that way throughout the entire animal kingdom. The strong care for the pack, the herd, the flock. Whatever. Real strength is inside you—in the kind of person you are."

He reached in the box and pulled out a twenty-pound dumbbell and joined me in curls. Talk about making me feel weak and puny. I figured my dad could have pulled any weight he wanted out of the box and casually started curling it. He worked outdoors at the campus most of the time and he was really strong.

"I'll tell you from experience, just lifting isn't going to do you much good unless you get on a program and get some guidance. Besides, that makes it more fun. Is that what you want to do?"

"Not really," I said. "I don't like the gym teacher yelling at me all the time. I'd rather work alone."

"Hmm. I understand that. There are other kinds of activities that could build your body and get you active without an annoying guy with a whistle," he said.

"Like what?"

"Well, there's skating. I don't mean rollerblades around the lake, though that's a good activity. I was thinking of figure skating. Building up your body to do jumps and spins. Or Karate. Martial arts have a good focus on building your body and inner discipline. Gymnastics. Did you see the guys at the Olympics in gymnastics? Man, are they strong. And, of course, there's bodybuilding with a good coach who will coach you through it and not scream at you."

"Where would I get any of that?"

"Hmm. I don't have all the answers. Why don't you do some investigating and see what you find? I know there's a skating rink downtown. A martial arts dojo up on Hennepin. Oh, the other direction on Hennepin, there's a gymnastics and tumbling center. It's probably the closest thing to us here. Check them out and if you see something that interests you, let me know. We'll see if we can get you in."

Dad was like that. He'd make suggestions, but if I didn't follow through on them, it was my tough luck. My arms were going to burn like hell tomorrow because I kept curling the whole time he was talking. I put the dumbbells away and went to my room to look up the places online.

I HADN'T REALLY paid much attention to the 2016 Olympics in Rio de Janeiro. I was only ten at the time and they seemed like a world away. But weightlifting, figure skating, martial arts, and gymnastics were all Olympic sports, though not all in the summer. I settled in and watched a bunch of events online. They each had something going for them.

The weightlifters looked so musclebound they couldn't bend over to tie their shoelaces. I wanted to be strong and muscular, but I didn't want muscles piled up on top of other muscles until the only thing I could do was lift weights.

Figure skating was cool and the jumps and spins looked great. I could just imagine, though, that if anyone found out I was figure skating, they'd think I was gay. That's what I thought. It was a really girly sport, even though they were obviously strong. So were the girls. I didn't need to give anybody new ideas for harassing me.

Martial arts. *Wow!* I could just imagine myself twisting a little and throwing a 250-pound football linebacker over my shoulder. As I watched, though, I realized that in order to get to that level, I was going to get punished. A lot. I was already getting beaten up. I didn't think my best bet would be to invite more of it.

Finally, I got to the gymnastics events. Some cute girls, basically dancing on a beam or doing somersaults on a mat. Nice butts that were just about fully exposed. But the guys. *Wow!* I'd never seen such self-control. Their bodies were sculpted. They stretched and pulled. The gymnasts could hold their bodies in any position and then just press to a different position. Impossible positions.

I stupidly tried to do a handstand in my room and fell flat on my back.

"You okay?" Mikey asked from my doorway. "Sounded like you just crash-landed."

"Good way to put it," I mumbled, picking myself up off the floor.

"Oh, God! That guy is gorgeous!" she said looking at my monitor. I didn't think my sister was all that interested in guys, but if that was her opinion of a gymnast, it was worth considering. I *did* want to attract a girl someday.

I KNOW YOU probably think this is going to lead up to me and my sister getting it on. *Yuck!* I love my sister. She's cute. But sex with her? No. *Just yuck!* There are a couple of girls she hangs out with I'd like to see more of. Much more of. Like completely naked. *Oh, geez, yes.*

Even when I was lifting up Penny Layne my first week of cheerleading and her legs were dangling in my face, I wasn't particularly turned on by her I mean, sure, she's athletic, but she's really skinny. I'm sure if I'd been holding Georgia Nichols like that it would have been different. Georgia was in my class until a year previously when I extended my term in tenth grade. Now she'd graduate a year ahead of me. Georgia had boobs. And a butt that looks so soft and round. I sometimes imagined lifting her up like that, only she's naked and I look up at her as she does the splits. That's enough to get me hard in an instant.

Not that I'd ever actually seen that view. Except in porn. I don't know why they keep cluttering up perfectly good porn with overendowed guys' dicks. They really spoil the view. But Georgia. I can just imagine taking her clothes off. I know she wears a pretty sturdy sports bra when she's cheering—all the girls do—but I'd dearly love to see those beauties unleashed.

Of course, Georgia had a boyfriend, and it just so

happened that he's one of the football players who once shoved me in my locker. Still, taking Georgia away from her boyfriend would be just as good as shoving him in a locker.

A COUPLE OF days after my conversation with Dad— yeah, we're back to when I was twelve—I stopped by the Hennepin Gymnastics and Tumbling Center, a few blocks from my home.

"Hi. Welcome to the Hennepin Gym," a guy said when he spotted me standing inside the door looking. People were all over the gym working with several coaches. Mostly girls, but there was a guy on the pommel horse doing a routine while a coach watched him and called instructions. "Interested in learning gymnastics?"

"Like... um... How old do you have to be before you can do that kind of stuff?" I asked, pointing at the guy on the horse. He was bald, but I wasn't sure that was an indication of age. He might just shave his head. He was sure built strong.

"Eric is twenty-nine," he answered. "I'm Coach Dawson, by the way. I'm forty-seven. We've got guys in here as young as six, learning basic tumbling. When you're devoted to a sport like Eric is, you continue to grow and progress for a long time. He could do a routine like he's doing now when he was fourteen. He does it a lot better and more confidently now."

"I'm Paul. Twelve. Do you think I could learn to do that?"

Coach Dawson surprised me by tossing a bean bag thing at me. I caught it and it gave off a big puff of dust. I tossed it back and got ready to catch it again if he threw it.

"That's chalk. Good reflexes. That's one key," Coach said. "How strong are you?"

"Not very. I've been lifting weights lately. Trying to get built up some."

"Weights can be helpful, but remember, there is one weight you carry with you all the time, and which you have to support through every gymnastic exercise. That's your body. Push-ups, sit-ups, pull-ups, step-ups. They'll not only build your body; they'll build the muscles you need to be a gymnast."

"I didn't even think of that," I said.

"If you're trying to do it all on your own, you're unlikely to think of things like that."

"I looked at bodybuilding and weightlifting as a possible way to grow, but the guys all looked musclebound—like they wouldn't be able to tie their own shoes."

"You don't know how true that is. We call it hypertrophy and gymnasts have to train carefully to avoid it. There are two more components that we emphasize: flexibility and endurance. When you work in a program here, you will have balanced training in five areas: balance, reflexes, strength, flexibility, and endurance."

"I just want to grow big enough and strong enough to not be picked on at school all the time."

"There's never a guarantee of that," Coach sighed. "I truly wish there was. We don't teach self-defense. But being healthy and strong will make you confident, and confidence is a good defense in itself. Anyone who sees you perform will respect you physically."

"How do I get started?" I asked. I was ready to go try my hand at the pommel horse right now.

"We'll need a parental authorization first. You know, I hate to mention it, but someone has to pay for training. We also need a doctor's statement that there are no signs that you would be hurt by athletic training. Then we need to set up a program that is customized to your goals. How much are you willing to do? How hard are you willing to work? Those aren't judgments I make for you. That's a difference between Hennepin Gymnastics and a lot of other training programs around. There's no pre-defined color of belts you earn like in martial arts. There are levels of expertise, but they indicate when you've gained a specific skill, not when you've beaten a certain person. I want to make you as good as you want to be. If you just want to be stronger and healthier, we can do that. If you want to compete in gymnastics, we can get you ready for that. If you want to compete in the Olympics, like Eric's goal, we can get you ready for national and international competition. It's really all up to you and how much you want to work."

"I want it all," I said. I reached out and touched his biceps. "I want this. And I want that," I said, pointing at Eric, who had switched and was standing on his hands on the rings. Yeah. I wanted it all.

2
WORKING OUT

DO YOU HAVE any idea how much work it takes and how long it takes to change from being a sixty-eight-pound weakling to a strongman? I didn't get 'all that.' I mean, not right away. I got results, though. I felt stronger and I even grew a few inches in height. I didn't get winded walking to school—even in winter. Gymnastics was hard work. Coach Dawson was so encouraging and so gentle in his ways that he soon became my best friend.

At first, either Mom or Dad accompanied me to every workout. I get it. They'd sit in the bleachers and read a report or surf online. They were putting their tender young boy in the hands of men who coached him and worked with him and made him their friend. We'd all been given a class in internet safety and knew the signs of grooming. Better than most adults who panicked over having a gay teacher or letting kids read a book about transvestites. That's not grooming, parents. That's just education. It's not like going to church.

But Coach wasn't like that. He never touched me inappropriately or made any lewd suggestions. He worked the same way with both boys and girls, and there were always several coaches in the gym. I even got instruction from a couple of the women coaches.

I started going to the gym every day after school, once Mom and Dad had decided it was safe. It was what made my day worthwhile. I still had a thing about not going into locker rooms or showering at the gym. I went home for that. I trusted the coaches, but I wasn't sure about some of the guys who worked out there. Or some of the girls. I think a couple of the girls could have stuffed me in a locker without much problem.

Almost everything I did in that first month or two was getting me strong enough to do other things. I used the apparatuses to build strength, but you sure couldn't call anything I did a 'routine.' I supported myself on the parallel bars and did dips and leg raises. I hung from the rings and did pull-ups. I turned somersaults on the mats, and did jumping jacks. I did push-ups, v-ups—a kind of sit-up where you raise both your shoulders and your legs until you can touch your toes above your head—hanging leg-lifts on a high bar, and pegboard exercises. Those take a while to learn and actually be able to do them.

I didn't lift weights anymore. Coach told me that lifting tended to create the hypertrophy we were trying to avoid. He wanted me to stay flexible, so we did stretching exercises every day. I also jumped, and did backward and forward rolls. I really missed the gym on days I had off.

Nothing was automatic. Just exercising wasn't enough. I was still skinny, even though I'd put on a little weight. Coach said that was just replacing fat with muscle. When I asked Mom for healthier meals, she looked at me and told me to get in the car. She took me to the grocery store and made me select the food I thought we should eat, then she stood over me in the kitchen to teach me how to prepare it. Before long, I was pretty good at half a dozen different meals and I took my turn in the cooking rotation.

Mikey wasn't as enthused about that. Oh, she liked my cooking, but if I was cooking a couple of nights a week, she had to cook a couple of nights a week, too. I traded helping her in the kitchen with her helping me with my homework.

Oh! And did I ever start sleeping well! I used to stay up late at night playing on my computer. Then I'd be half-asleep through my morning classes. But by the end of seventh grade, I was zonking out as soon as I got in bed. Half the time, I didn't even masturbate! And I got up early enough to do my morning exercise routine before school.

I took a test at the gym, and according to Coach Dawson, I'd achieved a Level 4 Junior Olympic rating. I didn't know what it meant exactly, but it sounded impressive.

I don't know if I actually had more confidence in school, but it didn't bother me as much anymore. I still barely scraped by with the lowest possible passing grades. I still avoided every athlete I could identify in the halls, and there was a fair share of tough guys on the route home after school. The only time I got beat up, though, was when I stepped between a bunch of guys and my sister with her friends.

The guys didn't appreciate it. I got slugged in the stomach and punched in the nose. Oh, I fought back, but I don't think I landed any lucky punches before the school security guy came rushing up and broke it up. My mom wasn't happy and would have spent all afternoon yelling at the principal if I hadn't been bleeding and she needed to take me to the hospital. I was out of school for a week with cotton stuffed up my nose, and then had a metal bridge guarding my nose for a month while it healed. That sure helped my popularity at school—dipshit with a broken nose.

I still went to the gym every day to work out, and I didn't see that particular group of toughs around school again. I noticed that a couple of my sister's friends got boyfriends to join them as they walked home, and I was always included in the group. Not on purpose, I don't think. I was just going to the same place Mikey was. They could scarcely tell her brother to bug off. Besides, the girls I'd taken a beating for at least tolerated my presence now, even though they didn't really talk to me.

"You know, I'm impressed with your work and dedication," Coach Dawson said that summer. I was afraid he was going to tell me I was abusing my gym privilege by hanging around all the time. That wasn't it. "I think you could become a real gymnast if you wanted to work that hard at it. Think about your goals and let's arrange a meeting with your parents to talk it over."

A real gymnast. I immediately had a vision of myself hanging from the rings in the Olympics and wearing a gold medal. I talked to Mom and Dad and invited Coach over to dinner one weekend before school started in August. I cooked so he'd know I was following the diet, too.

"We know Paul is in better condition and we're all eating better," Mom said as we sat at the table. "What do you mean when you say upping his training?"

"As is usual, we've spent a good year in basic physical training," Coach said. "Paul is stronger and he's grown some. What's your weight and height now, Paul?"

"Five feet and a hundred even," I said proudly. My voice chose that moment to split on me and go in two different directions.

"And you're maturing," Coach nodded.

"Are you going to be a soprano or a bass?" Mikey teased. Everybody laughed and I just shrugged it off.

"By upping his training, I mean shifting from the Junior Olympics track we've been on and starting seriously to build routines on the apparatuses as a Junior Elite. Paul, you have good flexibility and reasonable strength. Now we want to put it to work. There are Junior Elite competitions this fall I think you should participate in."

"Please, Mom?" I asked.

"Frankly, I never thought you would be interested in anything beyond playing *Fortnite*," Mom sighed. She looked at Dad and he nodded.

"It's good to see you develop a healthy interest," he said. "You know eighth grade is a critical year before high school and isn't going to be easy. We don't want you to shirk your studies."

"That said, I guess it's okay to work out a more advanced training program," Mom said.

Mikey gave me a high five.

I GOT MOM to buy me a regular uniform with the gym logo on it. Coach made sure I got one that fit and for the very first time, I went into the locker room to get dressed for my training. I changed into my spandex tank top and stretch pants. I stood admiring myself in the mirror. I wasn't just a skinny guy anymore. I was wiry. I liked that term. You could see my arms weren't just sticks. I wasn't built with huge muscles, but I was doing okay.

I headed out to the gym to start my warmups. Coach had given me a complete routine he wanted me to do every day before we started really working. I headed to my usual mat and started stretching.

With the beginning of the school year, there was an influx of new kids in the gym. A lot of elementary school kids started with the beginning of the school year. So, the majority of those in the gym were young. That went for both boys and girls. I guessed most of the girls were between eight and eleven years old. I understood there were special classes for pre-teen girls who were self-conscious about their bodies and only women were in the gym during their training time. Most of the teenage girls worked out then, too, or assisted with the younger ones. I was always gone by then.

There were a few boys in the eight to twelve range, but as they got older, there were fewer and fewer who continued. Even at that, most of the kids were better than I was at almost everything. Then there were a few guys I only usually saw when they were working out early in the morning before school. High school guys who kept pretty much to themselves. The rest of the guys were above high school level, anywhere from college to Eric's age.

Anyway, I was stretching and warming up when I saw the group of four or five girls, younger than my sister, watching me and whispering. Then they outright laughed. Nice. Real nice, little bitches. I could see the ridge of bra straps through their leotards. Training bras for girls who had nothing to train.

"Hey, partner," Coach said. "Come over to the desk with me for a minute." He motioned me around behind the front desk of the gym and grabbed a pair of scissors. "You missed a tag on your new uniform." He efficiently clipped off the tag and handed it to me. I sighed and tossed it in the trash. Then I looked at him and we both snorted. "Let's get started on the parallel bars," he said.

Oh, well. Why would I care about what a bunch of ten-year-old girls think? I went to work and actually managed a couple of the moves coach had me try. It was the first time I managed a swing up to a handstand. It was a short handstand, but I made it. I was proud my arms could hold my body upright like that.

"HEY, DUDE!" ONE of the guys coming into the locker room said. Four of the high school gymnasts—senior elite, I was told—had followed me in. I tensed, ready to defend myself if I had to. "Nice handstand on the p-bars today," he continued. "You're coming along."

"Keep up the good work," said another. "Andy is going to be a senior next year and then we'll be looking for a replacement for him on the team."

"I see you work out every day, man," the one identified as Andy said. "That's what this sport is all about. Keep working every day. You'll get this."

"Thanks, guys," I said. They went on to their own lockers and for the first time in my life, I felt accepted.

I REMEMBER THE first time I asked a girl on a date. I know, this is out of order again. I was fourteen and in ninth grade. It was damn near the last time I asked a girl out. I don't think I heard anything in class all day because I was thinking about how to ask her out. It was the New Year, 2020, and I was determined that I was going to start remaking my image. I was nearly five-three now and I was pretty strong. I wasn't going to be a wimpy little pissant. I caught up with Cathy at the end of the school day on Thursday.

"Um... Hi, Cathy."

"Hi?"

"Um... Yeah... uh... Paul," I said, pointing at myself. "From your English class."

"Oh, yeah."

"I was wondering... um... if... uh... you might like to go to the game... and uh... the dance after with me... um... tomorrow night? I'd... uh... walk you home afterward."

Cathy looked like she was about to be attacked by a madman. I could see her shrinking in front of me. I looked around to see if we were about to be attacked and I guess that didn't help.

"No!" she practically shouted. "I mean, I can't. I can't date until I'm sixteen. And I'm not. Even close. So, no. Bye, Paul. See you in English."

She didn't quite run, but I was pretty sure the direction she headed off in wasn't toward her home.

Okay. Fine. I wasn't fifteen yet, either. I didn't think that made a difference when you were just going to an event at school and walking home together. And I sure didn't think the first girl I ever asked out would just turn and run away from me.

I sniffed at my pits, but I couldn't smell anything through my parka. One thing was sure. I wasn't going to do that again. *What the fuck?* I didn't know how to dance anyway.

I headed for the gym, and I might have worked out a little harder than I usually do. I was late getting home and getting dinner ready.

EVENTUALLY, LIKE FOUR years later when I was finally a senior and eighteen, I did ask a girl out and she accepted. Dana was cute and bubbly. I thought she'd be a lot of fun. And she was. We saw a movie and shared popcorn. We laughed as I walked her home and she took my arm to steady herself when she almost slipped on an early patch of ice.

We got to her house and I wasn't quite sure what to do, but I figured starting by saying I had a good time would be all right.

"Thanks for going out tonight. I had a really good time."

"Me, too. It was fun."

"Would you... um... like to plan something for next weekend?"

"Oh. Well... I don't think so. You're a nice guy, Paul. I had fun. But I'm, like, not into you like that. Thanks for the nice evening."

And then she darted into her house and closed the door. *WTF?* I tried to figure that one out all the way home. I put in a really intense day at the gym the next day.

WELL, ONE THING was for sure: I was progressing in the gym. After my first rejection when I was fourteen, I'd started spending even more time working out. I could do some pretty good flips in both tuck and pike positions in my floor exercises. I'd even placed in a Junior Elite competition for my level. It was my first medal. I was getting a good feel for the pommel horse and was gaining confidence on the parallel bars. Coach Dawson introduced me to Coach Anders. Coach Anders was working on my rings and horizontal bar work. Those were the two aerial events and were the ones that required the most upper body strength. I hadn't done more than the required vault yet, but that really felt like flying.

In case you didn't pick it up, there are six apparatuses in men's gymnastics: Floor, pommel horse, still rings, vault, parallel bars, and horizontal bar. Yes, the floor is an apparatus. It actually has springs under the floor and mat. You get a lot more bounce on that than if there was just a mat on the gym floor. That's the big difference between cheer and gymnastics. Cheer doesn't use a sprung floor. You only have the lift you get from your legs and hands. There's nothing that bounces you up farther. I'd learn a lot about that difference when I started cheerleading.

About half my daily exercise was on routines. The other half was all building the skills and strength needed to create a routine. I did two or three hundred push-ups and sit-ups each day. I walked all around the gym on my hands. I did jumps and flips. I supported myself on the p-bars and did dips and raises. And every single move was done slowly and deliberately. I was getting to the point I could stand straight, then flex my knees and propel myself into a full back flip without touching my hands to the floor. Forward flips required at least a couple of steps to launch, but I could do them.

I realized I was becoming a real gym rat. Any time I had available was spent in the gym. I'd been late to school a few times because I lost track of time during my morning workouts. Mom and Dad noticed.

I GUESS I'M all out of order again. Let's see. I turned fifteen on March 16, 2020. Coach told me I was doing really well and I'd be ready for more advanced competition this spring. It was possible I'd have my first Senior Elite competition this year.

I don't know if it was good or bad, but life intervened. I mean, I know it was bad. Awful, really. Two days after my birthday, the Governor ordered all schools closed and all non-essential businesses closed. Guess what isn't an essential business. The gym was ordered to close. I didn't care about school. It just meant I had to listen to the teachers drone on over my laptop. Mikey latched onto the process like it was designed for her. All our classes met online and she could work as far ahead as she wanted to. Occasionally, she'd pause to help me catch up.

Uptown was a ghost town. And then the riots hit after the cops murdered George Floyd. Mostly, I tried to stay low when I was outside, and not be seen by any police. You never knew who they'd kill. Or why.

I went crazy fast. My body craved the workouts. I found myself back in the garage doing push-ups and sit-ups. There was only so much I could do on the concrete floor. I did pull-ups from the rafters. We'd been told the shutdown would only be for two weeks, but it kept stretching on. All the competitions I might have been in were cancelled.

It was no easier for Mom and Dad. Mom was home from the office and working remotely. Dad had to get us a faster internet connection because three of us were online all the time. He still had to go to work. Being a campus engineer was considered an essential job. He was responsible for keeping buildings operating and problems dealt with.

As the lockdown stretched on, I rigged makeshift bars and rings in the garage. Dad got mats to put under me, but they were right on the concrete floor. Whenever I got tired of working out, all I had to do was go inside and turn on my computer to get the day's lessons. As if...

"You passed, but barely," Mom said at dinner the weekend after Memorial Day. She was looking at the printout of our school reports. "You'll both be sophomores next year. Yes, Michelle, we'll approve the AP courses you have requested for next year. Don't ask yet about the International Baccalaureate. We can consider that course of study when you're a junior. But you need to find some non-academic interests as well. You know colleges look at your extra-curricular activities as well as your grade-point."

"I know. It seems so stupid, but I'll find something to get involved in. As long as it doesn't take time away from studying," Mikey said. I kind of snorted and Mom and Dad both glared at me.

"You, young man, are going to need to cut back on gym time to focus on your grades," Dad said.

"No!" I exclaimed before I could get control of myself. I knew they would suggest something stupid like that. Mikey and I had talked it out and she hissed at me. "I mean... Um... Like... maybe there's a solution without cutting back on gym time," I said. "Um... Actually, I'm really doing well as a gymnast. Coach Dawson and Coach Anders both say I'm on track to compete in senior elite by next spring. Mom. Dad. It's the one thing in life I'm good at. Please don't take it away!"

"Dad, you guys are giving me the opportunity to excel academically. Thank you," Mikey said. "And I'll try to add that extracurricular stuff so colleges think I'm more attractive. But it wouldn't be fair if you denied me the opportunity to take AP courses until I became a cheerleader or some stupid thing."

"That would be a stupid thing," Dad laughed.

"It's just as unfair to deny Paul the opportunity to excel at something he's really good at because his grades aren't good."

"Even with a sport, though, no college will admit a student with grades like this," Mom said.

"I'm not interested in college, Mom," I said.

"Where would you compete after high school?"

"If I can make the grade as an elite gymnast, I don't need to have a college team. There are several independent gyms in the country that train elite athletes for professional competition all the way through to the Olympics. College is just one route. And you know, only a dozen or so colleges even have men's gymnastics teams. It's the same with things like figure skating and martial arts. Those just aren't big NCAA sports. Oh, women's gymnastics is, but not men's. There would be no reason for me to attend a college to be a gymnast."

"Why can't you learn your math and history as well as you learn your sport?" Mom sighed. I glanced at Mikey and she nodded.

"You and Dad could teach me," I said quietly.

"What?"

"You guys are smart. That's a great idea. Why don't you home school Paul?" Mikey jumped in enthusiastically.

"What makes you think we'd be more successful than the school?" Dad chuckled.

"Um... school just goes too fast," I said. "I learn the stuff, but by the time I learn something, the class is two more chapters ahead of me. If I could just limit what I studied to the necessities and not rush it, I know I could learn it."

Mom and Dad were silent. I could see the wheels turning in their heads. It was all I could do not to burst out with another argument, but Mikey had warned me about that.

"If that's really what you think you want to do, we'll investigate the possibility," Dad finally said. Mom nodded. "That isn't saying it's a done deal. We need to find out what the standard is and how we can manage a homeschool curriculum. And you'll need to show as much motivation to achieve the standard academically as you do physically. And son, you need to also be prepared to take longer than your classmates to get through the next year of high school. If we take a year to home school you, you might not be at the level that your current class is. You've got some catching up to do. In other words, your little sister might graduate with your class while you graduate with hers."

Wow! That was a sobering thought. I was a crappy student, but I'd managed to keep up with my year— though just barely. It was going to be a huge adjustment.

Or not. I was always considered behind in class. My teachers had pretty much given up on me keeping up with the class and were passing me anyway. They didn't want me around an extra year.

ON JUNE SIXTH, Coach Dawson called me.

"Paul, I'm going to open the gym to select trainees. There won't be more than a dozen people there at a time. And we'll all have to wear masks and wipe down the equipment every time it's been used. This COVID thing is serious. We've got a couple of coaches down with it. But with all the precautions in place, you can start coming back in to work."

"That's great, Coach. I can come right over."

"Easy, sport. We won't be open full hours and right now, no one is there. Let's plan on starting next Monday at ten. If you need more exercise, go out and run around the lake a couple of times. Then do all your body weight exercises. Just keep your mask with you."

"Okay. I'll do that. I'm kind of going stir-crazy here already."

"They say we've weathered the worst of it," he said. "Just be careful."

3

IDOL WORSHIP

I'**LL PROBABLY GET** back to talking about the lock-down and how it affected school and all. The remote learning environment on the laptop made home schooling supplemental. I did okay, but with just half the course curriculum. With that load, I could keep up. I was spending around six hours a day working out. As predicted, I ended up taking two years to finish tenth grade as Mikey went zooming past me. But I actually got it. I wasn't unable to learn. As Mom predicted, Mikey graduated with my class in 2023 and I officially became a member of the class of 2024. And a cheerleader.

Then, my senior year, I met the most beautiful woman I'd ever seen. It wasn't long after my one lone date with Dana that I arrived for cheerleader practice and saw Tara White with Coach Cook. I was instantly in love. I'd seen her in the Acrobatic Gymnastics World Championships in Geneva. You wouldn't believe the obscure sports channel I had to subscribe to in order to watch that on my laptop. It was beautiful.

But Tara had been injured in the dynamic routine

30

qualifying round and was carried off the floor on a stretcher. There'd been a flurry of stories about the extent of her injuries—unknown—over the next several days, and then the story dropped out of the news until it was reported that her partner, who had dropped her in the routine, had passed away.

The woman I saw talking to Coach Cook looked far more elegant, refined, and beautiful than the little girl I'd seen in the competition three years ago. She also sat regally in her wheelchair. I wanted to rush over and bow at her feet.

I restrained myself when Penny grabbed my arm with a grip hard enough to leave a bruise.

There was nothing between Penny and me except our cheer partnership. She had a boyfriend. She was still possessive. I have to tell you that Penny wasn't the only flyer on the cheer squad. She was the smallest and did some of the most difficult tricks with me, but two other girls were often the ones who mounted my shoulders or stood on my hands. I was the all-round base for the team. If all three girls were flying, or standing on top, the other two were each supported by two more girls.

I didn't cheer at ballgames or other sports events. From the first day I walked onto the gym floor with the cheer team, it was made clear I was there for their competitive routines where they did more acrobatics than when cheering at a game. I wasn't the only one. There were sixteen of us on the competition team. Usually, only five cheered at a sporting event. They were the ones who bounced up and down with their boobs flying and slept with the football players. No thanks.

"Paul, come here, please. Penny, you, too. Flyers and bases," Coach called to us.

"Yes, ma'am," I said as we ran up to stand before her.

"I'd like to introduce you to our new acrobatics coach," she said.

"Tara White," I finally broke in. I was too excited to see the phenomenal acrobat in person. "I was so afraid you wouldn't survive three years ago. I'm so happy to see you."

"Well, you have a fan," Coach Cook laughed. "For the rest of you, this is Tara White, one of the world's top acrobatic gymnasts until a tragic accident at the World Championships three years ago. She has recently relocated to Minneapolis and has volunteered to help coach our cheer squad this year. She will work primarily with our five bases and three flyers, but will have choreography suggestions for the entire team."

"Happy to meet you, Miss White," Penny said politely.

I thought Tara's smile was a little forced. She didn't really look much older than any of us. When I did the calculations, I finally decided she wasn't more than a year older than I was. Like all the tops in acrobatic gymnastics mixed pairs, she'd looked twelve when I saw her perform. I glanced at Penny. She would be eighteen soon and still looked twelve, as well. Tara looked *much* more mature.

We moved to a separate area where Tara rolled her chair to work with the acrobatic cheerleaders. We all did tumbling and flips, but only the eight of us did formations that involved two levels, lifts, and throws. We'd had some discussion as to whether we could do a three-tier pyramid formation, but hadn't come up with an answer. We weren't far into demonstrating our moves when one of the girls asked Tara if she'd teach us a pyramid. I saw her heave a big sigh and drop her head.

When she raised it, there was fire in her eyes.

"Paul, would you be kind enough to remove your shirt, please?"

I was really surprised. Our uniforms weren't even form-fitting. There were cheerleading rules about what we could wear and high schools were instructed to de-emphasize form-fitting tops and ultra-short skirts. There were specific rules about what panties girls had to wear and instructed men to have full-length bottoms. We all had to wear specific shoes.

But I'd probably do anything for Tara White. I pulled my shirt off.

Since I didn't dress with the girls, I couldn't think of a time when any of them had seen me bare-chested. It was a little embarrassing—not that I have anything to be ashamed of in that department. There were a few gasps or catches of breath. I'd been training in gymnastics for six and a half years now. I was not the skinny runt I was in seventh grade. I had a six-pack and nice set of pecs and guns.

"Ladies, I detect that you have not seen this shape revealed before. I want you to notice the musculature and the core strength. Paul, please bring your partner to your shoulders so we can see the muscles at work," Tara said.

Penny stepped up to me and did a stairstep mount to my shoulders. When she stood up, I held her ankles next to my ears.

"That move requires every muscle in the upper body, and several in the lower body I won't ask Paul to show you," she said. There were some giggles. "So, when any of you can show me comparable musculature and control, I'll discuss building a pyramid with you. You can gain that strength, by the way, by working in your trios on artistic formations. Anyone care to show me now?"

"Hardly," said one of the girls.

"You can come down now, Penny," Tara said.

Penny gave a little bounce and jumped off my shoulders into my arms. I set her on the ground.

"I want you to know that this is what happens to a flyer when her base drops her." Tara used her hands to lift one of her legs and then let it drop. It was completely limp. She maneuvered it back onto the footrest of her chair.

"Oh, shit. I mean... I'm sorry, Miss. I didn't mean to be vulgar," Penny said. She turned and looked me up and down.

"It's something I say on a regular basis," Tara said.

"What happened to your base?" one of the other girls asked.

"He killed himself rather than come to visit me," Tara said. "I'm not telling you any of this to make you feel bad. It's been three years since the accident and I'm more mobile than most paraplegics. I have strong arms and torso muscles, and even limited use of my legs. I want you to know, though, that I am deadly serious when I talk about the importance of your strength and support for each other. Now, let's work on some other formations you can do with a top and a base—or two bases."

During the COVID pandemic—I said I was going back to that—I didn't have to go to school. I mean *at* school. We all thought everyone was going back in the fall, but the damned plague just kept on and on. It was fine with me. Mom and Dad had agreed to help me at home for my sophomore year, even if it took two years. And it did.

Dad and I finished converting the garage into a gym for me so I could work out when I couldn't go to the gym. The gym was permitted to open in June, but on a limited basis. My time there was strictly for coaching, then I had to leave so they could get someone else in. I averaged only two hours a day. But I had a six-hour training regimen.

Dad borrowed a set of parallel bars, a pommel horse, and a set of rings that were being stored at the university. The rings were strictly for exercises, not for practicing a routine on. The rafters in the garage weren't high enough to do a routine. I practiced rings, vault, high bar, and floor exercises at the gym. I also got a pegboard and we laid a wrestling mat he salvaged on the floor.

Dad and I installed a metal carport from Home Depot in front of the garage and he made it clear that I was responsible for seeing that snow was cleared between the door and the carport and out the driveway to the street. We had about eight inches of snow on the ground from November through February, but it started melting off then with only a few storms through April. I never stopped to think about what all this was costing my parents, or to make a special point of thanking them until much later.

Between being locked down inside and my time in the gym or garage, I didn't have anything really to personally spend money on, so my allowance just got dropped in a dresser drawer. I had no idea how important that would become in the future. I was really lucky to have parents who were employed at a pretty high level and believed in providing for their kids. I've often mentioned that to them as I got older.

As soon as I had a space, I moved my laptop to the garage with me. When I took breaks from working out, I did my assignments for the day. I took classes on the school's remote access, like Mikey did, and we studied some together. Mom and Dad both checked over my homework each evening to be sure I was doing the studies and not just 'hanging from the rings.'

I couldn't do routines on the rings in the garage. There just wasn't enough height. I could do exercises on them, but... People don't realize when they watch a competitor on the rings, his coach is giving him a boost up to the rings which are hung 8'2" off the floor and 20" apart. But the rings are hung from straps anchored 18' off the floor. If you figure the angles and relative force it would take to press your body into a cross with your arms straight out, you'd be pushing the rings roughly five or six feet apart. You'd be forcing the straps out at a much higher angle if they were only anchored three feet above your head. You'd practically have to be touching the anchor.

Mom made me figure this all out in a geometry lesson. She's done that with a lot of the equipment. It was some of the stuff I understood best!

The rings in competition are called 'still rings.' That's as opposed to swinging rings, I guess. Part of the artistry is that the gymnast is supposed to do his entire routine without having the rings swinging from that eighteen-foot-high anchor.

I tell you all this to explain why, three years later when I was a senior and told to take off my shirt, my chest and arms were something to look at.

But... Oh yeah. Back in 2020 when I was doing two-thirds or more of my exercises in the garage, I was just building upper body strength on the rings, not doing a routine.

The same was true with the pegboard. Think of approaching a climbing wall. You find a new handhold and pull yourself up with your foot pressure and the pull of your arms. Two differences between that and the pegboard. First, you don't use your legs at all. Your feet are dangling. Second, there aren't multiple handholds. There are multiple holes for the pegs. To move up or across the pegboard, you have to pull one peg out of the hole while you are dangling from the other, then put the peg into the next hole and pull yourself up on it.

There's just enough height in our garage that I can do a limited routine on the parallel bars or the pommel horse, except I have to be careful with dismounts. Have to be careful regardless because I'm working without a spotter. I don't have a death wish.

DAD TOOK US all to the university to get vaccinated in September. We were back a month later for the second dose. It didn't look like people were taking it seriously, though, and cases started increasing again. You guessed it, the gym was closed again. Coach Dawson met with me by video link every day for the rest of the year.

There was a big protest to demand businesses reopen just before Christmas. The gym didn't. It wouldn't have made a difference to me because Mom and Dad wouldn't have let me go anyway. They took the whole warning system seriously. That didn't prevent Dad from coming down with the damn plague right at Christmas. He was home, but Mom was the only one who ever saw him when she took him meals in his bedroom where he isolated. We all wore masks in the house—and everywhere else. I know the masks were to protect other people, but even with our precautions, it was always possible we'd be carrying the virus and inadvertently expose someone else.

Because he was vaccinated, Dad's case was mild and in two weeks he tested negative and went back to work.

Too bad for his end-of-year holiday break. Mikey didn't return to school yet either, even though they were doing some kind of alternating days thing so only half the students were in class at a time. It actually looked like I might be keeping up with my class for a while. Except it was only in three subjects. I was considerably behind in everything else.

It wasn't until May of 2021 that I returned to the gym. Coach Dawson was on me from day one. I'd maintained my body building and stretching, but was way behind on my routines. And there were competitions coming up in June. He really wanted me to test and see if I qualified for Senior Elite.

I didn't. I would compete at the Junior Elite level for the summer and some of that was a stretch. I worked out nearly every day, doing my routines with a spotter. The gymnasts took turns doing their routines and spotting for each other. We worked hard and even though I didn't yet qualify for Senior Elite, I spent my workouts with the high school team at the gym. It looked like there wouldn't be a team the next year at that level. I was the only male gymnast working up to that level from our gym. The other guys I knew had graduated or didn't stick with things through the shutdown.

Things were almost what I called normal by January of 2022. I was going to the gym every day for six or seven hours. Then I studied for four or five hours, doing the lessons Mom had left for me. She'd returned to work, but was the primary parent monitoring my studies. I think she was depending on Mikey to help keep track of things.

Regardless, I was told that I needed to return to school in the fall. I'd managed to get far enough that I was considered a junior with a lightened workload so I could continue to train. The trade-off was that I needed to join the cheerleaders.

"Hey! I know you have to put your hand there to support me, but you don't need to squeeze," Penny complained to me after a lift.

"I didn't mean to," I said. "Really. It was just kind of a reflex."

"Boys! If I brushed a pacifier across your lips, you'd start to suck, wouldn't you?"

I had to think about that. *Well, maybe.*

"I guess, I'm sorry."

"Paul, you're okay, but every girl on the team thinks you could force yourself on her. We know you've got muscles that are ten times what we have. Just try to make sure there's no reason for any of us to be afraid of you," Penny said.

"I wouldn't hurt any of you! I'd never try to force myself on you. Jeez! What kind of asshole do you think I am?"

"I hate to be the one to tell you this, but you are a really strong and not very smart jock. At one point or another you have to touch nearly every girl on the squad. Some of us have to let you put your hand on our butts or inside our thighs or practically across our breasts. We just don't need you to be squeezing when you do."

"Oh, shit. I didn't even realize it."

"What? You don't realize you have our butts or our breasts in your hands? Be real!"

"No! I mean... You three are like little girls. That's the only reason I can lift you like that. What do you weigh? Eighty pounds? How would I even *know* I had my hand on your breast? How is it different than anyplace else on your ribs? Hell, I feel guilty if I even have a stray thought about one of you—like I'm a pedophile. I'm not interested in any of you like that."

"Strangely, that makes me feel more insulted than comforted. I am *not* a little girl. So, I'm small. I'm seventeen years old. I'm a woman. Stop thinking of me as a little girl!"

"Wait! I don't want to think of you like that! I don't want to always be wondering if my hand is on your breast. I don't want to think of your butt as more than what you sit on when I'm picking you up. Jeez! You want me to think of you sexually? No!"

"Oh, crap! That sure turned out backwards. I started out telling you not to think of me that way and then I complain that you aren't. Okay. Just, for what it's worth, no matter how you think of me, remember I've got a boyfriend and I'm just plain not available."

"I..."

"Don't say it! Even when it's what we want, we don't want to hear you actually say we aren't desirable."

"I will never in a million years understand girls," I said.

WHICH BRINGS ME back to Tara White.

Believe me, when I saw her compete, I thought she looked like a twelve-year-old with too much makeup on. But when I saw her in the gym, I got a completely different impression. For one thing, I would never mistake exactly where her boobs were. They were right there. The rest of her frame was still slim, but I understood the signs of atrophy in her legs. She was strong and the top half was absolutely gorgeous. I think her face had matured, too, and she didn't wear as much makeup. Of course, she wasn't performing. No one wears that much makeup unless they're performing.

Except Brenda Wilson in my civics class.

I remember when I first met her when we were freshmen, I thought she was kind of cute, but she had red hair like a burning bush and enough freckles to populate Manhattan. And I think she was really self-conscious about them. Guys weren't always kind to girls who were a little different. I commented on it because I thought she was kind of cute and Dad told me that redheads got a freckle for every soul they ate, so to be careful. Well, I never got around to really talking to her after I asked Cathy to the ballgame and dance and found out we weren't supposed to do that until we were sixteen.

Then when I came back to school as a junior, Brenda was a senior and had gone through as much of a transformation as I had. She was nearly eighteen, had an absolutely stellar figure, had colored her hair black, and found some kind of makeup that covered her freckles completely. She used a lot of makeup to get what girls called 'the goth look.' Pale skin and dark outlines around her eyes and lips.

Of course, at this point, I was a year behind her in school and she didn't even know who I was anymore, if she ever had.

When Tara asked me to take my shirt off and pointed out my physique to the other cheerleaders, I got a real shiver of pleasure. I think even Penny was a little awed when she took my hand to mount up to my shoulders. And Tara was going to work with us to develop some new routines. This was going to be a great year!

At least that was one thing to look forward to.

I'd competed at the Senior Elite level the previous summer—2023—and did okay. I didn't win any medals and I'd certainly not scored high enough to qualify for the upcoming Olympic trials. I'd asked Coach Dawson about entering some of the competitions after the first of the year that could qualify me, but he didn't hold out much hope for me this year.

"You could compete at the Nationals in Fort Worth or at the Winter Cup in Louisville, but you'd need to place on the podium to get an invitation to the Olympic trials. Remember all the gymnasts who have been competing in college will declare themselves as pros before those competitions and will have an edge on you."

I was disappointed, but more determined than ever to get there. I was doing well, but I wasn't at that level of competition yet.

So, I was excited to have a real competitor at the World Games level work with Penny and me. It took me a while to get Penny on board.

"Well, like what, for example?" she asked when I'd suggested upping our routine a bit.

"You know how I hold you up in the air on one hand?" I said.

"Yeah. Thank you for having not squeezed my butt lately."

"You're welcome. It wouldn't be an issue, though, if you were standing on my hand instead of sitting on it," I said.

"If I was... You mean you could lift me, or support me while I was standing on your hands? Really?"

"For me, it would be about the same as you sitting there. It would all be about your balance, really. I mean, you weigh the same up there whether you're sitting or standing."

"I'd be up... I mean... My feet would be... um... around six and a half feet off the ground. That's a long way down!" Penny said.

"I think that's why Coach White was emphasizing the importance of not being dropped by your base. We could do all kinds of formations if we worked on it. And I know neither Coach Cook nor Coach White would ever allow us to attempt something like that without a spotter," I said. "Preferably a couple of them."

"That could be kind of cool. Okay. I'm up for it. Geez! Don't ever drop me."

"I promise I won't."

Tara White was a good coach and knew exactly where to start us. She had me lie down on the mat with my hands palm up on either side of my head. Then Penny stepped onto my hands supported by spotters on either side. It took us a few tries before we succeeded, but eventually, I was able to rotate my forearms to a vertical position with her standing on my palms. Can't tell you how many times she started to lose her balance and bailed on me. Fortunately, she only jumped *on* me once.

Penny had been all concerned about me squeezing her butt when I held her up, which I'd managed to discipline myself not to do. But this was a completely different challenge. When I raised her up on my hands I was looking straight up between her legs. Well, that was a view I'd imagined a few times—with other girls—but I never actually saw the shape of that crease right above my face. Maybe three feet above my face. I actually saw what was known as a camel toe.

The first time I became truly aware of what I was seeing, my lower body started to respond. When she jumped off of me, I got up and made an excuse to leave the gym and use the bathroom. I stayed in there until Paul Junior managed to relax.

Of course, working with Penny wasn't enough. Lana and Melina wanted to work with me, too. There was a bit of competition developing to see who would get to be the lead flyer. And the view of all three girls was inspiring. From this angle, I couldn't see that they looked as young as they appeared from the top. I spent more time with my eyes closed while we were working on that move than I care to remember.

From having them stand on my hands with my elbows on the floor, we progressed to me pressing them up until my arms were fully extended. By that time, I was working hard enough not to notice what was in my hands. I was basically just bench-pressing a hundred pounds. In fact, Coach White had me raise and lower them several times.

All this took a couple of weeks before we really worked on any cheer formation that involved lifting the girls to a stand on my hands. I was wondering if we were ever going to progress to something we could really use.

AND THEN ONE day, my world changed. I walked into the Hennepin Gym to start warming up and saw Tara working out on the mat. She motioned me over and I sat next to her to do stretches.

"I came to Minneapolis for just one reason, Paul," she said. "To work with you."

4

PORTALS OF OPPORTUNITY

IN SIX YEARS of training, no girl ever expressed the least bit of interest in me. The girls on the cheer squad tolerated my presence, about the same way they'd treat a table if they had to stand on it. They had parties and went to events together, but I was never invited to go along. It was too much like asking a boy out, I guess.

I'd once been working out in the gym when one of the coaches called to me.

"Paul, please go spot for Andrea. I don't want her trying this flip without a spotter."

"Sure, coach." I dismounted the parallel bars and rushed to the vault where Andrea was set to try a new vault.

"It's okay," Andrea said, waving me away. "I don't think I'm ready for this today." She turned around and headed for the locker room.

"That wasn't directed at you, Paul," the coach said. "Andrea's been having some confidence issues lately and it was just the idea of someone other than me watching her that set her off."

"Yeah... um... sure. No problem," I said. Except it *was* a problem. It was the typical shun I got from girls. She had her hands chalked and was bouncing at the start until the coach said my name. Then she spun away so fast she must have left her shadow on the mat.

I don't get it. What was so terrible about me that girls couldn't stand to be around me? I showered daily—most of the time twice daily. I'd always been polite and tried not to stare at any girl. I mean... shit, I was eighteen. I couldn't help but *notice* girls. I just wanted to be treated like a human being, you know?

"I came to Minneapolis for just one reason, Paul," Tara said. "To work with you."

"Uh... What do you mean work with me, Miss White?"

"Oh, please, Paul. I'm the same age you are. You can call me Tara. Let the bitches on the cheer squad keep calling me Coach White. It keeps them from sassing me. But I want to be um... friendlier... with you."

"Tara? I guess maybe you don't know who you're really talking to. I have no idea what you mean. I don't even want to think you might mean what I think you might mean. I've only ever been on one date in my life! And it was a disaster. I mean, the date was fun, but she never wanted to see me again. I'm a year older than everyone else in my class because it took me two years to finish tenth grade. I'm dumb as a box of rocks. And I think I'm going to hyperventilate."

I started gasping for air. What the hell was my idol suggesting? Friendlier? How friendlier?

"I'm sorry, Paul. Wait! Don't panic. I'm not more experienced at that kind of thing than you and I proba-bly came off meaning something way differently than I meant. I mean sounding like it. I want to work with you. On gymnastics. Together. I need a partner."

"A partner? Um... What do you mean. Can you still perform? That's incredible. I'd do anything to see you perform again!"

"Thank you. I'm not *completely* crippled. I've been in physical therapy for hours every day for three years. I'm in PT or training most of the day still."

"That's really wonderful! How can I help?"

"I accept that I'll probably never be the performer I was before the accident. But I want to perform again— even if only once. It will show people that even though I use a wheelchair or crutches, I can still be a coach. But I can't do it alone. I need a partner who is strong and steady and sure. I need someone I can trust."

"Why me?"

"I saw you at the Chicago Elite Competition this summer."

"I sucked."

"Not so bad. You were less experienced than just about everyone else on the mats. I called your coach and he told me you were working with the school cheer squad. That's as close to Acrobatic Gymnastics as you can get without actually being in training from cradle to grave."

"I don't really know anything about performing in mixed pairs. But if I can help you, I will. Where will you perform?"

"*We,* Paul. We'll perform at the Gymnastics for All National Championships and Gymfest. In June."

"That's at the National Olympic Trials. I didn't qualify," I said. That was a disappointment. I just didn't have an adequate point total.

"You didn't qualify as an individual for the Olympic Trials. But the Gymnastics for All Gymfest isn't an

Olympic Trial and it won't advance anyone to higher level competition. Specifically, we'll participate in the HUGS program."

"Isn't that like for special needs kids?" I asked stupidly.

"Uh... Paul..." she held her arms out to the side. "Who do you think I am?"

I gasped.

"Oh, geez! I didn't think of... I mean... I thought they were all... You just don't impress me as being handicapped even when you're in your chair," I spluttered.

"Thank you, I think. HUGS stands for Hope Unites Gymnastics with Special Athletes. When I damaged my spine, I became a special athlete. There's no way I could compete again in mixed pairs, or in any individual gymnastic event. And there is no mixed pairs category in the HUGS event. I've petitioned the committee to allow a special demonstration. Pending a review of our performance, they've agreed. We have five months to put together our routine and make it work. There's the Winter Cup qualifier in Louisville in February. We won't be on the program, and we won't be announced. We'll simply demonstrate our routine for the judges."

"Tara, I'm flattered that you think I could do this with you. Why don't you want a real competitor to work with you? There are several guys in the gym who are a lot better than I am," I said.

"Honestly? No one of a higher rank would be the least bit interested in working with a cripple. It would take time away from preparing for their own competitions. Paul, you aren't a last resort, but you're my best hope. Please say you'll work with me."

I just wanted to pick her up and carry her around— be the legs she didn't have working. Do whatever she wanted. All I could do was nod my head yes.

I wasn't expecting her to wrap her arms around my neck and give me a hug. I really wasn't expecting her to pull herself around until she was sitting on my lap. I about passed out when she kissed me on the cheek. Then she whispered in my ear.

"And I won't care if you squeeze my butt when I'm sitting on your hand," she giggled. "I might not feel it, but I won't care."

WHAT HAVE I done? I just agreed to work with a national champion mixed pairs acrobatic gymnast who only has partial use of her legs. And I'll have to dedicate the next nine months to her. And still get through school and cheerleading.

This whole thing had catastrophe written all over it. I needed to talk to my sister. That would be the smart thing. She was living in a dormitory on campus, but she never turned her cell phone off. It was almost dinner time, so I was pretty sure I could catch her when she wasn't too busy. She never missed a meal.

"Mikey! I'm glad I caught you. Can we get together?"

"You mean in person? Hmm. Yeah, that would be a great idea. It's Friday night. I know you don't cook on Friday. Meet me at the Lucky Dragon buffet in half an hour. We'll have dinner."

"Wow! I didn't expect you to be so fast. Especially on a Friday night."

"I'm trying to slow down on dating so I can keep track of guys' names," she laughed. "I'm at the library right now and a librarian is giving me the stink eye. I'll see you in half an hour."

"Okay."

Whatever the subject or the mission, my sister could

take over and get it organized. I guess that was what I was hoping for. I hadn't been anywhere near as organized this fall since she moved over to campus. I needed to make sure I left time this weekend to get my statistics assignment done. I only had four classes to complete for my diploma. That was due to taking school at a slower pace, but having class year-round.

My English course was focused on reading comprehension. We had to read something and then answer questions about it. A lot of the kids in that class were non-native English speakers, but it was a pretty good course. I had statistics for my math course. I was pretty good at math as long as I didn't skip any steps. I was getting along in world history. The biggest problem with it was having to read so much. And then there was my US Government class. We joked a lot about it being almost obsolete since our government was abandoning the constitution and legal precedents of cases. But we'd all be eighteen and able to vote before the next general election, so the course was taught from that perspective.

I got vocational credit for my gymnastics work. That was cool. I had to sign a paper that said I was working toward a career in gymnastics and had to list ten jobs that a gymnast was qualified for. That stretched my mind a bit. And it made me think about what I was going to do with my life. I started gymnastics to get strong, but now that I was strong, I was doing gymnastics because I loved it. It didn't feel like I needed a big goal. I would keep training for national competition and hope to advance next year, and eventually compete in the Olympics. I was teaching a Saturday morning toddlers' class, but that didn't really pay much.

I jumped off the bus at Seven Corners and walked quickly to the Lucky Dragon. College students loved this place. It wasn't badly priced and once you were in, you could just keep eating as much as you could hold. I'd have to restrain myself so I didn't overeat. The food was good.

Mikey ran to meet me outside the restaurant and give me a hug. I thought that was a little more demonstrative than we usually were. But we hadn't seen each other in a month, so I guess it wasn't that strange.

"They have the best spicy string beans here," Mikey started at once. "The food in the dorm is all bland. I miss your cooking!"

"I miss having you at the table," I chuckled. We went inside and immediately stacked plates with our first round of food. "How come you're available on a Friday night? I figured you'd be out with some guy for your usual date and I'd have to settle for seeing you for breakfast sometime tomorrow afternoon."

"Things change, Paul. After a few weeks of dating college guys, I kind of swore off. They just want to fuck a seventeen-year-old like they never managed in high school. It's like, if I want to actually *watch* a movie, I need to go alone or with a girl. And some of the girls I don't trust much. I just quit dating unless I want to fuck. Then I'll choose a nice enough guy and go out with him. We do just enough to convince him that he deserves to have me put out, then we screw. I go back to the dorm and I'm fine for a couple of weeks."

Mikey was always pretty blunt about her activities. I knew she'd been screwing guys for a couple of years while she was in high school. I'd never really gotten used to hearing her talk about it.

"Well, I'm glad you're on an off week," I laughed. "I think I got myself in over my head."

"Whoa! What? Is someone picking on you? Can't you

defend yourself now? Just having dinner with you will be good to keep guys away from *me* for a week. You're strong!"

"Yeah. That's the problem, I guess. It's a girl. I don't mean the classic girl problems—except that I can never say no to one. There's this super gymnast who I practically worship and she's asked me to be her partner."

"Partner? You mean live together?"

"Not that kind of partner. Mixed Pairs Acrobatic Gymnastics. I'm afraid I'm nowhere near good enough."

That got us started and I told her all about Tara and the idea of being her partner for a demonstration of a partially disabled woman still doing gymnastics. Tara had showed me a few moves in the afternoon, and even though I had to lift her in order to get her to stand, she was pretty stable once she was on her feet. What she couldn't do was walk without support. Mikey came right to the point when I told her about the HUGS program at the Nationals.

"Hmm. You spent thirteen years of school struggling through classes and regular curriculum when you could have had assistance by being classified as a special needs student. You did that because that kind of classification would follow you all through your life. But you're considering entering a demonstration in a special needs gymnastics program when you're perfectly capable of doing full performance artistic gymnastics at a senior elite level? Would people start looking at you as though you were one of these 'special athletes' who needed to be patted on the back and told you're wonderful?"

"Wow! I didn't even think of that! I was more worried about whether I'm really *capable* of doing what's necessary. What if I can't support her right? What if she got injured again because I dropped her. You know, her last partner killed himself after he dropped her.”

“Oh, man! Whatever happens, you just have to promise me you wouldn’t do a thing like that. I would never forgive you,” Mikey said.

“She doesn’t talk about it much, but I gather Tara never forgave her partner. For killing himself. I think she forgave him for dropping her. She is so strong and fierce that she didn’t let it stop her from getting back on the mats to perform. She did a handstand on her crutches this afternoon. But she can’t really walk without support, so all the usual tumbling routines are out. She can hold her legs in a position—though not as perfect a position as she used to. But she can’t use them to propel herself. No pushes, jumps, walks, or running,” I explained.

“You always made fun of the girls in pairs acrobatics. Even your partner in cheerleading, Penny. If I remember correctly, you said they looked like twelve-year-olds with too much makeup trying to act grown up.”

“That still gives me the shivers,” I laughed. “I guess I’ve kind of gotten used to Penny, Lana, and Melina on the squad. To them, I’m just furniture. There’s a new freshman on the junior varsity squad and I’d swear she was ten. I’m glad I’ll be out of school before she wants to be a flyer for varsity cheer. But Tara... Um... I try not to be an obsessive boy, you know? I mean...”

“I see. Tara has boobs,” Mikey said.

“Yeah. Really nice. They get flattened down in her sports bra and leotard, but... Oh, God! I asked her.”

“You asked about her breasts?” my sister exclaimed in disbelief.

“She started it. She asked what bothered me about working with the cheerleaders. I told her about the twelve-year-old thing and she started laughing. I said, 'You're not like that!' And she was all, 'No kidding!' She said that after the accident, she was laid up with no exercise for nearly a year before she could start really working. Her breasts grew when she wasn't working out."

"And they came to stay," Mikey laughed. "I bet that was something to get used to. How old is she?"

"Nineteen. But I'll be nineteen in the spring. It's not much of an age difference."

"I wasn't thinking of that. I started becoming aware of my sexual characteristics way back, even though they didn't develop fast. I was this big two years ago. I'm just imagining her being my age now and having not developed, then suddenly having them thrust upon her, so to speak."

"I'm sure it was an adjustment. She told me she wouldn't care if I squeezed her butt when I lifted her, though she might not really feel it. That was unpredictable. She didn't say it was okay to squeeze her breast," I said, blushing.

"Don't try it. She might have lost some feeling in her legs and butt, but there's nothing wrong upstairs." Mikey paused and looked at me curiously. "Is that why you want to work with her? I don't mean, like, I think you'd try something with her because she's crippled. I mean you really *like* her, don't you? Paul, are you in love?"

"How would I know the answer to a stupid question like that? Yeah, I like her. She's beautiful and smart and funny. And... um... she kissed me. I mean, on the cheek, but still."

"Oh, my! My brother has a crush on a girl! Go for it!" she said suddenly. "Treat her like a princess. Do the routine she wants you to do. Talk to her and be friendly. I'll bet she hasn't had many guys trying to pick her up since her accident. You might be just what each other needs."

"I don't *need* a girl. I've done just fine without. I mean, I still like her. She's sweet. But I don't *need* her."

"Okay. Forget I said that. I still think you should do it. There's something different about you when you talk about her and what you can do together. I think it's worth a go," Mikey said, pushing herself back from the table. "Those cream-filled red bean buns are to die for. You've never thought of beans for dessert, I'll bet. Whatever they do to them, they're as good as any Danish you've ever had."

We got dessert from the buffet and it was every bit as good as advertised.

"LET'S TRY THIS from a kneeling position now, Paul. Penny, approach from behind and spotters assist her as she steps up to Paul's shoulders. Good. Balance! You both have to be steady. Paul, hands next to your shoulders, palms up. Penny, use your spotters to steady yourself and step out to put your foot in his hand. Good! Good! Deep breath. Feel your stability. When you feel you are stable, release your spotters and take your position with arms out to the side, then up in a vee."

Tara gave us instructions at cheer practice. When Penny was standing on my hands with her arms raised in a vee, the whole squad cheered and applauded. Tara nodded at me and Penny didn't even notice as I pressed my arms up until they were fully extended. She was standing two and a half feet above my shoulders when she realized she was up in the air.

"Spotters!" Tara barked. I lowered my arms and Penny wobbled off her platform to jump down, assisted by the girl on each side of us.

"Woohoo!" Penny shouted. "I did it!"

I clapped my hands for her, even though I wasn't sure what she was so proud of. All she had to do was stand there. I was the one who did all the lifting. Penny was all anyone would really see, though, if we did that kind of lift in a routine. I'd watched every acrobatic cheer and gymnastics routine I could find online. No one ever noticed the base. They saw the top, way up in the air, posing in a victorious stance. I wondered if Penny could do the move on one foot. Could I lift her with just one hand? Yeah. That wouldn't be a problem.

Of course, both Lana and Melina wanted to try mounting and standing on my hands. I got a real workout lifting and pressing the weight of our lightest cheerleaders. It was kind of silly, but I was really having fun. Tara made sure of it.

My four morning classes were out by eleven and I ran to Hennepin Gymnasium. The weather was getting pretty darn cold as we approached November, but we hadn't had snow yet. I went straight to the locker room and changed clothes. I was on the mat stretching and warming up by eleven-thirty.

Tara was already in the gym and I could tell she'd been working with her trainer already. Once I was stretched and warmed up, she hobbled over on her crutches and smiled at me.

"You're here early!" she said. "You don't usually get here until after cheerleading."

"Well, this means I'll have to be back in two hours for practice," I said.

"So will I," she said. "I'll give you a lift."

"I've decided," I said in a rush. "I'll do it if you really want me to work on a routine with you. It was never really a question, I don't think. I just had to talk myself into believing it. Tara, I'd love to work with you."

"That makes me very happy, Paul!"

She lifted her crutches so she could wrap her arms around me and we hugged. *Wow!* I had never had much experience hugging someone with breasts. Or anyone else, for that matter. I could have held her like that all afternoon.

"Uh... Paul? If we're going to work together, maybe we should stop hugging and get started."

"Oh! Yeah. Sorry. I just... Never mind. Where do we start?" I asked.

"This isn't so far from what we *should* be doing. We need to learn to move together. You need to learn how my body moves, and I need to trust you to keep me from being injured."

"How do we do that?"

"Dance. A lot of Acrobatic Gymnastics overlaps with Acrobatic Dance. I'm wearing my knee braces. That seems to be where I'm weakest. Jennifer—my therapist and coach—says that while I'm weak in my legs, my core strength is still good. Or is good again. Let's start with a basic promenade. I'll move my legs and you'll be my crutches."

And that was how we started. I held my right arm around her waist as she had her left arm around mine. We held hands with the other arm across our middle. And we walked. It didn't take long to figure out what she meant by being her crutches. She could move her legs, but she couldn't move them and support her weight as she came down on them.

I'd never been in physical contact with a girl—a woman—for as long as I held Tara that afternoon.

5

I'LL HAVE A TWIST, TOO!

THERE'S A GREAT scene with Steve Martin in the movie *L.A. Story* that Mom just loves. A bunch of Hollywood elite are sitting at a table and start one upping each other with their coffee orders. Martin finally says, "I'll have a double decaf, half caf, with a twist of lemon." Everyone immediately jumps in with "I'll have a twist, too." Mom just howls when she watches that movie and every morning, I end up presenting her coffee saying, "Double decaf, half caf." She always responds, "With a twist!" That's even though she just drinks black full caffeine coffee.

She really likes old movie classics, so we watch a lot of them at home. That one was from way back in the 1990s, last century.

Remember, even as a senior in high school, I'd never really dated. That one time I thought everything was going well and then Dana said she didn't want to go out with me again. So, Saturday night family entertainment was often watching old movies in our home theater.

Tara and I had been working in the gym together for almost a month and were progressing pretty well.

59

I could pick her up and hold her over my head as she took various poses. One of them that was working out really well was when I held her on one hand over my head with her lying back, completely stretched out and one leg crossed over the other. It's not a pose you'll find in many acts.

Anyway, we were finishing up on a Saturday afternoon at the gym and Tara just turned to me all of a sudden and said, "Want to try out that new Mediterranean restaurant over on Lyndale?"

"It sounds pretty good," I said. "I might try it."

"Let's go."

Call me dense, but I didn't realize she was *inviting me out* when she asked if I wanted to try it. It was almost like my sister was there, telling me where to meet her. The more I thought of it, the more I thought my sister was probably the only person who had ever made that kind of suggestion. So, I just figured Tara wanted to talk something out or maybe go over a new pose and how to get into it. I just followed her to her car and got in as if we were going to the school for cheer.

I can drive, but I don't have a car. Tara's car is a little intimidating and I wouldn't offer to drive it. For a small woman, she drives a big car. She can't depend on the speed, accuracy, or pressure of her legs, so she has hand controls that are a little confusing. I suppose I could get the hang of it eventually, but she told me she nearly crashed every time she got in the car the first month she was learning it.

We parked in a handicapped space. She had Arizona DP plates which are for disabled persons. If she was just moving from one place to another, she usually used her crutches. If she was going to be in someplace for a while and needing to sit, she used the wheelchair. I got out of the car and ran around to get the wheelchair out of the back seat and open it up for her. She positioned it and slid over into the seat.

Unless there was a problem, like a curb or snow, I knew enough not to try to push her around. Tara was really independent and could wheel herself. I stood by and closed the car doors. She pushed the button to lock them.

The restaurant was nice, but not expensive. I was making a little money by giving toddler tumbling lessons on Saturday mornings, but at almost nineteen, I was still mostly saving the allowance my parents were giving me by tossing it in a drawer. They said they'd continue that as long as I was still making progress in school, and I was. I always carried a little cash, but most of my allowance for the past few years had been tossed in that drawer.

"It all looks so good," Tara said. "What are you going to have?"

"Me? Well, I've always been partial to shawarma. I figure if I don't pig out on it and go sparingly with the tahini, it's a good meal," I said.

"Oh, shawarma sounds good. With pita."

"Yeah. I'll have pita, too."

"Look, they have hummus with raw vegetables."

"Mmm. I love hummus."

"With a twist?" she asked.

It took me a full beat to realize she'd quoted my mother's favorite movie. I just stared at her.

"You know that movie?"

"Loved it. Jennifer introduced me to it. You can't imagine how many old movies I watched when I was basically bedridden."

"That must have been a really tough time," I said.

"I was doing okay at first. Then Jackson killed himself. God damn him! We could have gotten through it together. Please promise me you'll never do that. No matter what!"

Tears were in her eyes and threatened to spill if I didn't make a definitive gesture.

"My sister said if I ever did that, she'd kill me," I said.

Whew! Disaster averted. It was the right thing to say and Tara started laughing.

"I think I'll like your sister. When do you think we can meet?"

"She's in her first semester at the University, but I think the semester ends December 21 or 22. She plans to come home for the break. Will you be going back to Arizona?"

"No. I figure we'll have a lot of opportunity to work during the break. We should be able to get some good workouts in."

Our food arrived. The kitchen just served a platter of meat and vegetables with tahini, a platter of pita, and a bowl of hummus and veggies. We served ourselves from the middle of the table. That was pretty cool.

We talked and I found out a lot about Tara I didn't know before. She'd started training as a gymnast when she was four! I guess maybe some of the kids I was teaching on Saturday mornings might grow up to be like her. It boggled the imagination. Her entire life she'd been tutored instead of attending school, because she loved gymnastics so much; she wanted to be in the gym all the time. That part sounded familiar. I guess when the bug bites, you get infected fast. Her parents were pretty wealthy and lived in Scottsdale. A gym there took her on until she was twelve and then she moved to Frisco, Texas where the US National Gymnastics team trained. She was selected for the under sixteen team.

That was where she'd been encouraged to try mixed pairs acrobatic gymnastics and met Jackson. They'd trained and competed together for three years, getting to the Worlds just after they turned sixteen. Then the accident cut everything short, ultimately including Jackson's life.

"That really sucks. Tara, I can't tell you how happy I am that you've recovered this much, and that you came to Minneapolis, and that you chose me," I said.

"Before you get too enthused, there's one more chapter you need to know about me," she said. "Um... a week before our accident, Jackson and I became lovers. It was a natural culmination of our relationship with each other. But it affected our performance. We paid more attention to our lover relationship than to our routine. That's why Jackson killed himself, I think. He could probably have stood injuring his partner, but he couldn't stand having hurt his lover. That's what I tell myself."

"Oh, geez, Tara. That's terrible. I mean, not that you became lovers. I think that's great, but that it impacted your performance and your lives that way. I'm just so sorry."

Now I was about ready to cry. I could just imagine the horrid impact that would have had on them. Not just the accident, but the thought that he hurt the one he loved.

"That's why I want you to know right now that we aren't going to be lovers," she continued.

What? She couldn't know I'd fantasized about that, could she? I was floored and about to bolt from the restaurant. She kept going.

"We can date and do fun things. I'd like that. We can even kiss sometimes and hold hands. We need to keep it out of school, but other than that, I like it when you put your arm around me and when you help me in and out of the car. I like it when you spot my exercises and when you look into my eyes. We just can't be lovers if we're partners. Are you okay with that?"

I was in way over my head! I had no idea how she expected me to respond. Sure, it was okay. I never thought there was even a possibility of becoming lovers. That was just something in the back of my overactive imagination. But dating? We could actually date each other?

"Please say you'll still be my partner, Paul."

"Y-yes! Of course, I'll be your partner. That's what I signed up for. I never thought about... We could date?"

"Um... What do you think this is?"

"It's um... We're um... Wow! This is a date?"

"I didn't think it would take you that much by surprise."

"I've never really dated. I just... Yes!"

"I'll try to be a good girlfriend, but I really don't have much experience dating, either. And I kind of have this baggage," she said, tapping her wheelchair. "But before I decided for sure that I'd ask you to be my pairs partner, I spent a couple of weeks coaching you with the cheerleaders to be sure I really liked you, you know? We wouldn't have had the first meeting in the gym if I didn't."

I laughed.

"I went straight from that meeting and had dinner with my sister. I needed to talk out whether I was making the right decision to partner with you. She started teasing me about having a crush on you and then said I should go for it. Honest, I never thought of anything other than being the partner you needed."

We didn't have any plans, but neither of us was eager to have our first date end. We ordered a piece of *basbousa* cake and a cup of coffee for dessert and kept talking for what seemed like hours. Finally, we each contributed our part of the check and tip and I opened her door when she unlocked the car.

"You can lift me in if you'd like," she said.

I'd lifted her out of her wheelchair on other occasions, so I knew the basic routine. Instead of rolling the chair up tight against the car so she could swing herself in, I got between the chair and the car while she locked the wheels in position. Then I bent over her and slid my hands under her legs while she put her hands around my neck. I lifted her, swung around, and carefully lowered her into the driver's seat.

Once she was in position, though, she didn't let go of my neck. Instead, she pulled me toward her and placed a long gentle kiss on my lips.

Oh, wow! A crush? Infatuation? I'm in love!

I folded her chair into the back seat and went around to the passenger side to get in the car. I looked at her and grinned.

"You know, a guy never forgets his first," I said.

"I thought that was the girl's line!"

We laughed and went for a little drive around all three lakes before we got to my house. By my sister's criteria, it was still early for a date to end. She never got in before midnight. But we'd both worked hard all day before going out and it was likely we'd be asleep by the time our heads touched our pillows—even with the coffee we'd drunk.

She pulled into our driveway—still with the carport in front of the garage, though Dad had been saying it was time to close up the garage gym and move the cars back inside.

I turned to Tara and she held out her arms. I folded her in mine, across the console, and we enjoyed another, longer and more loving kiss than the first.

"I wanted you to remember your second, too," she whispered. Then she let me go and I said goodnight.

"Who was that who brought you home?" Mom asked as soon as I entered the house.

"Oh. That was Tara. She's um..." It was at exactly that moment that I realized I'd never told my parents I was working with a partner in gymnastics. Dad stood in the doorway with an eyebrow raised. "Well, you see, she started as a volunteer coach for the cheerleaders because she's very experienced in pairs, where the guy lifts a girl. You've seen the routines I do with Penny. She coaches those."

"And?" Mom persisted.

"She's a gymnast, and we've been working together on a mixed pairs routine that we plan to perform as an exhibition at the Gymnastics for All Gymfest in June. It's not a competition. They don't do mixed pairs for the competition. This is a special performance to show that she is still a performer, even though she was injured a few years ago."

"And is kissing part of your routine?" Mom asked.

"No... um... She became my girlfriend tonight. We were out on a date."

"My son has a girlfriend," Dad said, nodding his head.

"I don't know about this," Mom said. "How was she injured and why are you doing an exhibition at Nationals instead of competing?"

I sighed. There was no way around things. I pulled off my coat and shoes and went into the living room where Mom was sitting with a book and a clear view out the front window.

I started to explain things from the beginning, taking them through the whole story of the injury, her rehab, the extent of her injury and why she thought she could still perform. I had to explain why I'd been working with her for close to two months without telling my parents. Of course, they wanted to know how old she was and I think they breathed a sigh of relief that I wasn't dating a twenty-something, even though I was almost nineteen.

"We'd like to meet her," Mom said.

"Um... sure. You could come over to the gym anytime."

"I think we should have her company here for dinner. Let's plan on it after your sister gets home. I'm sure Michelle will be surprised to hear about this." Mom paused. "She already knows, doesn't she? I must have words with my own daughter."

"She knows we're partners in gymnastics. She doesn't know we're dating," I defended her.

"I'll bet she's already figured it out," Dad laughed. "Probably knew it long before you did."

I couldn't respond to that. Knowing my sister, she probably did.

AT THE GYM Monday, I asked Tara if she thought having dinner with my family would be too uncomfortable or moving too fast. She giggled and blushed when I told her my mom had seen us kissing in the driveway.

"You know, if I was ashamed to be seen with you or to meet people, I wouldn't have asked you on our first date," she said. "I'd love to have dinner with your family."

"That's great! My sister will be home for the winter break. I talked to her yesterday and she's dying to meet you," I said.

"Maybe we can at least get another date in this weekend before we jump in the fire. Okay?"

"Yeah. I don't know much about what to do on a date other than have dinner and maybe go to a movie."

"Okay. I'm happy with that. Let's have dinner Friday night and see what's playing," she said. I had no idea dating was so easy!

"PAUL, I NEED you tonight," Penny said at practice the next Friday.

"What do you need?" I asked. Tara and I had a date planned. We'd been riding to and from the gym together and I'd been helping her in and out of the car now that we'd had some snow. Of course, that usually involved at least a little kiss as I got her settled, but we kept it outside the school.

"I need you for a double date."

"Uh... Maybe. I'll ask..." I said.

"No, I have a date for you. You just need to show up."

"But... I have..."

I looked up at Tara and she was laughing and shaking her head. I had no idea what I was supposed to do. I'd never been asked out before and twice in two weeks I was being asked for a date.

"We'll leave from here after we get showered and dressed."

She turned abruptly and headed to the locker room. I went immediately to Tara.

"What do I do? I can't go out with her!"

"I can't say I'm not a little disappointed. I was looking

forward to this evening."

"Me, too! I don't want to go out with Penny. I'm going to march right down there and just tell her I don't want to go," I said, turning.

"No, wait. Let's have some fun. Find out where they're heading and tell her you'll meet her there. We'll just show up together and see what happens."

"You don't mind being open and declaring that we're dating?" I said.

"Is there any reason I should mind?" Tara asked.

"No! Absolutely none at all."

I came up with the idea of going home to change clothes and shower instead of using the school locker room. I hardly ever went in there. On the way home, I texted Penny and asked her to send me the address and I'd meet her there.

She was upset that I wasn't at school and I just said I didn't have any date clothes at school and needed to go home.

Of course, at home, I didn't want to leave Tara in the driveway, so she parked behind Mom's car and used her crutches and me to get up our walk to the door. I called for Mom and introduced them.

"It's lovely to meet you, Tara," Mom said. "It's nice that Paul started dating someone so well known. I was able to Google you and find out all about what hap-pened. Would you like a cup of tea while Paul gets show-ered and dressed?"

"That would be lovely, Mrs. Bradley. I was looking forward to meeting you. I didn't mean to crash in before the dinner on the twenty-third."

"Oh, don't think a thing about it. Go ahead and shower, Paul. Tara and I will entertain each other for a few minutes until you're ready."

I wasn't sure if that was a good thing or bad, but I trusted both Mom and Tara to be nice. I hurried through a shower and dressing and downstairs again. They were laughing at the kitchen table.

"Did you find out where we're going, Paul?" Tara asked. I checked my phone.

"Not far. Lago Tacos. We can eat pretty well there."

"It's nice that you're meeting friends," Mom said. We just smiled.

I helped Tara up from the kitchen chair and handed her the crutches. We got our coats and shoes and carefully navigated our way back to her car. I lifted her in and got a kiss for a reward.

"I hope that wasn't too painful an experience," I said.

"Oh, your mom is a sweetheart. She did absolutely nothing to dissuade me from dating you."

"I'm glad to hear that. Now let's hope we can survive our surprise coming out party at the restaurant," I said.

I HAD ABSOLUTELY no idea what Penny was thinking. She'd never expressed any interest in doing anything socially with me at all. I'd heard her make a comment that I had no personality. She must have been desperate to fix a friend up with a blind date and chose whoever was closest.

We consulted briefly and Tara decided she'd be most comfortable in her chair in the restaurant. I lifted her into it and rolled it through the slushy snow to the door. When we were inside, I told the hostess we were meeting friends and stepped around the corner to see if I could spot Penny. She immediately jumped up and waved me over to a table.

"Paul! You know Ethan, my boyfriend. This is Madison, my sister."

"Hi. It's nice to see you all. This is Tara," I said as she rolled up behind me.

"What are you doing here?" Penny asked rather rudely. "I mean, um... hi."

"Tara and I were going out tonight," I said. "You kind of took over like it was an emergency."

"It is. I needed you to meet Madison. You're perfect for each other."

I looked at Madison. The truth was she looked marginally older than Penny and I wondered if she was an older sister. She looked kind of familiar, too.

"Oh, I know you," she said looking at Tara. "You're the crippled girl who works out with Paul at the gym. That's what gave me the idea to partner with him."

"Uh... Tara's my partner and my girlfriend," I said firmly. We sat at the table, which only had four chairs. It was smart for Tara to wheel in.

"What? You're dating? Can you even do that? Miss White is one of our cheerleading coaches," Penny said. I noticed that Ethan was sitting back with a kind of smirk on his face. I knew who he was because he'd just gotten all-conference honors for football something or other. Nice that they could still honor players who were on losing teams.

"I think at a casual gathering like this you can dispense with the Miss," Tara said. "It would be silly to have Paul be the only one who calls me Tara."

"Why would you date *her*? Or you date *him*?" Penny persisted. "Like isn't it even illegal?"

"Finally found one who couldn't outrun you, hey Paul?" Ethan cracked.

"He found one who had no desire to outrun him," Tara shot back. "I'm not a school employee and I'm about the same age as Paul. Why wouldn't I want to date him? The girls in school can be pretty dense about such things."

"I'm not," Madison said. "I knew I wanted Paul from the first I saw him on the rings. I just assumed he was only into artistic gymnastics and not acrobatics. Not until I saw you working together. We'd be a perfect pair."

"I'm committed to Tara," I said.

"Well, we're not actually married," Tara laughed. "I take it you are *trying* to get into acrobatics?"

"Yeah. I had another girl as a base, but she's decided I grew too much. I mean, I'm five-three and most of you tops are under five feet. Penny's only four-ten."

"Don't rub it in," Penny growled at her sister.

"I love my little spinner," Ethan laughed.

"You'd better," Penny shot back.

"That's all great, but Tara and I are preparing an exhibition for the Nationals in June," I said. "Between that and cheerleading and school, I don't have time for anything else."

"You mean you're actually going to perform those stunts you've been doing?" Madison asked. "I mean, we could do the actual acrobatics together. Penny's told me how strong you are. I'm sure you could lift me... and put me in about any position you want."

"I'm not looking for another partner. I don't know what might happen after our exhibition, but I don't think I have time for anything else right now," I said.

"We could probably work in a few practice sessions over the next six months. You wouldn't be ready for a qualification run in time for the Nationals in June in any case," Tara said.

"You said you're preparing for it," Madison said with a little pout.

"For an exhibition in the special athletes section. It has nothing to do with the selection competition."

"I guess it will all depend on schedules and whether we can work together, then," I said. I wasn't sure I wanted to move on this at all. Penny could have arranged a meeting without going through the pretense of a blind date. It didn't sit well with me.

"I'll do anything," Madison said.

That made me even more uncomfortable.

6

LEARNING TARA

I **HELD MY BREATH** all day the Saturday before Christmas. Figuratively. I know, I know. I'd never taken a girl home to have dinner with my family. It wasn't like I was worried about any of them. Well, Mikey, a little. But the whole thought that *I* was bringing my *girlfriend* home for a holiday meal was just too intense to comprehend.

I didn't have a toddler class that morning. We were all but closed for the holidays. Only those of us seriously working toward a program or competition showed up at the gym. Unfortunately, that included Madison. It had been two weeks since I agreed to spend some time working with her. Coach Daniels, who worked with Madison, showed up as well and started in on us as soon as we set foot on the floor.

We started with some synchronous tumbles and flips, just to see if we were at the same level. No problem there. I thought I could do any move on the mat Madison could do and probably a few more. Which is what Coach Daniels tested next. We started with a

74

couple of throws—something I wasn't doing with Tara for obvious reasons. Lifts, though, were both easier and informative. The big difference between lifting Madison and lifting Tara was that Tara couldn't help by jumping more than a little bounce on the sprung floor. Our lifts were all static. Madison could practically jump to my shoulders. She was more athletic than her sister Penny and was unafraid to stand on my hands, even on one foot. Her coach had me work a few times on a pose called a table—lowering myself to the mat, where I was supported on one hand while I held Madison over my head with the other. That was definitely more difficult than anything I'd done with either Tara or Penny, but we managed okay.

"We need to work every morning," Coach Daniels said. "We'll start at eight, so be warmed up before that."

"I can't do that," I said

"What?" the coach snapped.

"I already have my regular partner I'm working with and we'll be spending most of our time on our routines," I explained. "Didn't Madison explain that I can only work with her occasionally?"

"There is no such thing as an occasional partner in mixed pairs. This requires dedication."

"I'm sorry. I thought that was understood. I am dedicated to my partner, Tara. I can't be dedicated to both," I said.

"Not dedicating yourself to this means we can't compete at the Winter Cup in Louisville and we won't have a bid for the National Team in June," the coach said.

"I'm not offering to even attempt to qualify for Nationals with Madison," I said. "Tara and I are performing in Louisville to get approval for our exhibition at Nationals."

"Well, that's just fine. You can't possibly need as much time to prepare for that. I've seen your routine. It's basic. You could prepare that in an hour a day and have plenty of time to work with Madison. It would do you much better to actually be in a competition than doing an exhibition."

Coach Daniels had no intention of taking no for an answer. I thought I was done with bullies. Apparently not. Madison had a smile on her face as though she'd already won. A single glance over to where Tara was working with her physical therapist, though, and I knew exactly where I was going.

"I'm sorry you've wasted your time this morning," I said. "I need to go work with my partner now. Good luck, Madison."

I left the mat and an animated conversation between Madison and her coach.

"You know, she might be right," Tara said when I told her and Jennifer what had gone on in the session. "We could probably do everything we're doing now in an hour a day instead of three. If you really want to compete with her, I'd be willing to make the adjustment," Tara said.

I was horrified.

"No! I mean, we're making progress. I'm finding out more about what you can do every time we practice. I need to gain confidence that I won't hurt you and we could do all kinds of things," I said enthusiastically.

"Don't take that thought too far," Tara laughed. "What do you think, Jennifer?"

"I think that if Paul really wants to learn what you can do, he should join our PT sessions. We could let him gradually take over some of your exercises and training," Jennifer said.

"Could I do that?" I asked.

"I couldn't turn you into a physical therapist," Jennifer laughed. "I had to get a doctorate. There's no way around that."

"I didn't know you're a doctor!" I said. "I'm going to graduate from high school with the bare minimum requirements. It would take forever for me to learn everything to be a doctor!"

"Maybe, though from what I've seen, you're smart enough. Have you considered becoming a personal trainer or massage therapist? You might not be ready to coach senior elite gymnasts, but I've seen you with the toddlers. You could coach the lower levels and kids who are just getting started."

"I could talk to Coach Dawson about expanding that role," I said. Knowing that I wasn't in line for a shot at this year's Olympic Games in Paris, made training for the next Olympics seem like a long time from now. I was going to need to earn some money eventually.

"Okay. You can start by helping me massage Tara's legs. Tara, go to the massage room and get ready. Leave your leotard on. Paul, just follow what I do and I'll teach you what you need to know," Jennifer said.

Tara went into the massage room and a few minutes later, Jennifer knocked. I heard Tara say, "Okay." We went into the room where Tara was lying face-up on the table.

"Um... Is this okay, Tara? I mean for me to massage your legs."

"Hey! Maybe you'll awaken more feeling in them. Have at it. Massage some life into these dead sticks."

"Don't let her fool you," Jennifer said. "She does have

life and feeling in her legs. It's reduced, but still there."

"If I'd known you were going to invite him to massage my legs, I'd have shaved this morning," Tara laughed. She was blushing a little. I think I was, too.

She was wearing her usual workout leotard, so she was completely decent. It wasn't the first time I'd touched Tara's legs, obviously. I lifted her, swung her, held her, and propelled her. But it was the first time I'd touched her legs with the intent of just touching them, and rubbing them, and feeling the muscles in them, and feeling how soft and smooth they were. I had to go inside myself to where I went when I was working with the cheerleaders. I had to not think about her as a sexual being.

I followed Jennifer's instructions and copied her movement. It was funny that I could almost see in my mind how all the muscles were connected and where the damage was. Once I got to that point, it was a lot easier to focus on the intent of the massage instead of the feeling of her body.

We worked on her legs for half an hour and then had her roll over onto her stomach so we could work on the backs of her legs, her butt, and lower back. Of course, we worked outside her leotard, but it was cut rather high and I found that I was not only squeezing her butt, but actively working on it to find the connections Jennifer was pointing out.

So, maybe I could control my reactions while I was working on her, but somehow, I knew a very active fantasy was waiting for me to get to bed that night.

JENNIFER WAS OUR coach as well as Tara's therapist, but we'd had another woman working on our choreography.

78

After the therapy session, we warmed up and then went to work on our routine. There were a couple of figures we could get into, but the transition wasn't smooth.

For example, if I supported the small of her back, Tara could bend over backwards and put her hands on the floor. Bent double backwards! We'd worked on having me lift her in that position and it was fine. But the classic figure would have her with her hands on mine and bent in that pose horizontally instead of vertically. Getting from one pose to the other was just impossible.

"Let's try your handstand, Tara," Jennifer said. "Paul, on your back, hands up. I understand you've done this with your cheerleaders standing on your hands. This will be similar, but Tara will be standing on her hands."

"Cool," I said.

I lay down and Tara took her position. It took us a few tries before we got the right height for my hands to be so Tara could use her phenomenal upper body strength to pull herself up. She wasn't quite able to get her legs up, but standing on her hands in a folded position was still good.

"Okay, switch to one hand," Jennifer commanded.

I wasn't sure of what she was going for until I felt Tara let go of my left hand and move both her hands onto my right hand. This was really cool. I'd held Penny once with both her feet in my right hand, but Tara was doing a handstand on my hand.

"Paul, keep your arm vertical and stable as you elevate your body into a table with your left hand."

I'd seen this figure in videos and had just done the table with Madison. I knew the objective was that the line from the bottom hand of the base to the tip of the top's—in the videos it was a foot. With Tara it was her butt—should be perfectly straight and vertical. I elevated myself so that I created a right triangle with the mat, my body, and my arm. Above me, Tara stayed steady on my extended right hand. We held it until I felt Tara start to tremble. Jennifer stepped right in and caught her as she dismounted.

What a rush!

After our workout, we stretched and I rubbed Tara's shoulders and arms. They'd been worked even harder than usual. We each headed for the locker rooms and showers to get ready to go to my house for dinner with the family.

I HELPED TARA to the door of the house. After asking if I minded carrying her at times, she decided to leave the wheelchair in the car and just use her crutches. I didn't mind carrying her, anytime. I'd kept the walk shoveled and clear of ice, so I suppose I didn't really need to carry her to the door, but I did.

Let me emphasize that Tara had some use of her legs and she was nineteen years old. She was beautiful and she sure showed it on this day. She wore a skirt that came to mid-thigh, knee-high black boots, and a form-fitting red sweater. She was wearing a little more makeup than usual, but nothing like the stage makeup girls wear when performing. In short, she was gorgeous.

I set her down inside and took her coat before my sister practically knocked us over, rushing to hug us.

"I'm home!" she yelled as she grabbed me. I kept one arm around Tara to stabilize her. "Oh, I just knew you'd be beautiful! Hi, Tara. I'm Mikey."

"I knew you'd have more energy than all of Paul's five-year-old tumbling class!" Tara laughed. "It's nice to meet you, Mikey."

"Michelle, at least let them come into the house," Dad said from the living room. "We don't need to overwhelm them. Let the floods rise slowly."

"Come on in," Mikey said contritely. "Mom's in the kitchen. But I was the only one who hadn't met you."

"Can I help with anything?" Tara asked as we followed Mikey.

We stopped at the living room so Dad could give us each a hug and welcome us, then continued to the kitchen. Mom was whipping potatoes in a big bowl and everything smelled incredible.

"We're almost ready to set things on the table," Mom said. She turned to us and hugged Tara. "It's nice to see you again. I'm glad you could spend some time with us before you go home for the holidays."

"Oh, it's a welcome treat. I'm not going back to Arizona over the break this year. Two weeks off was too good an opportunity for Paul and me to work on our routine. We made some great strides today."

"We sure did! I'm sure we can take that all the way up to a stand. You were phenomenal!"

"Oh, you're staying here in town? Do you have people here? You are more than welcome to join us for Christmas, and whenever else you'd like."

"Thank you. I don't want to impose," Tara said.

"I have a feeling the only way we'll see my son is if you are here," Dad laughed. "Make this your home for the holidays."

That was a lot more of an invitation than I ever expected. I probably needed to explain some things to my parents or they'd assume things that weren't true.

IN FACT, DAD managed to maneuver me aside when the

women went into the living room. Mom really loved the living room because the big window in front looked out over the lake. Her reading chair was positioned right where she could look out at the various lights on the other side of the lake.

"We've never had this discussion, son, and now I feel it's a little rushed," Dad said. "First, your mother and I talked. You're almost nineteen and we don't want you feeling you're a stranger in this house. You have your room and bath. It's well separated from your mother's and mine. Don't feel like you have to sneak around to be together. You have a home here and we'll welcome your girlfriend in it. Second, please tell me you know about safe sex and you're using protection."

"Dad! Tara and I are dating. We aren't sleeping together! That's not an option right now," I said.

"I didn't realize her injury prevented sex," Dad said. "I'm sorry. What do you plan to do?"

"Wait! I don't think her injury prevents sex," I explained. *Damn! I did not want to have this conversation with my father.* "Tara and I agreed that as long as we're performing as partners, at least, sex is not an option. It has to do with her previous partner and we'd rather not discuss it with the family."

"Oh. Oh. I see. I'm sorry. I shouldn't have made assumptions. The only example I had was your sister and to her 'dating' means 'sex.' I should have known you had more common sense than she has," Dad said, shaking his head.

Me? More common sense than my sister? You've got to be kidding. If sex had been an option, you bet I'd have gone there. I was in love with Tara. I would do anything with her or for her.

WE PLAYED SOME games as a family and Tara was very competitive. Of course, games meant getting to the basement to the family room and home theater. Mikey carried Tara's crutches down the stairs and I carried Tara. She chose to ride on my back and I deposited her on the sofa next to where I'd sit. Mikey started to sit there until I scowled at her and she giggled before moving to the chair.

After the game, Mom and Dad went all the way upstairs to their room. Mikey stayed with Tara and me for a while, but seemed to figure out that I wanted a little time alone with Tara.

"You know, you can stay here if you want," I said. "I don't mean with me. We have a guest room and everything you might need, I think. I hate the idea of you going out in the cold to go home."

"That's sweet of you," she said.

We finally got around to kissing, which was probably what my sister expected we wanted to do. There was just something about being on the sofa together instead of reaching across the console of the car that made kissing a lot more like I imagined making out to be. The kisses were a lot hotter than anything we'd had before.

"I'd better get going," she whispered. We were both out of breath. "I have a night routine that requires a little help. Help I don't think I'm ready to have you do."

"How do you handle it at home?"

"Jennifer is my physical therapist, my coach, and my helper companion," she said. "We try to make sure we each allow the other her independence, but there are a few things I just need to have help with."

"I had no idea. I wondered where you lived."

"There's an assisted living residence not terribly far from the gym. If Jennifer needs a break or is out on a date, there's always someone there who can help. During the day, I'm pretty independent, but Jennifer helps me dress and shower in the locker room. She really is a godsend."

"I didn't even know people like her existed," I said.

I carried Tara upstairs with her crutches and helped her into her coat. Then I took her out to her car and shared another long lovely kiss when I got her into her seat.

"Goodnight, girlfriend," I said.

"Goodnight, boyfriend," she responded.

I stood outside in the cold, watching her drive away until she was out of sight.

I ADMIT, I wasn't all that sure what to do with a girlfriend. I mean... Yeah... I was eighteen years old—almost nineteen—and I'd watched enough crap on my computer to know how the parts fit together, but what do you do with a *girlfriend*? Especially one who is partially disabled? We were clear with each other that we weren't going to have sex anytime in the next six months, at least. We liked kissing, but we didn't do any feeling each other up. And besides, that wasn't what I meant by what to do. That's all just the sex and romance stuff.

What do you do?

Well, Tara and I talked a lot. She told me what life was like for a dedicated gymnast on an Olympic track from an early age. Her dad was some kind of political muckymuck in Phoenix and got there through his wealth, the way Tara told it. But that was also what enabled her to have private tutors and hours of dedicated training every day from the time she was little.

"One day, my tutor told me I had an assessment test to take," Tara told me. "I figured it was just one more thing I had to do and rushed through the stupid thing so I could get back in the gym. A couple of days later, my tutor showed up with my diploma—a GED certificate—and said, 'Congratulations. You're out of school.' And that was it. My tutor left and all I had to do each day was work out in the gym."

"I might end up having to try that," I laughed. "If I get a successful completion in the four courses I'm taking this spring, the school says I can graduate. They've already had me on the books for an extra year. If I don't graduate, they don't really care. I'll be nineteen and no longer required to go to school. I guess, for that matter, I could quit school now, but my parents would be really upset if I did. I'm still depending on them to pay for my training and home."

"I turned sixteen a week after I got my GED. My father set up a bank account and trust fund for me that would last a normal person for years, then went with me to the courthouse to file my emancipation papers. The day they were approved and I became an emancipated teen was the day Jackson and I went all the way. It was kind of a celebration. We'd grown so close through two years of training together that it was a natural step."

"I can't even imagine how hard the past three years have been for you. Do you have enough money now that you aren't performing?" I asked.

"Oh, yeah. My father didn't wash his hands of me. He just wanted me to have the freedom I needed to pursue my life goals. After the accident, I went back to live with him for a while and he found Jennifer for me. She is a regular full-time employee of his company. I don't know what I'd do without her."

"Um... Do you mind if I ask what about your mother?"

"That's one that only brings up a kind of wistful emotion when I wonder what it would have been like. I never really knew my mother. She was killed in a drunk driving incident before I was a year old," Tara said.

"I hate hearing about drunks killing people on the highway. Can't they have the least decency not to get in their cars?" I said, thinking I was supporting Tara with my declaration.

"Yeah. My mother never should have gotten in the car. She was depressed, on drugs, and drunk. I'm just glad she didn't kill anyone else when she went."

"Oh my God! Your mother was the drunk driver. I'm so sorry. I didn't mean to be offensive," I backpedaled.

"Take it easy, Paul. You weren't offensive. It's true. Drunks shouldn't get in their cars. Someone will be hurt or killed. In my case, my mother was killed and my father and I were left behind. He had enough money to hire a couple of nannies and enough awareness of my life to let me pursue gymnastics. Now, tell me something about your family."

"Hmm. Well, I guess my mom, dad, and sister used up all the intelligence our family was allotted and left me with nothing to show for it."

"Come on. You aren't stupid," Tara laughed.

"No. I'm just slow. I think I'd have done fine in school if the subjects were stretched out over the full year instead of nine months. But my family is all *really* smart. Dad's an engineer. Mom's head of human resources for a manufacturer in Bloomington. My sister thinks she'll become an environmental engineer and is only seventeen and a freshman in college."

"What's made the difference for you?" Tara asked.

"I think when I discovered gymnastics, life really

changed for me, you know? Not exactly the way I thought it would. I thought if I got really strong, no one would bully me. I saw the athletes at school and how popular they always seemed to be, so I thought that becoming strong would make me popular, too. And if I was popular, I'd have no trouble getting dates and finding a girlfriend. It's all a lot different than I expected."

"Are you popular now?"

"No. If anything, I'm kind of an odd man out, you know? They still think of me as the dumb kid—just big and dumb instead of little and dumb. Held back so I didn't graduate with my class. Scary to the kids who are all younger than me."

"Are you still getting bullied?"

"Um... No one is stuffing me in a locker, if that's what you mean."

"What do *you* mean?"

"Well, I get bossed around a lot. The cheerleaders treat me like a servant who is only there to pick them up and carry them around. And Madison's coach—well, none of my other coaches have ever tried to humiliate me into doing something. Is that bullying?"

"Maybe so. What about getting girls to pay attention and having a girlfriend?"

"Sneaky. Having a girlfriend means I don't really care about any other girls paying attention to me. It makes me really happy. I'm glad you are my girlfriend."

"So am I."

7

THE GIRLFRIEND VS. THE PARTNER

TARA AND JENNIFER came over to spend Christmas Day with us and stayed with us through Tara's twentieth birthday on the twenty-seventh. I went crazy trying to figure out what to give her for Christmas/birthay and Sunday, Christmas Eve, after our workout, Mikey took me to Southdale to shop for something special. We'd only been dating for just over a month, so I knew that items of clothing and jewelry were out of the question. As were things that were really expensive. I set a fifty-dollar max on what I should buy her.

I knew what kind of cell phone she had and considered getting a cool protective case for it, but Mikey said those were as personal and intimate as jewelry and clothing. *Sheesh!* Then we passed one of those kiosks that aren't in any store, but stand alone out in the mall. It had some really beautiful candles. They'd been hand-dipped and shaped out of multiple layers of wax and one was shaped almost like an abstract couple embracing with one lifted up. I knew that as soon as it was lit, the illusion would go away, but I liked it. Mikey approved.

88

I knew Jennifer liked to read, so Mikey helped me pick out a new release. I certainly wouldn't have just walked into a bookstore and picked up *The Fairytale Life of Dorothy Gale* on my own. But Mikey assured me that this takeoff on the main character from *The Wizard of Oz* was a sure winner. I bought it.

I learned a few lessons about what I could do with a girlfriend over the holiday. Tara and Jennifer stayed with us for three days and we all headed for the gym together on Thursday. In the meantime, we played games, watched movies, cooked, and went through old family photographs. Tara couldn't believe how scrawny I was before I started my gymnastics training.

When we got to the gym, Jennifer told me to change clothes and meet her at the therapy room. I figured I'd be helping massage Tara's legs again. Jennifer had more in store.

"We're going to progress slowly and you'll work on Tara's back today," Jennifer said. "Eventually, after the two of you become comfortable with it, I want to teach you to do full body sports massage. I've talked to Coach Dawson, and he agreed that the gym could use a massage therapist. And you need a job."

"I don't know when I'll be able to work while I'm keeping up with school, cheer, and our routines. Plus, Madison and Coach Daniels. If they have anything to do with me after the vacation."

"Oh, they'll be waiting for you, I'm sure," Jennifer said. "She's not the kind that lets people just walk away from her." We went into the therapy room and I saw Tara stretched out on her stomach on a massage table with a sheet over her. "Now, we'll start with extremities to get you used to touching Tara without getting lost in the sensations."

I was already lost in the sensations. Jennifer pulled a corner of the sheet back and exposed Tara's shoulder and arm. Bare shoulder. Tara wasn't wearing anything under the sheet. It took me a minute to keep from hyperventilating as I let that soak in.

"Tara's arms do the normal work of a gymnast's arms, which you know is a heavy workload in itself. But they also do at least half the work of her legs. I'm sure you've noticed how strong she is," Jennifer said. I nodded. "So, it makes sense to pay special attention to her arms and shoulders in a massage. Here's where you'll start."

She began showing me how the muscles connected and where tension was likely to build up. I followed the instructions and before too long, I was able to concentrate on the muscles and tension, and not so much on who all that skin was connected to. I could hardly believe Tara was willing to let me touch her like this, but as long as I kept the principles of therapy and care in mind, everything was okay.

When we'd finished working on her arms and shoulders, Jennifer pulled the sheet down farther so we could work on Tara's upper back. Man, was Tara strong! I had a reasonable understanding of my own strength. My back, shoulders, and arms were built to support my body on bars and rings, to vault, and to propel myself in floor exercises. I routinely held Tara above my head, and before Christmas had held Madison on one hand above my head as she did a needle stand—that's vertical splits.

I could certainly understand why Tara needed this kind of massage work with the extra work she put on her upper body.

We moved to her lower back and I was a little relieved to encounter the top of a pair of panties. She wasn't completely naked and that made me relax more. Of course, when we moved to her legs and butt, I discovered how minimal those panties were. I did close my eyes for a moment as I was massaging her gluteus maximus. Then I was able to let the feeling go as I moved down her legs and massaged her feet.

I was released from the massage room to go warm up for our routine and get a workout in before Tara joined me, while Jennifer turned Tara over to massage her chest and abs, and down the fronts of her legs.

WE GOT A good workout in and made some progress on our routine. Jennifer wanted us to get to the point at which Tara could actually lift her legs to a vertical handstand. She could support them okay, but balancing them was the problem. She wore lightweight knee braces that helped to hold her legs straight.

The biggest difference between Tara's routine and that of Madison was that Tara couldn't jump to get started on a lift. As a result, she had to press herself up using just her arm and torso strength, like I did on the rings. Once you were on the rings, you couldn't swing. Everything had to be a controlled movement.

I had to support Tara's weight steadily in my hands, but it was Tara who had to lift her weight over her head. We were working on her coming straight up with her feet above her head. We worked the exercise repeatedly as Jennifer moved around us, spotting and helping as needed. She gave advice and encouragement. We finally reached the point where Tara was straight up on my hands with my hands at shoulder height.

Then the unthinkable happened. Her left arm started shaking and before Jennifer could move, she collapsed on that side, dropping toward the floor head first.

Dad sometimes told a story about Mikey when she was a toddler falling backwards down the stairs. Dad, who was across the hall from her at the time, managed to get under Mikey on the stairs before she hit. He considered it to be a gap in time that allowed him to move through space faster than gravity was drawing Mikey. He couldn't explain it any other way.

I understood now. There was no time to think about what I should do. Part of my training for the past seven years had been to enhance my reflexes, but I don't think that affected the faster than life move I made to get myself under Tara and hold her to my chest as I fell to the mat and she landed on top of me.

The wind was knocked out of me, but I managed to scramble around and gasp, "Are you okay?" as Jennifer quickly checked us both over.

"I'm... I'm fine!" Tara said. "I'm not hurt! You didn't let me fall! Paul! You protected me. Are you okay?"

"Just a little out of breath. Oh, Tara. Thank God you weren't hurt."

I gathered her into my arms and kissed her like my life depended on it. At that moment, I thought it possibly did. She was safe.

"Uh... I appreciate the enthusiasm, but that isn't really appropriate in the gym," Jennifer said. I thought there was a little shakiness in her voice. It had all happened so fast that we were all in shock. "Now, can you tell me what we learned from that."

"To always stay under my partner, no matter what," I said.

"Um... Not to try to scratch my nose while I'm in a

handstand," Tara breathed. The draining of adrenaline from our systems finally left us in giggles.

"I think you also learned there's a limit to the number of times you can try a move in a row," Jennifer said. "I think we've reached the limit for this practice. Locker room, Tara. I want to check to see if you're bruised. Paul, use the mirrors and let me know if you spot any significant bruises. You didn't hit your head. We should be okay."

TARA AND JENNIFER were treated like family and stayed New Year's Eve and New Year's Day with us. Jennifer brought her boyfriend, Bob, with her. He was a nice guy, around fifty or so, I guess—my parents' age. Of course, so was Jennifer. Mom and Dad weren't going to object to her having her boyfriend with her and we had plenty of room.

We aren't usually big partiers—except Mikey. She was off to a New Year's Eve party and not expected to come home before the next day. So, the six of us—Mom, Dad, Jennifer, Bob, Tara, and me—had a pretty laid-back New Year's Eve. It ended up being the old-sters upstairs, playing cards at the dining table, while Tara and I watched a movie in the entertainment room downstairs.

Around eleven, Jennifer had me bring Tara upstairs so she could get ready for bed, but then I took her back to the basement to count down to midnight. Everybody else gave up and went to bed. Yeah, real party people. Neither Tara nor I was eager to leave and go to bed. I had an arm around her and she leaned against me, holding my hand in hers.

At midnight, we kissed. And then we didn't really stop kissing.

We'd been working together for almost three months and dating for a month, but we hadn't really spent more than a few minutes at a time making out. We did things on our dates. We went out to eat or went to a movie or went to a concert. We spent a little time in the car kissing, but even over Christmas, we hadn't just stayed in the entertainment room making out.

Tara was in her pajamas. There is something really different about holding a girl dressed in jeans and a shirt with a winter coat on and holding a girl who was in just her pajamas... with nothing underneath them. I mean, I'd been massaging Tara's bare skin all week. Saturday, Jennifer showed me a draping technique that kept Tara's modesty while I worked on the front of her legs.

But holding her and kissing her and running my hands up and down her back and side was a new and exciting experience. I think it was true of both of us. She was so soft and squeezable I was lost in the sensations.

"I can definitely feel you squeezing there," Tara whispered.

"Oh, my God!" I breathed, trying to snatch my hand back away from her breast. "I'm sorry!"

"Kiss me more," she said, holding my hand to her breast. I did.

Somehow, we managed to slow down a little. We just kissed and touched each other lightly, pretending to watch some stupid after midnight movie until we fell asleep together on the sofa.

Waking up with my girlfriend in my arms was the high point of my winter break. It wasn't easy getting up, but we managed and Tara got to the bathroom about the same time Jennifer came out of her room and rushed to help her.

We were well-behaved for the rest of the holiday. I cooked and had fun with Tara helping me in the kitchen. The day was way too short as the last day of vacation always is. I was back in my classes the next morning to start the new semester. There was a change of teacher in my English Literature and Composition class. He seemed okay and was interesting to listen to.

I got back to the gym for practice at noon and back with the cheerleaders at two-thirty. I was beginning to feel like cheer was a real waste of time. Of course, I didn't dare quit. I could have, but Dad drilled into me that I should never let my team down—even when they didn't care about me.

For example, I could lift Penny over my head with her standing in my hands, then toss her and catch her when her pose was over. She never even looked at me. No thank you. No touch of my arm. Just down and away. The other girls were pretty much the same. Lana was the most decent of them, but that wasn't saying much. She did a dismount and gave me a quick hug once, before she ran off to the girls' huddle.

"Paul's really nice," I overheard her. "He puts up with all our shit and never complains. And God! What a body."

"He has no personality," Penny scoffed. "Really, he's like a Goomba. You know his younger sister was in our class but skipped a grade and graduated last year. In the meantime, he got held back a year. D-U-M-B. I don't know what my sister sees in him."

"She just wants someone to stand on," laughed Melina. "He *is* a good base."

"He should wake up and get with Madison. She'd be sprawled out under him in a second."

"Isn't she only, like, seventeen?"

"Almost eighteen. Our parents couldn't wait to start again after I was born. So what? I started having sex with Ethan when we were sophomores. I don't think that Tara White woman is even capable of sex," Penny continued as the girls went past without even recognizing I was there. "I mean, what would she do? Just lay there with her legs spread? Maybe that's the most he could deal with."

"Let's hit The Uptown Creamery for ice cream," Lana said as they walked out the door.

I guess I was probably the only one left in the building. I went out and walked toward the gym. All three of those girls drove their hot little cars. Any one of them could have offered me a ride. They all knew they'd drive right past the gym on their way Uptown. What a bunch of stuck-up bitches.

"Good, you're already dressed," Madison said when I walked into the gym. "Coach Daniels wants us to work on a cannonball mount straight to a handstand. This is the way it should be done. That slow motion stuff you've been doing with Tara is for the birds."

She dragged me to her mats and I stripped off my shoes and coat. *I should really warm up more.* I didn't see Tara on the mats yet, so I supposed I could spend a few minutes working on a move with Madison.

Madison's coach started in on me right away.

"You'll stand with your feet outside the width of your shoulders so Madison can swing between your legs. We'll start once with Madison lying down behind you and you reach back to grasp her hands and swing her forward," Coach Daniels said.

I kind of dragged her along the mat until she was in front of me. Not pretty.

"You're too short!" Daniels said.

I don't know what she expected me to do about that, but she warned Madison that she'd need to keep her arms bent to pull herself off the floor. Well, the problem *could* have been that Madison was five-two and that was about five inches taller than most of the mixed pair tops. Nonetheless, we started working with her getting into position and me just swinging her between my legs.

In order to do that, she had to pretty much fold in half at the waist with her feet above her head as she lay on her back. Then she reached up and I reached down to join hands. From that position, we pulled her up off the mat and I swung her back and forth between my legs. It wasn't too difficult once we got the hang of working together on it and keeping our arms bent so she was off the mat.

The next step was to get enough swing that I could swing her all the way up on my hands at shoulder height. Believe me, we failed more times than we succeeded, but we did finally manage to get her into a handstand on my hands with her legs straight up. The rest of the time, I simply caught her when she came crashing down.

"Now we need to reverse the direction and swing with head and feet back instead of forward," Daniels said. "You will be able to do different mounts and throws in this position."

I saw Tara and Jennifer come out of the locker room about then and begged off any more.

"I have to go work with my partner now," I said. "I can probably work with you this weekend."

"Oh, come on. We need to get this down. She can work later," Madison complained.

"Can't anymore today. I'll see you tomorrow," I said.

If she thought she was just going to change my schedule and my time, she had another think coming. I guess I did, too.

Tara and I had a good workout and we actually progressed to doing a swing mount—the cannonball—too. I could feel Madison's eyes burning a hole in my back since it was so easy to swing Tara up to the proper position. We used it for a throw and Tara did a full tuck flip and I caught her as she landed.

Jennifer and Rachel, our choreographer, said we had all the poses down for our balance routine, but we needed to work on transitions and getting into the positions. That was going to take as much work as just learning the poses in the first place.

I have to admit that sometimes I felt like I was tossing around a doll and balancing her on my hands. Tara's knee braces kept her knees from giving out when she was going into a stand, and a lower back brace stabilized the base of her spine at the cost of some flexibility.

The first time she went up on her hands from a cannonball, her feet didn't make it above her head and she ended up in a full layback fold with her feet and head pointed in the same direction. Jennifer was enthusiastic about the position, called a Mexican arch, and wanted us to practice it for the routine.

I was worried that I'd break her in half, but all the female tops could get in that position, so I guessed it wasn't too bad.

I WAS STILL managing to get individual workouts on the apparatuses in. I found that working with Tara made me even more enthused about progressing on my other routines—especially my floor exercise. Coach Dawson was spotting me on the rings and I was doing pretty well. I was just a little short of horizontal on my iron cross, but I'd managed to hold where I was for three seconds. I dismounted and was ready to switch over to the pommel horse when I saw Madison and her coach come in.

"You need to go work with your partner," Coach Dawson said. "Coach Daniels has complained that you aren't fulfilling your commitment to her. You need to shape up on that."

"Wait. What? My only commitment was to work out with her sometimes," I complained. "I have a full-time partner I'm working with and my individual routines. I try to work with Madison once or twice a week."

"Coach Daniels and Madison say you promised to work with her as a partner. I admire the work you are doing with Tara White, but that isn't going to get you far. We know it's temporary. You could still make the competition in Louisville with Madison and stand a chance at the trials in June."

"Coach, I'm going to Louisville with Tara. We're auditioning our routine there and that's when they promised to decide if we can perform at the trials in June. I never promised any partnership with Madison before June. I don't even like her that much," I said. Maybe I was being a little whiny. *Yeah, I was.*

"You might not realize it, but Madison needs you as much as Tara does. You're one of the only bases we can field who is strong enough to support her. Being five inches taller and ten pounds heavier than other tops is a disadvantage for her, but you can lift and throw her. She has some real talent and you can likely go further as a mixed pair than you can as an individual gymnast,"

Coach Dawson said. "I'd really hate for you to get a bad reputation by slighting your working time with her."

I was pretty mad about the whole Madison thing. More like twenty pounds heavier. I didn't like her and I didn't like Coach Daniels. But Tara wasn't out of her physical therapy session yet, so there was nothing to stop me from going over to work with Madison for a while. Except that I really wanted to practice my pommel horse routine.

Still, the implication from Coach Dawson was that I would damage my reputation in the gym by not working with her. We all worked everywhere in the gym. The expense of my gym time and coaching was defrayed by the time I spent working with younger gymnasts, spotting for seniors, and teaching the toddler tumbling class. Reputation was a big part of success in the gym and in paying my way.

I headed over to Madison and Coach Daniels. If they'd said anything about my commitment, I'd have lost it, but they didn't. We just went straight to work. Coach Daniels was definitely trying to get us into some choreography as we moved through the pieces. I had to admit that Madison was talented. She had good balance and was reasonably easy to support. Tara required hyper-diligence because I had to help balance her. Madison was able to do a throw with a full pike flip with a rotation and I could catch her as she landed to support her.

We worked hard. I wasn't going to give Coach Daniels an excuse to complain, but after two hours, I said I needed to go work with my 'real' partner. I think the little dig went by both of them. Madison rushed up to me before I got off the mat and kissed me—right on the lips. It took a second to shake her off.

Some people just can't take no for an answer.

8
MOUNTING TENSION

I **HEADED FOR THE** mat where Tara and Jennifer were waiting for me. Jennifer wasted no time getting us started, so I didn't really have a chance to talk to Tara before we started working. She didn't seem to be in much of a mood to talk, either, so we just buckled into our routine and started working on those transitions.

We were only four weeks away from the Winter Cup competition in Louisville where Tara and I were intending to preview our routine for the USA Gymnastics Committee to get approval for the exhibition in Minneapolis in June. Coach Daniels had also let slip that she'd already entered Madison and me in the qualifier round for the mixed pairs. I wasn't enthused.

Jennifer had sat with Tara and me to get our travel arrangements made. When Madison mentioned that we'd be traveling together, I was only too happy to inform her that I already had my travel and lodging arrangements made. My parents had decided to come down to Louisville to watch, too. I intended to spend as little time as possible with Madison and Coach Daniels.

"I'm tired," Tara announced. "We can pick up tomorrow."

"Would you like to go out to dinner?" I asked.

"No. I don't feel much like being sociable right now. I'm sure you can find someone else to do." She turned and grabbed her crutches, heading for the locker room as fast as she could. That was really strange. Jennifer just shook her head and followed.

Having an extra hour to myself before I had to get home and help with dinner, I immediately headed for the pommel horse to pick up my interrupted routine from the morning. I was combining a Russian flop followed by double splits and into a high dismount. I ran the routine three times and was pretty pleased with myself the last time I came off the dismount.

I headed toward the gymnastic mat to practice my floor routine and got into the flips and turns. I never got to do this kind of thing with the pairs routines. The tumbling was more basic and limited to things we could do in sync. Madison and I could synchronize a flip or other roll, but Tara didn't have the leg strength to propel herself. If I did a flip, it had to be coordinated with a somewhat static move of Tara's that I could catch her in before she fell. Madison and Tara could get as much height as I could throw them. That wasn't too much with Tara because I also had to control her landings. Madison had to balance herself when she landed.

I really wanted to do a double pike with a twist, and I needed the sprung floor and a run-up to get the height I needed. I did a few warmups either without the twist or a single pike salto. I set myself in the corner and ran across the mat. Midway, I launched into the move.

Unfortunately, I didn't get quite the height I needed and I landed without having fully rotated. I caught part of my weight on my hands and then landed on my back. I lay there for a couple of seconds, analyzing what I'd done wrong. In that time, three coaches had come running from different parts of the gym to check on me.

"I'm fine. I just didn't get the full rotation," I said as I sat up. "I was just trying to figure out what I did wrong."

"You tried a new move without a spotter, Paul," Coach Dawson said. "You know better than that."

"Yessir. I should have waited."

It didn't make any difference whether I needed a spotter for this move or not. The right answer was to wait. In that way, gymnastics was just like school. You had to give the right answer in order to stop the lecture. Unfortunately, it wasn't enough this time. I had to undergo the lecture anyway, with a couple of other coaches chiming in about not being stupid in my workouts.

I finally got off the gym floor and into the locker room to shower and dress.

"How'd you manage to get everyone so mad at you today?" Andy asked in the locker room.

Andy had been one of the senior gymnasts who graduated from high school about the time I started in high school. I hadn't seen him much because he went off to college somewhere. But he was taking a term off this spring to prepare for the trials and had come back here to practice. He was a star in the gym.

"Is everybody mad at me?" I asked.

"I just heard Coach read you the riot act. Earlier today, Coach Daniels was complaining to Dawson about something you'd done or not done. And when Tara headed to the locker room an hour ago, she looked steamed as hell. The only thing they all had in common was you," Andy said.

"I have no clue. Everybody wants something different from me. They're all ragging on me."

"That's a tough one. If you actually landed that last flip you tried, you'd be a contender in the qualifiers. It's too bad you're spending all that time with the pairs routines. They're circus acts—not gymnastics. Usually, the only people who do acro-gym are those who can't master the apparatuses," Andy said.

I'd heard that before and even believed it. In fact, I'd made the same comment once or twice myself. If you couldn't master the apparatuses, then you could do pairs or group acro gym on the floor. Still, I couldn't discount acro gym being more fun than artistic gymnastics. I kind of felt the acrobatic gymnastics were more artistic and artistic gymnastics were more technical.

"I did a qualifier event in Chicago late last summer and didn't qualify," I said. "Coach said he didn't think I'd progressed far enough to qualify this spring and that I should take the opportunity to help Tara. I don't mind that. In fact, I like it a lot. I just try to keep working on my routines so I can get back to it after the exhibition in June."

"What's with the other chick you're working with and Coach Daniels?" Andy asked.

"Don't ask. I said I'd help her out after her previous partner quit on her. I thought it was just going to be an occasional thing, but Coach Daniels thinks I'm her full-time partner and has us registered to compete in Louisville. I don't know how she managed to convince Coach Dawson."

The more I let all this out, the more depressed I was becoming. Andy thought I could have qualified in one of the events this spring. I really didn't mind helping and working with Tara. I liked it. She was my girlfriend and I wished we could spend more time together. But I missed doing real gymnastics and it irritated me that I had to sacrifice my workout time to practice with Madison.

"Well, I'm not your coach," Andy sighed. "All I can say is do the best you can and don't give up your routines. I think you've got what it takes, but you're still young as male gymnasts go. There's a lot more pressure for the women to get in the game in their teens. There aren't that many like Simone who can hold a career together for ten years."

"I'll make Team USA for Worlds by 2026."

I wished I was as confident as I sounded. After this year's trials were over and Tara and I had done our exhibition, I planned to spend all my time getting ready for fall artistic gymnastic competitions.

IN ANY CASE, I didn't have time to worry about any of it. I received word from my school counselor that it appeared my grade average had slipped below the standard required for participation in sports at school—like cheerleading. I don't know how they measured that. The most recent grading period had ended at Christmas and I had sufficient grades to continue. They weren't great grades—I was still no genius—but they were good enough to continue.

On top of that, I'd been studying more than what was in school. My four classes seemed unimportant compared to the study Jennifer had assigned me to become a massage therapist. From the first time I did a guided massage on Tara's legs, Jennifer had me keep track of every hour I put in studying massage. I was putting in a good twenty hours or more a week learning therapeutic massage.

I watched YouTube videos repeatedly to support the reading and had a one-hour practice session each day on Tara. That was a real trial by fire, so to speak. I'd learned to control my natural physical response to her. She was my girlfriend, and even though we hadn't had much time together in the past week or so, we still kissed and I was really attracted to her physically as well as emotionally.

Something seemed to be bugging her lately and we just weren't finding time to talk. Or anything else that wasn't in the gym. It bugged me, but I couldn't figure out what to do about it.

Now there was this school thing that blindsided me.

"Paul, Mr. Fields is concerned about your progress in his class," Ms. Brown, my counselor, said when I reported to her office. "He says your responses in class are not in keeping with the rest of the class and he feels your writing is elementary."

Mr. Fields was my new English teacher. My last term in high school, and I get a guy who thinks everyone in his class should be a Rhodes Scholar. My previous two English classes had mostly been kids who had English as a second language, so the workload was adjusted accordingly.

"He assigns a lot of reading and I can't get it all done. I just don't read that fast," I said. That hadn't been a problem the past year and a half. My teachers had tested me on the lighter reading assignments. I guess Mr. Fields wasn't with the program. I knew a couple of the ESL kids were struggling.

"This is the work the class is assigned. Everyone else is keeping up just fine."

"I don't read that fast. Isn't there a class that isn't as accelerated as this one?" I asked.

"I'm not sure what we can do about that. Mr. Fields is of the opinion that athletes and second language learners need to keep up with the curriculum just like everyone else does."

"I don't think there are any other athletes in my class. And I don't think all the ESL kids are keeping up, either."

"We have complaints on file from you and your parents that indicate your unwillingness to be in classes with the athletes you are referring to. The school has done its best to keep you out of classes known to cater to athletes who have limited time to study."

"So, you keep me out of classes I'm capable of passing so I won't get beaten up by the others you've chosen to give special treatment to? I don't think I need to worry about getting beaten up or stuffed in a locker anymore."

"Your presence in those classes could be considered an incitement. If there was violence, you would be considered at fault for not having stayed in different classes. Besides, you are older than the rest of them."

I'd be nineteen in a month. The school wanted to be rid of me.

"Great. So, my choice is to go someplace where I'd end up being expelled for other people's actions, or stay where I am and fail based on a different standard. That doesn't really seem fair."

"Avoid conflicts and keep up with the rest of your class. That sounds like the same standard all other students are held to."

Well, shit.

"Mr. Fields, I'd like to do better in your class," I said. I'd had to cut all my afternoon training in order to be at the school when he had a period free. He looked at me critically. I could see 'big dumb jock' written all over his face.

"Well, that's a good first step," he said. "I understand you've received special treatment in the past. That's something I'm not in favor of."

"I've paid dearly for the slower pace of my classes. It's taken me a year longer than my classmates to get this far in school, but I've done the work and passed the classes," I said. "I'd rather not take another year. My only real sports interest in school is the cheer squad, and I'm nearly out of eligibility for that. The state cheerleader competition is March first. I turn nineteen on the sixteenth. That ends my eligibility."

"And today is February twelfth. Hmm."

He looked at a calendar and shuffled some notes on his desk. I recognized the signs of someone thinking a problem through because it was exactly the way Dad acted when he was faced with a tough decision. Somehow, that was comforting. Mr. Fields was actually thinking about the situation.

"Why are you in my class, Paul? Nearly every other jock who can't make the grade point is in Mrs. Dunham's class. Why aren't you?"

"It's kind of a long story, sir. Are you sure you are interested in it?"

"Yes. Remarkably, I am very interested. You've been in the—shall we say—accelerated classes for the past year and a half. Certainly not AP or IB classes, but most of the people in these classes are intending to get at least a community college education. Even the ESL students. I'm pushing them to get ready for college. The less accelerated classes are expected to go into trades or manual work of some sort. Why have you been in the college prep courses?”

It was the first I knew I was in the college prep classes. It's not like they made a thing about who were the smart kids and who were the dumb ones. Since I got some 'trade school' credit for my work at the gym, I assumed I was being prepared for a trade rather than academics. I'd chosen gymnastics as my trade with massage as my occupation.

I told Mr. Fields my story, starting from being a dumb wimp and progressing to being a dumb jock. Nothing had made me smarter, obviously.

“So, for five years your teachers have just been passing you without you doing the work?” Fields demanded. He looked steamed. It got me mad.

“No! I did the work. It just takes me longer and my teachers accepted the lowest standard. During Covid, I spent two years at self-guided pace with my parents monitoring my progress and administering tests. I've passed the tests. I learned the material. I just can't read that fast.”

“How fast *do* you read?”

“Not very. That's why it takes so long to get the work done. Even in math, I understand the concepts fine. I might remember them better than the students who study for the test and then forget about it. I just have to, like, prove every step before I get it.”

“Interesting.” Mr. Fields seemed to be puzzling over something. “You're studying to be a massage therapist?”

“Yessir. It's one of the ways I pay my way at the gym so I can continue to work on my gymnastics.”

“You're a competitor?”

“Sort of. I didn't qualify for individual events at the national level this year. I hope to next year. I'm still a senior elite gymnast. But that means it will be three more years before I can qualify for the Olympic trials. This winter and spring I've focused on working with Tara White, the pairs gymnast who was injured three years ago. I also work with Madison Layne on a pairs routine. She thinks we can qualify for trials at Louisville next weekend."

"You don't sound enthused."

"I don't much like her or her coach. They think of me as a convenient footstool instead of a partner. Like the cheerleaders do. Tara is my real partner."

"Okay. Do the work I assign and I will pass you so you can compete at the Louisville qualifier weekend after this one, and for the state cheerleader championships the following weekend. I want you to try something. I'm assigning you a book by Neil Gaiman. It's not on the class reading list, but it's a fun book. I think you'll enjoy it. You won't be dealing with the same material as the rest of the class. The book *American Gods* came out in 2001 and won several awards. I think they made a television series out of it, but that wouldn't help you with this assignment. I want you to read and understand this book, Paul. I'll be asking you relevant questions about it every week. That means you need to keep me informed of exactly how far in the book you've gotten each week. That way I'll have the right questions ready for you. Now, have you used an audio book before?"

"I'm not on a program that allows for assistive technology," Paul said. "My parents felt that would be detrimental to my future."

"Audio books aren't assistive technology. They are a valid publishing format for literary works and are every bit as common as print books and eBooks. I'd like you to try listening to the book *as you read*. Try that out for

110

a couple of weeks and see if it helps your understanding and progress. You can buy the eBook and turn on the screen reader. Your Kindle will read the book to you while it highlights the words. You might call it assistive technology, but they are equally available to all students. I know there are several students who listen to their books instead of trying to read them. Give it a try."

"Yessir." I wasn't sure it would help, but Mr. Fields was giving me a chance I didn't expect to have. I'd take it.

"Good luck in Louisville."

"Thank you, sir. And thanks to your wife for the cookies."

He snorted and I left.

I GOT TO the gym and ran straight to Tara, just in time for our practice session. Madison and her coach tried to wave me over to them, but I really wanted to see my girlfriend.

"You should probably just go to your partner," Tara said. "She isn't going to let us work and you'd rather be there anyway."

"What? I don't care what she or her coach wants. I want to be here with you. You're my partner and she can just go to hell as far as I'm concerned. What do you mean I'd rather be there?"

"I saw you kiss her. Don't try to deny it," Tara burst forth. "You go straight to her as soon as you come into the gym. You don't even come in for massage lessons. You'd rather have her."

"That is so untrue. The only time I kissed Madison, I didn't even kiss her. She attacked me and laid one on me. I was so surprised I ran away from her. And the only reason I've been going to her first on most days is because Coach Dawson insists. I'd much rather be massaging you."

"Is that true, Paul? Do you really want to work with me? I told Jennifer not to complain to Dawson because I thought you wanted to spend time with her and we could limp along with our demo."

"Tara! First off, you asked me to be your partner back in October, and I agreed. Second, you are my girl-friend and I would never cheat on you. To think that you believe I'd do it with her? Yuck. And third, you went with me to the initial meeting with Madison and sug-gested that I could work with her while still working with you. I never wanted to work with her in the first place. I have a hard enough time working with her sister on the cheer squad."

"But you're doing so well!"

"Not because I'm putting any great effort into it. You know it's the same with her as with the cheerleaders. They all think they should be put on a pedestal and I'm a convenient hunk of marble. I don't know why I ever wanted to become strong in the first place. I'm not even a human anymore. When I'm working with you, I feel like I'm part of something. Something beautiful."

"I'm so ashamed," Tara cried, clutching me tightly.

"No. You don't need to be ashamed. I understand how you could think that, but it's like what I want doesn't even count. All I want is you."

"Okay. One quick kiss to make up and let's get to work," Jennifer said. "We're going to move the twist throw up a notch."

I gave Tara a quick smooch and we promised to go out to dinner after our workout. As soon as we were in the middle of the mat, I saw Madison and Coach Daniels marching across the floor with Coach Dawson in tow. Jennifer stepped between us and them and told them in no uncertain terms that they needed to leave us be so we could work on our routine.

"We need him on Madison's routine," Coach Daniels said. "They're competing at Louisville."

"Only if you think they're ready now," Jennifer said.

"Paul needs to work with Madison in order to maintain his competitive edge," Coach Dawson said.

"No, he definitely doesn't and you've betrayed his trust as his coach," Jennifer responded. "Paul works much harder with Tara than he does with Madison. In fact, the amount of artistry required for Madison's routine could be handled by a stepladder. You know as well as I do that there isn't a ghost of a chance she'll qualify for nationals. She has no more chance of that than Tara has. You're just milking a money cow by sacrificing one of your best gymnasts to her."

"Now just a minute, Jennifer. That is not remotely true," Coach said.

"Isn't it Phillip? I know what the gym has charged *us* for our training time and use of Paul. You haven't reduced that despite shorting us on the time. Are you telling me she isn't paying just as much? We agreed to a maximum of an hour a day, four days a week for Madison. The rest of Paul's time is ours. You've been keeping him two to three hours a day, six days a week. You owe us training time."

"Paul, you have to speak up here. I've been guiding your career since you wandered into the gym as a scrawny twelve-year-old. You know Madison offers you a better opportunity to succeed than Tara does," Coach Dawson said.

First off, I had no idea the gym was charging Tara

and Madison for my time as their partner. I needed to really think that through. But the important issue right now was training time with each.

"No, Coach. Four hours a week. That's the limit of my commitment to Madison," I said. "And that's more than my initial agreement. Take it or leave it." My heart was racing so fast I was afraid I'd pass out. I felt like I was that same twelve-year-old getting stuffed in a locker.

"Phillip, you have to talk some sense into him."

"I'm sorry, Coach Daniels. I can't force him to give you more time," Coach Dawson said. "You should take what's offered. Dr. Martin is right. Paul's commitment to Tara was well before you started putting demands on his time. I'm sorry, Paul. I should never have approved any of this."

Coach Dawson ushered Madison and her coach away from our mats and Jennifer started working Tara and me on the three throws in our routine. We worked hard for three hours, then Tara and I went to dinner.

9

COMPETITION

"ARE YOU SURE** you'd rather be with me?"

"Tara, I don't know why we're even talking about this. Is there some way I can be clearer about how I feel about you and about what we're doing?" I asked.

"I just don't understand why a guy who is fit and strong and talented would rather be with a crippled girl who won't put out than take up with an obviously willing and able beautiful girl."

"I never see you as crippled," I said. "The throws we were doing today? You were spectacular! I don't think we'd have to do our bit as an exhibition. We could compete."

"Thank you, but that just shows your lack of experience with pairs acro-gym. There are too many things I don't do and can't do."

"I thought you wanted to return to competition," I said.

"I thought I did, too. I need to be honest with myself and with you, though. I'll make a splash because I dared return to the mat after the disaster almost four years ago. But it wouldn't qualify in a competition. *You're* why I can be out there. There were other potential bases we looked at. They just didn't stack up. Some were too full of themselves to even consider working with me. Others just weren't strong enough to do the things you can do with me. Bases have to be strong and well-balanced, but you can surely feel the difference between working with me and working with Madison—or even with her sister cheerleading. I can't land without your help. I can't propel myself in tumbling. I only minimally help balance myself. I might as well be a plastic doll."

"Oh, believe me: I don't think of you as a plastic doll at all. Sometimes I feel like a juggler a little, but what does a juggler have to do first and foremost? He has to not drop anything. I'm juggling a precious living woman and all I want is to keep her in the air and show people how beautiful she is."

"Do you want to kiss me right here in the restaurant?" Tara giggled. "That was beautiful. But don't drop any of your other partners, either. I love the way you make me feel and how you talk. I don't want to hold you back."

"*If* you were holding me back, it sure wouldn't be from working with Madison or the cheerleaders. For me personally, all I need is a little time to stay in tune on the apparatuses. You're keeping me strong enough and there's no real chance I could qualify for individual gymnastics in time to make the trials. That means I'm on a track for next year, not anything that interferes with us and the exhibition."

"I promise that after the exhibition, I'll set you free."

"I don't really like the sound of that. Um... You know, if you decide you need to break up with me, I guess I understand, sort of. No other girl would have anything to do with me. I scare them. And Madison doesn't count. She thinks if she was with me... you know... sexually, then I'd have to do whatever she wants. She's pretty obvious about that. But... if you do decide... you know... to break up, please tell me directly. I'm terrible at reading clues. I didn't understand you were upset with me until today. I just... Please don't just shut me out. I really really like you."

"I really really like you, too, Paul."

In fact, I was in love.

I suppose we could have gone to either of our homes and just relaxed and made out as much as we wanted. I think we both knew that after New Year's Eve, we could get carried away if we did that. And I really didn't want to get carried away with Tara with either my parents on the next floor or Jennifer in the next room.

I could sure imagine getting carried away with Tara, though. Except, not over the console in her car when the temperature was eighteen degrees.

In all fairness, I had to squeeze out more practice time with Madison in the next week as well as with Tara. I wasn't happy that Coach Daniels had signed us up to compete in Louisville without asking me. She wasn't happy that I wasn't traveling and staying with her and Madison. That's the way it was.

I have to say we all made a lot of progress that week and we were confident in what we could do in Louisville. My parents decided to travel down for the weekend, too. That was pretty exciting because they didn't often get to one of my competitions. Mikey decided the event was just two weeks before spring break, so she couldn't take time off. She promised to watch us in June. Tara,

Jennifer, and I flew with my folks, but I'd need to go to the arena as soon as we got to town, while they went to the hotel to relax.

There are five events in acrobatic gymnastics: women's pairs, men's pairs, mixed pairs, men's group, and women's group. I guess the pairs are self-explanatory, but the women's group is defined as three women, while the men's group is defined as four men. A maximum of ten teams are assigned to the US National Team. That's two from each of the categories. But they don't *have* to have that many. I guess there have been years when they only took one team in a category and even a couple of times when no one qualified in a particular event.

The mixed pairs competition in Louisville was so small that it didn't even appear on the event schedule. Only three mixed pairs competed. If that sounds like it should have been good odds for qualifying, you're wrong. Each team is held to an independent standard that includes how ready the judges deem the team to be for international competition. The same judges that assessed whether Madison and I qualified for the national team trials in June, would determine *if* Tara and I merited an exhibition.

We got to Louisville on Thursday afternoon. I was cutting two days of classes to travel to this event. We had a practice time set Thursday night with Madison and early Friday morning with Tara. As soon as I turned my phone on after my plane landed, I got a text message from Madison that she was waiting at the arena for our practice time. I took off for the arena directly from the airport. Mom and Dad said they'd check me into the hotel and took my luggage.

Each team had only forty-five minutes of practice time to run their three programs. The competition included three events, judged on different scales. The first was the balance event. It was all about the poses and positions we could get in and hold where I was supporting Madison above me. She was pretty good at those. All I had to do was hold her steady. The second event was the dynamic event. That emphasized our synchronized tumbling, throws, and swings. It was considerably harder because Madison was so tall. We both had to keep our elbows bent on the between the legs swing, the cannonball, so she didn't drag her butt on the floor. If her partner had been six feet tall instead of five-five, it would have been easier. On the other hand, we didn't look ridiculously mismatched like some of the pairs where the top didn't even come up to the shoulders of her base. Finally, there was the combined routine which was the most artistic.

I think Coach Daniels started yelling at us the minute we stepped onto the mats and didn't stop until we were out of the arena. Nothing seemed to please her, even though I thought it was the best we'd ever performed our routines. We were off-beat on the music, we weren't perfectly vertical in a pose, we were out of sync in our tumbling run. We worked hard and fast for the full forty-five minutes and I was glad to get off the mat and into a shower in my hotel room. Dad gave me my key when I got there and told me they'd meet me in half an hour for dinner.

As soon as I was in my room, I called Tara and asked if she'd join us for dinner. She said Jennifer had already made the reservation for the five of us and that they'd meet us in the restaurant at seven.

Of course, once I was out of the shower, there was a message on my phone from Madison telling me where to meet her and Coach Daniels for dinner. I just sent her a text that said 'Already committed. CU at breakfast.'

You can imagine how well that went over. Her response made me shiver.

Part of having grown up small was learning not to talk back. My parents were fine about it and administered appropriate discipline. But at school, saying no to someone could get a guy a bloody nose. As a result, I still found it kind of gut-wrenching to say no to someone. And someone like Madison was going to make it even harder. I turned my phone off when I met Mom, Dad, Jennifer, and Tara.

Breakfast with Madison and Coach Daniels would be at nine. Tara and I had our practice time at five. It was like we didn't really merit the time because we weren't competing. In fact, we were only doing one combined routine rather than the separate balance and dynamic programs. We had two minutes and thirty seconds for the exhibition, just like the combined competition.

"Are you ready for this?" I asked when we got to the arena.

"I'm nervous. I know I'm not the same as the other athletes. When I was on the national team four years ago, I didn't even need to qualify. Our coach just petitioned the selection committee with a video and they sent an invitation to the trials," Tara said.

"Jennifer?"

"No. Jennifer became my coach and caretaker after the accident. My coach down in Texas was actually on the selection committee, so he had an inside track. Then the next year, we were qualified by virtue of having been on the under-sixteen national team the previous year."

"We're going to do great," I said. I sounded more confident than I was, but once I was on the mat with Tara, everything seemed to be right. I had to work harder to balance Tara than to balance Madison, but Tara's lines and movement flowed with artistry that Madison lacked.

We had our thirty minutes—less time than the competitors because we were only rehearsing one program instead of three. Then I had a light breakfast with Tara and Jennifer before joining Madison and Coach Daniels for my second breakfast. I still ate sparingly. The mixed pairs would perform balance and dynamic routines on Friday and then do their combined routines on Saturday morning. Tara and I would have our demonstration after the last group competitors Saturday at noon.

The convention center where the events were held was basically a bunch of big empty spaces that could be configured any way they wanted. I snagged a brochure that said it held 7,000 spectators for a college basketball game. I figured it was set up for maybe a couple thousand at the gymnastics convention. The rest of the hall was divided into sections for different events and practice. By the time we got to our first performance about noon on Friday, other gymnastic events were already underway in the rest of the space. That's another thing about gymnastics in general; each event is on its own schedule. No one waits for other events to finish.

I wasn't sure how many teams were competing in acrobatic gymnastics. I understood some of them were junior elite and some were senior elite. All I knew was that when Madison and I stepped on the mat for our balance routine at 11:45, it was showtime. Two minutes and thirty seconds later, there was polite applause from the few spectators who were there for our event—mostly parents and teammates of the competitors.

We went to the sofa where Coach Daniels joined us and waited for our score.

Scoring in gymnastics and especially in acrobatic gymnastics is arcane. You're judged on artistry, execution, and difficulty for a total of 31.5 'possible' points. The thing is that the 1.5 points assigned for difficulty isn't really a cap, so you can earn more points for extra difficulty. There wasn't much chance Madison and I would gain extra points for extra difficulty. We were counting on execution to get us in the top tier. Artistry counted for ten points and execution counted for twenty. I thought we did pretty well on our execution and when our final score of 23.685 was posted, I thought we were in good shape.

"If you had smiled at the same time, you would have had two more points," Coach Daniels reprimanded us. "You need to connect more. The judges need to see you working as a unit." She shook her head as we went to the ready room to relax until our dynamic routine was called.

In a lot of really big competitions, there is a qualifying round before the final round. In international competition it is usual to qualify for each event: balance, dynamic, and combined. The Winter Cup didn't attract enough teams to merit a qualifying round.

The balance routine was based on getting into static poses of varying difficulty and holding them for three seconds. You were always supposed to be in touch with each other. We'd even been measured after our practice the night before because you get a deduction if your heights are more than 11.5 inches (29cm) different. The greater the difference in height, the greater the deduction. I knew there were some pairs that had to be taking a full point deduction because of the extreme difference in height. With Madison and me, it was only two inches, so no deduction.

The dynamic routine was only two minutes and was based on flight, both individual and assisted. Where the balance elements required that the partners be in touch at all times, the characteristic of dynamic elements was that they involved flight and contact between the partners is brief and either assists or interrupts the flight. In other words, throw and catch and release. We were required to have at least six different dynamic elements in our routine.

We warmed up at 3:30 and were called to the mat at 4:00.

For me, the dynamic routine was just fun. In the balance routine, I had to constantly hold and support Madison while she balanced in an arabesque or splits or a Mexican arch. In the dynamic routine, I got to throw her in the air so she could do a straight back flip or a pike or tuck or twist. I'd come to really like the cannonball as either a mount to balance or as a throw. We'd learned to keep our arms bent enough so she didn't drag on the floor and we could get some serious height for her saltos.

We got right into the routine, but on the second throw had a bit of a stumble. That got us off a beat from the music. Of course, we'd get a deduction for the stumble and when we didn't finish right on time with the music, we got another half point deduction. I still thought we did okay and our score showed 24.675.

Of course, Coach Daniels had a hundred notes to give us about what we did wrong and blamed me for the stumble. I don't think I could have prevented it, but I was glad to get free of them and join Tara, Jennifer, and my parents for dinner.

"I'm afraid you aren't going to win this one," Tara said. "She's got potential, but she moves like a wooden board. I should talk, since I move like I have no bones, but she really needs to loosen up."

"How was I?" I asked. "I really can't do anything about Madison."

"As always, I'm impressed with your strength and balance. You are steady and sure. I always know that when you are holding me, but it's comforting to see it," she said.

"This is very different than what we saw you do in August in Chicago," Mom said. "How do you feel about it?"

"Um… Working with Madison is okay, though I don't really like her coach that much. I don't think she should be doing our choreography. Even Jennifer has a professional choreographer who works with Tara and me," I said. "Working with Tara and Jennifer is great. I feel like we get all the connection Coach Daniels says is missing between Madison and me. I guess we are just more connected."

Tara giggled a little and I blushed. We were connected, all right. Mouth to mouth whenever we could. I wondered why it was so different with her previous partner that it was all screwed up when they made love. When I was holding Tara, I felt like there was no way I could ever drop her. Well, tomorrow would tell the tale of whether we were going to perform in Minneapolis in June. That was for both of my pairs.

Madison and I did our combined routine at a little after nine Saturday morning. Shortly thereafter, we stood on the podium to receive our bronze medal. Third place out of three. Our cumulative total points did not qualify us to go to the trials in Minneapolis by a long shot, but we weren't that far behind the second place team.

"I'm really sorry we didn't place higher. You know, I wasn't trying to torpedo your chances," I said.

"Hush. Coach is pissed, but I'm not," Madison answered. "Our score was higher than anything I got with my previous partner when we did women's pairs. When I grew and Susan quit, I didn't think I'd be able to ever find another partner. I didn't even realize you were in the gym until I saw you in a cheer competition with my sister. Um... I could still come over to your room later, you know. Maybe it would help our connection. I'd like to connect with you, you know."

"Madison, you know that isn't going to fly. I need to go change to my other uniform now. Tara and I need to warm up."

"Yeah. Well, thanks. Really. I mean it." She headed in for another kiss and I saw it coming in time to turn my cheek to her.

"See you later."

"You did good out there, and look, you got a medal," Tara said when she met me to warm up.

"Yeah, they give medals for last place now," I laughed.

"Don't be hard on yourself. The first place pair barely qualified for the trials in June. If I believed that was the best the country had to offer, we'd be competing instead of doing an exhibition."

"That's not really encouraging," I said. "Somehow I don't believe you think we're that good."

"Oh, I believe *you are.* I think the judges felt the same way. I sat near them and listened carefully. You know when they do the measurements, you are supposed to be within 29 centimeters of your partner—about eleven and a half inches. But the standard is so weighted toward a large base and tiny top that they felt you and Madison were unevenly matched. They thought she was too tall and you were too short to be together. That is something you and I won't need to deal with. I'm seven inches shorter than you, not three."

"I heard one of the coaches at the gym once say I'd be more proportional if I was three inches taller. I don't think there's anything I can do about that."

"Lift me. Swing me. Throw me. I think we have a good connection."

We finished our warmup under Jennifer's watchful eye. She checked Tara's shoulder muscles and the positioning of her braces. We'd chosen to wear matching black unitards with gold braiding on the legs, arms, and chest. I'd noticed that most of the women, whether in pairs or groups, chose a leotard with bare legs and arms. A couple wore short skirts. But if Tara chose that, her braces would show. In the unitard, the leggings covered the braces. The gold braid against the black fabric was a requirement so judges could see how straight the line of the legs was.

The last of the Men's Group had just performed and they were going to be presenting the medals for that event shortly. I saw a shuffling at the judges' table as a different group replaced the judges for the previous event. One of the judges came across the floor to talk to us before we performed.

"Tara, it's wonderful to see you back," he said. "Are you sure you are up to this?"

"I've been working on my rehab for three years now. I feel strong, though I can't do some of the moves. That's why we are only planning an exhibition and not competing. I'd like to believe we could compete someday, but that isn't likely," Tara said.

"Dr. Martin, the tariff sheet looks... um... ambitious for the extent of Tara's injuries. Do you believe this is safe for her?" he asked Jennifer.

"Yes, sir. I have monitored Tara's physical rehabilitation as well as her coaching and she is fully capable of this program," Jennifer said.

"Well, if we see enough development and artistry in your performance, we'll approve you for the exhibition in June. Shall we get started?"

He didn't really even look at me. He returned to the judges' table and took his seat. In a few seconds, they nodded to us and that was our signal to take the floor. There were no announcements or any other indication we were going to perform. We walked to the center of the mat with our arms around each other. That way, I could support Tara as she walked. As soon as we were in our starting position, we stopped and turned our heads away from each other.

There was a single tone and we began to move with the music that followed it.

The artistry our judges were looking for had to do with the story-telling aspect of our performance. Between the music and our moves, we were supposed to tell a story. You might think it's a pretty loose interpretation, but all the moves, mounts, and poses had to fit with the music and the story. That's why Jennifer had called in a choreographer who was experienced with both acrobatic gymnastics and figure skating to put together our performance. I never did know what the story was in my performance with Madison.

Of course, all the talk and analysis of what we were

doing was nothing when we actually started our performance. We were the music and we were each other. I could tell when Tara needed a little extra support and when I could set her free. She did extremely well on her 360 twist and our cannonball mount to a handstand was perfect. Instead of trying to balance straight up, she went into splits, and then into a Mexican arch. I was able to throw her into a flip and support her as she landed in front of me.

Our ending pose had me supporting Tara with one hand as I leaned one direction and she did a one-arm bridge in the other direction. It was a position I could pull her up from into my arms as we walked off the floor.

As soon as we were off the floor, Tara smashed her lips against mine and gave me a deep and sincere kiss.

10

CHEER

WE RECEIVED A letter on Tuesday with an official invitation to honor the national team with an exhibition showing that injury need not always be the last step in an athlete's life.

I didn't practice with Madison at all that week and my practice time with Tara was limited. Saturday would be the State Cheerleading competition in St. Paul. We practiced after school every day and I had to be there, even though I was only competing in the Coed Group Tumbling division. We weren't going three high in our pyramid, but we were doing something I understood was unique. While Lana and Melina would mount to the shoulders of the two bases each girl had next to us, Penny was going up on my hands and then on a single foot on my hand with the other raised in a needle split. It was pretty impressive and we had practiced it a lot.

Of course, that wasn't the only skill we were showing. There were jumps and turns. I also caught Lana as she ran to me and placed one foot in my hands. Then I flipped her into the waiting basket of our other bases.

The other six girls on our team did lesser tumbles, including cartwheels and flips, but mostly they served as spotters for the tops.

Of course, that was only for the tumbling competition. I wasn't in any of the other events, for the same reason I didn't cheer at ballgames. I was a guy and was only needed for my strength. On the 100-point judging sheet, ten of the twenty-five points for partner stunts were for 'Difficulty: Level of Skill, Use of Coed Skills, Number of Stunts, Number of Bases, Creativity, Transitions, and Variety.' That's right. One mention of Coed Skills in a ten-point segment of the 100-point score sheet.

Coach Cook said that other than the stunts where I was lifting, throwing, or supporting a top, I should focus on not detracting from the girls. I don't know how she could have made my importance any clearer.

There were eight schools in Division I and eight in Division II. We were in Division I, so our competition started at ten in the morning. We were on the bus at school at eight in the morning and at the Riverside Center thirty minutes later. We had to go through registration, music check-in, and warmups. Then the girls did the sideline routine, fight song, and spirit routine. All that happened before eleven-thirty when the group tumbling got started.

We were the fifth team to take the floor.

I thought we did a pretty good job. No one missed a running pass or any jumps. Throwing Lana was perfect, right into the basket. Then the other four bases and I rolled into our line. Our three tops mounted, supported by our spotters from behind. Lana and Melina got to the shoulders of two bases each. Penny was on my shoulders. There was a big round of applause when she stepped onto my hands and I lifted her straight up over my head. Then she shifted her weight and swung her left leg up in a catch-foot splits position.

And that's where it fell apart. I could feel her wobble a little and shifted to support her, but she never stabilized.

"Spotters!" I called as I felt Penny's weight leave my hand. I dropped my hand rapidly to make her descent as vertical as possible. If she'd done a nose dive, it would have been disastrous. Lana and Melina lost balance as the spotters rushed between us, but they both jumped into a dismount supported by their spotters and bases. I saw Penny coming down and reached out to grab her under the arms. She straightened with her hands on our two spotters and I got her to the floor almost gently.

That ended our routine. There was scattered applause, but everyone knew we'd failed our last stunt. Penny brushed my hands off her and stalked off the mats refusing to even look at the rest of us. Three more teams performed after us and there was a ten-minute pause as the judges compiled their scores. By some miracle, we still managed second place. I thought that was pretty good. The girls didn't.

"You dropped me!" Penny screamed when she rounded on me at the bus.

"I didn't drop you," I said as calmly as I could. "You fell and I caught you."

"I wouldn't have fallen if you'd been steady. You dropped me."

"I was steady. When I felt you teetering, I tried to stay under you."

"You grabbed my boobs!" she screamed. That was really too much.

"How was I supposed to know that?" I spat back at her.

Not the nicest thing to say to a girl, I suppose, but she was really flat as a pancake. Next thing I knew my cheek was stinging from where she slapped me, Penny was crying on the bus, and every other girl on the cheer squad was scowling at me.

I stood outside the bus staring at the door.

"Better get on the bus so we can get home," Coach Cook said. I balked.

"I'm going to ride home with my parents," I said, backing away.

"Normally, I wouldn't approve that. It's technically against school rules," she said, glancing back at the bus. "Maybe in this instance it's better, though. They're here and know to look for you?"

"Yeah. They'll pull around in a minute or two," I lied. They'd been at the competition, but I hadn't even dug my cell phone out of my bag yet. I assumed they were still in St. Paul someplace.

"Okay. I'll see you at school," she said.

No. I didn't think she would. I wouldn't be going back to the cheer squad. There was no reason to. This was the last competition and I wasn't interested in seeing any of the little bitches again.

I started digging in my bag for my cell phone. If I lost that, I'd be taking a city bus home for the next couple of hours.

Not two minutes after the bus left, while I was still digging in my bag for my phone, Tara pulled up and asked if I wanted a ride. *Hell, yeah!*

"I didn't see you in your usual seat when the bus left," she said. "Not to worry. You did great and they'll figure that out eventually."

"Who cares? I don't have to work with them again," I said. I was thinking uncharitable thoughts about

Penny. I bet if I saw her stark naked, I wouldn't know which side was up. Yeah, that was nasty and I'd never say a thing like that, but if I hadn't caught her...

"Hey. You caught her," Tara said, reaching over to touch my hand. "That's what I taught you. And the rest of the routine was beautiful."

"Not that it gains me anything," I sighed. "They're all mad at me and blame me for messing up the end of *their* program.

"They got second place for the event. That's higher than they placed in any of the other events. They'll figure it out eventually."

"You know, the only one who matters is sitting beside me," I said. "If you think I did okay, then I'm happy."

"Well, I think you did better than okay. If you hadn't caught her, she'd have been injured. Ankle if nothing else. Because of you, she hit the mat like a feather."

"She's light as a feather."

"She'd have discovered how heavy she is," Tara laughed. "Believe me, I know. Hey. Let's pick up a pizza and go to your house to watch TV."

"Sounds good to me."

WE ATE THE pizza and turned on the TV, but don't ask me what was on. My focus was all on Tara.

"You know I'll never drop you, Tara. I promise," I said.

"I take you at your word. I'm going to try to never test that. But I saw what you did today, Paul. I trust you more than ever."

"You know, I'm in love with you, Tara. I don't know how to say it in any other way. Maybe I have no idea what love is, but I'm sure what I feel for you is love," I said.

"Oh, Paul. I hope one day we get to explore that in all its ramifications. Kiss me."

We kissed. In fact, we made out like we hadn't done since New Year's. We were humping against each other on the sofa in the TV room—still mostly dressed, but our clothes were loose. I was thinking it might be time to lose some of them completely. That's when we heard Mom and Dad get home.

"Mmm. We need... to put..."

"Mmmhmm. Let me help you."

"That's not helping."

"Sorry."

"Zip. Zip."

"Oh, yeah."

We were mostly back together when Mom called down to see if we were there.

"Just watching a movie," I called back.

"Okay. Good performance today. Will Tara be here for dinner?"

"We had a pizza. There's still some in the fridge."

"Well, if you get hungry, let me know. We're going to have those shrimp skewers you like so well."

I consulted with Tara and told her what they were. We agreed.

"We'll join you!"

"I thought so."

Joining Mom and Dad for dinner got us out of the basement and away from temptation. After dinner, Tara excused herself and said she needed to get home—even though it was only about seven-thirty. She said she'd see me early in the morning at the gym.

I went to my room, exhausted from the emotional

roller coaster of the day. I opened my Kindle and continued reading *American Gods*.

I was enjoying this story, which was saying something. I didn't enjoy reading all that much. It took me too long to process the letters on the page into words and the words into sentences. But with the screen reader reciting the words as the yellow highlight moved down the page, I was able to keep up with the thoughts being expressed.

I found it odd that the main character, Shadow, didn't really seem to do anything. He just let things happen to him, maybe acknowledging the beings around him were gods and maybe just humoring them. Regardless, he just let life happen to him.

When I was young and weak, I just wanted to be strong. I was a lot like Shadow in prison. He had big plans for when he got out, but everything he planned turned to shit. His wife died. He found out at her funeral she'd been giving his best friend a blowjob when he crashed his car and killed them both. Shadow found himself traveling the country with one of the old ones. Like me, he just did what he was told to.

Maybe I was going to figure out what was missing in my life. I wanted to say no one picked on me, but Penny had laid a really good slap on my face today. Coach Daniels was constantly ragging on me and berating my level of commitment and my skills. It wasn't like everyone stopped picking on me just because they couldn't slam me into a locker anymore.

And all the girls I thought would flock around me because I was strong—wasn't that what happened in the movies? Girls went gaga over the muscular guys on Muscle Beach or wherever. Girls seemed to avoid me unless they thought they could get something from me. Penny just wanted a base for her cheering. Madison just wanted a base who could lift her now that she was taller and heavier. Even Tara just wanted a base who could support her crippled body in an exhibition.

Well, that wasn't completely true. Tara wanted... I could only hope, Tara wanted me.

I fell asleep dreaming about weird creatures who claimed to be gods and wanted me to do something for them. All the gods were female.

TARA AND I worked even harder at the routine we were preparing. She was convinced there were additional moves she could make if I supported her in specific ways. I no longer went to any cheerleading practices. Nothing else changed. When I passed one of the cheerleaders in the hall, she ignored me, just like they'd always done.

Mr. Fields checked with me each week to see how far I'd gotten in the book and was pleased with my progress. He'd ask me what I liked and disliked. I told him about the weird feeling I got about Shadow and he nodded. He made a mark in his gradebook and that ended our five-minute conversation. I left the classroom.

"You think it's cute to grab my girlfriend's boobs?" a voice snarled as I was thrown against the lockers. Ethan, Penny's boyfriend, had his hands on my shoulders pinning me back. He was seven inches taller than me and weighed in at close to 200 pounds.

"I'll tell you the same thing I told her," I said. "How was I to know I had my hands on her boobs? There's nothing there."

"Your smart mouth is going to get you a broken nose and some missing teeth," Ethan growled back.

That was it. Something inside me just popped and I

grabbed him around the waist with both hands. Well, both hands would almost completely encircle Penny's waist, but I had a damn good grip. I pressed my thumbs into his gut until I had made a handle for myself.

"Let go of me, you freak!" Ethan yelled.

I lifted. Yeah, he weighed more than twice what his girlfriend did, but I could hold my own body in an iron cross for five seconds. Lifting his weight wasn't that difficult. I walked him across the hall and into the lockers on the other side.

"Don't you have some kind of college scholarship you'd lose if you could no longer play football?" I growled. "Maybe you should spend some time living in your locker to think about it."

"Put me down!"

"Paul! Put him down and step away," Mr. Fields barked from the door of his classroom.

I looked up into Ethan's eyes, a good foot above mine, and just let go. He dropped down half a foot and lost control of his knees for a second as I backed away.

"You bastard!" Ethan yelled, starting toward me.

"Stop!" Fields yelled. "You've both made your point. Ethan, back off. Paul, back into my classroom."

"He attacked me," Ethan insisted.

"I think you have the story backwards," I said.

"You'll hear from my father about this."

"Is he as big a bully as you are?" I shot back. Fields shoved me into his classroom and Ethan stumbled down the hall with his hands holding his sides.

"This isn't going to go well," Fields said when he was in the classroom facing me. "What on earth got into you?"

"He grabbed me and slammed me against the lockers, accusing me of groping his girlfriend," I said.

"I saw you slamming him into the lockers with his feet six inches off the floor."

"You came out long after it started. He grabbed me as soon as I left your classroom."

"What's this about groping his girlfriend?"

"At the cheerleading competition last week, Penny fell from on top in a statue pose. I grabbed her under the arms to keep her from falling on her face. She claims I grabbed her boobs. If so, I didn't notice. She doesn't even have anything to put in a training bra," I said.

"Did you tell her that?"

"Not in exactly those words," I said. "Didn't stop her from slapping me."

"This could get serious, Paul. Two popular athletes with a grudge against you. You're older than they are?"

"I'll be nineteen next week."

"Be prepared. You may be expelled."

"Then I'd never have to come back, would I?"

"You *could* never come back. You will have a hard time becoming a massage therapist without a high school diploma. Look up what it takes to get a GED. You might need it. For what it's worth, you're doing well in my class."

"Thank you, sir. I can't believe I'm in this situation. I've tried my best to just avoid getting picked on. I thought getting strong would be the end of it. I was wrong."

"Some people just see that as a challenge."

HELP CAME FROM an unexpected quarter. I came out of the massage room after my lesson with Jennifer and Tara to find Madison waiting for me. She looked pretty steamed.

"What did you do to my sister?" she demanded as I emerged. I closed the door behind me so Tara and Jennifer would have privacy to dress.

"Nothing," I said.

"She said you assaulted her on the gym floor."

"Madison, how possible is it to assault your partner on the gym floor during your performance?" I asked. "I caught her when she fell. She says I grabbed her boobs. She's full of shit."

"You mean during the competition Saturday? That's what she's going on about?"

"That and I guess I insulted her by asking how I'd know if I grabbed her boobs."

Madison burst out laughing.

"Oh, geez! She is way too sensitive about her little buds. I wish my boobs were her size. Um... You'd know if you grabbed them, if you ever want to try."

"No, thanks."

"I know. I know."

"She sent her boyfriend to try to rough me up. I wasn't gentle with him," I said. "It will probably get me kicked out of school."

"Ha! Serves him right."

"What's going on?" Tara asked as she came out of the massage room ready to work.

"I'm getting ready to save your boyfriend's bacon," Madison said. "He's going to owe me, though. I promise not to use him up."

"Oh, please," Tara said.

"You were at the competition Saturday," Madison said. "Did anything about the end of that performance seem less than right?"

"Aside from Penny losing her balance and not know-ing what to do. She kicked one of her spotters in the face on the way down and Paul caught her before she landed crooked on her other foot," Tara said.

"Exactly. Paul's action kept her from being injured. We can tell the school," Madison said confidently.

"That won't do any good. All the cheerleaders hate me anyway. They'll back up Penny's story."

"Hmm. Not in the face of the evidence," Madison said.

"What evidence?"

"The video. The performances were all recorded. All we have to do is play the video and it will clearly show Penny losing her balance and you catching her," Madison said.

"I don't have the video."

"The school always orders a copy. I'm sure Coach Cook has it."

AFTER THE WAY Coach Cook cut me loose in St. Paul to find my own way home, I wasn't sure she'd provide the DVD for a hearing. When I was called into the principal's office to discuss the incident with Ethan, I immediately said that he attacked me because his girlfriend claimed I grabbed her boobs and that I had evidence that it wasn't true.

That put the whole conversation on a different level. Penny and Coach Cook were called into the office and Tara was there with them. The DVD was played and it was pretty clear that I saved Penny from a possibly serious injury. With that decided, Ethan and his father were asked if they really wanted to pursue the conflict in the hallway. It seems Ethan's scholarship could be in jeopardy if I made a big deal out of it. The school would have to report the incident to his college.

They huffed a lot, but finally left. Penny and Coach

Cook turned to leave, but Tara blocked Penny and pointed back at me. She turned toward me and heaved a big sigh.

"I'm sorry, Paul. I got too wrapped up in myself," Penny said.

"I'm sorry I insulted you," I responded. "I really didn't mean to."

"Do something great with Madison," Penny said. "That's enough."

"You know what Madison is going to want," Tara said when she got me home. We went down to the TV room, but didn't turn it on.

"I suppose she's going to want more training time and another shot at a qualifier," I said.

"Maybe. She's going to want another shot at you."

"Me?"

"Yeah. As much as she thinks she can control you better if she's involved with you, I think she's got a serious crush on you, too. I'll talk to her and get her talked down until at least after June, but if she tries to kiss you again, let her. Just don't enjoy it too much," Tara said.

I looked at her with horror.

"I can't..."

She met me with a kiss of her own.

"I assure you, whatever she puts into it, I've got more."

We didn't spend the rest of the day making out— though if it hadn't been nearly dinner time, we might have. Mikey burst into the room and called us up to dinner as we were kissing and touching each other. It was spring break at the university and Mom and Dad had firmly denied Mikey permission to go to Florida. She was, after all, still only seventeen.

"Why aren't you two just using Paul's room when you screw around?" Mikey asked. "The entertainment room is pretty exposed. Is that what you like? Are you exhibitionists?"

"Mikey!" I said. Sometimes my sister could really be a pest. She'd followed us out to Tara's car.

"Little sister," Tara said softly. The term coming from Tara's mouth stopped both Mikey and me in our tracks. We turned to Tara. "Yes. I hope you think of me as a big sister. So, I'm going to give you some sisterly advice. Paul's and my relationship is none of your business! Since you are being so nosy, I'll tell you that all we ever do is make out, so if that satisfies your voyeuristic impulses, I'll get you a written invitation next time. You knew full well what we were likely doing when you came running into the entertainment room—something your parents never do. And you didn't turn around or even blush. Don't accuse us of exhibitionism when you are a voyeur. The only place we put on an exhibition is on the floor exercise mats."

"I'm... I mean... I didn't mean to be a voyeur. I was just teasing you," Mikey said. "Do you really think of me as a little sister?"

"With about the same amount of exasperation that Paul has at times like this."

"I was just teasing. I'm sorry," Mikey said. "Would you like to... um... go shopping sometime? I never have anyone who wants to go to the mall. All the college girls consider themselves too old for that."

"I love the mall," Tara said. "Want to go Sunday?"

"Yes!" Mikey squealed. "I like having a big sister."

Of course, I got dragged along, too. Somebody had to carry the packages.

11

ON TO NATIONALS

JENNIFER WAS EXPANDING our routine, based on the letter she'd received from the qualifying committee. They suggested that with the lack of jumps Tara could do, we emphasize more of the throws that look like she's jumping. We worked on a new entry for our cannonball mount and tried going into a pike position double salto. The pike position worked well for this because as soon as I launched her, Tara could grasp her legs and hold them in the proper position. I caught her as she landed in front of me.

We got pretty good at the move, but we still had to figure out how to work it into our routine. Another thing the committee said in their letter to Jennifer was that even though our storytelling was good for a normal routine, we needed to up our artistry even more to compensate for the lack of elements that required Tara to land unsupported and to propel herself in a jump.

When I first started training, Coach Dawson had drilled me on building my strength with body weight. I did pushups, pull-ups, sit-ups, knee bends, and any

144

other exercise that used my body weight. Most of the men's events depended largely on upper body strength, so my chest and shoulders and core really developed well. Of course, that didn't mean I ignored my lower body. The vault and floor exercises depended on lower body strength as much as the rings and high bar depended on upper body strength.

Tara had been in great physical condition at the time of her accident, but after that she went through a long and arduous process of regaining control over her lower body—a process that still continued. She didn't slack off on her upper body work, though, and was almost as well-developed in the torso and shoulders as I was. Um... With the rather attractive addition of her breasts that she said grew during her time of enforced rest. Believe me, I'd never mistake whether I had hold of her boobs or not. I'd touched them a few times while we were making out and they were spectacular.

Oh. I wasn't intending to get side-tracked there. I just... I'm a nearly-nineteen-year-old male. What else can I say?

I meant to talk about her upper body strength. There was a real difference between what she could do with her arms and shoulders and what Madison could do. Madison depended on her legs to get her in flight as much as she depended on me launching her. Tara helped in the mounts and throws with her arms. In our balance routine, she could slowly push herself up as I lifted her into a handstand, but in the dynamic routine, she could use a slight bounce on the sprung floor while I supported her to give her enough momentum to vault into position with her arms. It was pretty amazing. Her core strength was phenomenal!

I wasn't clear on exactly the nature of her injury.

Jennifer said the extent of her recovery was off the charts. She wasn't expected to walk again at all. It was a sign of her determination and possibly stemmed from her upset at her partner's suicide. I just knew that I loved her all the more for it.

Love. I didn't think I'd ever actually said that out loud to her. Everything else in my life took a back seat to what I felt about her. But was that love? How were you supposed to know? I knew what lust was. I wanted her. I wanted to spend more time caressing her breasts while we kissed and then go further. I wanted to make love. That was my lust. I was willing to wait until she was ready. I guess that was my love.

I KEPT WORKING with Tara every afternoon. I no longer had to take time out to go to cheer practice. I was through with them. I went to my classes in the morning, worked with Tara all afternoon, and studied all evening. My work with Tara also included massage instruction. Jennifer said that most certifications required 500 hours of practice. I was getting about an hour a day. And then things changed a little. I went into the massage room after knocking as usual and found another person on the table.

"It's time you started working on more bodies than just your girlfriend's," Jennifer said. "We've posted a notice in the front of the gym asking for volunteers for a massage. You'd be amazed at how fast our schedule has filled up. Today, your first new client is Coach Anders. He's used to giving you instruction on rings and high bar, so he'll be providing feedback as you work on him. I will continue to be in the same room, monitoring your progress and giving instruction as needed."

"Welcome, Coach," I said, moving to the side of the table. "Ready to relax?"

"Bring it on," he chuckled. "We've been talking about expanding the services here in the gym and are beginning to attract more adults."

"That's good. I wouldn't want to be working on any children," I said. "I'm sure they'd be fine, but I just see too much potential for miscommunication and problems. I'm glad to have a guy for my first new client."

The massage went well, I did the same work on him as I usually did on Tara and discovered he could take more pressure than I used on her. A lot more pressure. His muscles were incredibly strong and it took some significant work to get them to relax. Like me, he was really strong through the torso, shoulders, and arms. Not that he had weak legs, but he specialized in aerial events and they really required upper body and core strength.

It also showed me more clearly that working on the body in massage was absolutely non-sexual. It was easy for me to drift off into a little fantasy when I was working on Tara. She often gave me a kiss after a massage. She was my girlfriend. There was no fantasy with Coach Anders. I didn't think there would be any with any other clients, either.

After the massage, I went out to work on the mat with Tara and Jennifer. Rachel, our choreographer, was waiting to work with us. She had a tariff sheet with our moves on it and we talked for a long time about our story. She started working with us on some very specific poses and throws she wanted to work into a song about flight. That sounded pretty cool. We didn't have an idea of the music yet, but she was working on sequence and transition before we got to rhythm and synchronization.

She said she didn't want us limited by the music before we'd had a chance to develop the moves.

Rachel gave the sequence and Jennifer worked on the execution of the pieces. Even working without the music, we could tell the piece was really emotional. Occasionally, we'd get into a throw or something when Tara was balanced up on top of me and Rachel would shout "Fly!" We got the message. This whole piece was about Tara flying. Our ending pose was going to be unusual. I was to lift and hold her in a flying pose as if she was truly taking off.

We worked hard and then headed back to the massage room. This time I worked on Tara's very tired body. By the time I was done, I was exhausted. Tara was feeling more energized. We headed for the locker rooms and then met to go to dinner at her apartment. It was fun to be in her place instead of with my parents. Of course, Jennifer was also there, so it wasn't like we were tempted to skip dinner and jump each other, but we were all feeling pretty wistful and dreamy after the session.

It was the new pattern for our workouts. School. Massage client. Mat work. Massage. Dinner. And on the weekends, I worked in a little time for Madison.

SATURDAY THE SIXTEENTH, I was surprised that after my class of toddler tumbling, and my two-hour session with Madison, and an hour of working on my own routines, I had no massage session and no working time with Tara. Instead, I was told to get showered and dressed. We were going out.

Maybe I was a little dense, but I'd completely forgotten it was my nineteenth birthday. Mom, Dad, Mikey,

Jennifer, her boyfriend Bob, and Mikey's date of the week Dean all joined Tara and me at Charlie's for my birthday celebration. Wow! That was a fancy meal.

The original Charlie's Café was long before my time. I guess it was pretty special, but closed last century sometime. This one is located in the Minneapolis Club, a kind of exclusive membership club frequented by a lot of politicians and company presidents. Dad's boss at the university was a member and did a great job of promoting us to the club to get a seating for us on a Saturday night. Usually, non-members can only be seated during limited hours on Tuesday through Friday.

Dad's boss had told the club that a national champion gymnast and her new partner were celebrating a birthday prior to the Olympic Trials in June. It would be a great opportunity for the club to do a little promotion of their support for Minneapolis athletes. I don't think anyone there actually knew either Tara or me, but the sales job was sufficient to get us a Saturday evening reservation. The décor included the bar and frieze from the original Charlie's and the furnishings were just plain elegant. The whole building was over a hundred years old and had an athletic club, library, guest rooms, and meeting rooms. Tara and I were photographed for a promotional poster the club planned.

Okay, so I was suitably impressed that my parents thought enough of me to take eight people out for an expensive dinner at this place. It made me even more determined to do well in our exhibition in three months.

I rode with Tara, of course, and that meant we had a pretty delicious make-out time before she dropped me off at home. It was getting harder for both of us to restrain ourselves from going someplace to book a room and not come out for a few days.

NINETEEN OR NOT, I was still in high school and I was making progress. Spring Break was the first week of April and I was determined to use the time to finish my English Literature assignment and to at least make sure I was completely caught up on my other coursework. Life didn't agree.

First off, Jennifer was scheduling three massages a day for me to practice on. She kept a timesheet and at the end of each massage she had the client sign it and give an evaluation score. The client could comment on the service as well. I asked her about it, not understanding the significance.

"Certification, which is required in some areas of Minnesota and in most other states, has a recommendation of having completed 500 hours of practice and education. This is how we're tracking your progress," she said. "And we need to get you graduated so I can assign your anatomy coursework to you."

"Are you an official teacher?" I asked.

"Yes, in fact, I am. Arizona requires 700 hours of schooling for licensing. It's national board certification that only requires 500 hours. I taught at the Phoenix LMT Institute for a few years before taking the challenge of working with Tara," Jennifer said. "I've served on the National Board for some time."

"Okay. I'll do whatever you say," I said.

"You always do," she chuckled.

That gave me some additional motivation to get finished with high school. I needed to start the coursework study for my massage work. Somehow, 500 hours seemed like a lot. I didn't even know how many I had so far. It turned out Jennifer had been tracking my time from almost the moment we met.

I massaged an older woman—I mean lots older, like seventies—and after I was finished, she sat with Jennifer and me and assessed everything I did. I found out later that she was on the Board of Directors of the state massage therapy alliance and had pretty much written the state laws on requirements. I might have learned more from her in the hour after her massage than I ever learned in high school. She was cool.

She had a few good-natured jibes with Jennifer, including saying that the only people who truly benefited from licensing massage therapists were massage schools. They are the ones who make money from training the initial 500-1000 hours required by the state and the additional 20-50 hours required every two years to renew the license. While Minnesota did not require a license, she recognized the sense of my getting National Board Certification if I didn't know where I would live in the future. Certification was a requirement in most states that had licenses.

Around the first of May, Mr. Fields had me set up an appointment to talk about *American Gods*. We'd had five or ten-minute chats all term, but this was an hour. I'd finished the book and really learned a lot. Reading was actually fun, thanks to the screen reading software.

He jumped right in when we met and asked me for a summary of the book. Then he asked questions I'd never heard in class before. How did that scene make me feel? What was the significance of the gold coin? Did the gods win or lose? They were questions that really made me think. Not only did I enjoy reading the book, but I enjoyed talking about it. I told Mr. Fields that when we finished and he nodded his head.

"Tell me about a passage that really spoke to you," he said.

"There's this place when Shadow is in Cairo at the mortuary, where he thinks back about his childhood and that he was a scrawny kid always being picked on. Then, all of a sudden, he grew. Bullies stopped bullying him and he was recruited for swimming and weightlifting teams."

"He became popular? Had all the girls? Protected the weak?" Fields asked.

"No. I think that's what got me. I marked the passage."

> *He liked being big and strong. It gave him an identity. He'd been a shy, quiet, bookish kid, and that had been painful; now he was a big dumb guy, and nobody expected him to be able to do anything more than move a sofa into the next room on his own.*
>
> *[Gaiman, Neil. American Gods: The Tenth Anniversary Edition: A Novel (p. 186). HarperCollins. Kindle Edition.]*

"I do like being strong. I'm not 'big' like Shadow. But people still treat me like I'm just a big dumb guy incapable of doing anything but move a sofa... or in my case, lift an acrobat over my head."

"But Shadow is a lot more than that."

"Yeah. He's just so used to believing he's still that scrawny little kid that he doesn't know how to use his strength yet," I said. "That really got me thinking about my life. I really don't know where I fit."

"Sometimes teachers forget that the most important thing about a class like this is to make you think. You scored an A for the class. Congratulations."

And that was it. There were still three weeks of school, but I was through with English Literature.

Late Friday night, I was on my way home after dropping Tara off from our date. We'd gone to see *Dune 2*. I was more enthused than Tara was, but the love story hidden in the war story was nice. My cell phone buzzed just before I got home and I pulled over to look at the text.

"Help! I'm at a bad party and need to escape."

I hadn't been expecting a message from Mikey! I thought Tara was calling to wish me a good night. I scrolled to the next message which was the address where Mikey was in trouble. A couple of clicks and the GPS was routing me out south of town. I texted Mikey and said I was on my way.

It took me twenty minutes to get out to the rural area southeast of Minneapolis. I pulled into a farm that had lights on in the house. I shut mine off so I wouldn't attract attention. Mikey's message was that she was hiding in a toolshed behind the house. Things must have gotten pretty serious for her to run away from the party and hide in a toolshed. I left Mom's Caravan and made a big circle around the house, so I wasn't too close to anywhere people might see me.

"Not in the barn," a voice said as I reached the back of the house. "The bitch must be in that shed."

"How'd she get out?" another voice asked.

"Donovan is so blind drunk she probably walked right past him."

"She's not gonna go far naked. She wouldn't dare even call 911. Not that there's police out here."

It seemed there were only two of them out looking for her and I was following along behind them, sticking to the shadows. If Mikey was naked and hiding in a tool-shed, this would be tricky. I didn't know any martial arts, but I was strong. I'd have to depend on that when I took her away from them.

They reached the door and pulled at it. It was either stuck or locked.

"Paul?" I heard my sister's voice. "Is that you?"

"Yeah." One of the guys yelled. He and his buddy laughed. I heard some movement inside and the door yielded to the guys' pushing. "Got ya!"

"No!" Mikey screamed. "I'm not going with you!"

"Hey, this is the end of term celebration. You've fucked eight guys from our house and then refused to see them again. We all want another go. Now come on out with us."

I heard some metal clang and one of the guys yelped. Good on you, Mikey. I got to the door right behind the guys.

"Bitch. Put the shovel down or you're going to get hurt."

"Get away from me!" Another strike of the shovel and then my sister yelped.

"Grab her feet and let's get her back to the house."

One of the guys backed up out of the shed holding Mikey's kicking feet. This was it. I'd never really fought before, so I had no idea how to be most effective. As he backed out of the shed, I just kicked up between his legs as hard as I could. He dropped Mikey's feet.

"Ow! Goddamn! How'd she kick me in the nuts? Fuck!"

He backed up another step, hunched over to protect his midsection. As soon as his head was clear of the door, I just punched as hard as I could at his face. Damn, that hurt. He staggered back and fell down.

"Danny! What the hell?" his buddy said. "You think I can hold this wildcat by myself?"

He emerged from the shed with Mikey held in front of him with his arms around her arms and chest. Mikey saw me and lowered her head as far as she could against her chest. I put everything I had into a punch and connected with his face. He let go of Mikey to protect himself, staggering back a step. His buddy was getting back to his feet.

"Car's at the end of the drive. Go!" I barked at Mikey.

I couldn't see what kind of condition she was in, but she stumbled off behind me. I couldn't spare a glance for her ghostly white body. Both guys were after *me* now.

"Son of a bitch. I don't know who you are, but you just walked into the wrong party," the one I'd just hit said, lunging at me.

I caught a punch to the gut, but it takes a bit to get hurt past my abs. I swung wildly at him again and connected with his head just as his buddy threw a punch that hit me in the left arm. Somehow, I didn't think these guys were completely sober. Their punches didn't seem that powerful. It was my turn to attack and I grabbed Danny's arm—the one that had just hit me— and twisted for all I was worth. He screamed out as I swung him into his partner.

Even if they were drunk, I knew I wouldn't last against them if they kept coming at me. The second guy lunged. I didn't let go of Danny's arm in my left hand, but reached out with my right hand and grabbed his friend by the throat. He had reach on me, but I guess when faced with strangulation the first reaction is to try to protect your throat, not to hit your assailant.

It took all my strength, but I swung the two of them and cracked their heads together. They both went limp.

I needed to get out of there and get Mikey home, but my sister was in the car naked. One of the guys had a university sweatshirt on, so I just grabbed it and ripped it off of him. He started to struggle and I gave him a kick in the nuts to match his friend's. He dropped back and I took off running for the car. I saw the back door of the farmhouse open and guys come staggering out. They were apparently all drunk.

"Danny! Dave! What's going on? Where are you?" one yelled.

I just kept running and grabbed the door handle of the car. Of course, Mikey had locked it.

"Mikey! Let me in!"

I realized I had the key in my pocket and punched the unlock button. It popped open and I jerked the door open as I saw a bunch of guys streaming around the corner of the house.

"Mikey, are you in here?"

"In back," came her weak voice.

I tossed the sweatshirt back to her and started the car, punching the lock button as I did. I spun on the gravel backing out of the drive. It didn't look like any of the guys were sober enough to get a car door open and chase us.

I took Mikey straight home.

"I just beat up two guys," I moaned as I drove Mikey home.

"You saved me," Mikey said.

"How did you end up in that position?"

"Ugh. I didn't want to get tied down to a guy, so I only dated them a couple of times. Then, after we'd had sex, I just cut them off. I didn't know any of them were taking it that bad. They'd gotten what they wanted and I got what I wanted. These guys took rejection personally and decided to pay me back for it all in one weekend."

"Mikey, you don't have to keep living like that."

"Says my virgin brother. Sorry, Paul. I'm just not cut from the same cloth as you."

"It'll end up this way again."

"You'll come and rescue me. It was impressive to see you take them down. You're so strong!"

"That's not the reason I got strong. It was supposed to be to stop kids from picking on me, not to beat others up. I'm no better than they are."

"You came to my rescue. If that's not the same as stopping kids from picking on you, it stopped them from picking on me," Mikey spat.

"I never did anything to make them *want* to pick on me," I whispered. "They picked on me just because I existed in their space."

Mikey didn't respond.

"Remember when the three boys wanted to take us girls and make out?" she asked. "We were in eighth grade. You stepped in front of them and refused to let them close to us."

"They beat the shit out of me. Mom would still be in the principal's office yelling at him if she hadn't needed to take me to the hospital."

"There wasn't a ghost of a chance that you could stop those boys. Why did you try?" she asked.

"What else could I do? They were threatening you and your friends. I figured the security guy would get there before it got too bad."

"When he got there, you were lying on the ground bleeding," Mikey said. "I don't think we ever said thank you. Thank you for that. And thank you for rescuing me tonight. I'll try to make sure I never need rescuing again. I promise."

"I worry about you, Mikey. What if I hadn't been where I could respond? I'd only just dropped Tara off. Your lifestyle is... dangerous."

"Yeah. I would have been gang-raped. And no one would believe me if I tried to press charges. I'd given it to each of them before," she said. "I'm moving home next week. The semester is over on Wednesday and the dorms close next weekend. Anything I can do to help you to graduation? I'll write your papers for you if you want."

"I appreciate you helping me study, but you've never done my work for me. I finished my lit class. Mr. Fields said I passed."

"That's great. I know you've got a lot more, though."

"Jennifer has me starting on anatomy. I'm studying to become a massage therapist."

"You can practice on me."

"I'm getting a lot of clients at the gym. Thanks anyway."

"Hmmph," she snarled.

12
EXHIBITION

I GUESS I DIDN'T look great when I showed up at the gym for my toddler class Saturday morning. I had a bruise on my left cheek and another on my left arm.

Tara and Jennifer were especially concerned when they looked at my hands. My knuckles were scraped and my hands were really stiff. I had to tell them about what happened with my sister. Tara was horrified.

"You can't do that kind of thing!" she said. "If you were accused of some kind of violent behavior, the committee might rescind our invitation. And you'd have real trouble finding any partner willing to work with you. You have to be careful. Bases are known for their strength and for working with small tops. Most people would think of us as fragile. We might not be as fragile as the public thinks, but if you were known to have been fighting, people would pull away."

"I didn't want to," I said petulantly. "What could I do? My sister was in danger."

"I know, Hon. And I think you did the right thing. It's just really frightening and dangerous on so many levels.

If Madison asks you about it, just say you fell during a practice routine."

Of course, Madison *did* ask and that's what I told her. I don't think either she or Coach Daniels believed me.

WE HAD A party at the house on June sixteenth. Some of the folks from the gym came. Of course, Tara and Jennifer and Bob. My family. Mikey was without a date. The occasion was my graduation from high school. I hadn't had to attend anything since Memorial Day, and I chose not to attend the school ceremony. I was sure the school was happy to have me out of their hair and didn't need the embarrassment of having me seen with a bunch of real students.

There were a few of those other students I knew had graduated with a doctored transcript. There were plenty of students who were no smarter than me, and a number of athletes who simply didn't need to try. I wondered how many of them would actually succeed in college when professors refused to pass them so they could play basketball or football.

But Mom and Dad wanted to have a celebration that I'd made it, so we held that on the day of graduation. There were some gifts. Most were pretty modest. I didn't expect people to bring me a lot of loot for having passed the lowest standard of public education. Mom and Dad, though, had taken me out the previous week and bought me a car.

It wasn't one of the popular teen cars. Sure, I'd love to have a RAV 4 or a Volkswagen, but I was more concerned with the ease of getting Tara in and out of my car. We still usually took her car on dates. It had been an unusual evening when Mikey called me and as it happened, I had Mom's car. So, I agreed with getting an inexpensive Chevy Trax. It had a more spacious interior and was still low enough to the ground that Tara could get in and out easily.

Mikey got me the next most elaborate gift. I think Mom and Dad might have had something to do with it. She got me a portable massage table. Well, I didn't really have much in the way of clientele that I'd go to visit, but I was progressing nicely and maybe after the exhibition, I'd be putting more time in on massage.

I guess she must have coordinated things with Tara and Jennifer. Tara bought me a selection of massage oils and Jennifer got me a full set of linens for the table. I needed sheets for under the client and to drape. Then I also needed towels so they could wipe themselves off if there was too much oil. The gifts were all very thoughtful.

We had a great time, and after everyone left, Tara and I spent some time 'testing' my table. That led to some pretty heavy making out and eventually I got her dressed and out to my car to take home. I was very near to just carrying her up to my bed.

We were only a week away from our exhibition.

ON JUNE TWENTY-FIFTH, Tara and I approached the floor at Target Center in Minneapolis to do our routine. I definitely felt we'd upped the level of our acrobatics since the Louisville competition, and I thought our story was really beautiful. I wasn't expecting the turnout for our exhibition that we had, though.

Like at the Louisville competition, the general space at the arena was divided up with the kinds of events that would be held in each of them. The special needs gymnasts had all performed and had all received their medals. Some of the routines were so simple as to be over before I realized they'd begun. For example, a girl carefully approached the mat and stood at the edge. She breathed deeply before jumping about six inches off the floor and landing on both feet. She raised her arms in the air in a perfect pose for a gymnast after sticking a landing. Then her trainer rushed to the floor and caught her before she collapsed. She was carried back to her wheelchair and waved at everyone.

On the other hand, there were some kids with less obvious handicaps. They did routines on the uneven parallel bars that were only performed on the low bar, for example. A Down syndrome girl did a whole tumbling exercise across the mat, and then landed in her final pose. When she started to walk off the mat, though, she wandered as if the whole thing had made her dizzy and her coach rushed to help her off the mat.

Nearly all the other events that were happening that day were over and competitors were just practicing on the equipment when there was a general announcement over the arena PA that former national champion Tara White and her partner Paul Bradley would be performing at the acrobatic gymnastics station. The announcer proceeded to inform everyone about the tragic accident that occurred four years ago and of Tara's valiant effort to overcome the restrictions imposed by her injuries.

It was a lot different than what we'd prepared for. We were told there would be no general announcement and that those who were there would see us and those who weren't would miss it. Instead, the stands emptied from the rest of the arena and filled the area surrounding the acrobatic gymnastics floor. That included all the other teams that would be competing in acrobatic gymnastics the next day. The stands around us were filled—many of the gymnasts having joined the spectators just to show support for one of their own who had been injured.

My parents and sister were out there. I knew Madison and her sister Penny, and Coach Daniels were attending. At one point, I thought I saw Mr. Fields, my lit teacher, in the stands. When everything had quieted down, we got the nod and approached our starting positions.

Our black unitards were perfect for this routine. Our new choreography was elegant and the music was stunning. The choreographer had chosen an old Paul McCartney song, but it was a new rendition by a female artist. When the tone sounded and our music began, I started to circle Tara, lying on the floor. Then I reached down to bring her to a stand and swing her around slowly. When the words started, our routine really took flight—so to speak.

> *Blackbird singing in the dead of night*
> *Take these broken wings and learn to fly*
> *All your life, you were only waiting*
> *For this moment to arise*

Then I launched Tara into the air and she looked like she was truly taking flight. Usually, audiences are respectfully silent during an acrobatic gymnastics routine so as not to distract the performers. But when Tara took flight, there was a sudden and loud cheer from the audience. Tara was back.

When the final reprise played, I used a cannonball launch to put Tara into her double salto. Instead of letting her reach the floor for her landing, I caught her above my head with my hands around her hips. Our ending pose was with her over my head, her arms outstretched like wings and her legs out straight behind her. We held that pose for the three seconds to the end of the music and then for another couple of seconds as the audience applauded. Then I brought her down into my arms to stand and bow to the audience.

There was quite an ovation for the girl who returned to perform in her chosen art and I was happy just to have been part of her triumph.

Of course, even though the competition and events were over for the day and no score was posted for our routine, we weren't finished. They had things set up for a post-performance press conference. I guess they often interview the champions in various classes. Regardless, Tara, Jennifer, and I were led to a small dais with microphones on it and a dozen or so reporters were there. I was told it would be streamed as well as recorded for television and newspapers.

Wow!

"Tara, how does it feel to be back?" asked the first reporter.

"Yeah. Well, I'm just so thankful for the people who believed enough in me to make me do the work to get back to this point. I hope I'll be able to show them how much I appreciate them."

"Tara, what are your plans next? Will you compete?" asked another reporter.

"Um... Yeah. I mean, that's a tough decision. I'm twenty years old and if you check the ages of the competitors on the national team, I don't think you'll find a top anywhere near that old," she said. I noticed that she didn't indicate it was because of her abilities. "I'll be looking for ways to help other gymnasts achieve the dreams I missed four years ago because of the accident. I've been taking instruction in coaching and I think I have a good perspective to bring to that side of the game."

"Paul, what was it like working with Tara. This was your first time out in this kind of setting, right?" asked another reporter.

Shit! I didn't expect to be asked any questions!

"Tara is phenomenal. Every day she grew more confident and agile. If she decided she wanted to compete again, I'd be begging her to continue as her partner."

There was more, of course, but it all sounded pretty much the same from there.

WE WENT OUT for dinner with our family. Jennifer handed Tara a folded-up paper as we sat at the table. We weren't competing in anything, so no score had been posted at the arena. The judges, however, actually compiled a score sheet for us!

We didn't score over thirty. I was pleased, however, to see that our score was better than what Madison and I had done in Louisville. I didn't think I'd share that with Madison or Coach Daniels.

After dinner, I took Tara back to her apartment. Jennifer had said she was spending the night with Bob, so we had the apartment to ourselves.

"Paul, you've been a perfect partner," Tara whispered as we sat on the sofa kissing. "You've never asked for more than I was willing and ready to give. I know that I've carried the baggage of what happened to Jackson and me, and I've held you more distant than I wanted to. But I love you, Paul. Will you spend the night with me?"

"Tara? You mean...?" I couldn't even go on. I was kissing her and she was nodding.

"Yes. Make love to me."

"What about... Will we be able to work together?"

"We'll have to see how that goes. I'm not anticipating doing more performances, but we might be able to do some work in the gym."

"You're not? Why?"

"As wonderful as everything we did today was, we still wouldn't have made the cut in a competition. There aren't a lot of places where we could do exhibitions. I mean, even the international federation, FIG, wouldn't approve us doing another exhibition here. We might get one or two regional exhibitions, but we've had our moment of glory. I showed what was possible with determination and a loving partner. Now, I want to enjoy and appreciate the other things life has to offer. Like being lovers."

"Yes," I said. "Tara, I'll be whatever you want me or need me to be. I think I love you."

We'd always been careful to keep a layer of clothing between us. Sure, we'd managed to get our hands inside that clothing, and we'd both climaxed from the loving we gave each other, but undressing with Tara was a completely new and almost otherworldly experience. We showered together and I relished just letting my soapy fingers glide over her body. And she explored me just as thoroughly. When we rinsed and stepped out of the shower, I carefully and gently dried her before carrying her to her bed.

And then we made love. Not all at once, but continuing to explore each other and the wonder of our bodies touching. She pulled me on top of her with her legs spread wide and guided me into her. I couldn't believe what I was experiencing. Only staying focused on her eyes as we moved together kept me in the same world. We went slow and when I'd come the first time, I continued to move and stayed hard enough for Tara to follow soon after. Then we rolled over so Tara was astride and she worked herself up and down on me as I supported much of her weight. I felt her and kissed her and loved on her breasts as we both rose to another climax and settled into each other's arms in the bed.

"I love you, Tara. I've known it for a long time now, but was always afraid to tell you. I promise I'll never be afraid to tell you how I feel again."

"Maybe I've been foolish to insist that we not be lovers until after our exhibition, but this was so wonderful. I will always cherish this night."

"You know what I said the first time you kissed me," I laughed. "A boy never forgets his first."

We talked and laughed and made love again.

THE NEXT MORNING was only Wednesday, but we didn't go to the gym. Most of the morning we spent in bed, just relishing the feeling of holding each other. Of course, we couldn't stay there all the time. We showered again, dressed, and went to the kitchen to debate the merits of cooking something that was in her refrigerator, or ordering food to be delivered. We finally opted for the latter, just so we wouldn't need to clean up so much.

When the delivery person rang her bell, I was surprised to find Jennifer standing behind the delivery, also waiting to come in. I took the food and ushered Jennifer into the room.

"I thought I might get home in time to cook for you," she said. "I see you have no need for my services."

"Sit down, Jennifer. I think we ordered enough for everyone without even trying. Everything on the menu just sounded good," Tara laughed.

"Did... uh... everything go okay last night?" Jennifer whispered to Tara. There was no way I couldn't hear her.

"It was so wonderful, Jennifer. I only wish we'd started months ago."

"I'm sure it was for the better."

We opened packages of Thai food and set out plates. Then we sat at the table and served our food to begin eating.

"You were reviewed," Jennifer said. "There's an article alongside the main report from Nationals in the *Star*."

"Were they kind?"

"Not unkind. It's pretty much what we assumed. But there is a nice little statement about you possibly being available to coach."

"Oh. That's nice."

"You'll need to be doing something," Jennifer said. "Your moment of glory would be wasted if not."

"Of course, you're right. I haven't wanted to consider that before we did the program. The only thing I planned for was last night."

"I hope that isn't all there is to it," I said, holding her hand.

"No, not at all. Let's read the review."

In 2020 the career of Tara White and Wesley Jackson, the reigning Mixed Pairs Acrobatic Gymnastics US National Champions, came to a sudden end in Geneva when the two fell from a difficult figure. White was reported as paralyzed and her partner, suffering from unnamed injuries, passed on later that year.

So, imagine the surprise and delight at yesterday's Gymnastics City USA when White returned to the floor for a flawless performance with her new partner, Paul Bradley. Months of healing and years of therapy have gone into White's recovery and the performance in front

*of 2,000 fans at Target Center left spectators
breathless.*

*The artistry of choreographer Rachel Levine
showed through in the performance as one of
the most moving pieces this observer has ever
seen. Set to the popular Paul McCartney tune
of "Blackbird" breathily performed by Tiffany
Alvord, White seemed to come alive with the
music echoing the theme of her broken body
learning to fly again.*

*And her partner, Bradley, kept her in flight
and well protected against mishap. His throws
and her spins were perfectly timed to the
music. The most stunning of all was having
White come out of a double pike salto high
above Bradley's head. Rather than let her land
supported in front of him, Bradley caught her
in the air and held her above his head as she
appeared to truly be ready to fly away. A stunning performance.*

*Of course, critics and the curious will ask
why they were performing in an exhibition
instead in the Acrobatic Gymnastics competition, which begins this morning at eight o'clock
at Target Center. No, my friends, heartbreaking
as it is, Tara White will never be up to the stunning quality she was at four years ago. While
thriving on the artistry of this performance, the
keen observer could note pain etched deeply in
the features of this remarkable talent.*

*The two did no synchronous tumbling—a
requirement of mixed pairs in competition—
because White's legs, supported by knee
braces and a pelvic brace beneath her unitard,*

Tara gripped my hand tightly as Jennifer finished reading the review. Tears were streaming down her cheeks. While the reviewer had praised her to the heavens in his article, he had also deftly condemned her. She would never be a true gymnast again.

ALL TARA AND I wanted to do for the next few days was make love. At least, I think we were of one mind on that. It was usually me following her to the bedroom.

Jennifer, however, cracked the training whip and got us out of the apartment to watch the rest of the competition. We had missed the morning rotations Wednesday, but we were at the arena and in our seats for the afternoon rotations. Lots of people came up to us when we entered the arena, congratulating us—Tara, mostly—on our performance.

She was readily identifiable, even if not dressed in a uniform. She could get along without support for short periods, but knowing we'd be up and down all day, she chose her walking canes for support. Well, that was enough to draw attention, and sitting in reserved seats in the front row completed our visibility.

The rotations at nationals did not focus on a single discipline at a time. Women's pairs, men's pairs, and mixed pairs were interspersed with men's and women's groups. It did help to keep the competition interesting, but made it harder to compare one act with another. Tara explained that was intentional. Each performance was to be judged on its own merits according to a uniform scale. It was not supposed to be judged as a comparison of acts.

It would be cool if we had a political system like that. Imagine the candidates each being evaluated based on an independent scale that simply determined who had the highest score as being the most suited to become president. Of course, we could never get even two people to agree as to what that scale should be. I was nineteen and this year would be the first time I voted in a national election. My civics class had been all about the voting system and making sure we all voted in the election. It was our civic duty.

It was pretty obvious, though, that nothing Madison and I had done in our one competition outing would come close to any of the qualifiers who were competing in the nationals. And Tara quietly pointed out all the different moves and poses she couldn't do. It was eye-opening. By the end of the day, I could even understand some of Coach Daniels's criticisms of what I did with Madison. I guess I was translating too much of what I *needed* to do with Tara into what I *could* do with Madison.

The competition stretched out for three days and we sat in the stands every day. Friday, the senior individual gymnastics events started. I wanted to go observe some of the men's events, since that was where I considered my future to be. I was happy about Tara's and my performance, but I wanted to get back to competing on the men's apparatuses.

Andy Warnock had qualified and would be competing for a spot on the men's Olympic team. These were really the crème de la crème of male gymnasts. Eric Reynolds had also managed to qualify, but it wasn't likely he'd get past the first round. The guy looked twice as old as any of the other male gymnasts—and I guess he was twice as old as some of them. He was thirty-three and had been pursuing this dream all his life. He was a good role model. He never quit, even when he was past the age of having a chance to qualify for the team.

And he passed that ethic on to the rest of us he coached. It was a shame our gym hadn't qualified a full team to compete for team honors. If I had qualified, we'd still have needed two more minimum. We really needed to attract more guys to the gym. There were some younger teens who might be ready for the next national trials.

Tara had openly declared that she wouldn't be performing again. After seeing the other mixed pairs and even the women's pairs and men's pairs, what she was capable of—as remarkable as it was—wasn't going to win a competition. Maybe we'd still practice some routines, but several people had approached her right there in the stands about coaching them. Jennifer had thought ahead and had business cards made up that Tara could give to people who were interested.

At the end of the week, she had several leads for new gymnasts to coach. She'd be busy testing them in the coming week.

13

IT'S ALL NEW

MY TIME WAS my own now. I could really focus on my individual routines. Well... and massage. I was definitely too far into my training to back out of that. According to Coach Dawson, he was planning to book massages every morning so I wouldn't be practicing much in the a.m. Massage was proving to be one of the top selling services offered at the gym.

Jennifer no longer felt it was necessary to be in the room with me for every massage, which made me proud, but was also a little scary. I didn't really know most of the people I was working on. We usually had a brief sit-down and talk session before their first massage, but mostly that was to get them used to me and to find out if there were any special needs, injuries, or sore spots.

My increased massage schedule meant I was finally earning a dependable income. Since I was still new at it, Coach sold the sessions for $50 an hour. I got paid $25 per hour-long massage. It was a real bargain. I had three and sometimes four each morning. Up to $100 a day in income. That would go up eventually.

I knew Madison was going to want more training time with me, but I wasn't sure I wanted to spend time on being a base instead of doing my own thing. And dealing with her coach wasn't conducive to a good relationship.

There were so many things up in the air at the moment that I really needed to talk to my family. I headed home on Sunday.

"I wondered if we were going to see you here again," Mom said when I came in for Sunday lunch. "I know you've been back because you didn't have enough clothes with you to stay forever. And all your toiletries are gone."

"I let you know where I was," I defended myself.

"Yes. That was all we asked," Dad said.

"My little brother has a lover!" Mikey exclaimed, grabbing my hands and dancing around. "He isn't a virgin anymore."

"You're making assumptions," I growled. "And I'm your older wiser brother, not your little brother."

"And what makes you wiser than me?" Mikey teased.

"I only have one lover and intend to keep it that way."

"Ouch! I'm just trying to find the right guy."

"Come and eat," Mom said. "Tell us all about this week."

"Well, we've spent nearly the entire week at Target Center. It was good to watch the competition and Tara got a bunch of requests for information on becoming a coach. I think she's going to end up with a few students. That's cool. We've been so tired after the day that we've just gone back to her place to collapse and start over the next morning."

"Pooh!" Mikey interjected.

"And stuff," I sighed, causing her to grin.

"As long as you are both okay and being careful, we don't need to know about *the stuff*," Dad said. "Is everything okay with her?"

"Yeah. You saw the review Wednesday?"

"They seemed to like you," he nodded.

"Mostly. The thing is, they also pronounced the end of her gymnastics career. While praising her recovery and her courage and the example she has set for recovering gymnasts, the guy also basically said she'd never be a real gymnast again. That hit pretty hard."

"Is that what led to you spending the night?" Mom asked.

"No. We didn't read the article until the next day. I think we always wanted it to work out that way. She's so sweet and loving."

"A big responsibility," Dad said. "I understand she has recovered to the point where she might no longer need a full-time caretaker, but she still has special needs."

"Yeah. That's one of the things we need to figure out. Her apartment is a little crowded with three of us in it. I don't think I can just stay there. And having me there might impact the terms of her lease negatively. It's an assisted living complex. It was fine with her and Jennifer because Jennifer was a full-time caregiver. I don't think I qualify."

"Well, we could certainly make some accommodations here," Mom said. "But wherever you decide to live, you'll need to start sharing in the expense."

That was one of the big issues. My income at the gym probably wouldn't cover half of Tara's rent. And Mom and Dad had been up front all along about supporting me through high school and my competition. I couldn't expect to live at home for free either.

"You aren't making me pay to live at home," Mikey insisted.

"You are not yet eighteen," Dad said, scowling at her. "And you have an internship that doesn't pay well."

"Paul is training for a career." Mikey was pushing a little hard and I patted her hand to get her to calm down.

"How is your training going?" Mom asked.

"Good. I've got about a hundred hours or so left before I can take the certification test. Jennifer has been great about keeping a log of my time and coursework. Usually, I have one session a day when she's in the room and quizzing me on some aspect of massage or the human body. She had me recite the muscles as I rubbed them. The next day she had me recite the names of all the bones."

"Are you earning anything from your massage work?"

"A little. It's pretty cheap because I'm not certified yet, and the gym keeps half of what people pay for a massage. I only get about $25 each," I said. "I talked to Jennifer about all the time she's spent teaching me. I haven't paid her a cent—and neither has the gym."

"That doesn't seem right. You have some educational funds available. Get her to tabulate the bill," Dad said.

"That's just it. When I talked to her, she said I didn't really understand their whole relationship with the gym. She knew I wasn't being compensated for any of my work with either Tara or Madison. When Tara and Jennifer negotiated training at the gym, they paid for their gym time, therapy time, my time, and other miscellaneous fees. She said she was of the opinion that as long as I agreed to it, she could use my time as she pleased."

"They paid the gym to have you work with Tara?" Mikey exclaimed.

"Yeah. And the gym never even talked to me about it. All my conversation was with Tara asking me if I'd work with her. I was pretty enthusiastic about saying yes," I laughed.

"That still doesn't sound like a very ethical thing for the gym to do," Mom said.

"The thing is, there have been hints that Madison paid the gym for my time, too. I'm not really happy about that because I felt coerced into working with her. I don't know what I'll do about that. I mean, I learned a lot working with Tara and I know I could improve Madison's and my performance. I'll keep working with her for a while and see if we can work out a balance that allows me to go back to work on my own apparatus routines and get ready for competition this fall and nationals next year."

"What's next in life?" Mom asked.

"I don't really know. Part of why I wanted to be here for lunch today is to talk that out. It's like everything for the past few years has been leading up to this week. Now I need to figure out the whole meaning of life in a day or two."

"Good luck with that," Mikey snorted.

I started laying out the pros and cons of my options. I was especially confused over how committed I was to continuing as Madison's base in acrobatic gymnastics and how to allocate enough time to what I loved in artistic gymnastics with what I needed to put in for massage. I already had a partner waiting to be my top. And if I started working with Madison more, Tara had already said she'd help coach and choreograph. There was little Tara could do with me when I was working on the pommel horse or stationary rings.

Then I had the classes and coaching that I was doing at the gym. I really liked working with the little kids and teaching them how to roll and tumble. And even though I only had one class a week, it paid pretty well. I could probably pick up more of that, but it would conflict with my massage time or my training time.

Of course, in the background was how to most effectively make Tara's and my life together work.

Tara and I had begun that talk a couple of times, usually just before we fell asleep after making love at night. As a result, we hadn't gotten very far. We were going to have to dedicate some daylight hours to the conversation. I thought perhaps we were moving a little too fast by having me spending every night with her. She hadn't really invited me to move in.

But I sure loved being there.

"Um... We're kind of in a new phase of our relationship," I started at dinner Monday.

"Yes. We're lovers. Are you happy?" Tara asked when we sat down.

"Unbelievably happy. I never had a notion of how truly wonderful it would be. I love you, Tara."

"And I love you. But that's not why you started this conversation. I can tell."

"Yeah. Well... um... New in something I have no experience with. I don't know what the... I don't know... rules are?" I ventured.

"Rules? Do we need a tariff sheet?"

"No. I just don't know how it all works."

"Okay. Rule 1: Don't fuck Madison."

"Oh, God no! That isn't even... No way!"

"Or anyone else but me. Okay?"

"Of course that's okay. There's never *been* anyone but you. Ever."

"I know. I was sort of teasing. But I do want you all to myself."

"Agreed."

"What else?" she asked.

"Well... um... Did you want me to move in with you? Or to move in with me?" I asked.

"Oh! Wow! We have been spending a lot of time here, haven't we?"

"Yeah."

"How do I put this? Uh... Even though our lives overlap more completely than other couples, we do have lives apart from each other, right?" she asked.

I grabbed a sheet of paper and drew two overlapping circles on it.

"What's that?"

"Venn Diagram. Mom made me draw one after lunch on Sunday. You're this circle and I'm this circle. Some things we have in common. Um... Like being pairs partners and um... making love."

"Yeah. That is definitely in this area," Tara laughed pointing at the overlap.

"Then we each have things the other isn't exactly part of. Like, for me, learning massage. We overlap when you get a massage from me."

"Which we might want to do here instead of the gym next time. I have ideas."

"I like the sound of that. But at the moment, my home is over here and your home is over there. We don't share a residence," I said.

"Gotcha. And don't think I'm trying to maintain distance from you or something bizarre, but I think for now we should keep it that way. We're in this part when we visit each other's home, but we live in these parts," she said. "Before you say anything, let me explain. My apartment here is in assisted living. Since I moved here, I've continued to get stronger. I've had Jennifer with me, but she needs a break now and then. Bob is pretty understanding and he doesn't come here to spend the night. But Jennifer goes to his house once or twice a week. If I need something, I have a call button that will bring a staff person to me fast. I am technically not allowed to shower alone. I think that will change soon because I'm so much more stable these days. Except after we make love. I swear the muscles in my legs turn to jelly. But you're here then."

"I understand, and that was one of the things I was concerned about. I know a lot about your body and want to learn more, but I certainly don't know all the things you need help with or the things you want me to keep my hands off of," I laughed.

"I don't mind where your hands are now," she whispered as she leaned over to kiss me. I stroked up and down her bare thigh. I didn't mind, either.

"Also, there's the privacy issue," I said, trying to catch my breath. "Like, I'm always a little embarrassed when Jennifer catches me coming out of your room. I know it's the same when you visit my house. I mean, my parents' house. They'd welcome you there, but it's still a little strange to me that they know I have this beautiful girl in my room and the door is shut and anything they imagine we might be doing probably falls short of what we're really doing."

"I can take it in small doses, but I don't think I could live with it."

"Same."

"So, let's plan on spending time together at one of our homes to do all those unimaginable things and spend the night, but let's not make a formal declaration of living together. I'd like you to leave a toothbrush and a change of clothes here, so you don't have to rush home just because you need something, but otherwise, don't move all your precious items—medals and diplomas and model airplanes and stuff—over here. I'll do the same with you. A couple changes of underwear and my overnight bag at your place so if we're watching a movie late at night, we don't have to close everything down and go home."

"I don't have any model airplanes," I said, puzzled.

"It was just an example of boy stuff," she giggled.

"Oh. But you should have things you might need… um… like tampons or stuff… at my house. I know that's girl stuff, but it's living necessities, not options."

"So kind of you."

By this time, we were kissing as much as we were talking. Dinner was forgotten. No matter what our living arrangements turned out to be in the future, it was the first time we really started talking about having a future together. It was pretty damn sexy.

I left the Venn diagram on the table and picked Tara up to carry her to the bedroom.

ONE OF THE things we discovered pretty quickly was that our schedules were significantly different. I had to be at the gym by 7:30 in the morning to be ready for my first massage client. Sometimes they scheduled one even earlier. I was used to being at the gym early because I always did a workout before school. There was no way to get a workout in before I started with massage clients. Some of the kids had training starting as early as six-thirty. Their parents were frequently my clients.

Tara didn't rise so quickly in the morning. Jennifer

started working with her physical therapy about nine. I was happy to see that even though Tara said she was retiring from gymnastics, she was still working on all the moves and exercises. Sometimes we did a little together, but we weren't really practicing a pairs routine. About one o'clock, after I'd had a bite to eat, I was demanded by Madison and Coach Daniels.

Daniels pointed out there were competitions late in the summer and she wanted us ready for them. Everyone was focused on the Olympics in July and the small fall competitions weren't getting much publicity. The good news for me was that Coach Daniels had attracted a couple of younger pairs and couldn't spend all her time with Madison and me like she wanted to. We got our two-hour session and instructions on what to work on, then Coach was off to work with a poor ten-year-old waif and her burly fifteen-year-old base—both girls. The little one was quick, agile, and cute. I identified with the base, of course. She was a rock that the little girl climbed on, jumped on, jumped off of, and left exhausted.

I got some time to work on my apparatus routines, and then my sweet girlfriend spent an hour working with Madison and me. Coach Daniels had finally consented to use an 'artistic' coach and figured I'd respond well to Tara. I did. And our routine advanced. We actually got better at a lot of things, but especially getting in touch with each other emotionally. Nearly all the critiques of Madison and me as a team had cited our lack of connection and emotion. I was beginning to feel more relaxed about working with Madison without Coach Daniels yelling at us all the time.

I was ready for my first appointment on Friday morning late in July. The Olympics would begin that day and Tara and I planned to watch the opening ceremonies and parade of champions in my family's home theater. For the most part, the past month had been good. I felt I was progressing with my artistic routines. I was nearing completion of my massage curriculum. Even Madison and I had made good progress on our mixed pairs routine. Mom and Dad weren't collecting a huge amount of rent for my space in their home, but I was able to contribute.

That all changed when I opened the door of the massage room that Friday morning.

Madison lay on the table, completely naked and uncovered.

"I'm yours this morning," she said smiling at me.

"No!" I practically yelled. I never let the door close behind me. "Absolutely not!"

I backed out of the room, closed the door, and headed for the front of the gym where Coach Dawson was looking at the day's schedules.

"I will not take her as a client!" I shouted at him. "You have to get her out of the massage room. I won't do it."

"Whoa! What is wrong, Paul? You work with Madison every day. There shouldn't be a problem with giving her a massage," he said. I swear that I think my coach is sometimes more clueless than I am.

"She's lying on the table completely naked without so much as a sheet covering her. It isn't a massage that she wants," I fumed. "That is completely against the rules."

"Well, Paul, did you knock before you opened the door?"

"Of course. She said she was ready."

"And you're sure she didn't just misunderstand how she was supposed to be covered?"

"You gave her the instructions. I didn't even know who was on the schedule this morning."

"Coach Daniels and I thought it would help the two of you connect if you worked on her as a massage therapist. Tara concurred. You'd learn how to communicate with each other better."

"Oh, she communicated, all right. I'm having no part of it. That's illegal!" I screamed.

"Really, Paul..."

"She isn't even eighteen. If I'd gone into the room she could accuse me of anything. And whether the accusation stuck or not, I'd be ruined. If you think it's all fine, *you* go in and massage her. I'm out of here."

I didn't bother to change clothes from my slacks and T-shirt that I worked in. I went straight to my car and drove away.

I DROVE AROUND for an hour, ignoring the phone calls that were buzzing my phone non-stop. If this was the way my coach was going to try to get me to connect, I was through. I couldn't believe Tara had thought I'd connect better with Madison if I massaged her. Jennifer would be upset to hear what had happened. Maybe I was over-reacting. I didn't think so.

Madison had taken every opportunity to let me know she was available as more than an acrobatics partner. Why was it that everyone seemed to think my relationship with Tara was expendable in order to become a better pairs partner with Madison? I didn't trust any of them.

I finally found a place to park near the rose garden at Lake Harriet and just answered the next call that came in.

"Hello."

"Paul! Honey, are you okay?"

"How could you think that having me massage Madison would be a good idea?" I barked at Tara.

"I didn't say that! Coach Daniels asked me if I thought having you work on me with Jennifer had improved our connection. I thought it had."

"Jennifer never let me massage you without her present. Even that was hard enough. After we became lovers, I massaged you at your apartment and it was a kind of foreplay. I mean, I love just massaging you and would do it without any thought of having sex with you, but we do have sex after most of the time and it's great. I walked into the massage room and Madison was just lying face-up on the table with nothing over her."

"That slut!"

"I don't know if I can even go back there."

"I'll talk to Jennifer about what happened. I know Coach Dawson and Coach Daniels have both been in touch with her about your 'unprofessional conduct.'"

"Fuck them!"

"Don't worry, honey. We'll get it straightened out."

I disconnected and continued to sit there in the parking lot as calls from Coach Dawson, Coach Daniels, and Madison continued to ring on my phone. When I saw Jennifer's call, I answered again.

"Hello."

"Paul, you should have stayed here to defend yourself. Did you assault Madison on the massage table?" Jennifer demanded.

"I didn't even go into the room! When I saw her on

the table, I backed out and just yelled, 'No!' Then I went to see Coach Dawson."

"That's what I thought. I've had an uneasy feeling about Madison and Coach Daniels for a while now. Like they might be looking for some leverage over you. I'm at the gym now and will settle things down here. Why don't you come to the apartment... No. Better yet, go home. I'll come there to meet with you. Take whatever time you need. I'll be a couple of hours yet before I get there."

"Jennifer, I really abide by the rules just like you taught me. I didn't do *anything* to Madison."

"I believe you, Paul."

I GOT HOME a little before noon. I'd stopped and had a Big Mac and fries on the way. Really off my training diet. I didn't care. I hardly remembered what they tasted like; it had been that long since the last time I had junk food.

I didn't know what to do while I waited. I was always at the gym all day long. Being home alone in the middle of the day was strange. Even after eating, I decided to go back to some of my routines from when we were in lockdown.

I started with pushups. After a hundred, I switched to sit-ups. Then I did squats, vee-ups, and went back to pushups.

By that time, the lunch I'd eaten caught up with me and I ran to the bathroom to throw up. My body just wasn't used to that measure of grease. I almost missed the doorbell ringing while I was in the bathroom.

I opened the door to admit Jennifer.

"It's okay, Paul. When Tara got to the gym and con-fronted Madison, Madison admitted that she made up the story about you assaulting her. She definitely wanted more control over you. There was very nearly a catfight on the tumbling mats."

I wanted to laugh at that thought, but Tara would have come out on the short end of that stick.

"I'm through, Jennifer. I'm not going back to work with her again. She'd just try something else," I said. "All I want to do is work on my artistic routines and compete with those."

"I don't blame you for that. You're a great base, and with the right partner, I think you'd go far. I don't think Madison is the right partner."

"She and her sister are both unbalanced," I said. "Mentally. They've got pretty good physical balance."

"Tara and I are leaving the gym. I told Dawson that if his facility wasn't safe for the therapists as well as the clients, I didn't think massage should be offered there," Jennifer said.

"I agree. I just don't know what I'm going to do for clients and training now," I said. And massage had been most of my income since I graduated from high school. I really needed that.

"Well, for one thing, I'll sign off on your hours and you can take the certification test. With a certificate, you can go to work most places in Minnesota. Offering massage is a big thing at most health clubs these days. And they pay better than what you've been earning."

"It's good for that part. Maybe I can find someplace else to train. I'll have to look over the various clubs and see if I can find a new coach."

"Tara will be looking for a place as well. She has two other teams besides you and Madison that she's been working with, but most of her inquiries have been out of state."

"You mean, you think you'll be leaving?"

I was near panic. Tara leaving the state? What about *us*?

"I will be. I've been talking to Tara for quite a while now. She hasn't really needed me much since she stopped training for a new routine. The physical therapy we do in the morning could be done by any competent therapist. She doesn't really need a live-in caretaker any longer. Not one who's a doctor of physical therapy, at least. You'll have to talk to Tara about what she wants to do, but you really need to decide what *you* want to do."

"Right now, I want to go to bed and hide under the covers. I can't believe Coach just let Madison and Coach Daniels walk all over me."

"Maybe she has something on him, too," Jennifer chuckled.

With Madison's actions that morning, I had to take that notion seriously.

14

ADJUSTING TO A NEW LIFE

"THERE AREN'T MANY gyms in the Twin Cities that are equipped for good senior elite level training," Tara sighed. She'd arrived a few minutes after Jennifer left and I wondered if she'd been waiting for a signal. I greeted her with a kiss and she asked me to take her to bed. We were in my room, but we were just talking. Mostly.

"There are a few gyms that cater to kids," I said. "I wonder if we could get one of them to give us a time to train elite athletes. Maybe during the day when the kids are supposed to be in school."

"That's a possibility. My athletes are all in school, too. Only you and Madison were training for *senior* elite pairs at Hennepin Gym," she said. Then she kissed me before I could say anything. "No. I don't expect you to go back to work with her. In fact, I'd be a little worried if you did. I guess it's time for you to really focus on your individual routines. I'm so sad because I really loved working with you. We're a great team and you're a really good base. If you had a good flyer to work with, you'd be

190

a candidate for a world championship."

"Not now. Maybe someday. Now, I'll need to find a coach. At the very least, a spotter. I've got ideas for my routines that are a little risky to practice without a spotter," I said.

"That worries me a little, but I'm not strong enough and stable enough to be a spotter for you. We'll have to launch a search."

We kissed for a while and started shedding our clothes. *Wow!* She still just blew me away with how pretty she was and how enthusiastic about loving me she was. We took it slow and easy, but it wasn't really long before I felt myself sliding into her and her little catch of breath as I opened her. The feeling always brought me to the brink of tears. She was just so unbelievably wonderful. If everything else in my life went to hell, I'd still be okay as long as I had Tara.

We were out of bed and preparing dinner when Mom, Dad, and Mikey got home from work. Us being there was a surprise and we had to go through the whole story and situation at the dinner table. Mikey was furious. Dad was quiet and I thought he might be mentally preparing a lawsuit. Mom was the MC of the questioning, even pointing to which of us she wanted to answer a question.

We finally begged off any more questions so we could go downstairs to the entertainment center and watch the opening ceremony from Paris. It was pretty spectacular. It wasn't even in the stadium, but was right downtown along the Seine! Well, we'd have plenty of time this weekend and next week to watch the gymnastics and other events as they were broadcast from Paris.

After the show ended, I carried Tara to my bedroom and made love to her again before we settled to sleep in each other's arms for the night.

I WAS SITTING in Mom's favorite chair Monday, reading. I couldn't believe I was reading a book, just for pleasure! After finishing Neil Gaiman's *American Gods*, I downloaded the sequel, *Anansi Boys*. I was just getting into it when I saw a car pull up in our driveway and, to my horror, Madison got out and headed for the door. I thought about just not answering it, but decided I'd better get this over with once and for all. I wasn't going to face her alone, though.

Unfortunately, after spending two nights with me, Tara went back to her apartment. We were both pretty depressed about basically losing our gym, but gymnastics is a sport that requires a huge amount of trust, and we just didn't trust anyone there now.

I had my cell phone in my hand and simply switched to camera and started recording. The bell rang.

"Madison. You shouldn't be here," I said when I opened the door.

"I need to talk to you," she said. "Can I come in?"

"No. Say what you need to say and leave."

"You have to come back. Coach Daniels said that if I don't have a partner there's nothing for her to coach me on and she'll leave," Madison said.

"Good. You'd do better with anyone else. But find a girl and do women's pairs. No boy is ever going to trust you."

"I apologized and told them all that you didn't assault me," she said.

"And that's supposed to make me trust you?"

"I thought if we had sex, it would make us closer and we'd improve our routine."

"You ruined my job and my training. That didn't make us closer."

"How can I make it up? Honestly, Paul, I'll do anything for you. You can make me your personal plaything. I'll do routines with you while I'm completely naked. I know you liked what you saw Friday. Let me in and I'll give you a blowjob right now. You can have me naked and do whatever you want with me. I need you. I need you as my partner."

"What part of 'No!' do you not understand? I'm not interested in you, Madison. I never have been. I've never wanted to be your pairs partner. I don't like and I don't trust your coach, you, or your sister. And now I don't trust Coach Dawson, either," I said. "Now, leave."

"All right, you bastard! I tried to make it nice for you and give you what every boy wants. I'll get what I want eventually. You don't know my father. Let me tell you that with my story and Penny's story from cheer, he'll make sure you never work or train in the Twin Cities again."

"Go away."

I closed the door.

She rang the bell half a dozen times and then pounded on the door. I made a call.

"9-1-1. State your emergency."

"There is a crazy woman trying to break into my house. She's already threatened me. She won't go away."

"Domestic dispute. I'll have a patrol car come by, but please try to settle your differences before they get there."

"There's nothing domestic about it. She doesn't live here and I have no relationship with her. She's a former work associate."

"Okay. A car is on its way."

Of course, after Madison had kicked the locked door a couple of times, she turned around and headed for her car. I'd have had a lot to explain to the police if she'd just gotten in her car and driven off. Instead, she dislodged one of the bricks that line our walk to the door and came running toward the house.

What kind of damage can a 110-pound woman do with a brick? Well, don't forget that Madison is a gymnast with incredible upper body strength. She rushed the house and heaved the brick at our front window, just as the patrol car pulled up. The lights came on and the siren wailed as the glass in the big picture window crumbled out of the frame. Two cops got out of the car, one circling wide and the other headed directly to Madison. She screamed and turned to run to her car where the other policeman trapped her and immediately cuffed her, pushing her against her car and quickly patting her down.

That'll get him a lawsuit for sexual assault, I thought.

Then she turned around and I saw it was a female officer. She marched Madison straight to the squad car as her partner knocked on our front door.

"Are you okay?" the officer asked.

"Yes," I said. I came out of the house and closed the door behind me. There was no reason to invite the police into the house.

"What did you do to her that set her off like that?" he asked.

"What did I...? *I* didn't do anything. She showed up here a little while ago to try to convince me to return to the gym and be her partner. I refused. I don't think anyone's ever said no to her before," I said.

"You know, with a big strong guy like you, it's going to be hard to sell that you didn't do anything," he said.

"I have video of the whole encounter."

"Why did you do that?"

"I was sitting over there reading when I saw her pull in. She made a false accusation against me Friday that resulted in me quitting my job and leaving the gym."

"Is that under investigation?"

"No. As soon as I left, she retracted the accusation."

"What were the circumstances around that?"

"I'm a massage therapist. I knocked on the massage room door and she said to come in. When I opened the door, I saw her lying entirely naked and exposed on the massage table. I immediately backed out while yelling 'No!' When she dressed and came out of the room, she accused me of molesting her."

"And you didn't?"

"I didn't even go all the way into the room. The door was never closed."

"So, why did you leave your job?"

"My coach and her coach sided with her. I can't do gymnastics in a gym where I don't trust anyone. Now she's threatened to get her father involved—whoever he is—and make sure I can't work or train anywhere in the Twin Cities."

"And you got all that on video?"

"Yes. Do you want to see it?"

"No. If I saw it, I'd have to take it and log it as evidence. Since we don't have any charges yet, other than property damage, that would be unnecessary. Save it for when the father tries to press charges. I assume you will want to charge her with the property damage?" he asked.

"My parents own the house. They're both at work right now, but I'm certain they will want some action."

"Okay. Probably better call them and get one of them home. You'll need to get this boarded up. I'll give my report to a detective and he'll come by to talk to you. Since we actually saw her throw a brick through your window, we have grounds to arrest and hold her for vandalism and property damage. I wouldn't have thought someone so little could create so much damage."

"Be careful. She's an acrobat. She's a lot stronger than she looks."

"No matter what gripe your daughter has with my son, the fact is she threw a brick through my living room window. That was witnessed by two police officers who were coming to investigate the 9-1-1 call my son made because she was pounding on the door and had threatened him," Dad said on the phone. Mom, Mikey, Jennifer, Tara, and I sat nearby listening in.

"My daughter is under eighteen and your son molested her. I can easily plead that the brick was an aggravated attack," Mr. Layne, Madison's father, shot back.

"You'll have a difficult time proving that in the face of the video that recorded the entire encounter. But if you want to have a go at my son, that's between you and him. The fact remains that your daughter, who you have said is a minor and therefore you are responsible for, threw a brick through my window. I expect to have the expenses of having it replaced and cleaned up covered by you. I've had an estimator out to give me a price for a replacement like the one that was broken. If you'd like a second estimate, let me know when your estimator is coming to assess the damage."

"Tom, you're making this more difficult than it needs to be. You know I'm the best civil law instructor at the university. I'll have to make it really hard on you."

"Neal, you've let your daughters run wild. Don't threaten me with what you can do at the university. You know who keeps the lights on in your building. Who makes sure there's heat. Who knows where all the buried lines are, where they come into your office and how close you are to a bathroom that's prone to flooding. You have an easy way out with me. Pay for my goddamn window. If you insist on going up against my son, I'll enlist Dr. Abrams to defend him. It's just the kind of case he'd like to use as an example in his classes."

"I'll have an estimator at your house tomorrow at noon. Just understand, your son is going to have a hard time getting a job in the Twin Cities ever again. There's nothing Abrams can do to stop that."

"We'll see. Have a good day, Neal."

Dad hung up the phone and we gathered around the dining table for a family conference.

MADISON'S FATHER WAS one of the most renowned law professors at the university. Unfortunately for Madison, my dad knew nearly everyone in the law school because he supervised the re-engineering and updating of the building they were in. Several of the professors felt they owed him for the state-of-the-art facility they could now work in. They'd pressed business cards into his hands when the building was re-opened and told him if he ever needed legal help to just call on them.

Madison's father had been one of those law professors.

Of course, neither Madison or I knew that our fathers knew each other. She might have been a little slower invoking his name if she'd known. It was apparent, though, that he'd bailed both his daughters out of several sketchy situations. I'd heard Penny and Ethan were headed toward a rushed wedding before he went to off to college because Penny was pregnant.

"Nonetheless, you need to take his threats seriously," Dad told me. "He doesn't teach a legal ethics class. He teaches how to do the most damage to your opponent."

"That's vicious," Mikey said.

"It's unfortunately the way a lot of the world works," Mom said. "There are people out there who don't even care if they win, as long as they do the maximum amount of damage to those who oppose them. You found that out when you were taken to the farm."

"Don't remind me."

"Just know that we'll back you," Jennifer said. "There's already a rumor that people have started to leave the gym. When your Saturday morning class showed up and you didn't, parents started asking questions. I was given this list of names and addresses to contact if you can start the class somewhere else."

"Don't worry, Babe. You never let me fall. We'll never let you down," Tara said.

I SPENT THE rest of the week studying for the National Certification Exam under Jennifer's tutelage. Tara was my only massage client that week and she got a couple of really long massages as Jennifer quizzed me on every move.

We also spent time calling other gyms and athletic facilities. I told one gym that I could bring a dozen kids for a tumbling class on Saturday mornings and they immediately enlisted me for that. It was a small gym that didn't really have any of the men's apparatuses. They were equipped for girls to get their start. They did have a sprung floor for exercises, so I got to do a little work after my class Saturday morning. The gym had gone to work getting more kids in and Tara came to assist me with the eighteen kids in the class.

Interestingly enough, the full-time job that sounded most promising for me was a potential job with the local women's basketball team. They used athletic men to practice against to toughen them up. It was mostly because men tended to be more physical than women when they played. They were harder to push around. I told them that as a gymnast, I was very strong and hard to push around.

I went back to Hennepin Gym once that week. I had a locker there and I wanted my things out of it. I thought I'd be in and out before anyone really saw I was there, but Coach Dawson was at the front desk when I came out.

"Paul. I'm sorry to see you cleaning out your locker. You know you don't have to leave here. You can keep training and even keep massaging. You have your certificate now?"

"I passed the test," I said. "I wouldn't feel safe working here."

"That was just a little misunderstanding. Madison was just shocked that you came into the room before she was covered."

"Jesus, Coach. Are you still holding that line? I knocked at the door per protocol and she said to come in. She wasn't in the process of covering herself. She had no intention of covering herself. She was there to get me in a compromising position. And you supported her and her bitch coach against me. How could I come to train here? Who would I trust? I wouldn't even trust you to be my spotter, let alone my coach," I ranted.

"Well, you're doing a good job of burning your bridges,

young man. I brought you from being a scrawny weak kid to the athlete you are now. Don't forget that."

"And then when a bigger opportunity walked in, you sold me off to her as your part of the deal. You abandoned *my* training and relegated me to a pairs base. And I'm the last senior man you have in the gym. You betrayed me, so don't lecture me about burning bridges."

"Take your gear and get out, Paul. Don't come back."

I left.

I HAD VISIONS of myself flipping burgers as I walked to the office of the women's basketball team. I hadn't received many invites for interviews. As we approached the end of the Olympics break, a lot of college guys that worked for the team were headed back to school. I wasn't certain how much work I'd have with the team after the season ended.

"Paul Bradley? Come in. We may have made a mistake inviting you here. I see you are only nineteen and a recent high school graduate. That's a little young for working with us. Where are you going to college?"

"Ma'am, I am not an intellectual powerhouse. I don't have any college prospects. It took me an extra year to get out of high school. I've spent the past eight years becoming a gymnast. I hope to return to it in the future."

"Why are you out now?"

"I had a falling out with the management at the gym. I need to find a new coach and place to practice."

"And you figure we might keep you in shape?"

"I'd like to believe I'd help your team stay in shape," I said.

"Hmm. That's a refreshing perspective. You know we use men on our practice teams to add bulk and strength. You look small to go up against six-foot-four women. You might get pushed around a lot."

"It takes quite a lot to push me around," I laughed. "Though I was used to it as a kid. I can jump. Pretty high. From a stand or a single step."

"Well, we can try you out. Understand, though, that we are in the middle of the women's basketball season, just coming back from the Olympic break. While we want you to be physical and present a barrier for the women to get around, we don't want our players hurt. The pay is not too generous. This is women's sports, not men's. It's looking better this year than in the past, but our pay scale is negotiated with the union."

"Would I need to join a union to work here?" I asked.

"No, you wouldn't be a member of the union. It's a players' union. But you would still be governed by its pay scale."

"Gymnasts aren't represented by a union and have notoriously low compensation," I laughed.

"Let's go to the gym and get an assessment."

My 'assessment' included putting on some pads to increase my footprint on the floor. I had a pad that extended my arms a foot so my reach was longer. Then I was given a station, not a player to guard or anything. My station was along the arc on one side of the court. Whenever a player entered my station, I joined whoever was guarding her to up the difficulty of her escaping or getting a shot off.

It was hard work. I was used to women who had a lot of upper body strength, but the legs on the basketball players were incredibly strong. I didn't think any of them would ever be afraid of me. I was a little worried about them.

It wasn't long before I was being challenged in my

station. I mostly jumped around and took up space, but eventually the player decided to try a three-point shot. The first time, I was caught flat-footed and the ball sailed over my head into the net. One of the trainers stepped up to me and hollered that I was supposed to be able to jump and keep my pads in front of the player's face.

I did. The next time a player launched a shot from deep, I had both hands up in the air and jumped straight up to block her. Even at that, I barely touched the ball as it sailed by, but it was enough to knock it off course. I worked with the team for half an hour with one trainer or another or a coach or something shouting instructions to me as I maintained my blocking stance.

Once, a player tried to go right through me. She found that I was harder to move than I looked like I'd be. She fell back after hitting me and instinct kicked in. I dove behind her and caught her in my padded hands before she hit the floor.

That was the end of my tryout.

"Not bad," the manager said as she watched me strip off the pads. "I'll show you to your locker and you can get cleaned up. We'll provide a uniform and laundry service. The locker rooms are fairly well supplied. $22.50 an hour to start. You will be working eight to ten hours per day. Sometimes in a practice session like the one you just participated in. Sometimes, you'll be engaged one-on-one. Sometimes you'll just be retrieving the ball during a player's shooting practice. Sometimes we'll need you on a Saturday or Sunday. Sometimes, you'll just be told to do something else. People will give you instructions as you go."

"Thank you, ma'am. I'll work hard."

"Let's see how it goes this week."

I HAD A new job and it was physically demanding. I definitely would stay in shape. The team had a weight room with a couple of devices I could use for my own workouts, including a peg board and a bar for pull-ups. I was often in the room to act as a spotter for players using free weights. I got to use the room after most of the team had left for the day. There was always an attendant on duty, though, so a couple women would be around getting physical therapy or using the therapy pools.

I was on the high bar doing pull-ups one evening when Chantell saw me. She was a veteran baller in her fifth year with the team. I saw her watching me as I pulled myself up. Her mouth was open and she just stared.

In all fairness, there was good reason for her to stare. I did gymnastic pull-ups. On each rep, I didn't pull myself up my chin and then back down. I use the same muscles I used on the rings and high bar to pull myself up until my entire torso was above the bar to my waist. Then back down. I guess most athletes don't see that very often.

"How did you learn to do that?" Chantell asked when I finally dropped to the ground.

"Oh. It's pretty much required to be able to do that when you're a gymnast. Even my girlfriend can do it."

"Your girlfriend. If I could do that, I think my range would increase. I'm a good three-point shooter, but you wouldn't block my shots if I was shooting back four feet. Can you teach me?"

"Sure, if you'd like. It's really mostly repetition and engaging the entire torso in the lift. Most people work their arms and traps when doing pull-ups. In order to do the waist-high pull-up, you need to pass the engagement down the torso. You'll get a lot more work on your pecs and abs. I bet you could do one right now."

"You think? Coach me through it."

She reached up and did a little hop to reach the bar that took me a solid jump to reach.

"Okay, palms away on the bar and farther apart. You might be used to doing them with palms toward you or one each direction, but this requires you to use your pushing muscles." She took the position. "Now, regular chin-up and hold at the top. Good. Now engage wrist and triceps to push yourself on up."

She made it up to her shoulders before dropping back down.

"Let's try it again. Did you feel what was engaging as you started shifting your center of gravity to above your hands? I can help lift you so you can feel the muscles engage all the way up. I'd need to touch your waist."

"Yeah, that's fine. Let's do it."

She went back up and when she stalled out, I gave her just enough boost that she could pull herself the rest of the way up. At the top, she gave a whoop and dropped back down.

"I think I'll work on this in the morning, before we've done a full practice. I can tell this will make me sore."

"I can give you some tips on that, too," I said without thinking. "I'm a certified massage therapist."

"For real?"

"Yes, ma'am."

"Maybe I'll take it a little easier tomorrow so I don't need that service. We're traveling to Dallas in the afternoon," she said. "Uh, what was your name?"

"Paul," I said.

"Nice to meet you, Paul." She left and I finished my own workout.

15
CHARGING AHEAD

IN CASE YOU were wondering, this was not the beginning of a torrid affair with an older athletic woman. After all, I had a girlfriend and for all I knew, Chantell was married with children. Not that it would have made a difference, because I had a girlfriend, you know.

It was the beginning of a rumor that I could help in the training room as well as on the gym floor. Of course, none of the women who were playing a game or two a week wanted to be sore when they played, I often ended a training session with a six-foot-something Amazon stretched out on a massage table as I worked the kinks out of her shoulders, back, butt, and legs.

"Paul, I need to speak with you a minute," the manager called me away from the gym. I hustled to her office.

"I need verification that you are indeed a certified massage therapist and not just a nineteen-year-old getting his kicks on my players' naked bodies."

"I wouldn't do that. I have a girlfriend. I assure you that my attention has been strictly professional."

"So the women have indicated. Can you get me a

copy of your certificate so we can display it in the massage room?"

"Of course," I said. *Whatever.* I finished my work day and the next day brought the GM my certificate. She nodded and smiled as if she were very pleased with something.

"Your work here the past month has been exemplary, and we have seen you expanding your responsibilities steadily. Therefore, I'm pleased to announce the end of your probation and establishment of a new pay rate of $25.00 per hour."

"That's great. Thank you."

"That does not cover massage. As I indicated when you started here, the pay scale is set by agreement with the union. You are to log your massages and turn that in with your time card. You'll be paid $50 per massage, assuming that each massage is approximately fifty minutes out of a one-hour session. Will that be satisfactory?"

"Um... Yes, ma'am. That's very kind of you."

"You have worked on five of our women so far and I expect that number will increase to the entire team soon. We had a therapist on staff who decided the work was too irregular and there was really nothing else we could have her do between massages. Also, the team complained that she was too weak to do them any good. I hadn't gotten around to having her replaced until you came along. So, you'll be filling both roles as a training assistant and as a massage therapist. I will be monitoring the number of massages and to whom so I'm sure no one is abusing the privilege. You needn't worry about that. I'll remind anyone who is having too many massages."

"Yes, ma'am."

"Okay. To work."

I felt like I'd fallen in a pile of shit at the Hennepin Gym and swam my way to the surface of a rose-scented pool at the basketball gym.

"That's because you are talented and a hard worker," Tara said that weekend. She was assisting with my Saturday morning tumbling class again. This gym paid us enough that we both got a nice pay packet each weekend. "I've been making do teaching some other elementary gymnastics here, but it's too far for my pairs to come for training. The work is good, but it's not where I want to be. I trained all my life. I'd like to coach a pair or two to a national championship."

"I'm hardly fulfilling a life dream, though I'm making twice as much money as I was at Hennepin Gym. There, half of what I made went to pay for gym time and coaches—which I understand you paid for, too. Geez! I had no idea how sleazy the business was. I'm working now and it's good, but I'm not training for gymnastics," I said.

"I think we need to continue our search for someplace to get what we really need. You need to look for a coach. I need to look for a place where I can coach a winning team. And I need to be someplace where I can hire a part-time assistant. Jennifer has accepted a new position with a D3 college in Iowa. She's leaving me."

"I'm sorry to see her go," I said. "She really helped me a lot. What will you do now?"

"We're only nineteen and twenty years old. We have dreams."

That gave me pause. My dreams had been interrupted by the catastrophe at Hennepin Gym. Tara's dreams had been destroyed by an accident in Geneva.

She was building a new life with new dreams. I owed her my support.

For that night, we supported each other in the most physical and loving way we could. I was seriously thinking that maybe I should ask her to marry me. We'd known each other for nearly a year now. I didn't want to face the possibility of her leaving to go somewhere else.

THINGS WERE GOING well at work. I was a suitable obstacle on the court and the women were learning to kind of bounce off me in a new direction. Their shots were gaining altitude as they arched more. I was able to block fewer and fewer of them. That was especially true when Chantell started stepping back just before her shots.

The step-back three was not new. There were players who were known for it. But it was not all that used except by that handful of players. Most got as close to the three-point line as possible before they launched their shots. The coach commented on it and investigated the new training she'd been doing.

Chantell told her I'd been working on building her upper body strength and she was definitely feeling stronger.

I could verify that she was feeling stronger. I was seeing her the day before any game for a good massage. Most of the women who wanted a massage saw me the day after a game. No matter how much they practiced, playing for two hours against competition that was as determined as they were was a lot different than practicing against a padded dummy or even the several men who were actually basketball players and provided training. They'd evolved an interesting method in which the opposition at either end of the court in practice had six players. They had the normal five and me. I was simply there to create a moving obstacle on the court, so most players found themselves double-teamed.

It was during a break, when I'd stripped off my pads, that a ball simply rolled up and hit my foot. I saw Chantell grinning under the basket.

"Shoot it!" she yelled at me.

That was not something on my job-list and frankly, I'd seldom actually handled the basketball other than to swat it or nudge it over to a player. She was grinning at me in a real challenge, though, so I figured I'd have to do something. Several of the other players had turned to look. I decided that if I was going to make a spectacle of myself, I'd do it my way.

I trapped the ball between my feet, launched myself into the air in a forward flip, and sent the ball toward the goal with my legs.

This is no fairytale story about how I swished it or anything. I was fortunate that I managed to launch it in the right direction. It fell just a little short and Chantell picked it up. The rest of the team started clapping.

"That isn't how it's supposed to be done," Chantell laughed.

"I've never played basketball," I said. "I was a cheerleader."

That was only a little stretch of the truth. I was on the cheerleading squad, but I'd never joined them at a game. I was strictly there for competitions when they needed an acrobatic base for the flyers.

"Show us!" one of the other players called.

I figured since we were all on break, it would be okay, so I set off on a tumbling run across the floor, doing flips and twists, tucks and layouts. It was far more difficult than it would be on tumbling mats. The basketball court was not a sprung floor, but I'd worked on the hardwood before.

"Go team!" I yelled when I reached the far side, landed my jump, and raised my hands.

"Thank God he doesn't do that when he's blocking us," another player said.

It was kind of a moment of acceptance. We were headed toward the playoff season.

THE FIRST ROUND, in fact, was the next week. The top eight seeds at the end of the season played against each other on September 22 and 23. The four winners went to the semi-finals the next week. From that, two teams would emerge for the championship series. While the play-in was a one-and-done elimination tournament, the championship was a best of seven series.

In the same position our team was in the previous year, we were going against the number three team in round one. As the lower ranked team, we were traveling to our game and I was asked to go with them. I wouldn't be doing much in the way of workouts with them, but I was taking my massage table.

We got there on Sunday for the Tuesday game, and I had a massage with each of the twelve team members by the end of Monday. The team was feeling good when they went to their shoot-around Tuesday morning and then dressed for the game that evening.

I'll keep it simple. We lost.

It was a good game, but we just couldn't pull it together for the win in the last few minutes. Everyone crashed in their hotel rooms after the game—at least I did—and we headed to the airport first thing Wednesday morning for the trip back home.

"It was a good run, Paul," the GM said when I met with her Thursday morning. "You were considered on the clock for eight hours of massage on Sunday, Monday, and Tuesday. So, your final check shows a little more than you might have thought. What are your plans next? Will you be available next season?"

"Uh... Next season? You mean I don't have a job during the winter?"

"We don't have a team here again until May. I'd be happy to have you back with us, then," she said.

In all the time I'd been working with the team, it never occurred to me that they didn't continue to practice during the off-season! I was officially unemployed.

As time permitted, I'd been doing searches for gymnastic training that I could afford. There are not that many training programs for senior elite gymnasts and precious few coaches. The truth was that Hennepin Gymnastics Center was one of the lower tier facilities among those few that were available. It, like most of the gyms across the country, specialized in children's gymnastics, assuming their senior elite gymnasts would either go to a college with a gymnastics program or would be recruited by another training center. I hadn't had enough exposure in competitions to attract the attention of any other gym.

I made a list of three places I'd like to train at. I decided I'd tell Tara about them to see what she thought at dinner that night.

I picked her up when she got home from her lessons in St. Paul. We went to our favorite restaurant—a little bistro-style place just off Hennepin in Uptown. We could eat there for a reasonable price and the food wasn't all covered in fattening sauces.

Tara seemed a little reserved. I hadn't seen her since the previous Saturday before I traveled with the team. I had to start off by telling her I was unemployed because the season was over for our team. That drew a sympathetic pat on the hand and a loving kiss.

"You'll find something. Are you thinking of going to one of the clubs to offer massage?" she asked.

"I've been looking at resuming my training somewhere. I brought along a list of places to see what you thought of them. Anyplace you'd like to go to train?"

"Oh. Um… Let's see the locations." I pulled out my top three list and we went through the pluses and minuses of each of the programs. Tara was more familiar with some of them than I was because she'd been traveling and competing long before we met.

"Texas is good, but awfully hard to get into. You really need a top-level coach to recommend you and a record of competition wins. At least, that's how I got in."

"Were you doing acrobatics when you were admitted?"

"No. I was like every dedicated little girl who wanted to be a gymnast. I worked on the uneven parallel bars, the vault, the beam, and the mats. That's where they decided I should be part of an acrobatics team. I loved to tumble, though I was very good on the beam."

"So, they just put you with Jackson?" I asked. I don't know why I was probing more and more. These were things I didn't know about her.

"No. They tried me first with a girls' team. You know, three girls. The other two were very strong and needed a top. We didn't get along. That's when they decided my dynamic was not good for working with other girls. They convinced Jackson to try some things with me and we gelled almost immediately. We were really quite a team."

There was a wistfulness in her voice that let me know she really missed those days. Really missed Jackson.

"Denver's a little shaky," she said, continuing down my list. "I did some inquiries there as well. The current director is retiring. There seems to be a bit of a power struggle going amongst the others and some coaches have taken their performers with them and left."

"That doesn't sound good. You've been making inquiries?" I asked.

"Yes. This center in Florida sounds intriguing. And they have a residence program. It would give you a place to live while you train. I'm sure you could find massage work, though you might need a license there."

"Are there any good possibilities for me amongst the places you've checked out?"

"No. I'm afraid not. It looks like..." she just stopped and started over once or twice. "I've found a place," she said. "I'm going to move to California. There's a university in the Bay area that plans to expand their gymnastics program to include acrobatic gymnastics. They actually contacted me. I'm flying out there on Monday to look over the program and if it all looks like they've sold it to me, I'll move there the next week."

"The next week! Like ten days from now?"

"Yeah. I'm sorry, Paul. There's nothing here in Minneapolis for me. Without Jennifer, I've been at loose ends. I know I'm going to do it, so my apartment is mostly packed up. Maybe we could go to your house tonight?"

"Um... Sure. You... You're leaving me."

I was numb and unsure of anything else Tara said. After dinner, she came to my house with me and we made passionate love that kept the tears at bay. But in the morning, she packed the few things she had in my room and bathroom, and left.

SHE WAS GONE most of the next week, leaving Sunday evening for her flight to San Francisco. When she got back on Friday, she seemed happy. She spent the weekend with me, but we spent a lot of our time together packing her apartment. A freight company truck came Monday morning and loaded her boxes on a pallet, wrapped it in plastic wrap, and loaded it on their truck. She'd rented the apartment furnished, so everything she shipped fit into boxes.

"I can't believe you're leaving," I said. I'd almost convinced myself it was all a nightmare, but I stood beside her car as she was preparing to get in. "I want to come with you. I want to marry you, Tara." Tears were so close that I was choking on them.

"Maybe someday," she said. "I'm doing this for you as much as for me. You have a dream, Paul. I was an interruption. You need to follow the dream. Compete. Join the national team. Win the Olympics. My accident ended my chances of fulfilling my dream of a world championship. It's come near to ending yours. I won't let that happen. One day, maybe we'll find each other again. Not today, love."

She kissed me again and got into her car. She closed the door, fastened her seatbelt, and started the car.

"I love you," I said.

"I love you, too," she answered. Then she put the car in gear and drove away.

I love you.

I HADN'T ABSORBED much of the book I read that afternoon. I'd just reached Spider's confession in *Anansi Boys*, and Rosie breaking up with both him and Fat Charlie. She'd slapped him and stormed away. I had a pang of sorrow for Fat Charlie, who really hadn't done a thing and was now, presumably, in jail for not doing it.

On the other hand, it would have been a bit of a relief if Tara had been incensed over something I had done, would have slapped me in anger, and stormed off without another word. But she hadn't. She wasn't mad at me nor was I mad at her. Our parting had been sweet. Sad. The tears were still there.

Parting is such sweet sorrow.

I knew those words weren't in this book, and the reading program had progressed two or three pages since I last saw or heard a word of it. I quit the app and glanced at the clock on my phone. Noon. It would be one o'clock in Florida. I opened my phone and called the number of the training center there.

"WHAT? YOU'RE LEAVING?" my sister wailed when I called to tell her I was going to drive to Florida the next day.

"I need to go down to interview and audition. I'm actually late already. They run on a kind of school year down there and here it is October already."

"But I never want you to leave!"

"I know, Mikey. It's not what I planned either. Tara left for California this morning. I can't go back to Hennepin Gym. The basketball team is closed up for the season. If I don't do this, I'll end up flipping burgers. If I could get someone there to take on a big dumb guy. All I've got is my gymnastics. If I don't make something out of it, what good am I?"

"Have you told Mom and Dad?"

"No. I figure dinner will be interesting."

"I'll be there. I'm going to go catch a bus right now. Don't you leave without giving me a hug!"

"I won't."

I didn't realize that Tara leaving would be so traumatic for my family, too. I guess I should have known. It wasn't Tara; it was me. I was going down to Florida to audition, but I'd packed nearly everything I'd need if I decided to just stay there. Or to go somewhere else from there.

I included a limited amount of camping gear and didn't plan to stay in any hotels on the 1,600-mile drive. I figured if I left early Tuesday morning, I could be there by Thursday afternoon. If I didn't make it until Friday, oh well. I just couldn't stay in Minneapolis a minute longer.

I'd already filled my car with gas and checked the tires. Everything was in good working order. I stopped at Byerly's and got some steaks, potatoes for baking, and a salad. I got home and got the potatoes in the oven before Mikey arrived.

Even though I'd called her at three, I knew she wouldn't arrive much before five, even if she rushed to catch the first bus available. She was on the East Bank and that meant she'd have to go downtown to transfer. When she opened the front door, she screamed.

"Paul! Where are you?"

"Kitchen."

She came running through the house and threw herself into my arms for a big hug.

"That's not the goodbye hug," she said. "That one comes before you leave tomorrow."

"You sure you can get up that early?" I teased.

"Yes. I can't believe you're leaving!"

"You will. It is really the only logical thing to do. Since Madison made it impossible for me to work at the gym and basketball season is over, I have to go somewhere to get trained for competition."

"I know. And I know I haven't been much a part of your life for the past year or so because of college and your girlfriend and stuff. But I'm really going to miss you."

"I'll miss you, too. But we can call each other. You do have my number."

"Yes, dummy," she growled.

Mom and Dad got home soon thereafter and I put the steaks on the grill. Mikey served the salad.

"What's the occasion for such a good meal?" Dad asked.

Mikey scowled at me and kept her mouth shut.

"I've got an interview at a training academy in Florida," I said.

"Congratulations!" Mom said. "When?"

"Friday," I said. "I'm leaving tomorrow morning."

"What?" Dad asked. "Isn't this kind of sudden?"

"Tara left for San Jose this morning. There's no reason for me to delay going down to Florida for my audition," I defended myself. I just knew this was going to be time for a lecture from my parents about hasty decisions.

"This is what you want, isn't it?" Mom asked quietly.

"Yeah, Mom. I need to get back into serious training. The past couple of months not getting regular training is beginning to tell on me."

"Well, then, let's eat a wonderful meal together and get you ready to go," she said.

That was it about the suddenness of the decision. From there on, it was all about what kind of academy it was and whether I thought I had a chance of getting in. Dad wanted to go over my route with me and make sure I was allowing enough time. Mikey was online reading about the academy and showing her findings to Mom.

Then Tara called to tell me she was somewhere in the middle of Nebraska for the night and that she loved me. I told her I had an audition in Florida on Friday, but I didn't mention that I was leaving the next day. That's one thing about cell phones. You keep the same number and call the same way no matter where you are. I'd probably tell her tomorrow night that I was somewhere in Illinois or Kentucky on my way to Florida.

Before I left in the morning, Dad pressed a bunch of money into my hand.

"You might need to pay some expenses before you get settled in," he said. "There's $2,000 there. It should get you through the trip and a few weeks. I know you don't plan to come back after your audition. Just don't forget about us and come home when you can."

"Thanks, Dad," I said. "I'll never forget where home is."

16

AUDITIONING

I GOT INTO TAMPA Thursday afternoon in time to check into the academy. They were very kind to say that even though they couldn't pay my transportation to Florida, they would provide a room for me in the dormitory and perhaps I would meet some other interesting people. I joined the other students at dinner in the cafeteria.

They were festive. That's about all I can say I took away from the dining room. I met people. Lots of them. Too many to remember any names. They were all performers and it looked like they were *on* all the time.

I should say that this was a bigger place than I expected; it was called the Tampa Gymnastics Acrobatics and Circus Academy. Some of those at dinner were still in costumes and makeup from their training day or maybe a performance. Others were simply making contacts and getting to know each other. I was induced to do a couple of flips, but I wasn't prepared to do much in a cafeteria. I was wearing jeans and a T-shirt, which wasn't the best gear to do gymnastics in.

220

At one point a few were doing some kind of launch and catch that went wrong and I looked up to see a flyer flying toward me. I instinctively spun to catch her and suddenly had a very surprised girl in my arms.

"Thank you," she said. "I was going to just tumble out of it, but I couldn't expect you to know that, could I?" She had a light accent that I took to be British, but I wasn't very experienced with that kind of accent so it could have been Australian or some other place that talks like that.

"I'm sorry I spoiled your landing," I said.

"Oh, don't be sorry. I rather like being caught. See you in class tomorrow."

Then she scampered off and I realized we hadn't even exchanged names. No matter. I didn't think I'd be seeing her in any classes. I hadn't yet figured out how training and classes all fit together yet. That was why I was here to interview and audition.

THE ESCORT I'D had earlier in the day, who got me checked in and saw me to my room, knocked at my door at about eight o'clock that evening. He handed me a packet that included instructions for Friday, a schedule, and even what to wear and be prepared to do. He offered to show where things would get started and I accepted. It was obvious that Friday would be a long hard day.

I was up at 6:00 and started my morning warmup. Then I went to have a light breakfast in the cafeteria. I returned to my room, showered, and dressed in my best gym wear. At 8:30, I was in the interview room and one of the hardest days of my life began.

"Paul, when did you begin your training in gymnastics?" Raymond Davis, the director of the academy, asked. They hadn't actually introduced themselves, but I recognized him from the photos on the website.

"I've been training for eight years now. I began when I was almost twelve."

"Kind of a late start, wasn't it?"

"Yes, but I devoted myself to it and made rapid progress. I am rated a senior elite."

"Your competition record isn't very extensive."

"Not as a senior, sir. I had many good competitions before I achieved that rank."

"But your last competition was over a year ago. Why is that?"

"I was recruited to assist former national mixed pairs champion Tara White in an exhibition program at Nationals in June. I spent nearly all my time working with her and preparing for that exhibition," I said.

"Ah! Now I see. You're him!"

"I beg your pardon, sir?"

"Well, there was nothing in your resume that called out that event and I didn't associate the name with that excellent performance. Why didn't you put it on your resume?"

"I want to return to artistic gymnastics rather than continue in acro-gym now."

"Okay. We'll go to the gym and take a look at your form and condition. Understand that if it is not up to that standard, we might still recommend you train in acrobatics," he said. "Now, tell us about why you left your gym and coach in Minneapolis."

I explained the entire horrid sequence of events involving Madison, her coach, and my coach's lack of support for me.

"I left because I could no longer trust my coaches or the gym. Even though Madison Layne retracted her accusations, she still came to my house and threw a brick through my window because I refused to work with her as a base any longer. I didn't feel safe going back to that gym."

"Well, acrobatics is not a particularly safe sport, but we try to mitigate that with spotters and good coaches. Nonetheless, you should feel safe from attack by your teammates. I'll want to make sure we do not offer an audition to that performer. Let's head for the gym."

We got to the gym and there were already several stations occupied with gymnasts, acrobats, and coaches. The place was huge compared to the Hennepin Gym. There was one area that was obviously set up for performances and competitions with each of the six men's stations and the four women's stations positioned so they could be seen from stands. The center part of the gym had multiple units of each station so more than one athlete could work at a time.

I hadn't worked on the high bar, rings, or vault for a while, though I was confident that I could do my routines. I just hadn't had a place to practice. I'd managed to do floor routines at the gym Tara and I worked at on Saturdays. I had my pommel horse and parallel bars at home in Minneapolis, but no room to do a full routine. For all of them, I'd need to trust to muscle memory.

I started on parallel bars, which was a good warmup for me. The director and three other coaches watched and assessed my performances. I had one coach who stayed at my side as a spotter. After all, this was an audition, not an actual performance. After I'd completed my routine on the pommel horse, I felt ready for the still rings. My spotter gave me a boost up to the rings and I began my ninety-second routine.

I was a little shaky on my iron cross and didn't quite make it parallel to the floor, but overall, I felt good about it.

I chose vault next. I didn't do a very complex vault. It was more important to me to show that I could learn to master the apparatus than it was to have a degree of difficulty I couldn't depend on. Then, after the high bar routine, it was time for my floor exercises.

I bounced a little on the floor to get the feel for working on a sprung floor again. I loved the feeling. This routine was my favorite and I took off with pleasure. I didn't intend to do a lot of extremely difficult elements, but I was really feeling good as I reached the end. I did a one-and-a-half back flip and caught myself on my hands where I stayed stable and then took two leg positions while showing my strength. I flipped out of the hand stand into the splits and raised my hands.

There was polite applause from a few people who had stopped to watch and my auditioning committee. Then they beckoned me to the side and said we'd discuss things at lunch. I could hear a couple of the committee commenting behind me.

"That's a banned element, isn't it?" said one.

"I don't know if it counts as such. He didn't do a twist. The Thomas salto has the one and a half backward salto, but it also has a one-and-a-half out."

"No. I'm sure the 2017 rule book bans all 3/2 salto elements with reception by the hands. He did it beautifully, but I still don't think it's allowed."

I'd never even heard of the Thomas salto and determined that I'd look it up. I thought I'd invented the move. Certainly, none of my coaches in Minneapolis had ever mentioned it. I guess that shows how attentive they'd been.

There are two types of 'banned' elements. One is an element that is simply not in or has been removed from the code of points. In that instance, if you do the element without prior approval, you simply get no points for it. So, why bother? The other is to have a specific ruling that prohibits an element. If it falls in that category and you do it, you're disqualified. It was obvious to me that the coaches here knew the rules better than my coaches in Minneapolis. Even if that move proved to not be permitted, I felt more confident in the program in Tampa.

My lunchtime critique was generally positive. I was asked to explain my element selection and how much of it had been my own decisions and how much were from my coaches and choreographers.

"It was hard not to notice a lack of difficulty in your vault. You'd have scored the base level of points for completing the exercise, but would not have gained anything there. Are you uncomfortable with the vault?" asked one of the committee members.

"No, sir. The truth is that I haven't done a vault since mid-July, so I didn't want to bite off more than I could chew on my first time back."

"You don't say! Well, that's understandable. I'll want you to try one or two new things with me this afternoon."

"Yes, sir." I had no idea what I was getting into. My schedule simply said, 'work with coaches.'

It proved to actually be a working session with four different coaches on four different apparatuses. I did not work on either the pommel horse or on the floor exercises. I guess those were the strongest of my performances.

I learned so much from the vault coach that I couldn't possibly hold it all inside after one session. He worked with me on elements of increasing difficulty, pausing after each to critique it, make suggestions, and send me back to repeat it to see if I could follow his suggestions.

The rings coach had me do several slow presses into position and then several rapid transitions. You can't swing on the rings, even though they are hung from straps that would certainly allow swinging. In fact, when your coach lifts you to the rings, you have to hang from them and he steadies you to be sure you are still before the routine begins. Part of the art is to be able to hold the rings still while your body works. But you can swing your body, so you can start from a vertical position, then drop and turn completely around into a vertical position again. I was definitely tired by the time I finished. I had to explain that I hadn't been on rings in several weeks, either.

The parallel bars coach simply wanted to give me moves and see me go from one to the next as he called them out. It was a combination of finding out if I knew the moves and if I could execute them one after the other. Our workout lasted only about fifteen minutes and I was shuffled over to the high bar.

That coach wanted to see if I could change routines from one to another after receiving instruction. Then he'd have me do an element or two to see if I knew them before putting them together in a sequence. I think he was impressed when I started myself off with a waist-high pull-up—the same move I'd taught to Chantell on the basketball team—only I followed it with a press up to a handstand.

I got a little break and then was led over to a differ-ent part of the gym where I worked with a woman on a straight-line tumbling routine. The sprung mat for tumbling is twenty-five meters long and two meters wide, with a line painted down the center and bounding each side. There's a ten-meter run-up that is not sprung, and a landing area at the other end that's six meters long and three meters wide with a much thicker cushion for landing.

I'd never worked on a tumbling track because there just wasn't room for one in our gym in Minneapolis. My tumbling was all done in floor exercises. The tumbling track was a total of 135 feet long and had a safety mat at the end that extended another ten feet, just in case the gymnast couldn't stop. The coach had a couple of other tumblers do passes on the mat before she started working with me, just to show me what she was looking for. It looked like fun.

It was really exhausting. I loved my floor exercises, which are the artistic gymnastics equivalent of tumbling. This track was a lot longer than the diagonal of the floor exercise and people really worked up a lot of speed. The pass has to include at least three elements, which are all flips, twists, and somersaults. It's funny to me, but the one-and-a-half with a hand landing wasn't banned in tumbling because you just spring into another element. You could hardly call it a landing!

I never really got up to the full eight elements required in a competitive tumbling pass. They were basically what I did in cheerleading when I did somersaults across the floor. With a sprung floor beneath me, though, the elements really gained a lot of height. I thanked the coach at the end and said I really enjoyed that. She said she'd see me for more work on my floor exercises on Monday.

That was the first indication that I'd be invited to stay over the weekend and do more auditioning on Monday.

Finally, I was conducted to a sprung floor in the acrobatics area. Even though my heart was set on being a gymnastics competitor, I had to admit there was a certain satisfaction in the acrobatic lifts that I enjoyed. There isn't really anything that shows off strength like those lifts and balancing routines.

And, obviously, I'd been working more on those things over the past year than on my artistic gymnastic routines.

"Hi! I'm Sydnie Cragg," said a bright little girl, meeting me on the mat. Okay, so I'm still prejudiced, but her name was bigger than she was. She might be twenty years old, but she still looked twelve or thirteen. Once I really looked at her and put that together with her accent, I realized she was the same girl I caught in the cafeteria the previous evening.

"Paul Bradley," I said, shaking her hand.

"I'm part of a women's group," Sydnie said. "The top, as you probably assumed. They asked me to come over and work with you a little, but don't think of me as a future partner. Our group is getting really good."

"That's fine," I said. "I'm not really looking at getting into acrobatics, but it's part of my overall audition. I promise you my best at anything we're asked to do."

"Paul and Sydnie," said a woman approaching us. "I'm Coach Li, Paul. I already coach Sydnie and asked her to participate in the exercises this afternoon. The two women with me are her teammates, Lena and Eva, and will act as spotters. We're going to run through a few exercises to see how you move and what your level is. Paul, I'm aware of your experience, but the things you were asked to do with your previous partner had subtle differences to what a competition would require."

"I'm aware of that, coach. I did some work with

another partner during that time as well. I'm ready."

"Oh good. Let's get started, then. First, see if you can synchronize a forward flip in layout position. Take a minute together to coordinate your timing."

I turned to Sydnie.

"Let me see yours," I said. "I'll adjust to match you."

It was a simple enough move that I'd done often enough with Madison, though Tara couldn't support herself well enough to either launch or land that type of somersault. It only took us a couple of tries to have a pretty well coordinated flip.

"Now, do the same thing, but when you land, launch immediately into a double back flip with a twist. Together now. Ready."

She didn't give us time to plot the run, launch, or landing together. I hoped Sydnie needed to bend down to launch her back flip, and that she had good height on it.

We did it. Coach Li went right into balance exercises next. Sydnie mounted to my shoulders and to my hands. While I held her aloft with one hand, I got down on the floor and did a classic right triangle table with one hand down, one holding Sydnie up, and my body stretched out as the hypotenuse.

We did a number of balancing poses and combinations, then Coach Li moved us directly into throws. We did throws in which Sydnie did multiple somersaults and I caught her as she landed, then we did some throws up to a position above my head. Throwing another person upward with the right amount of force to let her complete her flip and still be high enough to land on my hands is a little tricky, but the spotters only moved in once to protect Sydnie from a potential fall.

I caught her.

We must have worked for over an hour as Coach Li gave us progressively more complex combinations to do. Sydnie was very good. I'd have to say she was way better than Madison could ever hope to be. That might be because she was six inches shorter and twenty or thirty pounds lighter than Madison.

"Good. Gather around here. We're going to resume on Monday. I want the four of you to put in a few hours of practice over the weekend. I'm not planning to put together a mixed pair with Sydnie and Paul, so the other two of you can relax about that. I'm using Sydnie because she is about the best flyer we have right now and I wanted to give Paul a chance to shine. The intent of your practice this weekend is to put together a two-minute combined program. Work your spotters into the routine so they can stay on the floor with you at all times. Got it? Good. See you Monday morning."

"What fun!" Sydnie said, grabbing hold of me and planting a kiss right on my lips. It was nice, but...

"Whoa. Easy. I have a girlfriend and I'm not in the market for another," I said.

"That's good," Sydnie said. "I'm not in the market either. I'm just friendly!" Then she dropped her voice so only the two of us could hear and growled at me. "But not *that* friendly. Don't try anything."

I put both hands in the air and backed up a step. Then our two spotters grabbed my elbows and started to march me off to the cafeteria.

"Dinner time! I'm starved," Sydnie said.

At DINNER, I finally learned the full names of Sydnie's teammates who had been spotting for us.

"I'm Lena Alexander," said the middle. "I'm from

Alabama, so I'm used to this heat. You northerners never seem to get used to it."

"Yeah," said Sydnie, "but you nearly froze to death at Nationals in Minnesota, and it was in the middle of summer there!"

"I'm Eva Evashchuk," said the base. "I was born in Ukraine, but we immigrated to the United States when I was young. I was not happy to leave my friends and my parents decided gymnastics would help me adjust. But then I grew, and now I support these two."

"That is quite a job," I said. "I trust you all do well, if Sydnie is an example."

"Oh, yes. We were only eighth in Portugal last month, but now we will train harder for next year," Lena said.

"You're on Team USA?" I said.

"Yes, of course," Sydnie said. "We spent the entire time from Nationals until Worlds training in Texas. But this is our home gym and we came back here as soon as possible. We'll return to Texas for pre-event training, but Coach Li travels with us."

"You're all so impressive. I've yet to qualify for the national competition. But, I'm only 19. Did you see the men's Olympic gymnastics in July? Most of the competitors are in their mid-twenties."

"You stand a better chance of advancing than I do," Sydnie said. "I'm seventeen, which puts me near the old end for acrobatic gymnastic tops. If I'd grown like Eva did, I'd be a circus performer already."

"Circus?"

"It's a common progression. Opportunity doesn't come knocking for older gymnasts. We go from being artistic gymnasts to acrobatic gymnasts to circus acts. It's not that we can't do the work anymore, but we don't look as young and innocent," Sydnie snorted.

"It's not like it's a hierarchy," Eva explained. "It's just that as you grow and mature, it's harder and harder to compete against younger gymnasts. And if you need to earn a living, you either end up teaching gymnastics, teaching physical education, or performing circus acts."

"I got my certification as a massage therapist, so I hope to earn my living in that. I know it's not much, though."

"Oh, please! I've had just one professional massage in my life and it was heavenly. I couldn't flex a muscle for the rest of the day," Lena said.

"Our motto is 'walk in, wobble out,' you know," I laughed.

"When can we get massages?" Sydnie asked.

"Um… I think in Florida I have to get a license before I can offer massage," I said. "I didn't really check that out before I drove down here."

"I bet that doesn't mean you can't give a massage if asked," Sydnie said. "And I'm asking."

"Let's get through our weekend training and find out if I'm even staying here. For all I know, they might send me home Monday."

"They'd have sent you home today if you weren't staying. And they certainly wouldn't have assigned members of Team USA to help you. Let's finish dinner and then go plot out what we want you to show in our routine."

It was going to be an interesting weekend.

It was far more than interesting!

I had worked with Tara, a national champion. I knew how good she was—or I thought I did. As far as moves are concerned, Madison was more advanced because of Tara's disability. But here I was working with three national champions who were at the top of their game and in peak health. What they could do was far more than either Tara or Madison could do. I assumed Tara had been able to do all of that four years ago, but not today.

"Okay, we've shown off a bit," Eva announced after our first hour or so of practice on Saturday. "But this is supposed to show off what Paul can do. Lena and I aren't even performing. It's just you two. So, what do you bring to the table, Paul?"

"Well, you guys are certainly worthy of all your championships. Just plain cool. Pretty much anything that you did with Sydnie on top, I think I can do. There are a couple of things I think we could do that I haven't really tried before, but I know I have the strength for."

"F'rinstance?" Sydnie asked.

"Well, in the combined routine, there's usually an element of coordinated tumbling. I love tumbling. Can you do a double front layout with a twist? That's usually a degree more complex than most pairs I've seen."

"Yeah. I can do that. Why'd we never think of putting that in our routine?" Sydnie asked her partners. They just shook their heads. We all four practiced the element, spotting for each other. Then Sydnie and I tried coordinating it together. I think we worked on that one move for an hour or more. We had to take a break and let our muscles recover a bit before we went to the next element.

"You know, one of the things I got from that is that Eva and Lena wouldn't have to just stand around waiting for us to fall," I said. "Like, we could all four do that tumble together, and then Sydnie and I could move directly to our next element."

"And what do you suggest?" Sydnie asked.

"Lena launched you into the air and you landed on Eva's shoulders. Well, you don't have partners to launch you. Can you launch yourself onto my shoulders?"

"How high would I have to get? Let's see. Um... I can't just jump up to them. I'd have to do a somersault to get up there. If I did it in a tuck position, I'd probably get there, but I'm not sure it would be a very pretty landing."

"How about if I was on my knees?"

"Yeah! I could totally do that."

"What else?" Lena asked.

"I was thinking that I always see one-hand lifts or poses with the base's dominant arm. Wouldn't it be cool to have Sydnie switch from one hand to the other?"

"You mean *your* hand, right?"

"Yes."

"That would count as a whole new pose, wouldn't it?" Eva asked. "I don't know if I can hold you in my left. Are you sure you can do it, Paul?"

"I gotta tell you, Sydnie weighs, like, thirty pounds less than either of my previous two partners. She's like lifting a feather."

"Thanks, bud."

"That's not a bad thing," I said.

"It sure isn't. If Sydnie weighed thirty more pounds, she'd need a different base than me," Eva said.

"I was also thinking that when we did the tumbling, we all four went together, right? What if you kind of reflected some of our other moves? Like, if Sydnie is standing on her hands on my hands doing the splits, you two could simply be standing on your hands doing the splits without being held up."

"Oh, that's a hard move for me," Eva said. "Remember, I weigh *fifty* pounds more than Sydnie."

"But I know you do the splits. You could mimic an inverse of the position."

"Could do that."

"Break time's over," Lena said. "Potty up and let's get back to work."

17

ACCEPTANCE AND REJECTION

I WORKED WITH SYDNIE, Lena, and Eva for four hours, took a two-hour break for lunch, and then went back at it for another four hours. We were really having fun.

That seemed strange. I tried to remember when I last just had fun in the gym.

I was still depressed about being 3,000 miles from Tara with no real hope of ever getting back together again. She was the only woman outside my family and Jennifer who ever treated me nicely. I don't mean just having sex, though I sure missed that, too. I mean... Like the cheerleaders did their best to ignore me and only recognized me to tell me what position they needed me in for them to climb on. Madison, I decided, was full-on psychotic. She wanted to control everything I did.

These three girls were actively working to see how good they could make *me* look. They were working hard *with* me. For those hours we were working, we were having fun. Some other students stopped by during the

236

day and a few gave us tips or suggested poses before they went to their own training sessions.

I guess... Well, the students here didn't just train together, most of them lived together. Several stopped to say, "Welcome to GAC! Hope you like it here."

I was going to like it just fine—if they liked me enough to offer me a place. And if I could afford it.

I talked to Dad Saturday night after we'd finished dinner and he said there were some funds set aside for my education that they didn't figure I'd ever use. He also said he'd cosign a loan if I needed more. I almost cried when he told me that. I didn't particularly want to go in debt for the expense of a college education and just get gymnastics training. But knowing the resources were available for me to follow my dream was important.

On Sunday, we worked on putting our elements together to some music the girls had. They said the academy had a library of pieces and when I was ready for music for my own performances, the librarian would help select and cut the piece of music of my choice. I hadn't really considered where music came from before. When I was working with Tara, our choreographer brought the music which set the theme for our performance. Madison had all her own music and never asked me about it at all.

After another hard day's work, we felt we had something we could show with pride. It wouldn't be perfect, but it would show what we could do. And we had an attentive Lena and Eva there to act as our spotters, just in case.

We didn't have time to really coordinate our costumes. When you compete, the rules say the costumes should be essentially the same or at least coordinated. They asked me what I had available and I said my best was a black unitard with gold braid and piping.

Sydnie said she had a black and gold leotard and that would work fine. Eva and Lena would wear white, indicating they weren't part of the act.

When they walked into the gym on Monday morning, though, they stopped as though they'd only seen me for the first time.

"Hey. You guys ready?" I asked.

"You're him!" Sydnie said.

"What?"

"It never occurred to me that it could even possibly be you! You performed at Nationals with Tara White!"

"Oh. Yeah."

"Why aren't you with her? What happened?"

That led to me having to explain that Tara couldn't really perform to the standards of national competition and she'd taken a teaching job in San Jose. I wanted to find a place where I could get back into my gymnastic apparatuses and possibly compete in the 2028 Olympics.

"I should have known just based on how strong you are," Eva declared. "You're right. Tara probably weighs twenty pounds more than Sydnie now. But you supported her through everything. There was no question in anyone's mind that while Tara was beautiful and wonderful, she wouldn't have been able to do any of that without you. You kept her stable."

"Thanks. I didn't think I should talk about what Tara and I did. I guess I'm glad you noticed."

"I got hours of lectures from Coach Li about what I could learn from you as a base. No wonder she wanted us to work with you over the weekend. And she was right. I've learned a ton."

"Well, let's get warmed up and show them what we can do," I laughed. We got started.

"THERE ARE A lot more people here than I expected," I said when we went to the performance mat.

"The coaches and your committee all have classes this morning, so they brought their classes with them. Just like I did," Coach Li said. "Are you ready?"

"Yes, ma'am," I answered. "You gave me great partners."

"Let's see what you've done with them."

She took our tariff sheet with her and shared it with the committee as we waited at the edge of the mat for our signal to begin.

"You may proceed," Coach Li said into the speakers.

We walked out onto the mat and assumed our opening pose. A few seconds later, we heard the chime a beat before our music started, so we were able to start our first pass cleanly with the music. This involved a couple of dancelike moves where Sydnie spun under my arm and our spotters turned a somersault to pose with their hands raised toward us. Then we were in action.

I did a cannonball launch for Sydnie and she did a pike position flip with a twist and landed with her feet in my hands. From there I threw her into a forward flip and caught her as she landed in front of me. I did a dead lift of her as she held her arms rigid with her hands in mine. Once she was over my head, she continued up into a handstand with a Mexican arch.

At one point, I heard some polite applause from the stands, but I just blocked everything out from my consciousness except our music and my partner. It came time for our tumbling pass and people were surprised to see our spotters go first across the mat. Then I went with my double layback with a twist. When I landed, I dropped to one knee. Sydnie was right behind me. She did a double tuck position salto and came down perfectly on my shoulders. I held up my left hand and she grasped it in both of hers, elevating herself into a splits.

As soon as our spotters were certain they were no longer needed, they went into their own handstand with the splits as I stood, holding Sydnie above my head with my left hand. I launched her into the air and she did a half flip to land on one foot in my right hand. From there she did a needle stand, which is a kind of vertical splits with her other foot vertical in the air and her extended hands above her head catching her foot.

That was the position she held as I returned to the floor and held her above my head as I put the other hand down on the floor and elevated myself into a table. That's the move I call a right triangle because my floor hand is supposed to be vertical and my body extending as the hypotenuse of a triangle to my feet. The hand supporting my partner is supposed to create a continuous line from my lower arm straight into the air and on into her position in the needle stand.

We hadn't done many throws at this point and Sydnie flipped from my hand onto the floor with her spotters watching carefully, but not needing to rescue her. From there, we went into a number of throws, each landing and going straight to another. At that point, Sydnie and I separated, spinning in opposite directions. Eva and Lena stopped our spin and sent us directly back into each other to collapse to the floor in our final pose.

There was considerable applause at that point. Without the music and concentrating on our moves, my hearing seemed to open up to the sounds around us.

"It's too bad there is no 'mixed group' category in AG," Coach Li said. "Well done. I especially liked the way you integrated your spotters into the action. It was obviously a pair, but the presence of two others on the mat did not detract from focus at all. Again, well done."

"That was certainly impressive," Dr. Davis, the director of the academy, said. "Paul, obviously we were gauging your strength and ability to work with others. Coaches Li, DiCello, Devault, Pleshenko, and Desmond all had good reports on your work Friday. The committee has all handed their decisions to me and I am happy to welcome you to the Tampa Gymnastics Acrobatics and Circus Academy. Congratulations, Paul."

The girls quickly gathered around me and Sydnie gave me one of her 'friendly' kisses. *Wow!*

Everyone in the gym had their own classes and routines to work on. I was escorted to the administration office and filled out a bundle of forms and enrollment documents. I had a high school transcript (which was not particularly impressive), my certification as a massage therapist, a letter of reference from the coach of the basketball team, and even a letter of reference from Coach Dawson at the Hennepin Gym. It was signed with his regrets that I'd chosen to leave Hennepin Gym and good wishes for my future as a gymnast. It was nice that he had come around that far.

When we got to the point of paying for my tuition, room, and board, I was stunned by the amount. I was pretty sure I'd need that loan Dad had promised.

"Paul, a resident gymnastics program is not cheap, as I'm sure you are aware," Dr. Davis said to me as we met with the bursar. "I don't believe anyone here can afford it. We are not a college or university, so state grants and academic scholarships are not available to us. We do, however, have sponsors. These are often companies associated with athletics who want to be associated with the US National Team and Olympic Team. They understand there is a risk involved in taking on an athlete. But the amount we are prepared to offer toward your time here will make a significant dent in what you owe."

He showed me a paper that held a promise of 80% of my tuition and board for my first year at GAC. I was stunned. Signing it held a promise that I would pursue a berth on the 2025 Team USA and the 2028 Olympic team with everything I could do. I signed the paper.

"I don't know what you were prepared to pay when you got here," the bursar said. "Will you be able to advance the remainder of the funds within ten days?"

"Yes, ma'am. I will arrange a wire transfer," I said. The remaining amount was within the limit of what Dad said was set aside for my education.

"I'm also told you are a certified massage therapist," Dr. Davis said. "You presented your certificate this morning. We'll sponsor you for licensing, but when you are employed internally, we don't need to wait for the license to get you started. We'll have a couple of tests from both students and coaches to assure ourselves that you are capable, then we'll approve you for specific massage hours. That will be worked out with your counselor for your schedule. The coaches will have input in your schedule as you will need to work into their schedules as well as a couple of general classes we want you to participate in. For now, head off to dinner and celebrate. I think everyone wants to meet and greet you."

I was exhausted, but the party atmosphere in the cafeteria was far more exciting than it had any right to be on a Monday evening. Sydnie, Eva, and Lena met me in the cafeteria and exercised their right to introduce me to as many people as possible.

I just hoped I'd be able to progress as well in the classes as I did in my physical development. I could see already that there was speculation as to whether I would be a gymnast or an acrobat. Well, I guess there were worse possibilities.

WHEN I WAS in Minneapolis, school, work, massage, basketball, all seemed like an interruption to the one thing I wanted to be doing—gymnastics. Suddenly, I was in an environment in which getting better at gymnastics was my primary task: To get stronger, more artistic, and more able to compete.

But you really can't work out twelve hours a day every day and expect to make progress. My training day was basically three hours early in the morning and three late in the afternoon. Wednesdays and Saturdays I had only morning sessions, and I had Sunday as a rest day.

I had to take a couple of classes in order to get my massage license. They were on Florida laws and regulations, but the licensing board recognized my education under Jennifer because she was widely known as a member of the certification board.

I didn't start any real classes at the academy other than my training until the second semester. So, mostly, I had Wednesday afternoons, Saturday afternoons, Sundays, and my evenings free if I wasn't in one of the massage classes. After a couple of coaches and students had tried my massage and approved the work, the school took over scheduling massages, much like the gym in Minneapolis and the basketball team had taken charge of scheduling me. With the tuition, room and board covered, I was able to bank the two or three hundred a week I made from massages at $50 an hour! That also meant that when Sydnie, Eva, and Lena suggested a movie or going to the beach on Sunday, I was free to go and had enough money to pay my way.

I also had my car, which was very popular with the girls. My car had plenty of room in it, so I never objected to having one or two additional invitees along. Somehow, those were always invited by the three girls, so were usually other girls. It was common for us to head out someplace with five girls in the car with me.

I didn't expect anything from them. The whole academy had about a three to one ratio of females to males in residence, ages maybe 13 to 26. In addition to that, there were day school classes for children who came for sessions to get started. Resident students usually taught those classes as their way of earning expense money while in residence. The classes I took during the second semester were focused on teaching gymnastics, coaching, and physical development.

When I started doing massages, I just set up my table in my dormitory room. Nobody considered that an ideal situation. There was a training and therapy center that had a few private rooms on the side and soon, I was given one of those rooms where I could leave my table set up and store my supplies—like clean sheets, towels, and oils.

Since my things were in the room and exclusively for my use, I did a little decorating, too. I put up a couple of anatomy posters, set a couple of lamps with low wattage bulbs in the corners so I didn't need the fluorescent overhead while people were trying to relax, and set a speaker up so I could pipe in music or nature sounds from my cell phone.

It was a pretty sweet setup and my clients appreciated the environment.

Time seemed to rush past. I didn't compete my first few months there. After the first of the year, though, I was included on the rotation of competitors heading to meets as part of the GAC team. We competed mostly in the southeast, but we did spend one week in the spring at a meet in Texas. It was my first opportunity to see the training center that Tara had been at when she rose to a national championship.

I guess that's when the loneliness really started to settle in. I'd been at GAC for six months and had only gone home to be with my family for a week at Christmas. Having a training routine that my body was really attuned to made it difficult to take a break anywhere I couldn't continue training.

My conversations with Tara had become fewer, degenerating into text messages or even comments on social media. I was reluctantly coming to the conclusion that we were no longer a couple. It broke my heart.

I returned to Tampa after the competition in Texas and tried to compose a letter to her, but I ended up just asking her for a time I could call and talk for a while. When Sydnie came to see if I'd take them to the beach Sunday, I just tossed her my keys. She looked puzzled and I just shook my head. We'd celebrated her eighteenth birthday a couple of weeks earlier and she'd moved into the adults' dormitory. It was really unusual for me to not want to go out with the girls. They were good company, but I was really feeling down and I wanted to talk to Tara.

I'd turned twenty in March and Tara and I hadn't

even talked. I got a 'Happy birthday' text from her. Now I punched in her number.

We talked. I wanted to know where she would go during the summer and if we could travel together a while. I just missed her so much. The conversation didn't go the way I thought it would. Me and my romantic brain.

"Why would you stop training for the summer? It was hard enough last year. Don't risk losing all you've gained this year," she said.

"But I want to see you," I complained. "I miss my girlfriend."

She sighed loudly enough that I could hear her over the phone.

"Honey, you've got to stop thinking of us as boyfriend and girlfriend. We just aren't anymore. I can't be where you are. I'm making huge progress with my team here. And there's nothing here for you. The university doesn't even have a men's program. Paul, you need to focus on yourself and your goals. Don't let thinking of being my boyfriend hold you back from what you have there. I know you go out with all those girls. I've seen the pictures on our social. Enjoy them. I can't be what you need right now. Oh, Paul..."

"I love you, Tara."

"I love you, too. Goodbye, Paul."

I WAS STILL crying in my room when the girls got back. There was a knock on my door and I opened it a crack to see Lena with my keys. Her face immediately fell and she pushed her way into my room.

"Paul! What's wrong? We missed you today. What happened?"

"I… um… My girlfriend and I… We broke up. I… um… Thanks for bringing me my keys. I'll see you tomorrow."

"Like hell. This is not a time for you to be alone. Talk to me and tell me all about it."

I felt like a real idiot. I talked a while and told her about Tara and me. I'd never told the girls who my girlfriend was. Lena was shocked to find it was the injured national champion. She insisted that I go get some dinner with her and when I said I really didn't want to see anyone, she grabbed my keys and just said, "Let's go."

I didn't argue with her about who was going to drive. I just got in the car and she drove us north and then west until we got to Tarpon Springs. We drove through a funky old town waterfront sort of place and then walked all the way out to the end of the wharf.

"Have you ever had a grouper sandwich?" she asked.

"Um… No. I don't think they serve them in the cafeteria."

"And none of the places we've all been out to serve them either. I save this for special times. If I ate like this all the time, Eva wouldn't be able to support me in the middle."

"Fish? That's not fattening."

"Not the fish so much as the hush puppies."

We were seated at a table covered with butcher paper and a brown bag of hush puppies was immediately set in front of us. Lena ordered before I even had a chance to see a menu.

"Grouper sandwiches are not the only reason to come to Florida," she laughed. "But they are a sufficient reason. Relax and enjoy. This is my treat."

Our diet Dr Peppers arrived and soon I was lost in the sensations of eating this incredible fish sandwich and the hush puppies. Lena was good company and she had comments that left me laughing.

"Ya know, the fishin' boats arrive over there on the wharf and the chef goes out and chooses the fish he wants by clubbing 'em over the head. Then he brings 'em back here and starts cooking." With just the two of us and being away from school, Lena's deep south accent was coming through.

I was busy licking my fingers.

"Ya know what we din't do this year? We din't go to any spring trainin' games. I din't think about it till I saw the number of Yankees at the beach on spring break. Most of 'em was sunburnt and drunk. Would you believe one guy tried to pick up all six of us who went out today? He said he was tryin' to set a campus record for the number of girls he could do in a single day. We said, 'Six?' and he said, 'Nah, eleven, but I've already got five done.' We laughed at him and told him to try some of the drunk girls."

"That takes a lot of balls," I laughed.

"More 'n two, I guess. I saw him passed out on top a girl who was out cold when we left. Din't look like they actually done anything other than drink."

We finished our dinner and Lena paid, declining my offer. Then we headed back to the academy. Sort of. Lena took a turn and we crossed the bridge and headed west instead of east and south. She pulled up at Sunset Beach just in time for us to watch the sunset over the Gulf. It was pretty nice, and before long, the darkness surrounded us.

This beach isn't popular with most of the spring break kids because it's kind of isolated and there are a lot of trees growing out of the sand, but really no services. You can't just pop into the bar for a drink or anything. Lena took my hand and we walked along the water around to a spot where we were pretty isolated from everything else. She pulled me down on the sand and laid back.

It was peaceful and I might have dozed off a little. I became aware of Lena cuddled up to me, gently kissing my face.

"Um... I... uh..." I wasn't sure what I thought I was going to say. She felt incredibly good in my arms. Wasn't sure when my arms had circled her. I knew her body pretty well because she'd had three or four massages. Of course, it never felt quite like it did while she was kissing me.

"You've been really stressed out," she whispered, losing her accent. I wondered how much of it had been put on. "Let me take care of you. Let me show you what you mean to all of us here in Florida."

I didn't think she could possibly mean that everyone I'd met in Florida would be kissing me, caressing me, and letting me feel what a luscious body she had in places that I never touched during a massage. Well, maybe Sydnie would kiss me like this, but that was kind of her thing—kissing people. Just being friendly.

Lena wasn't going to stop at making out. I didn't realize that for a bit because I was just lost in the sensations of having a girl in my arms and in my hands. Then she had my shorts open and was stroking my rigid cock.

"Wow! You're really ready for this, aren't you? I'll just... um... take the edge off a little before we get to the main course."

With that, she dipped her head and enveloped my dick in her soft warm mouth.

Yeah. Six months since the last time Tara and I had made love. I'm not really big on masturbating, mostly because I fall asleep before I get anywhere. But feeling Lena's mouth on me gave me just enough time to grunt a warning before I was firing my spunk into her throat.

"Mmm. There. Now you'll last a little longer," she said confidently.

She pulled my hand to her middle and I discovered that somewhere along the line, her shorts had been kicked down and off one foot. I knew what to do. I wasn't completely inexperienced. I found her moistening and spread that lubrication up and around her clit as we went back to kissing. I certainly wasn't going to soften up much with this going on. I didn't know exactly what I was getting into, but I knew it was soft, warm, and wet.

Lena straddled me and sank onto my cock with a moan—which might have been mine, or possibly ours.

"It's been a long time since I've had a guy in me," she breathed. "Sometimes I feel left out when Sydnie and Eva get going. This is nice. You feel so good in me. Don't think that just because we're making it on the beach in a romantic clear night that I want to be anything more than what we've always been. But I think tonight, I needed this as much as you did. Yes. Touch me there some more. I'm almost there. Can you wait for me? Just a little more."

She kept sliding up and down my cock while she continued to talk and plant kisses on me. Then I felt her begin to tense and she pressed her lips against mine and kissed deeply as she fluttered around my cock and whined into my mouth. I let go with a few really strong spurts up into her. It was unbelievable and she lay on top of me just breathing deeply and occasionally rising to kiss again.

"I don't know what to say," I said. "That was really wonderful and intense. I didn't mean to push myself onto you."

"You've got the positions mixed up, Paul. It's me who's on top. We just both really needed that. Thank you."

"Thank you, Lena."

10

LOSING MYSELF

I WOKE UP EARLY Monday morning with Lena looking into my eyes in my narrow dorm room bed. We were both very naked. Our adventure had begun on the beach, but it continued late into the night once we got back to my room.

"I... um... Hi," I said.

"Hey you," she answered. "That was some night."

"It sure was. I... uh... really don't have much experience with this. I mean, like, the morning after stuff."

"Mmmhmm. That's okay." She cuddled closer to me, as if there was any choice. I found my hand stroking her breast. "I suggest that we fuck one more time and then get our buns in gear to get cleaned up, fed, and off to our training sessions. I'm a firm believer in building all the memories I can. Who knows if we'll ever do this again."

"That's like... um... You don't expect to be my girlfriend now?" I asked. She'd moved my hand from her breast down to her crotch.

"God, no. You shouldn't have done that with Tara," she said and then hastened on. "I'm not criticizing. I know you fell in love and it seemed like it would last forever. I'm not going to fall in love with you, Paul. I hope we'll stay good friends and maybe we'll even repeat some of what we did last night and… mmm… right now. But I know our paths lie in different directions. I don't know when, but I know we'll be going our own ways. Oh! Yeah! Push into me. Ahh. Mmm. Better not to get too involved with each other. I'm going to want more massages from you and they need to be just as professional as you've always been. More. Yes. Faster. It's like… a special thing that we did once one night. Or half a dozen times. If it happens again, great. But don't be watching for it. We'll know if it's right. Right there! Yes! Now, baby. Now! I want it!"

We kissed some more and finally rolled apart. *Wow!* I finally got a really good look at Lena's body as she stood up to head for the bathroom. She was thin and muscular. Like me, she was probably only two or three percent body fat. That meant small breasts, but you'd never mistake this woman for a little girl.

"You can join me in the shower," she called. I did, gladly, and we washed each other thoroughly. "No more of that!" she giggled. "We'd miss our training sessions and have to explain to everyone that we were fucking in the shower." She pushed my hand away from her pussy and then kissed me before getting out of the shower. I finished washing my hair and stepped out to use the damp towel she'd used before me.

"I had a great time," I said. "Thank you for everything."

"Everything?" she asked.

"Well, I don't want to leave out the grouper sandwich."

She pulled her shorts and top on and carried the rest of her things as she scampered down the hall to the stairs and up to her own room.

I DON'T REALLY believe sex is a cure-all for whatever ails you. I felt guilty about having fallen into bed with Lena—having fallen into Lena—the same day Tara broke up with me. I still missed and mourned my relationship with Tara, but I had to be honest. It ended when she drove off to California and I decided to call the academy in Florida. I'd been living a fantasy that she was still my girlfriend. If we'd been more honest with each other at the time, we'd have broken up right after we made love that morning.

An unfortunate side-effect of my encounter with Lena, though, was that I started noticing the other girls in the academy. The numbers in the adult dormitory were slightly more evenly divided between men and women, but no one seemed to have a permanent relationship. Maybe some of the mixed pairs had something going on like Tara and I had had. But I didn't think any members of mixed pairs were currently in adult housing.

Then there was Sydnie and Eva. I hadn't really figured that one out before Lena filled me in on it. The two girls had become lovers nearly as soon as they met four years previously. Sydnie would have been only fourteen, but there were only two years difference in their ages. I'd once commented about Sydnie's 'friendly' kisses being incredibly enthusiastic. Eva had said, "Yeah. The first time she planted one on me I nearly sucked her tongue down my throat. We control that a little better now."

I guess that should have been a clue. But Sydnie planted that kind of kiss on just about everyone. Eva didn't seem to get upset by it at all.

I knew there were some adults who were in training every day but lived off-campus. Some of them were married or in long-term relationships. I'd read an article online (with the help of my screen-reader) that talked about how many female teammates transitioned into being a couple. Not just in gymnastics, but in basketball, hockey, soccer, and other sports. I guess it made sense and figured that there were probably just as many guys, but the media didn't dare talk about that.

Still… Tara. I was irrationally angry with her, hurt by her, in love with her. As much as I rationalized the sense in breaking up—who knew when we'd see each other again?—I still didn't *want* to break up. I wanted her as much as I loved her and I didn't see that changing soon.

I'D BEEN AT the academy for two full semesters when I was called into a meeting with 'the committee,' which included Dr. Davis, the director, and several of the coaches.

"Paul, most of us have had a chance to work with you this year and we've all observed your dedication and skill," Dr. Davis said. "It's time, though, to narrow things down a little. At this stage of the game, you need a single coach who will guide you through all your training and competition heading for LA28. We have assessed your skills and believe you can become a successful part of Team USA. You've medaled in a couple of competitions and improve every time you are out. The four coaches I've brought to this meeting have all agreed they would like to work with you as your primary coach, starting this summer. Of course, the others will still be participating on specific events. We want to know if you have any preferences regarding coaches you'd like to work with."

"Wow! I feel like one of those competitors on *The Voice* who have to choose their coach. I really appreciate all you've done for me this year. I feel more confident than I did when I moved here in October. You've each helped me more than I can say. Coach Desmond, you've brought my pommel horse and parallel bars to a whole new level, and I thought I was pretty good on those two before I got here. Coach Pleshenko, I really appreciate what you've done for me on the high bar and rings. I feel stronger every day. And thank you Coach Devault for your work on the vault with me. I learned almost as much the first day you gave me instruction as I had in all my training up to that time. I think I need to follow my love of floor exercises, though, if I have to choose a single coach. If you're willing, Coach DiCello, I'd like to keep working with you as my primary coach."

"Oh, I'm willing," Coach DiCello laughed. She was the only one of my coaches who was female. Nearly all male apparatuses are coached by men, but she'd been the first coach to work with me on my tumbling and floor exercises. "You understand that we'll be consulting with the other coaches on the other apparatuses, though. Are you sure you don't want one of them as your primary?"

"If I can continue to work with them periodically, I'd be pretty happy to have you as my primary."

"Let's do it, then," Dr. Davis said. "It's not a surprise to any of us. We wondered why you seem to get along so well with women. We have that report regarding the athletes and coaches both. What would you say was your primary influence in that direction?"

"I don't really know. Maybe it's because until I got here, the only women who ever paid attention to me were my mother, sister, and Tara White. Everyone else ignored me as much as possible or tried to take advantage of me when I couldn't be ignored. When I got here, Coach DiCello, Coach Li, the trio of Sydnie, Lena, and Eva, and just about everyone else I met were accepting and became friends. I'd have to say the academy was my primary influence in that direction."

"We'll meet together later this week to start planning out your training direction and competition schedule," Coach DiCello said. "Welcome to my team."

THERE'S A POINT in *Anansi Boys*—I finished reading it back in December—at which Fat Charlie discovers that Spider is a part of himself that was exorcised. Up until that time, all the fun and charming and magical side of him had been lost. I identified at first with Fat Charlie. I felt sort of like what Dad called a Sad Sack.

You'd think that doing what I loved and being accepted by the women and other male athletes around me would have made me as happy as I could be. It was really everything I ever wanted. But in that way, I was also like Spider. The fun and magical side of me was empty and had no relationships. There was nothing there that could really define me. I felt hollow and empty.

And I guess that my attempt to fill that hollow part of me spilled over into my training. I devoted twice the energy to it that I had before. Maybe if I won a gold medal at the Olympics, I'd feel validated, I guess. I'd be whole.

I didn't sleep with Lena again that summer. She, Eva, and Sydnie spent a lot of the summer in Europe, attending training camps and competing in the European championships. They did very well.

I competed in four domestic events that summer. They were all in the Southeast. It was nice that Mom, Dad, and Mikey came down for one of them in Atlanta.

"Tell me when there's a competition down here over one of my school breaks in the winter," Mikey complained. "How do you stand this heat?"

"It isn't the heat, it's the humidity," Dad chimed in. "We get days this hot in Minneapolis—once or twice a year—but it's a dry heat."

"I spend most of my time in the gym or massage rooms. The academy has good environmental controls. I even have air conditioning in my dorm room," I laughed.

At the word "environmental," Mikey's ears perked up. She was two years into her education and intended to become an environmental engineer. She hadn't quite decided what she intended to do with her degree, but a lot of her study had been on natural solutions to interior environmental control so the necessary pollutants of air conditioning, heating, and waste management were mitigated to some extent.

And that was everything I understood about what she was doing.

Mom and Dad put their foot down and told her it was too far to go visit the academy so she could just drop in and offer to assess their pollution quotient.

It was nice seeing them, and I sent a few of my medals home with them. I didn't keep any of my medals or awards at the academy. I didn't really have anything that personal or sentimental there.

THERE WERE, HOWEVER, a couple of interludes with the women I knew. I still made frequent Sunday afternoon trips to the beach with several of the women who had gone when the three girls had invited them. It was kind of cool to be a muscular guy on the beach surrounded by three to five athletic beauties in skimpy bikinis. Occasionally, we'd do some acrobatics on the beach. That always attracted a few watchers, even though we were just clowning around.

I've talked about how young some of the pairs performers were or at least looked. That is not just dependent on size. I mean, the reigning world champion in women's gymnastics was twenty-eight years old and no one would mistake her for a little girl. Still, she's only four feet and eight inches tall. And women gymnasts do incredible balance and acrobatic routines on the beam, floor, and vault.

So, it was no big deal for a couple to balance on me or have me throw them into a somersault. And those girls who had moved to circus training could do almost anything, including incredible contortionist exercises while supporting themselves with just one hand on my head. We weren't really performing or practicing, though. We were just playing and having fun. Sometimes, our antics were in the water and sometimes on the beach.

And once or twice, they led to acrobatics in bed. Lifting and balancing a girl is always filled with the awareness that someone could get hurt with a bad move. When we were both naked and balancing, it added a level of adrenaline rush that was otherwise missing. Most of these girls can do splits at more than parallel to the floor. That in itself can be an experience if you happen to be embedded in her as she stretches out!

But these occasional tête-à-têtes grew from our just having fun and carrying it on into the bedroom. There was nothing serious about them.

I WAS SURPRISED one afternoon to see my coach waiting for a massage in the training room.

"Coach DiCello? Are you here for a massage?" I asked.

"I think it will give me some insights into you and how you work that will help us in training. Do you have a problem with giving someone as old as me a massage?"

"No, ma'am. You're not old."

She snorted.

"I mean, um... When I was doing my 500 hours up in Minneapolis, one of my clients who reviewed me about once a month was in her mid-70s. I don't have a problem with people's ages regardless."

"I see. Well, I'm not in my 70s, so I'll accept your judgment that I'm not that old."

"Just... um... go on into the room. There is a basket and hooks for your clothes. When you are ready, slip under the sheet on the table and I'll knock before I come in."

She went into the massage room and five minutes later, I knocked and she said to come in. I always open the door and check the room before I actually enter. I learned that lesson from Madison. Coach DiCello was on the table, lying face down with the sheet over her and her face in the cradle.

I started my relaxation soundtrack and turned the lights down, getting rid of the fluorescents. I started by just laying my hands on her shoulders outside the sheet.

"Do you have any specific pains or problem areas I should know about?" I asked.

"No. Just need relaxation."

"Good. Let me know anytime you find my touch too deep or too shallow. Everyone has a different threshold."

I began to work, starting with her neck and shoulders, then moving down her back. After I reached her waist and did some full torso moves, I covered her back up and slipped the sheet under her left leg, exposing her left butt cheek and leg so I could work on them. Then I switched the covering and exposed the right leg and butt cheek.

Like all the gymnasts I'd worked on, Coach DiCello was extremely fit with low body fat and good flexibility. I held the sheet in a tent over her so she could roll over and then I started again at the head. I worked my hands under her and then drew my knuckles up on either side of her spine until I worked my way all the way to her skull. I held the position for cranial-sacral release and then went to work 'styling her hair.' That's a term my clients coined for the part where I work on their scalp and the top of their head. I'd had a couple of clients who came in for a short session fully dressed and asked me to just work on their neck and head.

From the top of her head, I worked on gently releasing her facial muscles. Then I pulled one of her arms out from under the sheet and worked on it for a while, eventually switching to the other arm and then up to the front of her shoulders. I worked down to her breasts, but not onto them.

"Do you want any abdomen and psoas work or do you prefer that I avoid that?" I asked.

"I signed up for the full treatment. Please proceed."

This part was a little tricky. On a man, I could just uncover the entire torso and work on the lower torso all the way to the pelvis. I had to keep a woman covered. I guess it didn't make that much difference, though, because I often worked with my eyes closed anyway. Working under the sheet wasn't that big a deal. I wrapped the sheet under one leg so I could work all the way from her rib cage to her foot. I started just below her breasts and worked the muscles of the rib cage, then directly to the abs.

I'd noticed that a lot of athletes have difficulty with the psoas muscle. It's a fairly large muscle that attaches to the femur and runs through the pelvis to the lumbar vertebrae. It is largely what makes homo erectus walk erect. In order to massage it, I had to be careful of the abdominal organs and kind of slide deep right at the pelvis to work up and down the muscle. Coach gasped a little when I got in there and I checked to be sure she was okay.

"I had no idea that was so tight," she said.

"It's not unusual," I said.

I switched sides and then did some soothing rotations on the surface of the abdomen before I moved down to work on the front of her legs and her feet.

"Just relax and take your time getting up," I said when I'd finished. "Don't rise too quickly. I don't want you fainting."

I left the room and waited for her to come stumbling out.

"I had heard from other coaches and athletes that you have great hands," she said when she finally emerged from the room. "Magic hands, I'd say. That was truly wonderful. Thank you."

"You're welcome anytime," I said.

I lost track of time. It was defined only by my workouts and interrupted by the competitions that I went to. Coach DiCello had some great improvements for my floor routine and vaults, but she contributed to choreographing my other routines as well. She also got me to work on tumbling passes. I really think they contributed to the height and speed I got in my floor exercises. I continued to meet with Coach Pleshenko and Coach Desmond once a week to advance my other apparatus routines, but I found Coach DiCello had a unique perspective on those routines that the men didn't have. I wondered why more male gymnasts didn't have female coaches.

There's a big difference between men's floor exercises and women's floor exercises. To start, the women's exercise is 90 seconds and includes a music background. The men's exercise is 70 seconds and has no music. As a result, the women's exercise contains dance moves and a lot more showmanship than the men's. The men tend to have three to six tumbling passes (with required minimum elements) and one strength demonstration. The sprung floor is the same for both men and women.

What Coach DiCello brought to my floor exercise was an element of showmanship that was missing previously. Of course, I was told that my one-and-a-half back flip landing on my hands was, indeed, an illegal move and I couldn't use it in competition. Apparently, there had been several injuries and one death while executing the move and that was kind of sobering. I hadn't even considered that when I was practicing it. Coach DiCello encouraged me to work it into a full double with the one-and-a-half twist, letting me land on my feet. That added a significant element of difficulty to my exercise without being illegal.

I took one week in the summer and one week at Christmas to visit my family, and then spent the rest of my time training and competing. 2026 was the first year in which I would be traveling to compete internationally. Assuming I qualified at the US Nationals in June, then I could head for Europe in October as part of Team USA. There were other Olympic qualifying events that I could compete in even if I wasn't on Team USA, but placing in the Nationals was my surest way in.

I was nothing if I wasn't competing in the Olympics.

IN FACT, I wasn't much anyway. I was even less when Sydnie, Lena, and Eva got first in the 2026 Worlds and received an offer to perform over in Orlando for three months. I got another erection inducing kiss from Sydnie and a place to put it from Lena. Eva waved good-bye as they loaded a small van with all their belongings and took off.

Even though I'd only made love to Lena maybe three or four times in the past two years, seeing those girls leave was almost harder than breaking up with Tara. But while they were in Holon, Israel for the championships, I was in Rotterdam preparing for the World Gymnastics Championship. I made Team USA in June, but my entry in Worlds was assured before that. Still, it was great that I'd be able to compete as part of the team instead as an 'also qualified.'

The level of competition here was higher than at US Nationals. These guys were the winners and champions of a dozen different nations—the best of the best. We were to follow the Olympic rotation, as most major competitions did. There would be twelve national teams that had qualified. The other thirty or so gymnasts who were not part of a full team would be grouped together in fives, the same number as on the national teams. So, there would be eighteen groups heading onto the six apparatuses. They would do it in three rotations.

The official rotation is floor exercise, pommel horse,

rings, vault, parallel bars, high bar. That's the order
we went through, but our team started on the rings.
That was probably my toughest event. Starting with the
floor exercises was always a confidence booster for me.
Once we finished the rings, we moved to the vault station. After everyone in our division had completed their
full rotation, we were done, but the next division of six
groups took their places.

In the qualifying round, only four members of each
national team competed in each event. It didn't have
to be the same four members. But three of us were
competing for all-around and so the three of us were
up each time with the other two rotating in on their
strongest events. The competition guideline is 'four
up, three count.' We had four people compete on each
event, but only the scores of the top three went into the
team score.

I placed fourth on our team on the rings. I knew that
wouldn't get me into an individual competition on the
rings, but I might still compete there if the team qualified. I got a team best on the vault. I'd have to wait until
the end of the day to find out where that ranked among
all the ninety competitors. We went through the same
process on the parallel bars, the high bar and floor
exercise. I got another team best in floor exercises, but
there was only 0.01 difference between my score and
our second best. He'd beaten me at Nationals.

In the final event, I stepped up to the pommel horse.
Coach Desmond had really elevated my level of competition on the pommel horse. Some say it is the most
difficult of all the apparatuses. I'm pretty confident on it
and consider rings to be the most difficult if you really
want to win. I did well, but not my best. I was third on
the pommel horse for our team.

There were national team coaches, but nearly every competitor also traveled with his personal coach—for me, Coach DiCello. We didn't find out until late after dinner what the final standings were. Our team qualified comfortably for the team competition. Eight teams would compete for medals in the finals. Each team could enter three of their athletes on each apparatus. This was a 'three up, three count' round. Our coach selected me for floor exercises, vault, and pommel horse—even though I'd done better on the high bar. We had stronger athletes on the high bar.

I did not qualify for the all-around finals. Twenty-four men were in that competition and I was number twenty-nine of ninety. I'd qualified individually on floor exercises, vault, and—to my surprise—pommel horse. I'd placed third on our team on the pommel horse, but our first three were all in the top eight in qualification. That dropped me out of the pommel horse event. I wouldn't have competed in the all-around anyway. Each country was entitled to only two entries in that event and I was only third on our team.

The top eight competitors, regardless of nation, compete in the individual apparatus championships. In case you got lost, that means that I qualified for three medal competitions: Team, individual vault, and individual floor exercise. It wasn't a bad showing, no matter where I ended up in the placing.

The second day of the competition was the team final. We did well. Our team stood on the podium and received the silver (second place) medal. It was my first medal in international competition. Day three was the individual events. I performed on my two and just missed a medal in the vault. I received my first gold medal in international competition for my floor exercise. Not bad for my first international competition. The final day of the competition was the individual all-around and our champion did the performance of his life on all six apparatuses to win the gold medal. Cool!

I called home to tell my parents and sister how I'd done. They were all super happy for me and promised they would have tickets for LA28. Dad said he'd already reserved a hotel room for the three of them. Mikey had finished her undergrad degree and was studying for a master's in Environmental Engineering. What can I say? She got the brains and I got the brawn. She'd also become engaged the past fall and I'd met the guy at her graduation in May. He seemed to be really nice and my sister had certainly settled down. I'd be going to their wedding over Christmas.

After dinner that night, I sat in my hotel room staring at my phone. It was only noon in California. I wondered what the chances were that I'd catch Tara where she could talk. I guess I kind of lost it. I mean, I just lost track of what I was doing and sat there blankly for three hours. At midnight, I thumbed in the number and surprised myself by calling Lena. The girls were in their dressing room preparing for an 8:00 show. All three girls gathered around the phone and squealed when I told them my news.

I never did call Tara.

19
GETTING TO LA28

ON MY TWENTY-THIRD birthday in 2028, I slowly realized I was pretty much the oldest guy in the academy adult dormitory. I'd been in the same room for three and a half years. It was convenient. I had a couple of sponsorships and a collection of medals that I'd sent on to my parents. I'd won a gold at Nationals twice for my floor exercise and had garnered silver in the Worlds in China. The Chinese team had been shocked when I nudged their competitor out of second place, so China took first and third.

I was traveling a lot for competitions and had to thank my sponsors for that. Between training and travel, I was making less from massage than I'd made my first year at the academy.

It was also becoming obvious that I was out of place at the academy. I'd need to move to Denver where the men's national team would be training for Nationals and LA28.

I'd had a massage client, Rachel, who I almost turned away, because I remembered her as a fourteen-year-old when I got here. She was eighteen now. I gave her the massage as a birthday gift. She felt fantastic beneath my fingers and I was reminded that I'd not had a lover, or time for one, since I started preparing for last year's Worlds.

I guess it was really brought home, though, when I had a meeting with Coach DiCello.

"What are you going to do when you grow up, Paul?" she asked bluntly. I wondered if she'd been talking to my dad. He'd asked almost the same question at my sister's wedding in December.

"I haven't had time to think of anything but preparing for LA28. The Olympics have always been my goal."

"I think by July you'll be a gold medal contender in the floor exercises. I'm betting you'll be in medal contention in three other events. That means a possible all-round. But that is only four months away. You need to start planning what comes next."

"The '32 Olympics?" I said.

"Where? Even if you are preparing for the next Olympic games, where are you going to do it?"

What she was saying finally dawned on me.

"My time at the academy is over?" I asked.

"Certainly as a full-time student it is. I can continue to coach you and you can buy training and practice time here, but having a dormitory room at twenty-three is a little extreme. And meals included. The academy is focused on second tier training and you've done well by it. But we don't lodge and feed professionals here. And you need to decide where you'll be working as a professional—possibly as an Olympic gold medalist."

"Oh. Crap."

"You don't need to have this all planned out today, but we need to get you on a track toward success in life, not just in the Olympics. I'd suggest you start looking at the circus training option. You've done some of that in your tumbling. But look at the aerial acts, too. You can continue to train and keep your gymnastics sharp while you are learning some new skills that are more marketable."

"Yes, ma'am. I'll look at it."

I WAS STILL making trips out to the beach with half a dozen girls about once a month. It was funny. None of the girls who piled into my car had been with Sydnie, Lena, and Eva when we started going out. I didn't know anything beyond the names of a couple of them. I wasn't even sure who was organizing the trips as it always seemed to be a different girl who asked me to drive them.

We still had fun. We played on the beach and in the water. We did tricks that kept a lot of the spring break kids entertained. Occasionally, I went to the beach with more girls than I brought back to the academy. They were pretty popular.

Rachel had come to my door to ask if I could take some girls to the beach on Sunday, but I told her I was planning to see the Twins' spring training game down in Fort Myers.

"I didn't know you liked baseball!" she said. "Can I go, too?"

"Sure, I guess. I was just going online to order my ticket."

"I'll pay for mine. And help with gas and stuff," she said excitedly.

She looked over my shoulder as we looked at the seating map of the stadium and chose good seats behind the Twins' dugout. They were a little pricey, but I knew from experience that these were concierge seats and we'd have service right in the stadium without getting up to leave.

"We won't catch any foul balls here, will we?" she asked. "Should I bother to bring my glove?"

"If you want. It's always possible. Even if we don't, you could get your favorite player to autograph your glove," I suggested. "They love beautiful young flirts."

"You think I'm a flirt?"

"I didn't say *that*. Did I?" I laughed.

We decided to make a day of it and really enjoy the ball park and Fort Myers. We might even drive down to Fort Myers Beach after the game. I wondered what the odds were that I'd be driving back alone.

I DIDN'T NEED to worry about that. Rachel had gone to work and got two more girls, Dorene and Lydia, to join us for the game. Of course, they didn't get their tickets at the same time we did, so they were seated a section away from us. Too bad that wasn't a concierge section.

We ate hotdogs and popcorn, slathered on enough sunblock to stop a direct hit, and Rachel got her mitt signed by one of the players. The Twins had just become her favorite team. I had no idea who had been her favorite before that.

We all agreed to go down to Fort Myers Beach for dinner. As I was driving, all three girls stripped in the car and put their bikinis on. That was a treat. I'd expected them to wait until we reached a restroom or at least to have me wait outside the car while they changed. Rachel was not only casual about stripping, she seemed to be in no hurry, making sure I had plenty of opportunity to glance over beside me and look at her. The other two weren't in much more of a hurry, but I had to catch glimpses of them in the mirror.

"Your turn," Rachel said, when I'd parked in a space that was just being vacated. It was after five and there was a shift change going on as spring breakers from the previous week rushed to the airport or packed cars to drive north, and spring breakers for the next week were still arriving and hadn't had time to get fully drunk yet. At least that was one thing I didn't need to worry about. None of us drank alcohol. It would definitely be bad for our training.

"My turn?" I said, not understanding what she was talking about.

"Strip and get your trunks on. You got a free show from all three of us. Pay up!"

"Oh. Um…" I put thoughts of being bullied out of my mind. She had a point. Fair was fair. If only I didn't have quite such a hard-on from the show they'd given.

I sighed, slid my seat back, and shucked my pants. I grabbed my trunks out of my bag and worked them up and over my cock, as the girls made appreciative sounds. I was redder than if I'd sunburned, but I'd get over it.

One thing we all did was wear skimpy bikinis or Speedos. There was no question we'd have tan lines. The idea was to have them where they wouldn't show when we put on our gymnastics uniforms. We grabbed our towels to take with us and I locked the car. Rachel had a small beach bag and dropped the keys in it along with our wallets. We headed out for a stroll along the water. The beach is a couple of miles long and we'd parked almost at the north end of it, so we had a really nice walk along the water, the girls attracting stares as we went.

"Let me up on your shoulders," Rachel said, handing her bag and towel off to Dorene and Lydia. I threw her from a cannonball and she landed on my shoulders without faltering. I thought she was just going to sit on my shoulders, but she stood there making quite a spectacle of herself up where everyone could see her.

Since she was perched up where she could be seen, I decided to have some fun and turned toward the water. I was already up to my knees before she realized what I was doing. I was up to my waist when she finally did a forward pike salto and dropped into the water. *My* waist. Where she landed, the water was fully up to her chin. I mentioned that she's a gymnast. That's almost guaranteed to mean short.

We had a little tussle in the water and my Speedos ended up rolled down below my crotch. It's not really easy to get a suit that tight off. Somehow, though, her top ended up in my hands without her in it. We were still deep enough not to be readily visible from the shore, but Rachel jumped at me and wrapped her legs around my waist, smashing her small breasts against my chest. She also smashed her lips against mine and gave me a kiss that was guaranteed to bring rigidity to where she was sitting.

"I hope you're planning to put that someplace useful tonight," she breathed. "Now give me my top."

I gave her the top and pulled my trunks up.

Dorene and Lydia were just sitting on the beach laughing at us and threatened not to give us our towels. They quickly relented when we began dripping on them. By the time we were away from the beach to a restaurant, our suits were dry enough to sit and enjoy fish and chips for dinner. They didn't have grouper sandwiches.

The other two girls jumped out of the car as soon as I pulled in to the dorm, yelling thanks for the ride. Rachel pulled my hand and led me to her room where she immediately stripped out of her bikini and 'helped' me get out of my suit.

"Are you sure you want to do this?" I asked. "I mean, I'm a lot older than you are."

"I hope that means you know what you're doing," she laughed. "Because from here on, this is all new territory for me."

"This is your first? Rachel, we should have made it special."

"What do you think we did? A ball game, a walk on the beach with a tumble in the water, and dinner. I don't think it gets more special than that. What... um... what do I do next? You're not the first naked boy I've seen, but I've never done anything with it."

"Let's just relax and let nature take its course," I said. "Maybe we should rinse off in the shower to get the salt and sunscreen off."

"Okay!"

That was the right place to start. We soaped and kissed and generally slid around on each other while we got things cleaned up. If we'd been in my room, I had spare towels because I washed my own for the massage room. In Rachel's tiny bath, we shared one towel and then tumbled into bed.

I was pretty nervous. I think Rachel was the first girl I'd ever been with who was less experienced than I was. We didn't do a lot of fancy stuff. We weren't making a porn movie. We just kissed and stroked each other until it was obvious we were both ready.

"You might want to be on top so you can control the speed and depth and all," I suggested.

"Really? I thought I just laid here and spread my legs. This is cool."

She had a couple of false starts, but I held her body weight with her butt in my hands until she got into a position where we could couple with minimal discomfort. Once she'd managed to get fully seated on my cock though, she kind of went wild.

"Yeah! Yeah! I knew it would be good. It's good! Isn't it, Paul? Is it good?"

"It's really good," I said as she bounced up and down on me. It didn't last long, but it was really fun. And from her perspective, it was as special as she wanted it to be.

The second time was just as fun. We lay there cuddling and kissing. Whispering together. Then she shocked me.

"It's nine-thirty. You should get back to your room. I need to get ready for bed so I can make my first session tomorrow. I'm teaching a bunch of six-year-old tumblers. Thank you for such a special day, Paul. See you around."

I dressed in my shorts and T-shirt, then headed downstairs to my room, feeling a little like I'd just been dismissed.

RACHEL DIDN'T AVOID me in the cafeteria or around the gym, but it was obvious that she considered what we'd done to be a one-time thing. I saw her hanging out with a guy who was part of a men's group team. That's four men who worked together and built pyramids, did throws, tumbled, and basically did everything Sydnie, Lena, and Eva had done. I thought the top she'd paired up with was really young, but I guess that was none of my business.

My old buddies had moved up to Montreal the previous summer and were working on a new show with a world-renowned circus company. I was really proud of them, but I missed them. They'd been so important to my first year or two at the academy.

Acrobatic gymnastics and then circus acts. That was the progression Sydnie had given me. I was the only person I knew of who had done acro and then went back to artistic gymnastics. I supposed the next stage would be circus. I began taking an hour of training time a day to learn some circus skills.

Circus acts use a whole different set of apparatuses. I stayed away from trapeze and rings for the time being. Not only were they risky while I was focused on artistic gymnastics, but swinging rings could mess up my routines on still rings. I just didn't want to get into that.

On the other hand, I rather liked the *corde lisse* and the silks. The *corde lisse* is a smooth rope, hung from the ceiling (or up high). It's great for climbing, but learning to create different shapes and positions, hanging from a foot, doing a flag, and other tricks was really fun. Silks replace the rope with special fabric ribbons. You can work with a single strand or multiple strands and a lot of the learning is of the different wraps and releases. It's also popular with two-person acts where one is on one ribbon and their partner is on the other ribbon. They can do combination poses, swing, spin around each other, and a variety of other tricks. Of course, I didn't have a partner, but I was learning the tricks.

All this did not take any significant time from my training for Nationals and the Olympics. There were four competitions leading up to the Olympics and I traveled to each of them, moving to Colorado to train with Team

USA. I was one of the strongest members of Team USA. I brought home more hardware.

More medals to ship home to Minneapolis. Mom and Dad 'stored' them for me. I'd discovered at Christmas that they weren't merely putting them in a box, but were storing them in plain sight in the living room in a special cabinet Dad built.

I spent most of April and May training with Team USA men in Colorado. I thought it was smart to work at such a high altitude. It really deepened your breathing. Supposedly, the new National Training Center would break ground in San Diego after the Olympics this summer. That was high on my list of places to move to when I could no longer really work at the GAC Academy

In May, the Nationals were held in Portland, Oregon. I felt good and strong, and my performance established me as one of the elite gymnasts in the US. I got two gold medals, a silver, and three bronze in the events. It wasn't common to medal on all six apparatuses. I received the gold for all-around. I was ready for the Olympics.

July in Los Angeles is hot and muggy. As Dad said, "It isn't the heat, it's the humidity." I was glad I had trained the past four years in Tampa. I guess July wherever the Olympics are held tends to be pretty hot. The Forum, where the gymnastics events were held, had new environmental controls and my sister and her husband managed to wangle a tour of the control room and equipment. Might've known. She was doing some good things with an architectural firm in Minneapolis to design some next generation environmental systems.

Of course, I hardly saw my family. It was exciting to march in the parade of nations as we entered the SoFi

Stadium. It was hot, but we scarcely noticed. Taking a page from the Paris Olympics, the parade actually started over a mile away from the stadium and spectators lined the street to watch the parade without having to pay admission to the stadium. Still, I was glad we were only walking a mile and then around the track in the stadium before we got to our seats. In Paris, the teams had floated down the Seine for four miles on boats with cameras on them.

I didn't carry the flag. The women's basketball team was one of the most popular teams in the world and one of their popular players carried the flag. She was someone I really looked up to, but I'm only five-five and 'looked up' to the whole team.

After the opening ceremonies and the parade, our team boarded a bus to Olympic Village at UCLA. The dormitories at UCLA were on a par with the dorm at the academy, but we were housed two to a room. I was with one of the other gymnasts and we got along pretty well. We'd roomed together in Colorado and Portland.

We were up early the next morning, had breakfast, and were bused back to The Forum for a day of practice before the qualification round began on Monday. It was a good session and the men were divided into teams and groups, as they had been at the Worlds a year ago. It took longer to cycle everyone through all the apparatuses because we were allowed two full run-throughs of our routines. There were a few hundred fans in the stands, mostly local, and most down on the women's end of the arena. We warmed up at the same time, though men and women performed on alternate days until the apparatus finals. Of course, there were warmup rooms available as well, but they contained standard gym equipment, not competition apparatuses.

After our practice session, we were bused back to UCLA and dinner.

We had one more sleep before the Men's Qualification Round.

Team USA was in the third subdivision of the qualifying round. That meant we didn't actually perform until eight in the evening. I spent most of the day sleeping until mid-afternoon when I needed to catch the shuttle to The Forum to warm up.

The subdivisions comprise six team and NOC mixed groups. I guess that is as clear as mud, as Mom would say. Twelve national teams from different countries had earned the opportunity to qualify at the Olympics. Each team had five members. In addition to that, the National Olympic Committees could submit up to three athletes to compete with final approval of the International Olympic Committee. So, there were sixty team athletes and thirty-six independent athletes, meaning they weren't competing as part of a national team.

In order to facilitate a consistent rotation on the apparatuses, the independent gymnasts were randomly assigned to one of six mixed groups. The result was eighteen total teams and groups. These were divided into three divisions, each with four national teams and two mixed groups. Six groups and six apparatuses. One group or team started the rotation on each apparatus and at the end of that round advanced to the next apparatus.

Each athlete got one shot at each apparatus and that determined if he (and/or his team) qualified for the final round of team, individual all-around, or apparatus finals. Only the vault was an exception. Each athlete got two vaults, but only the first was tallied for the team placement. The two scores were averaged to determine if the gymnast qualified for all-around or apparatus finals. Weird, but when you are competing, all you pay attention to is what apparatus you are on and the best you can possibly perform on it. The judges can sort out the fine points.

It takes a little over two hours to cycle each subdivision through all the apparatuses. Team USA started on the parallel bars. Then we went to high bar, floor exercise, pommel horse, rings, and vault.

We were competing with the best of the best. Team USA qualified as one of the top eight teams who would compete in the final on Wednesday. I missed qualifying for the all-around by 0.015 points. That was due to a mess-up on my pommel horse routine. I just wasn't feeling it. I would have qualified for being in the top twenty-four, but only two gymnasts per country were allowed, and I was third on our team. Individually, I qualified for the floor exercise, high bar, parallel bars, and vault finals.

No medals were awarded in the qualifying round. It just determined which eight teams, twenty-four gymnasts for the all-around, and eight scorers on each apparatus (with a limit of two per nation) would advance to the finals. My failure to advance to the all-around meant I wouldn't be competing on Friday.

It was disappointing, but I did well in qualifying for four event finals and would do my best to get to the podium.

WEDNESDAY AT 5:30 in the evening, we started the team finals. There were five members of each team; three competed in each event. My score counted toward our team final in the floor exercise, the high bar, and the vault. My teammates handled the parallel bars, pommel horse, and rings. We had three extraordinary athletes on the still rings who dominated the competition.

At the end of the evening—about eight o'clock—we stood on the podium as a team to receive the silver medal. I had my first Olympic medal.

I WENT TO the gym each day to practice and stay warmed up and loose. Coach DiCello worked as hard at keeping me calm and settled down as she did on my routines. The first two events of individual apparatus exercises would be held Monday evening. My high bar, parallel bars, and vault qualifiers came in third, seventh, and eighth. The top three qualifiers in each event were incredibly good and no one expected any of the other five qualifiers to make it to the podium. I knew that could happen, though, if any one of the top three faltered.

I had to do both the high bar and the vault Monday night. I had a stellar performance on the high bar and moved into a tie for second place. We were all shocked, though, when the fifth place qualifier had the performance of his life and moved into first. At the end of the event, I was tied for third.

Sadly, that doesn't mean they give two bronze medals. When gymnasts are tied, the gymnast with the highest difficulty score is declared the winner. It was determined the other gymnast had a higher difficulty than I did, and I was moved into fourth place by 0.01 points. *Shit.*

I'd barely edged out another qualifier in the vault and then stepped out of my landing in the final. I finished in sixth. I was done until Tuesday night when the finals for floor exercises and parallel bars were held.

20

THE CLIMAX

I'D HAD THE second highest score in floor exercises during qualification and the highest score in floor during the team finals. I had a floor element with an extremely high difficulty factor (H) in my routine. It was a back double pike salto with a one-and-a-half out. It came on my fifth line. The men's floor exercise comprises six tumbling lines, plus one strength exercise. My strength exercise was slated between the fifth and sixth passes.

Tuesday night finally arrived and I was ready for my floor exercise. My heart was racing. I'd received a silver medal as part of the team all-around, but had failed to qualify for the individual all-around, and had finished just out of the medals in high bar and vault. I had the highest floor exercise score in the games so far and I knew no one had as high a difficulty score as I had in the event. All I had to do was my best, and none of the others could touch me. Coach DiCello laid a hand on my shoulder before I approached the mat.

"Breathe," she said calmly. *Yeah, right.* I gulped in a lungful of air and headed to the floor.

When I stepped up to the mat to await the green light, I had adrenaline pumping through me like I'd never experienced before. My heart was racing. This was it. My best event and my shot at an Olympic Gold Medal. There was a tone and my seventy seconds of fame began. I stepped back on my first pass landing which was a deduction of 0.100. The second pass stuck perfectly and I took a deep breath to begin my third pass.

I don't remember my third and fourth lines. I think they were perfect. The fifth was where things took a slight deviation from my tariff sheet, submitted before the event. It was my highest difficulty pass, featuring the double salto in pike position with a one-and-a-half out that I'd practiced daily with Coach DiCello. I started the pass and did a forward layout salto with a half twist which gave me exactly the bounce I needed to launch the back double.

I guess that's where the adrenaline proved too much. I realized about halfway through the second salto that I was over rotating. My first thought was to save my neck and I immediately snapped open and threw my hands out above my head.

In practices, I'd often landed jumps on my hands. I'd never used one in a competition, though. The rules outlawed all moves that landed on the hands with a roll-out.

By some miracle, I stuck the landing on my hands. I went from that, directly to my strength exercise, holding myself on my hands, and doing the splits, then moving directly into a flair with a spindle and roll-out. The final tone indicating ten seconds remaining in my time sounded and I had to hurry into position and start my final line. I stuck it, and all-told, I felt I'd done a great exercise. I stepped off the floor after acknowledging the judges and Coach DiCello gave me a quick hug, letting the Olympics coach congratulate me. Coach DiCello immediately wanted to examine my hands and wrists. I hadn't expected a hand landing and wasn't wearing wrist braces. Bearing the impact of about ten times your body weight when you come out of a high flip like that can be murder on the wrists. She immediately wrapped them and used a brace because I still had my p-bar routine to go.

It took forever for my score to come up. It seemed there was quite a discussion going on among the judges. When they finally settled down, my scores were 0/0/0.

I'd been disqualified!

The coaches immediately went to the judges table to protest and appeal the decision. I had not done a roll-out. It had not been a 1.5/1.5 Thomas Salto as I'd rotated 2.5 and twisted 1.5. The coaches argued that the difficulty score should have been increased to a level I (the most difficult element) and that I had done it flawlessly. The judges, in principle, agreed, but said the move was a clear violation of the intent of the rules. The decision to disqualify me stood.

I was not only off the podium, I was last in the competition.

Fuck!

I didn't have time to really let it soak in, because I had to get to my p-bar routine. Unfortunately, Coach's assessment of my wrists was accurate and I was in pain through the entire routine. Even though I fought through it, I simplified my dismount to save my wrists, and that dropped my score enough to leave me with another fourth place finish.

WHEN I FINALLY got off the floor and collected my possessions, I found I had a flood of text messages on my phone. I think everyone I knew personally had sent me a message expressing outrage at the judging and congratulating me on a routine that was near perfect and should have been awarded a gold medal.

Nice. Thank you. Wish you were judging.

The message from Tara was simply a crying emoji.

Well, I'd sent her enough of those in my life.

I DID NOT stay in LA after the event. Wednesday were the rings and pommel horse finals, and I had no desire to watch them. I gave my silver medal to my parents, kissed them and my sister goodbye, and flew back to Florida. When I got there, I quietly packed up my dorm room and my massage room into my car. There wasn't any reason for me to stay at the academy. Coach DiCello had made it clear that I needed to find a new venue to continue my training. I just wasn't interested. It was so unfair.

If they'd said I'd blown the element and awarded no points, I'd have been mad, but I would have understood. I *had* blown the element. My tariff sheet said a double with a one-and-a-half out. I'd recovered, but the resulting move wasn't technically in the code of points. I would have needed prior approval for it and a judgment of how difficult it was before the competition.

But to disqualify me entirely based on it being a derivative of a banned element just wasn't right.

I was someplace near Atlanta when I pulled into a motel. It advertised a pool on its sign and vacancy. They told me the pool closed at ten, but it was only a little after nine, so I put on my Speedo and headed outside to it. It seemed there were a lot more bugs than in Florida, but I didn't really use a pool much while I was at the academy. We always swam in the Gulf. Well, the bugs wouldn't bother me in the water. I jumped in and began swimming laps.

There were a couple of other guests at poolside and some kids playing in the shallow water. I stayed clear of them and just swam laps up and down the pool, using the water to wash away my tears. I stopped when a guy shouted at me at the end of the pool. I looked up.

"It's ten. We're closing the pool," he said. "You need to get out now."

"Oh. Okay. Sorry."

"You a professional swimmer?"

"No. I just needed the exercise."

"Forty-five minutes of laps is a lot of exercise."

"Maybe I'll sleep tonight," I said. I got out of the pool and looked around. A couple of parents were herding their kids back toward their rooms. I grabbed my towel and hotel key and went to my own room.

I stayed there a couple of days, trying to figure out what the hell I was doing. The route I'd taken was one that would eventually get me up to Minneapolis, but I didn't want to shuffle into the city and ask my parents to take care of me. I had a pretty sizable bank account now. I didn't really have much to spend money on. My sponsors had awarded me sizable bonuses for each medal I'd brought home in the past three years. I hadn't really dated much. I still drove the same Chevy my parents bought me when I graduated from high school. I never thought much about clothing because I never went anyplace but the gym or the beach. And I'd had my expenses covered by sponsors. I'd earned money by giving massages.

Between finding appropriate food and swimming to keep fit, I researched places and found a national chain of fitness centers that seemed to have a good spread of locations and various degrees of gym spaces. There was one not far from the motel where I was staying, so I went over for a tour.

"Are you looking for a place as a trainer?" was the first question the club manager asked. "If you've got experience, we could probably use you."

"I was actually looking for a place where I could train and exercise as I travel around the country. I know I look strong, but I'm not a weight trainer. I'm a gymnast."

"We don't have a gymnastics area in our club," the manager said.

"I know. I'll have to search out gymnastic clubs while I'm traveling across the country. It's just important for me to have a place where I can work out for a couple of hours each day and that has nice facilities and amenities," I said.

"We have that. Two hours of workouts and you don't lift weights? I'd like to see your workout."

"Happy to show you. I'm still designing the routine I'll use as I'm traveling. It involves a lot of bodyweight training and floor work."

"Got your gear? Let's get you set up. I'll even arrange to let the next club on your route know you're coming."

That was cool. I grabbed my bag out of the car and followed the guy on a tour of the facilities. It was nice and I especially liked that they had a sauna and hot tub. I'd gotten used to using those at the academy. Unfortunately, they didn't have an ice bath. When I'd been through his orientation, I changed into a working uniform and began my routine with stretches and warmups. If I was on a two session a day gymnastic workout, I'd spend more time than the half hour I used getting warmed up. Then I started with my bodyweight routines. This club didn't have a peg board, which was too bad, but it did have a regular chinning bar. Like most fitness clubs, the bar had a platform so people could adjust how much of their bodyweight they were lifting. I put it on zero, jumped just slightly, and started underhand pull-ups. Those are the ones with the palms facing the body and develop the biceps and latissimus dorsi muscles.

I think he was a little surprised that I stopped at twenty-five, but then I switched to neutral grip pull-ups and did twenty-five of those. The neutral grip is with palms facing away about shoulder width apart. Finally, I did twenty-five wide grip pull-ups, which are hands wider apart, palms facing away. This is the position I use for doing waist-high pull-ups. He was really surprised when I did twenty-five pull-ups that went beyond the chin and up to the waist. By that time several people had gathered around to watch me just doing pull-ups.

I was specifically targeting my upper body that morning, so my next move was to use one of their yoga mats on the floor and do a handstand. I took a Japanese handstand position first, my hands spread wide apart as I lifted my body up. In the Japanese handstand, the top of your head is supposed to be a hand's breadth away from the floor. I moved to and held several different positions from that stance, then moved my hands in to the more common shoulder-width handstand. Once I was there, I started doing push-ups. I had to admit that after this, my wrists were really sore and I realized I probably did some damage to them when I landed that move at the Olympics.

I asked to use one of the hardwood floor rooms where they typically do things like dance aerobics, Zumba, yoga, and other such classes. For me, it was time for a limited leg workout. I started by simply making several circuits of the room in a squat position, thrusting my legs out and pulling myself forward. Then, because I thought the people watching deserved to see something gymnastic, I did a few single saltos in front and back rotations with pike, tuck, and layout positions. I wasn't going to do any multiples or more than a half-out without a sprung floor and a higher ceiling.

I'd been working for nearly two hours when I left the floor and said I thought I'd take a swim for a while and use the hot tub. The manager thanked me for the demonstration and gave me a schedule of when the hardwood floors were available. I told him I thought I'd stay in town for a few more days before I decided where to head next.

When I got back to my motel, I got a bucket full of ice and a couple of plastic bags. I wrapped my wrists in ice and just flopped on my bed for a nap.

I WOULDN'T SAY I'm a particularly social guy. But I really missed all the people chatting and showing off at meals at the academy. And Sunday trips to the beach.

Friends, I guess. It took me until I'd been gone a few days to realize that when I left the academy, I left all my friends behind, without even saying goodbye. Once I finished my workout for the day, I was at a loss for what to do. I took some long walks and went to see local sights. I found different restaurants to eat in that had reasonably healthy food—a little rare in the Southeast. And I spent time in my hotel room or in the pool, letting

tears just run out of my eyes. I wasn't sobbing or anything. I didn't even know for sure why my eyes were
leaking like they were. When it got to be too much, I
swam and washed them away.

I told the health club manager I'd be leaving the next
weekend and thought I'd drive north. He suggested that
I find a place in Winston-Salem, North Carolina, as he
knew the manager of the club there. I was easily influ-
enced, so said that I'd stop there in a day or two.

AND THAT BEGAN my days of wandering.

I kept my parents and Mikey up-to-date on where I
was and what I was doing. When I called Mikey Saturday
to wish her happy birthday, she yelled at me for leaving LA so abruptly before she'd had a chance to tell me
she was pregnant and I was going to be an uncle in
January. Mom was mostly concerned for my safety and
wanted to make sure I was driving carefully and staying in reputable places. I was, mostly. Throughout the
south, cheap motels had swimming pools.

Dad was the practical one and asked about my
finances and whether I could afford to take this kind of
'time off.' I wasn't sure what I was taking time off of. I
guess, just life. Then he suggested that I consider stopping up there in Minneapolis and taking a plane somewhere if what I was doing was trying to get my head on
straight. That actually sounded like a good idea, if I had
enough money. I told him I'd consider it.

I didn't hurry, though.

From Winston-Salem, I headed up to the DC area.
I stayed far enough out of town that I could find a
motel cheap enough for my budget—no pool—and a
gym nearby. It was also the first place I located a real

gymnastics training center and when I called, they were more than willing to have me come to spend a week training and giving classes or coaching. I was close enough to the nation's capital, though, that I could take a little time and go sightseeing.

I got all the way to Boston, staying in cheap motels near the local club and keeping up with my workouts. I got into another training center for a week in Massachusetts with much the same terms. I could train and get advice from their coaches, if I'd also give some training master classes to their students. It worked out well.

I called Lena to see if I could visit the girls in Montreal, but she said they'd just moved out to the Los Angeles area to join a show there. They were really enjoying their circus work after having won their world championship in women's group acrobatic gymnastics the previous year. I started considering whether I should start to focus more on being an acrobat. I was doing a lot of acrobatics in my workouts, just to stay fit.

I went to Stroudsburg, PA, Niagara Falls, and Pittsburgh. From there, I went to Indianapolis, and from Indy, I plotted a course through Chicago, Milwaukee, and back to Minneapolis.

Great timing. I'd been wandering from club to club and seeing the sights I never had time for before. I'd been gone from the academy for five months and had visited a dozen other training centers and another dozen fitness clubs. It was cold in Minneapolis, but I had a good place to stay. I decided I'd stay there at least until Mikey's baby was born. If she'd looked in LA like she did at Christmas, I would have known instantly there was a little one on the way. She looked like a nudge would cause her to explode.

I talked to the manager of the health club in Minneapolis and they agreed to let me offer massage in the club. They wanted fifty percent of the take for providing space. I agreed and set my price at $90. That seemed to be in line with what was being charged for most therapeutic massage in the area. I settled in for the worst of the winter.

Mikey's baby was born the 23rd of January. She named the little girl Polly Jeanette and everyone immediately started calling her PJ. Mikey confided that Polly was a nod to her baby's uncle—me—that didn't call attention to the fact as 'Paula' would do.

"It doesn't seem fair to saddle a baby with the name of someone who was always picked on in school and never amounted to much out of school," I said.

"Her uncle is an Olympic athlete," Mikey defended herself—and me, I guess. "And I'm very proud of him."

"Thank you. It's been hard to think of myself as having ever been to the Olympics. I was disqualified."

"That was rubbish. Your act was perfect."

"Not really," I said. "I didn't think they'd disqualify me for it, but the move I did was accidental. It wasn't on my tariff sheet. I was supposed to land on my feet. I thought they might deduct as much as half a point, but it was a shock to be disqualified."

"What are you going to do next, Paul?" She got PJ changed and handed her to me to hold while she slept.

"I don't know for sure. Dad suggested that since I'm traveling around, I should travel to other countries, too. I've got a few acquaintances I've made over the years in competition. I thought I'd start contacting them to get a month or two of training with their coaches to see what else I can learn."

"That sounds like a great idea. Where would you go first?" she asked.

"I thought I'd start in Japan and go from there. I'm not sure how much money I'll have to live on when I take off. Without the massages I do, I don't have much of any income."

"Your sponsors all dried up?"

"Not completely. One equipment manufacturer has kept me on a retainer. After all, I've got a couple of National Championships in addition to an Olympic Silver. I'm supposed to do a series of advertising photos for them next month. That will be a quick trip to Chicago for the photos. Then I'll come back here and plan to take off again in March."

"Just come back as often as possible," Mikey said, giving me a hug and taking PJ from my arms. "We want PJ to always know her uncle."

AN ADVANTAGE OF flying to Chicago for the photo shoot was having a week in the manufacturer's gym to work on the equipment, and extra time I could spend at the local training center where I'd been just a few weeks earlier. Lest you think there are no gymnastic training centers in the US, let me say that nearly every state has at least one. I'd visited several over the past few months.

Most, however, were focused on children and teens gymnastics. If they had a team they trained for competition, it was *usually* only girls. More and more universities had expanded into men's gymnastic programs, but there is a significant difference between the level of NCAA gymnasts and elite gymnasts. It mostly had to do with how many hours a day they could practice. More

293

than about seven or eight hours of active practice could be detrimental. But it often took ten to twelve hours in the gym to get the seven or eight active hours. College kids just didn't usually have the time to devote to the sport.

I worked on the equipment for a week before we actually got to the shoot. They had custom outfits they wanted me to wear that declared a team name as if they were launching a professional gymnastics team. I didn't mind. The gig paid well and I'd wear their team outfit wherever I trained and competed.

When I returned to Minneapolis, I made calls and got my ticket to Japan.

THERE ARE A few individual sports that accept the possibility of an athlete having different coaches at different times or for different reasons. Some team sports have that as well. When I was working for the basketball team in Minneapolis, I found that half the players were headed overseas to play for teams in other countries during a more traditional basketball season.

Gymnasts, figure skaters, runners and other field sports often spent time with a trainer for a specific purpose. A figure skater who is doing well, for example, might go to a skating rink in another country for as much as a year, just to work with a coach who could improve their spins.

I contacted Mr. Kimura in Osaka. I'd first met him at a competition in Japan a couple of years before and renewed our acquaintance at the Olympics. He'd invited me to come to Japan and he would improve my rings work. His athlete at the Olympics won the rings apparatus final. He helped me find a place to stay when I visited.

"Mr. Kimura sensei," I said when I arrived. "Thank you for agreeing to teach me for a while."

"Yes. Welcome to Japan. We will improve your rings and teach you to control your floor exercise. Come to the training room."

It sounds more abrupt than it felt. I'd found the family with which I was staying and they had helped me get settled, fed me, and showed me how to reach the gym. Mr. Kimura was as eager as I was to get started. I didn't expect to start where I did.

He took me to a weight room and started me with back fly lifts. I lay face down on a bench and lifted forty-pound dumbbells with my arms outstretched until I had them above the plane of my shoulders. I'd done very little with weights during my years of training, as it was considered to be too much muscle isolation for gymnastics. Mr. Kimura considered my upper back and shoulders too weak for 'real' work on the rings. We went from back fly to standing row and half a dozen other upper back and shoulder lifts. By the time I was finished, I was sorer than I'd been in ages.

That's saying something. People don't realize how brutal gymnastics can be. They see the final product and at most say, "That looks dangerous. What if he falls?" But they never stop to consider that a gymnast *does* fall—almost as often as he succeeds. We use extra levels of pads beneath us, so that when we fall flat on our chests or our backs, it only jars every bone in our bodies rather than breaking them.

In my first afternoon session, I felt like an absolute novice on the rings. My muscles were still exhausted, but that didn't mean Mr. Kimura went easier on me. It was the most grueling session I think I'd ever had.

Nor was he content to work me only on the apparatus

he specialized in. He had a staff who took me all the way back to basics on all the other apparatuses. When I returned to my hosts' house, they smiled at me, fed me, and sent me to bed. I was out like a light.

21
WORLD TOUR

OF COURSE, MY time in Japan was not all working out, but my typical training day was from seven in the morning until seven at night, with breaks for rest, water, and nourishment. I got a day off and went straight to training the next day. On that day off, my hosts made sure I saw the sights around Osaka. Their daughter, Mio, escorted me to clubs and karaoke. I met other athletes and civilians. I didn't participate in any drinking contests with my new friends, but they understood, even when we went to a club.

I didn't feel so short in Japan. At five-five, I was only a couple of inches shorter than the average man in Japan. The only place I'd consistently been around short men was at the academy or in competition. Everyplace else, guys seemed to tower over me.

It had been seven months since I was last in regular training. I think I must not have been doing enough to maintain my strength. At any rate, I could feel new strength flowing into my muscles and I began to see the results in my exercises. My iron cross on the still rings was perfectly parallel to the floor. I could hold the position for seven seconds with a neutral expression on my face.

That's another of the fine points of the differences between men's and women's gymnastics. No matter how hard or stressful the exercise is, men are supposed to maintain a neutral expression on their faces and not show the strain. Women in floor exercises are supposed to smile and be flirtatious. They all smile when they land their vault and uneven bars, no matter how serious and fierce their expression is during the performance. Guys aren't supposed to show emotion or stress in their exercises. Floor exercises for women included dance moves and music. Balance beam had a section of the code of points devoted to dance moves and was sometimes accompanied with music.

Of course, when I was working on acrobatic gymnastics with Tara, it was a whole different world. It was hard to tell where the dance ended and the acrobatics began. Smiles were fine if they went with the music and the storytelling. Our code of points included dancing and showing emotion.

I worked hard, made friends, learned a little Japanese. Six months went by incredibly quickly and, after a visit home, I found myself on a plane to Hong Kong. While The People's Republic of China owned Hong Kong, the rules there were significantly less restrictive. This was the result of the area being a British colony for a hundred years before being returned to China. Nonetheless, one of China's top gymnastic coaches had set up a training center in the densely populated city.

Mr. Chen welcomed me in much the same way Mr. Kimura had, though we used a translator when working together. He promised to make my vault a record-breaker.

It nearly broke me, as well.

I cannot say how many times I came out of my vaults in something far less than a stuck landing. Often, on my face or back. When I asked about a spotter, Mr. Chen said, through our translator, "It is a soft landing place. Protect your own head and neck."

I had my orders.

After four months in Hong Kong, I flew back to Minneapolis for my niece's birthday.

"Good grief!" Mikey said when she hugged me. "What have they done to you in Asia? You're bigger and stronger than you were before the Olympics!"

"I've been working hard," I said. "Every trainer wants to add their own layer of muscle to my body. But they all insist that I still remain flexible. Now where's my little niece, PJ?"

I was presented with the baby and just spent a long time looking at her and then playing with her on the floor as she showed me all her tricks.

Over the course of the next few days, I taught her to turn a somersault on the floor. She was barely standing up, so I couldn't teach her to do a full flip. It was cute and natural for her to tumble, though. She put her hands on the floor and walked her feet up until she'd made a bridge. Then I helped her tuck her head between her hands and go on over. She thought it was great fun.

"If she grows up to be a gymnast, I don't think I'll ever forgive you!" Mikey said.

"Tumbling is a good exercise. Becoming a gymnast requires more hours in a day than any smart person would have," I answered. "There's no way to study and dedicate the hours needed for training. I got by on the bare minimum of both."

"What you did was the minimum? And you still qualified for the Olympics?" Mom asked.

"You have to remember there are ten times as many girls competing for those five spots as there are boys."

"What's your next move?" Dad asked. "Competitions coming up?"

"No, not really. I mean there are competitions I was in two or three in Japan and one in Hong Kong, but I've been out of the country for almost a year. I resigned my position on Team USA, so any competition I go to now will be as an independent."

"So, where are you going next?" Mom asked.

"I don't know if you remember meeting Gerhardt Bohnert when I competed at the European Invitational. He's invited me to come to Switzerland to train for a while. I think I'll take him up on it."

"Meaning you already have your ticket," Mom snorted. "When do you leave?"

"I thought I'd stick around until after my birthday. The company down in Chicago would like to film me on the rings and vault to use in a new series of advertisements," I said. "I understand they have a new uniform they want me to wear while training abroad."

"Well, we have you for a few weeks, then," Dad said.

"So, TELL ME about your love life," Mikey said when I visited her at her home instead of her coming to Mom and Dad's.

"That's kind of personal," I snorted.

"Well, you knew every detail of my love life," she said. "It kept me honest. I had to tell Rob about everything from my past—even the attempted rape at that party down in Bloomington. I couldn't risk something coming up about a boy by accident."

"How'd he take it?"

"He married me. I'm really past the days of wanting anything other than the guy I married," she said. "Now spill it. A cute Asian girl got your eye?"

"I admit, there was a girl in Japan I hung out with sometimes. It was nothing serious, though. Everyone knew I was there temporarily and no one wanted to get involved seriously."

In fact, Mio had been my hosts' daughter. I'd been reluctant to get involved with her because I didn't want to lose my lodging. It was almost one of those ridiculous anime settings where I was the boy trying to fend off the beautiful 'sister' in the house. The second time we'd been out to a club on a Friday night and she crawled in bed with me afterward, I realized how ridiculous the whole thing was and decided to just enjoy it.

It wasn't a regular thing—well, maybe most Friday nights—but we did have some fun. Turned out she was kind of using me to get another boy interested in her and I got out of Osaka just in time to avoid a conflict.

"You shouldn't avoid girls just because you aren't going to be there a long time. You're almost twenty-five years old. You shouldn't have to live without a little company now and then."

"You know, I'm working my tail off. The training I've been on doesn't leave a lot of time for finding and dating a girl. Mostly, the only girls I meet are in the gym, and they're in the same boat I am. They work from sun-up to sundown. Everyone is too tired to do anything after we practice. And, I'm not really interested in getting tangled up with someone yet. I still..."

Mikey understood without me having to say it. I was still emotionally attached to Tara. If I made love to a girl, it just reminded me again that Tara was out there and might have a new guy. She never posted a relationship status on her social media, so I didn't know. I never posted one, either.

THE FLIGHT TO Zurich wasn't bad. I took off in the evening from Minneapolis, arrived in Iceland early in the morning with just enough time to change planes and take off for Zurich. The total trip took a little over ten hours, but with the time zone changes, the clock showed about eighteen hours elapsed.

My host was waiting for me at the airport and drove directly to a pleasant apartment in town. Inge was a single woman about five or ten years older than me. She lived alone and had a spare bedroom she'd often used to house gymnasts who came to train. She made it clear that her duty as a host ended at providing a room. I had kitchen privileges as long as I cleaned up after myself. She gave me a key and disappeared from the apartment while I got settled in.

The next morning, I followed my instructions to get from the apartment to the gym and spent the next three months under Herr Bohnert's instruction primarily on the parallel bars and pommel horse. Of course I was also given coaching on the other apparatuses. My gym time was paid for by my teaching several classes of young athletes, both boys and girls, each day.

Herr Bohnert made it clear that as I taught, I was to pay attention to fundamentals, and that I was then to apply those fundamentals in my own training. It was an interesting concept and I discovered several important bits that I'd let slide in my training as I became more advanced. I guess it is true of gymnastics as much as it is of other subjects, that the best way to learn is to teach.

At the end of June, I bade farewell to the Swiss and took a leisurely train trip to Sofia, Bulgaria. That was where things changed drastically for me.

I ARRIVED IN Bulgaria the first week of July 2030. I stayed much longer than I planned. Mostly, because of my lovely host.

I thought the arrangement was a little strange. I dragged my bags from the train station about a mile or so over cobblestones into town to a secure apartment building. I called my host and discovered once again that I had a woman with an extra room to let. Unfortunately, she was at work and could not get free for a while. I found a restaurant and had a nice meal of moussaka with a glass of dark beer. I gathered that the moussaka was a Bulgarian adaptation of a popular Greek dish. All I cared about was that it was delicious. It was a rare thing for me to drink anything alcoholic, but I'd been on trains for two days with a couple of layovers and little time to eat or drink.

Teodora met me at the apartment at eight in the evening and conducted me to a top (6th) floor apartment. She was a charming woman about my own age. I found she worked in a tech industry startup company and the hours were often long. She led me upstairs to my room, a fairly large empty space with windows that opened to a rooftop. There was really nothing in the room but a single mattress and springs on the floor and a small dresser. She said to make myself at home and come downstairs to the kitchen for a cup of tea.

There wasn't much to do. The bed was made and it took about ten minutes to put my clothes in the dresser. I couldn't complain, really. I would pay 30 Bulgarian *leva* a day for the room, which was only about $17. When I got to the kitchen, Teodora showed me around, including where tea and coffee lived. The tea was bags and the coffee was instant. But it was nice hospitality. We sat at the table and chatted over the cups of tea she made and she took it upon herself to instruct me in the Bulgarian language.

She drew a chart of the equivalent of Cyrillic characters and Latin characters. Then she showed me that there was significant overlap in the words of our languages, once you translated the characters from one alphabet to the other. Certainly not 100%, but it was closer to comparing Spanish to English than say, Kanji to English.

I didn't need to report to the gym for another day, so she invited me to go with her in the morning to her office and she would see that I got a good cup of coffee instead of the instant. I accepted.

Then came the surprise. I discovered that Teodora's bedroom was also up the stairs and she had to go through my very open space to get to or from her bedroom. My bath was back down on the same floor as the kitchen, while hers was an en suite. I debated for only a minute and when I finished in the bathroom and came back upstairs, I simply stripped off my clothes and crawled into bed. Her door was shut tightly, so I assumed she was in for the night.

I know I'm saying more about my arrival in Bulgaria than I have about any of the other locations where I'd trained. I guess it was more significant. Teodora did, indeed, get me a good cup of coffee at the espresso shop in the building where she worked. She told me to go exploring and be back at noon so she could show me a good local place to eat. I explored the lovely city of Sofia and was back at noon.

She met me and took me about two blocks from her office to a restaurant where she proceeded to call up an app on her phone that allowed her to translate what food items on the menu were and show me pictures of them. We had a great time chatting and she asked me where I'd visited, giving me several more suggestions of where to visit in the afternoon. Then, over my protests, she paid for our lunch.

My calculations said that she had paid almost as much for coffee and our meal as I'd paid for my first night in the apartment. I would have to do something about that.

I was already infatuated with Teodora. It was nothing compared to what was to come.

I THOUGHT I'D be there three or four months—the length of my study visa—and then move on to either Germany or Israel.

I might have done that if I were only interested in the training. Don't mistake me; it was great. Coach Karov helped me more with my floor exercise than anyone since I'd first worked with Coach DiCello at the academy. I worked hard at it and was often home as late as Teodora. I taught at the gym, much as I had in Switzerland. The difference was that most of the kids in Switzerland spoke at least rudimentary English. The kids in Bulgaria hadn't started English lessons yet. Still, we managed to communicate, and I learned as much from teaching as from practicing.

I learned the names of the gymnastic elements in Bulgarian first, so at least I could instruct kids on that. Then I started picking up bits from my coaches as they helped me—more complete instructions that enabled me to communicate more clearly.

Nor was all my instruction in the gym. Teodora and I spent whatever time we had available talking and learning about each other's goals and desires. By late August, we'd had a few days with temperatures over 80°, but the weather was really pleasant. I got 'home' from the gym and a light dinner about eight o'clock and plopped on the sofa to watch some TV. That was also helping me with my Bulgarian. My phone rang.

"What are you doing tonight?" Teodora asked.

"Just got in and sat down. No plans," I answered.

"Give me fifteen minutes and meet me outside. I'll pick you up. I want to show you something," she said.

"Sounds like fun," I said. It was Friday night and I had a lighter training day on Saturday, though I had a couple of afternoon classes I taught. In fifteen minutes, I was standing outside the apartment building and a few minutes later, Teodora pulled up in her little Dacia Sandero, a popular car in Bulgaria.

"I wanted to do this a little earlier. Sunset is wonderful, but dark is when everything comes on," she said as we took off out of town and onto a winding uphill road. The City of Sofia is built right up against a mountain on the south and before long, we were at an overlook, maybe a few hundred feet above the city.

We walked out to a viewing area and watched the lights of the city as they continued to come on—dusk turning to full night.

"I've wanted to show you this most beautiful thing in our country," Teodora said softly. "I have only just found the courage."

"I love it," I said. "It should not take too much courage to bring me here to see this wonderful sight."

"No. Not to see the sight. For this," she whispered as she leaned into me. For a moment or two, I wasn't sure what was happening, but then our lips met and I no longer had any doubts. Our first of many many kisses lasted nearly half an hour as darkness encompassed us and we glanced out over the beautiful city.

TEODORA LED ME up the stairs in the apartment, but didn't hesitate in 'my' room. We went straight through to her bedroom.

I'd been infatuated with her since I arrived, but it didn't take long for that to turn to love. We undressed each other and fell into bed as we continued to kiss and explore.

Eventually, we made love. It was sweet and gentle. Neither of us were complete strangers to sex. Perhaps we weren't as driven by it as some people, but we thoroughly enjoyed it and each other. I thought to ask her if she was protected or if I needed a condom. Birth control was almost a universal standard, but some chose not to use it. Teodora did and I slid into her welcoming body to unite with her for the first of many times. We kissed and whispered as we moved together, mounting slowly but surely to our climax. When it burst upon the two of us within a heartbeat, we gasped our pleasure into each other's mouth as we kissed some more.

And that changed my entire living arrangement in Bulgaria. I applied for a new resident visa on my visit home, and it was granted under terms of a study visa. I left my clothes in the little dresser in the open room at the top of the stairs, but slept her bedroom.

We found we both wanted a lot of contact when we first went to bed—always kissing and sometimes making love. When we were ready for sleep, though, we curled up or stretched out on our own side of the bed with no more than our hands touching.

And I stayed in Sofia for another year.

DURING THE SUMMER of 2031, Teodora had to do extensive traveling for her company. They were expanding rapidly and she was often a speaker at conferences and trade shows. While we loved each other, our relationship did not have the dramatic peaks and valleys that most had. We both worked long hours and met for interludes of intimacy. Even though we slept together most nights when we were both home, and shared in household tasks, we really didn't make love all that often.

In addition to Teodora's travel, I was competing at the events in Europe that summer. There were several FIG challenge events. The excitement and tension were beginning to build for the 2032 Olympics and I was doing well in the European and International competitions.

I was often the only American present at these competitions. Often, but not always. I met John Archer at one of the events and he told me I needed to return to America in order to have a chance at the team. Since he was the director of USA Gymnastics, the national governing body for the sport in the US, I took his instruction seriously. The organization had moved its headquarters with the completion of the new training center in San Diego.

"Come with me to America," I pled with Teodora.

"I can't come to America," she said. "I have a job. I am not going to give it up. Besides, it would take forever to get a visa to spend any time in the United States. Stay here and train with Karov. You like him."

"I can't stay here and compete for the USA in the Olympics. This is my last chance. I'm almost twenty-seven years old. I won't have another chance if I don't go."

"Go, then. You don't need to stay here."

That was a final dismissal.

Oh, we 'discussed' things frequently after that, with more passion than there had ever been in our relationship. I suppose if we had learned to disagree and argue earlier in our time together, we might have made it through the rough patch. We didn't.

I flew back to Minneapolis for a little time with my parents, Mikey, and thirty-two-month-old PJ—who was happy to show me she could stand on her head. By the end of October, I was in San Diego, working under the direction of the coaches for Team USA.

I petitioned the committee for inclusion on the USA National Team by virtue of my previous Olympic berth and record in Asian and European competitions over the past three years. They were willing to bring me on as listed on the team. That didn't mean I'd be selected for any of the team competitions before Nationals in 2032. There was still a lot of proving ground to be covered.

The national team is to have a minimum of fifteen members, but the upper limit is poorly defined. It's generally accepted that they could have as many as twenty members. Regardless, including me on the team didn't displace anyone else. Just before I returned to the US, there had been a FIG Challenge Competition held in Bulgaria. Coach Karov entered me as an independent from his gym. I won the all-around, the floor exercise, and the high bar. I got a silver and two bronze on the other apparatuses. I didn't place in the vault.

The world of gymnastics had changed significantly over the past few years. When I'd told Mom and Dad I didn't need to go to college for gymnastics training, there were only fifteen NCAA sanctioned college or university men's teams in the country—in all divisions! In fact, there were so few that the Div III schools competed directly with the Div I schools. It was widely assumed that if you were a college athlete, you were, by definition, not a professional.

The Elite Division of the USA Gymnastics were mostly paid and sponsored athletes. Even during my long residence in Bulgaria, my equipment manufacturing sponsor had kept paying for my training and for photo shoots when I came back to America for them. They paid for my transportation and expenses when I traveled. And after I won the FIG Challenge (FIG is the Federation Internationale de Gymnastique or the International Gymnastics Federation), I picked up two more high-profile sponsors as we headed for the Olympics.

At that time, athletes had to leave their college programs (after the NCAA championships) and declare themselves as professional Elite gymnasts. Of course, NCAA changed the rules governing amateur athletes in school with the advent of Name, Image, and Likeness (NIL) deals for top tier athletes. Now there was little difference in the categories of amateur and professional, except that the collegiate athletes had to make progress in school.

The number of schools offering men's gymnastics programs tripled and in 2031 the only athletes who bore the name of an independent gym were Junior Elites, most of whom were still in high school, and older guys like me who were past college years.

22

IT HAPPENED IN VEGAS

THE FIRST MAJOR competition to qualify for the Olympic Trials was the Winter Cup. And, yes, all the top college athletes registered for the competition as well as those in dedicated training at the center in San Diego and others who had not yet left their normal gym for the training center. There were fifty competitors in the men's division at the Winter Cup. It was a little different than some of the big competitions. An athlete did not have to compete on every piece of equipment unless he was going for the all-around title. Like I was.

We were randomly divided into twelve groups of four (and a couple of five) and the first six groups did their routines on the first flight in the morning, and in the afternoon, the other six groups did their routines. Day One was the qualifier round, determining which gymnasts advanced on which apparatus. I qualified for the final round in all-around, and for the floor exercises, high bar, and vault in the individual rounds. There was no team competition at this event. Out of fifty men in the open competition, eighteen qualified for the all-around

312

final. That was easier than dealing with everyone. The final was over in two hours.

I didn't win. You can't drop any scores in the final. When I fell flat on my face off the vault, that was really it for me in the all-around. I just lay there for a minute trying to catch my breath while a medic rushed to me to see if I'd broken anything. I hadn't, but I hurt like hell.

Most of the individual apparatus competitions had far more competitors. I almost withdrew from the vault because it was in the afternoon after my fall in the all-around. I went for it, even though I hurt in every part of my body. A handful of Advil helped to dull the pain. I completed a good vault, but I'd simplified my difficulty level enough that even with a perfect execution, I wasn't in the top three.

The next day, I placed second in the Floor Exercises, fighting through the pain of a full-chest bruise from my fall the day before. I launched my routine on the high bar with a chest pull-up in slow motion. When I reached the top of the bar with my arms extended to my waist, I kept pressing up into a handstand on the bar. That was a move I thanked Coach Karov for. Unfortunately, my double pike at the top of the next rotation left me short of the bar and I fell on my face again.

I was thankful for my one medal, but disappointed overall.

I WAS BEGINNING to feel old. Most of the men on the team were between twenty and twenty-three. That was because of the number of college kids who were now competing. I think there was only one other guy who was nearing thirty in age.

I'd worked hard over the past three years with coaches who drove me harder than any coach I'd had in the US. Their intent was to either make me a champion or kill me. It didn't seem to matter which. Over the past twenty years, USA Gymnastics had focused on less abusive training techniques. I guess in principle, I agreed with that. While the women's team had been the focus of the reform—and victims of the most egregious abuses—the men's team had also come under close scrutiny. Every training program and trainer in the country had been visited to be sure they were not physically or mentally abusive.

Mostly, I think the program benefited from that. My years in Asia and Europe had definitely taken a toll on me in some ways. I'd had various injuries and a surgery for a torn meniscus that kept me going easy on my knees for a while. It didn't stop my training in other events, though.

The US Classic was the next qualifying event. Technically, I was already qualified for the Olympic Trials, but the coaches and selection committee wanted to see consistent performance in competitions. I couldn't just sit idle for the next four months and expect to get selected for the Olympic team.

I did better at the Classic. Men and women competed on alternating days and there was a team component to this event. The colleges and universities entered their entire teams in the events. I think only one independent gym entered a full team. As far as I was concerned, that was a day wasted on a college event while the rest of us sat idle.

However, I got four silvers in the competition, including second in the all-around, floor exercises, high bar, and vault. It was good to show the coaches how much

I'd improved and conquered my problems on vault and high bar from one competition to the next. On the other hand, there were only three competitors on the vault. Getting second was a hollow victory.

THE NEW NATIONAL team training center and association headquarters was really state of the art with multiple stations for each apparatus. Two guys could work out on the vault at the same time, for instance. Four on rings and high bar, six on p-bars, and six on pommel horse. There were only two floor exercise areas because of the amount of space they take up. When we looked across the gym toward the women's area, we could see eight or nine beams, three vaults, six uneven bars, and three sprung floors. Well, the women outnumbered the men about three to one here and only had four apparatuses, so it made sense that they had more of them.

Coach Danilo Ryabets finally agreed to function as my principal mentor. He was Ukrainian, and immigrated to the US during the war when he needed to get his students out of the country. He approved of the training I'd had in Europe and Asia because it was closer to what he did in Ukraine. He did, however, comment that my routines were more acrobatic than other seniors. He thought that was okay, but warned me that some would discount that.

It was true, I guess, but I also had to thank him for an acrobatics move in my floor exercise that both increased my difficulty and assured a cleaner landing. We do six passes or lines in floor exercises in seventy seconds and have to sandwich a strength exercise in there somewhere. My most difficult element was still the double salto with a one-and-a-half out (twist). But when you get that much height and speed going forward, it's really hard to stick the landing. Coach Ryabets suggested I connect it to a single salto half-out, going the opposite direction.

I thought that was crazy until I tried it. Sticking the landing without taking a step or falling forward is hard enough, but sticking and reversing direction for a lower value element connected made sticking the final landing much easier. And I found it was actually easier to hit and reverse into another salto than to just stick the landing. Weird. It gave me another quarter point difficulty for that pass.

"Are you sure you don't want to switch to acro?" Coach asked me, pointing across the gym where a lone girl was working out. She was tiny.

"Coach, I did that for a while. Maybe when I'm old, I'll go back to it."

"Don't forget, you are twenty-seven. Think about what you mean when you say 'old'."

Yeah. He was probably right. I went to the training room and submerged myself in an ice bath with another handful of Advil.

I DID OKAY at the US Championships in Fort Worth, TX. I had solid performances on all apparatuses, but finished fourth in the all-around and got a gold medal for floor exercises. The next step was in New York City for the Olympic Trials at the end of June.

It wasn't a bad showing, considering that I was the oldest in the competition by three years. Some of the guys had started calling me gramps. A couple of the girls on the team had taken a year off to have a baby and then came back to compete, but they were having a hard time of it. I didn't think I was old enough to be grandpa to their kids.

The trials were to be at the Jacob Javits Center and the end of the event would include the announcement of the five men who would compete at the Olympics. There was a strong preference toward selecting the top all-around qualifiers so the USA would have the top chance at the Olympic team gold. But they had to balance that with who could win an individual apparatus gold. They could switch off who competed on each apparatus in the team competition.

Back in 2020-21, IOC rules said four persons per team. Any NOC (National Olympic Committee) could submit up to three nominees to the games. That was mostly for those countries who had no national team but had one or two great gymnasts. In 2021, Team USA had four gymnasts on the team, but also had one who was absolutely great on a single apparatus. The NOC nominated him as an individual on just that apparatus and he went to the Tokyo Olympics. I was a strong all-around contender, but I was the top favorite for the floor exercises.

In 2024, teams were changed back to five members, and countries with a national team were not allowed to submit an extra. Whoever they chose for the team were all that were going.

The Olympics in 2032 were in a part of the world I'd never traveled to: Brisbane, Queensland, Australia. It was only the second time the summer Olympics had been held south of the equator during the host country's winter. The first time was 2016 in Rio. The forecast said we should expect pretty mild, dry weather with temperatures between seventy and eighty degrees. It sounded like heaven.

Of course, temperatures in New York City at the end of June were expected to be about the same, but we could expect rain, rain, and more rain. Regardless, we were all excited to get on with this next chapter and find out who would be on the team for the Olympics.

I had pains where I used to only have aches. After the Olympics this year, I was definitely going to consider retiring and coaching. A gold medal would certainly get me more high ranking students.

THERE WAS THIS kid...

Damn, he was good. He was only seventeen years old and a junior in high school. He came from one of the top gyms in the country and had devoted time to his training like I had. The Olympic rules said a male gymnast had to be eighteen by the end of the year. Kevin's birthday was in October.

It seems weird to me that women's gymnasts only need to be sixteen in the year of the games. I guess it used to be fourteen, but there were so many injuries and abuses that the age was raised. I don't know when the age was raised for men. I guess it's assumed we just mature later than women. After all, I was the oldest man on Team USA at twenty-seven. It had been eight years since a woman that old from the USA had won a gold medal.

Anyway, this kid, Kevin, was wicked on the vault. I'd only seen him qualify at Classics and the US Championships. He beat me at both, but it was a narrow margin. And he specialized in the vault.

Well, the story is sad but true. I was in the final five in the men's all-around, but the selection committee decided Kevin was better for the team because of his vault. They dropped me and put him on, even though he'd been seventh in the all-around.

I wanted to appeal to the NOC for a place as an independent but, of course, that was no longer allowed. I was an alternate.

I flew back to San Diego to work with the team, but it was soon obvious that I wouldn't be called upon in my role as an alternate. The team would not pay for my transportation and lodging in Australia.

I packed up and drove back to Minneapolis to decide what my life would be like in retirement.

God damn it all, anyway.

IT WAS THE darkest time of my life that I could remember. And there had been some doozies. Tara leaving and then telling me we were no longer a couple. Being disqualified at the LA Olympics in '28. Leaving Teodora. And finally, not making the Olympic team for '32. I had no idea what I'd do with my life now.

I considered calling Teodora and asking if I could come back. We hadn't been on very good terms when I left, and just when I had screwed up the courage to call, I read her relationship status change on social media. She was now in a relationship with a guy who worked with her.

Shit.

I got my gig at the local health club giving massages back, so I managed a small but steady income. And when I wasn't working and my sister wasn't working, I hung out with her, Rob, and little PJ. I was doing that one evening when the elephant in the room trumpeted.

Well, I was playing with three-year-old Polly, helping her do a back bend and then kick to get over in a backward somersault. She kicked especially hard and blew her diaper out. We'd have had a real mess if she hadn't been ready for bed, which was the only time she was still wearing a diaper. She was devastated to have pooped her pants.

I followed Mikey into the nursery for the clean-up. For such a tiny girl, she could sure produce a lot of poop! We eventually took her into the bathroom and she got her second bath of the night. Once she was clean and in fresh jammies, she went to bed, promising to do it better tomorrow. I assumed she meant the back walk-over. She did a pretty good job on the poop.

"So, what are you going to do?" Mikey asked me as she poured us each a glass of wine. I didn't often indulge, but what the hell.

"Maybe I'll find a little studio to set up as a full-time massage therapist," I mused. "Might even ask Mom and Dad if I could pay rent and set up in the entertainment room."

"They wouldn't go for that, even if they weren't selling the place."

"What? When did they decide to sell their house?"

"Well, think about it. You've been gone for eight years except limited visits. I've been married for five years. They rattle around in that house. They've been talking about selling it forever and moving to something more compact. You know, Dad's been at the University for thirty years—almost thirty-five, I think. He can retire with his full pension."

"He's too young to retire!"

"He'll be sixty in the spring. Our parents aren't that young anymore."

"Man! I just never thought about them not being there in the house where we grew up."

"You often don't think about things. Like how happy you wouldn't be if you were only doing massage therapy and let this body go fat and flabby. If you don't keep working out at your intensity level, it won't be long before you start packing it on. Just look at what happened to me when I got married."

Mikey wasn't fat and flabby. She was, perhaps, a little fuller than she'd been when she was lighting hearts on fire in college. I credited that to having had a baby.

"There are a couple other gyms up here. I never considered them seriously before because they're both a lot farther away than Hennepin Gym is."

"Was. They closed the doors there two years ago."

"Wonder if I could buy it."

"Too late. It's been subdivided into half a dozen custom health and fitness businesses: Massage, aerobics, weight machines, Pilates. You know."

"Too bad I wasn't here then."

"You'd still be bored and getting fat. You need to do something that will use your talents. Don't you think you could coach?"

"Yeah. If I could find the right gym. If I changed my workouts, I could start training for a circus act."

"Why not do acro like you did with Tara?"

"Um... I'm twenty-seven years old. What little girl who's fifteen to eighteen is going to want to have a partner who is so old? In fact, I'd probably have to start working with a girl who is twelve or thirteen, so we could develop a partnership by the time she could qualify for senior competition. By that time, I'd definitely be too old."

"What then?" she asked.

"Coach Karov wanted me to get more into acrobatics and start developing a circus act. He suggested that when I was done chasing my Olympic dream, I move to Moscow or to Las Vegas. They seem to be big centers for training circus acts."

"Don't you dare go to Moscow. It was ridiculous having you in Bulgaria. We don't want you even farther away."

"I'll have to check out what's available in Vegas." I didn't mention that I'd already made a contact there. I wasn't completely set on becoming a couch potato.

In a way, it always seemed to work before, though some of my acquaintances said I was just running away. When Tara left me, I left for Florida the next day. When I was disqualified in the Olympics, I took off on a US road trip and then a world training tour. No one in the family was surprised when I loaded my old car and headed for Las Vegas.

In reality, I put a lot of thought into it. I'd met a coach from Vegas and he introduced me to the owner of a circus gym down there. She looked over my record and agreed it wouldn't be hard to turn me into a performer, and that she could use the coaching assistance in the gymnastics area of the gym.

Of course, there are circus acts that don't require acrobatics. A flame eater or sword swallower come to mind. Lion tamer, anyone? The LVC Gym, however, focused on various acrobatic acts, and you really had to train for gymnastics in order to get there.

Nicole D'Amour had been a circus acrobat with one of the big stage shows in Las Vegas and had toured the world with her act. She still consulted on shows and had established the Gym in Las Vegas specifically for those who wanted to work on the big stages. She'd been trained in Montreal, where the girls from the academy had gone to train. She still spoke with a rather thick French accent and I had to be careful to tune into her so I understood what she was saying.

Nicole had found a furnished 'bachelor pad' for me that was little more than a hotel room with a partial kitchen. I could rent on a weekly basis until I got myself established. The partial kitchen included a sink, refrigerator, microwave, and hot plate. After I checked in, I ran out and bought some basics for my meals, a frying pan, a bowl, and silverware.

Fortunately, both the room and the gym were well air-conditioned. I don't think there was a day the temperatures didn't reach 100 for a month after I got there in mid-August. Unlike gyms I'd worked at before, Nicole did not have me working with children, but rather with teen boys who were talented, but had gotten too late a start to seriously compete in gymnastics. When I started at twelve, it was considered to be a late start and only my devotion to being in the gym all the time made it possible for me to advance to the level I had.

But circus acts required showmanship, not just gymnastic skills. I could teach skills to guys who were dedicated to the show. Having worked with Tara, Madison, and the girls in Florida, I was comfortable training a young man to be a strong base or get him ready for an aerial act.

I had four students who were dedicated to the track and were in the gym every day. Four students is not many when they aren't in the gym all day. That gave me time to train with a couple of circus pros and I sampled all the apparatuses that didn't require actually flying. But I did work on the pole, the *corde lisse*, and aerial silks. I suppose it would have been a small step from there to pursue the aerial hoop, but it just didn't appeal to me.

Balancing on the rola bola was a trick that almost cost me my front teeth. The guy who was spotting me as I learned the trick managed to get his hand between my face and the floor before I hit. It hurt anyway. By late fall, I was advancing in a number of new skills, not the least of which were more acrobatic uses of my gymnastic skills.

Hmm. How to explain that. Well, in gymnastics, I could tumble across the floor, do a double salto with a one-and-a-half out, and land stably on my feet. As an acrobat, I adjusted that so I could land on a two-foot-high platform, make a back flip, and land on a four-foot platform. That's acrobatics.

And that was also when the next big change in my life occurred.

I WENT TO the gym and did my coaching sessions, did a massage, and headed out to the floor to work on my new skills. When I got to Nevada, I immediately checked on the licensing regulations and started my locally required classes so I could practice as a licensed massage therapist. The gym let me practice in a private room and I was now charging $100 an hour. The gym took only 20%!

Anyway, I'd just started my routine when my eye was caught by a kid doing multiple flips across the sprung floor. She looked familiar, but after seeing female gymnasts for ten years, all the tiny women looked familiar. Still, there was something almost haunting about her presence. She seemed older and determined, but the only apparatus she worked on was the floor.

Then she turned and faced me and we both had an instant of recognition. We ran across the intervening space like a parody of one of those slow motion commercials. She leapt from several feet away and landed in my arms with her legs wrapped around my waist and her lips smashed against mine.

"Sydnie! How great to see you! Are the rest of your group here?" I glanced around to see if Lena and Eva were nearby.

"Oh, Paul!" The happy girl was suddenly a bundle of sobs. "It's terrible! I'm so sorry!"

"What? Did your group break up?"

"Lena…"

Lena had been the one of the group who had rescued me the day Tara told me we were no longer a couple. We'd only occasionally made love, but I was always close to all of them.

"What happened? Did she leave your group?"

"We were on our way here to audition for inclusion in a new show—driving from LA, you know. Lena was driving and Eva and I were making out in the back seat. I don't know for sure what happened. We heard a loud bang and thought there had been a gunshot. The car went out of control and crossed the median, head-on into a semi-truck. Lena… She didn't survive, Paul. She died. I'm so sorry."

"Oh my God! Oh my God!" I panted. I collapsed to the floor with Sydnie still held in my arms as tears streamed down both our cheeks.

"Eva threw herself on top of me, but she was hurt and doesn't think she'll be doing acrobatics again. But Lena…"

"Oh my God!" I repeated. "She's gone?" Sydnie nodded against my chest.

For a long time, we just sat on the floor crying together. It had only been a month since the accident. The wound was fresh for Sydnie. For me, it opened a hole in a heart I thought was dead, and I bled for the bright Alabama girl who had once rescued me.

"Are you okay?" I asked. "And Eva is okay? Not seriously injured?"

"No, but she's not going to perform any longer."

"She's not crippled, is she?" I asked with visions of Tara's body in my mind.

"No. The stress was getting to her and honestly, this was going to be our last shot at the big time before we retired. Isn't that the dumbest thing you ever heard of? I'm only twenty-five and we were talking about retiring after this gig."

"Well, I'm only twenty-seven and kind of forced into retirement," I snorted. "I'm coaching here and learning more circus skills. Like you said once a long time ago: gymnastics, then acrobatics, then circus."

"Oh, God. I'm thinking the same thing. Our acrobatics had already taken a turn to circus acts. You can't just perform an acro gymnastics act for long and get bookings. We'd just been working on some new techniques, but not knowing what to do next. We just always thought we'd all be together."

"You and Eva are still together, aren't you?" I asked.

"Oh, we're married. That's not going to end. She thinks she might do some coaching if she can find a good opportunity when she's fully healed. I just had to find a place where I could get some serious workouts in. I don't know what I'll do."

"That's easy," I said without thinking. "Work with me."

23

BACK IN COMPETITION

"THAT'S EASY," **I** said without thinking. "Work with me."

"Work with... You mean acro gym or circus?"

"We can try acro gymnastics if you want, but I think I'm destined to become a circus act."

"I'm into that. Show me what you can do."

I got into my routines and each time I finished something, Sydnie jumped in and showed me something she'd been working on. We put a few of our moves together and liked the combinations. Nicole saw us working and came over to watch.

"Are you going to become an act?" she asked. I looked at Sydnie with my eyebrows raised.

"Yes! That's exactly what we're going to become!" she exclaimed.

"Good! Paul, I've been thinking for a while that you need a partner to work with. Sydnie is perfect. Have you worked together before?"

"Only once a long time ago. Sydnie helped me in my audition at GAC Academy in Florida. She was part of a

327

women's group, though, and I was working on becoming the world's greatest gymnast. We know how that one turned out."

"There is nothing to be ashamed of in your gymnastics career, Paul. But you are both too old to compete in acro-gym. Let me see what you can do together."

I consulted with Sydnie briefly and we lined up on the floor. I did a double salto followed by a single and dropped to my knees. Sydnie was right behind me with her double. Then she landed her single perfectly on my shoulders. I didn't even have to steady her with my hands.

"Yes!" Nicole said. "A good start. I will start designing moves for you. You will compete in three weeks."

"I thought you just said we were too old to compete," I said.

"To compete for USA Acrobatic Gymnastics, yes," Nicole said. "A new season of National Talent Search is beginning soon. You will audition here in Las Vegas for the next level. It is not a gymnastics competition. Musicians, singers, magicians, ventriloquists, acrobats, daredevils. There will be a little of everything. The top acts, as determined by judges and the audience, will be put together as a variety show for a year run at the New Trop."

"I've seen those talent-kind of shows before," I said. "They all seem to end up with impressive little children winning."

"Well, this is different. It's for a revue in Las Vegas. Children aren't allowed. You are over eighteen, aren't you?"

"Oh, God yes," Sydnie laughed. I just nodded.

"One always has to check these days. Okay. Work on what you've got so far and I'll join you tomorrow to review it and suggest some new things. I've been think-ing about this for years, ever since I left the stage myself."

Sydnie and I started working, putting some of our moves and ideas together, and ended up on the mats until eight o'clock in the evening. She had to rush home to Eva and tell her what was going on. We'd all get together over the weekend.

I FELT SOMETHING that night. After I stopped for a light dinner at a nearby casino, I went home and crashed. Lying in bed, thinking of what the day had brought, I felt... happy.

It took me a while to realize what it was. I was heart-broken about Lena, but working with Sydnie had woken something inside me. We clicked as quickly as we had when she fell into my arms in the cafeteria the first night I was in Tampa. Maybe I should have followed Coach Li's suggestion and become an acro gym partner then. I was so dead set on my goal of an Olympic gold medal that I shrugged the suggestion off, though she'd often asked me to work briefly with a new flyer to help build their confidence.

No. I wouldn't trade in the past eight years of my journey. I'd been challenged and trained by the best in the world. I'd won national championships, European and Asian competitions, received an Olympic silver for our 2028 team, and had traveled the world. But I'd seldom thought about being happy.

Even when I fell in love with Teodora, it was filling an empty place in my life and it left me feeling gladder to have company than it did happy. Maybe that was why we dissolved our love affair so quickly when we had career goals that took us in different directions.

The very idea, though, that I could help and support Sydnie when she was at her lowest, just made me happy.

I had no notions of sex with Sydnie, any more than I'd ever had with my sister. But I would do anything for either of them.

There was a pang back in the furthest reaches of my heart for having lost Tara. Working with her had made me happy. Being her lover had overjoyed me. Before I went to sleep, in those last moments before I lost my waking consciousness, I thought wistfully of Tara and hoped she, too, was happy.

THE FIRST THING Nicole did was move us off of the sprung floor onto just mats.

"The mats are for safety while you are learning things. While they provide some cushion for an unexpected landing, they aren't a soft and comfy place to land on your face or your back, not to mention your head," she explained. "But we can't move an entire sprung floor onto the stage for your audition. As soon as possible, we'll map out the stage area onto a hardwood floor and prep your performance there. If we have to spread mats before the audition, it will limit how much of the stage floor we can use."

"I don't think I can bounce high enough to get to Paul's shoulders without the sprung floor," Sydnie said disappointedly. "We'll have to work out a different mount."

"Ah! Just because you can't have a sprung floor, it doesn't mean you can't have a springboard. You might even get enough height to do a double for your mount."

"Oh, wow! That would be cool. What else can we do?"

"Throws," Nicole answered immediately. "Launching you into the air and having you land on his shoulders or even hands should be a breeze for Paul."

"We can do that," I said.

That was the first of Nicole's additions. By the end of the week, it looked and felt like Sydnie and I had been working together all our lives. She was a natural and had as many good ideas as Nicole had. I was glad to be able to make a few suggestions myself, including a Thomas salto. I'd done it with a two-and-a-half on the sprung floor. It didn't seem to be a problem to do a one-and-a-half and land on my hands on the mat as long as I was wearing wrist braces. I didn't try to stick it there, though. Without the cushion of the sprung floor, I decided the better, and slightly safer, choice was to roll out of it.

Nicole saw it and immediately made that my entrance piece. The trickiest part of it was that I had to launch myself from the springboard and stabilize quickly enough that Sydnie could spring, do her pike position salto, and land on my shoulders.

"We will need spotters working with you, even in the audition. I'm going to ask Jon and Steffan to join you. It will still be a two-person act, but I'm not willing to risk your lives for it. You look comfortable doing these tricks on the mat, but when we move to the hardwood next week, it will be a different story. Besides, we need to have someone who will move the springboard into position and remove it until you need it next."

"Will we need it again?"

"I think so. You've been working on flipping up a level. With the springboard, you could get much higher. If you threw Sydnie up even higher, she could jump off a level onto your shoulders when you get up."

We were being filled with new moves every day and by the end of the week, we had the structure of a routine. The next week, we'd add music and move to the hardwood. I was glad Nicole was managing our time at the gym and the people and spaces we'd need. She was also working with a *corde lisse* act that had been performing for two years. She'd registered us both for the auditions and saw to it that we were performing on different nights.

"The type of performance you are going for is normally done by a larger group," Nicole said before we broke on Friday evening. "If you have three or five or twenty performers, spotters are integrated into the action, the thrower and catcher need not be the same, and launches can be much higher. You have an advantage, though. Even with an unobtrusive assistant or two acting as spotter and equipment mover, a two-person act is much cheaper than a large group act."

Well, that was one edge we might have over other acts. I considered it as I took my daily ice-bath and ate Advil for dinner.

DINNER WITH EVA Friday night was a little strained. She was still moving slowly and said her broken bones had healed but everything was still sore. I offered my services as a massage therapist and she checked with Sydnie before saying she'd like that and would come to the gym on Monday.

"That's great. I'll let them know I'm expecting a client and then you can spend some time giving Sydnie and me some tips and pointers," I said enthusiastically.

"I don't think I can do that, Paul," she said quietly.

"What's wrong?" I asked naïvely.

"I'm happy you are working together. It means more than I can possibly express," Eva said. "But I can't help being a little jealous of you. I wanted so badly to be there for my Syd."

"Honey, you are here for me. I come home to you every night, bursting with news about what we're learning. You always perk me up when I'm down and give me tons of great tips. Am I hurting you by working with Paul? Paul, we might need to quit this."

"No!" Eva said. "I'm happy for you. I want you to continue and to succeed. I'll keep picking you up as long as you'll let me. I'll keep giving you tips. I'll keep loving you and always be there for you. I just wish I was the one able to help you and be your base. But I can't be the one anymore. My body was wearing out before the accident. It's never going to be what you need as an acrobat."

"I wish I could give you a massage like Paul can," Sydnie said. "At least we each get something from him. Now what are we going to give back?"

"Please, don't," I said. "I don't know how to say this, but I've been in a vacuum for weeks… months. I was working on becoming a circus act because that was all that was left to me. But when you came along, it gave my work meaning. It gave me hope. I'm going to be your base because you need it and I've discovered it was what I need, too. That's all I'm asking of the two of you."

Sydnie leapt into my arms and planted a kiss on my lips and well into my mouth. I started to splutter as Eva laughed.

"And sometimes…" Sydnie started.

"…a friendly kiss," Eva finished.

"Okay. Sometimes."

We were back at work again Monday morning. I think we all needed the weekend rest. I was at the gym a couple of times to use the ice bath and hot tub, but didn't do more than stretching exercises.

Nicole had mats out in the gym marked to the dimensions of the stage. It was larger than a competition floor. She emphasized, however, that we should use and fill the entire stage. Many acts benefit from being performed in a very tight area with everything around them being dark.

"If you were a roller skating duo competing for a spot on the revue stage, you would perform on a circular platform that is only eight feet in diameter. That makes it necessary for the pair to contain everything within that spotlight. But acrobatics like you will be doing require run-ups and passes that need to show you can fill the stage with just the two of you. And a few props," Nicole said.

We ran through our moves, getting used to the openness of the space. When we performed in the auditions, the audience would all be in front of the stage, looking in. It wasn't like a circus with a ring in a tent.

"Now let's start putting this to music," she said.

Nicole had access to about as much music as the academy in Florida and knew the catalogue inside and out. The music was mostly brisk, but started with a slow crescendo. This was going to be our big entrance. I did my double tuck salto with a one-and-a-half out to land on the platform, five feet above. I was no more than landed when Sydnie made her pass, launched off the springboard, did a single pike with a half out to land on my shoulders. If that didn't grab the audience right there, we had no hope of anything else moving them.

Like acrobatic gymnastics, we needed to be perfectly timed to the music. We had just three minutes max to impress the judges and then receive their votes. We ran that opening sequence a dozen times before we moved to the next move. In this one, I'd lift Sydnie on the platform and toss her into the air. She would do a single salto and land on the platform where I'd just vacated it. As soon as she was launched, I jumped off the platform onto the springboard and did a full layout with a one-and-a-half out, landing facing Sydnie as she jumped, did a single with a half twist and landed on my hands.

We were thankful for Jon and Steffan spotting us. It took several tries to coordinate throwing Sydnie from a cannonball into the air and vacating the platform so she would have someplace to land. Jon and Stef were up on the platform with us and we'd decided the surface of the platform could be padded. I launched onto the springboard and Nicole kept me from falling on my face several times. She was small, but as strong as any gymnast I'd ever met.

Stef and Jon removed the springboard and platform after that trick, but we were far from finished. By the end of our training day, we'd worked through just half of our routine. We saw Eva come into the gym just as we were finishing up.

After greeting her wife with an enthusiastic kiss, Sydnie excused herself to the therapy room where she took an ice bath. The work we were doing to prepare for the audition was the hardest either of us had worked on extending our abilities in a long time. We had our share of falls and stretched muscles. I'd get an ice bath when I was done with Eva.

"You really took some punishment in the accident," I said as I worked on her body. Even with the lightest of touches, there were places where she winced or even cried out. "I had no idea the extent of your injuries."

"I didn't tell anyone but the doctor," she said. "Please don't tell Syd."

"You can't mean to say she doesn't know!"

"How could I talk about *my* injuries to her when we'd just lost our partner? Lena wasn't our lover, but we'd been together for ten years. We shared everything. She kept us stable in more ways than in our formations. I thought... I was afraid Syd would divorce me when she found out I could no longer support her."

"Oh, Eva! Sydnie loves you." It wasn't exactly professional, but I took Eva in my arms and held her as she cried. "I mean she loves you like my parents love each other. They're always there for each other. They've been together for thirty-two years. You and Sydnie are going to last like that. The only thing it needs is for you both to want it."

I sounded like a marriage counselor. I hadn't been successful in my own relationships. It was just so easy to encourage my friends.

'Friends' was a concept that was taking on a new dimension of meaning in my life. Yes, I had friends among the gymnasts I'd trained with. I had friends among the coaches. But I'd had no friends in high school. At the academy, my friends were those who wanted a ride to the beach. On Team USA, my friends had been those who competed with me. But I felt a deep and comfortable friendship with Sydnie and Eva. I felt like *it* could last as long as we all wanted it to. I could see our friendship extending to going to the beach together when we were all in our sixties or seventies.

I realized that it wasn't just Sydnie I was here for. I was here for Eva as well. I would care for and protect both these women as long as they would have me around.

"Thank you, Paul. Thank you for being here for us. Take care of my Syd on the floor. I trust you with the most precious person in the world."

"I'll protect her with my life," I said.

OCCASIONALLY, THAT BECAME a promise I had to fulfill. Our stunts were incredibly difficult and we were no longer working with even a mat under us on the hardwood. Just like it would be on stage. And that stage was rushing toward us for a Saturday night performance. Nicole briefed us on the entire process. She had an 'in' on the production team for NTS.

"National Talent Search has been holding open auditions for the past months, with agents traveling from city to city to watch every level of talent and determine who would be invited to audition. This year that includes a guy who does bird calls, a fire eater, dozens of acrobats, magicians, contortionists, singers and dancers, and a guy who played the National Anthem in his armpit. There have been garage bands and professionals who make a living with their talent—no matter how meager. They'll all audition here in the next three weeks."

"So how did we manage to get into the audition tonight?" I asked Nicole.

"Talent scouts. This is Las Vegas. I was one of the agents who traveled and reviewed acts in the Southwest. As soon as I saw the two of you working together, I submitted your names for an audition. The only difference between this audition and the open auditions from around the country is there will be a single panel of four judges who will decide who goes to the next round, and there will be an audience. The open auditions were all private and several scouts went to hold them."

"I'm ready," Sydnie said, bouncing up and down.

"You're always ready, little dynamo," I laughed.

SATURDAY WE WERE ready by noon, but spent most of the day just waiting. Auditions took place in three blocks of three hours each. The audience was dismissed and a new audience invited in for each block. The poor judges were sitting through nine hours of acts during the day. I had some sympathy for them. Order was supposedly determined through a drawing, but I suspected there was some manipulation of that so they wouldn't have five singers followed by three acrobats followed by two dog acts and seven comedians. We were finally drawn for the last block of the day, starting at eight o'clock.

We weren't the first to appear that night. We waited backstage in a kind of cattle pen with all the other acts that were scheduled for the evening. I didn't count, but I understood there were twenty-five or thirty acts in each block, with the option of delaying some until the next day if the show ran long. The theatre had reserved VIP tables with eight people at them near the front, around the judges' table, and then rows of seats sloping upward. They could seat around a thousand people. There was a huge bar with waitresses serving all the tables in front, and the 'cheap seats' people getting drinks and snacks to bring to their seats with them.

What we hadn't been told before we arrived was there were cameras and the whole thing was being videotaped. We had to sign a release for the filming and a waiver of liability before we could be a part of it all. A close-up view of each act was projected onto big screens on either side of the stage to make it easier for people who weren't in the select seating up front to see.

At intermission, our number still hadn't been called. There had been some pretty good acts. On the other hand, we wondered why some were there at all. Apparently, the performers were immune to the hooting of the audience and the buzzers of the judges. They'd been on a stage with a thousand people in the audience and that was enough, I guess.

Finally, we were called and went to the front of the stage to face the judges for our introduction and round of questioning while Stef and Jon set up our equipment for the start of the act.

"How long have you been performing together?" one of the male judges asked.

"This is our first time in front of an audience," Sydnie responded. I was in favor of her answering all the questions.

"Have you worked together long?"

"We met and worked together about eight years ago, but our paths were different. Paul is a four-time national gymnastics champion in floor exercises and team silver medalist at the 2028 Olympics. I was part of a women's acrobatic gymnastics team with two World Championship gold medals and have been touring with the group for the past five years. Paul and I met again at the Las Vegas Circus Gym."

"And why are you with Paul instead of your women's group?" asked a blonde lady who looked vaguely familiar, like someone I should know. Her nameplate just said, "Donna."

I thought this judge was more interested in our background than she'd shown for most of the other acts.

"There was an accident and we lost one of our team. I'd rather not go into that any further," Sydnie choked out.

"Enough said. Take a minute to compose yourselves and good luck."

We stepped over to the wings and I hugged Sydnie. She, in turn, raised her lips and gave me a toe-curling kiss.

"Ready?"

"Let's do this!"

I signaled to the tech to start our music. At the first stab, I raced across the floor, did my double pike salto and hit the springboard perfectly, flipping with a one-and-a-half turn to land on my perch and wait for Sydnie. She was on her way and fifteen seconds into our routine, she was standing on my shoulders on the platform and the audience was cheering.

That's the last I was aware of the audience. We focused on our music and moved through each of the elements in our performance. I had no room in my head to spare for what was going on in the theatre. All my attention was on Sydnie.

The music ended and we ended on exactly the last beat in our final pose. Then the sound of the audience crashed in on us and we saw people standing to applaud, including all four judges. We stood to face their evaluation and judgment.

"Wow!" said the first. "My only question is how are you going to improve on that for the live show semi-final? Do you have anything else to give?"

Sydnie shoved the microphone at me.

"We believe it's our responsibility to give the best we have to offer at every performance," I said. "That means we have to get better each time."

"Well, you have my vote."

"I have never seen two people take up so much space in a performance!" said the other woman at the table.

"Our choreographer said we would be competing with some acts that had as many as twenty acrobats in them and we needed to be just as big," Sydnie said.

"I vote yes!"

The next two judges were also complimentary and we ended up with four votes to send us to the next round of the selection. We left the stage to more cheers and applause from the audience.

Offstage, Nicole, our spotters, and we were immediately conducted to an associate producer who explained the details of the next round. It would be in about three weeks, depending on what night that week our act was called back.

"The acrobatics director for the revue will meet with you and give you some coaching for the next round," The producer said.

That was news to me and I glanced up at Nicole. She nodded. Okay, then.

"What sort of coaching should we expect?" Sydnie asked, her nostrils flaring a little.

"She will have advice on preparing a performance for a Las Vegas revue. She won't be interfering directly in your training. She'll have ideas and suggestions for staging, decoration, effects, lighting, and music. You'll have the opportunity to consult with her on your ideas for the next round and she'll come to see your act again as we get closer to the event. Remember, the next round will be recorded for television broadcast and the audience will be voting for which acts should go on. You won't know until after the eight sessions have been recorded."

"That won't give us much time to prepare the next act after that," I mused.

"Oh, the semi-finals won't be held until all eight episodes of the next round have been broadcast. It will be a live broadcast and the viewers will be able to vote as well as the studio audience. So, you'll have about two months from the conclusion of the next round until the live semi-final round. The final will be a month after that, so all the acts have a chance to get fresh material after they know what competition they are up against."

"I guess we'd better get to work," I said.

We left the theatre.

24

NEW COACH, NEW PROBLEM

WE SAID GOOD night to Nicole and our spotters, Jon and Steffan. It looked like we'd be seeing a lot of them over the next month or so. I took Sydnie home and we went in to tell Eva the good news. She was truly overjoyed. I hadn't seen so much life and excitement in her since Sydnie and I started training together. They insisted I make a call to tell my family.

I hadn't really told my family I was auditioning for a show. I mean, why get them all excited when I might be eliminated in the first round. I called Mikey first and she wondered why I was calling her in the middle of the night. Oh. Midnight was no big deal in Las Vegas. It was two in the morning in Minneapolis.

"I did a thing," I said. "A pretty big thing. My partner and I auditioned for a Las Vegas Revue and we passed the first round of auditions. The next round will be broadcast on TV."

"What partner?" Mikey asked sleepily. Trust her to get to the interesting part.

"A few weeks ago, I ran into a woman I trained with

343

at the academy in Florida. We decided to put together an act that could be in a Las Vegas show. It's really good. That was what we auditioned tonight."

"Am I about to have a sister-in-law?"

Mikey was suddenly wide awake and alert. I had a feeling she didn't care in the least about our audition. She wanted to know about my partner.

"Heavens, no! She's my acrobatics partner, not my lover."

"Well, that can change."

"No, it can't. She's married and I love her wife, too. They are both listening in on this call. Sydnie and Eva, say hello to my one-track-mind sister."

"Hello, Mikey!" they chimed in.

"Oh! Married. To each other. I understand. Wonderful! I'll just welcome you both to the family. So, you auditioned and it went well?"

Once the interpersonal stuff was taken care of, Mikey wanted to know all about our act.

"I heard someone say the most popular acts would probably be posted online by sometime tomorrow," Sydnie said. "It's possible you'll be able to see it."

I hadn't heard that and it sent a shiver down my spine for some reason.

"I suppose I should call Mom and Dad and warn them," I said.

"Not until morning! Remember what time it is. Mom and Dad have been going to bed earlier every night it seems. Old people!"

"Well, I normally go to bed early, too," I defended them.

"Bet that changes when you're in a Vegas revue," Mikey laughed.

We got our goodbyes out and I said goodnight to Eva and Sydnie. I half expected to get one of Sydnie's friendly kisses, but when I turned at the door, I saw her and Eva engaged to the exclusion of the rest of the world.

I WENT OUT for Sunday brunch when I got up around ten the next day. I was alone, but not particularly lonely. I was happy for a little time to just absorb the high from what had happened the previous night. I had a nice slab of prime rib, a couple of eggs, fried potatoes, and just to celebrate, a mimosa.

When I got home, I started looking through social media posts and searching the web until I found postings of the acts from the previous night. Sure enough, I found ours. It was a little terrifying to watch through the eyes of the camera. I hadn't actually seen a video of what we were doing. Our coach told us what we needed to know.

I decided I'd better call Mom and Dad immediately.

IT WAS SUNDAY afternoon and Mom and Dad were in the entertainment room relaxing. They immediately found and watched the video as I told them about the competition.

"Paul! This looks far more dangerous than anything you've done before! Is it safe?" Mom asked.

"Um... Sure, Mom. You see the two guys dressed in black that scurry around on the stage moving equipment and watching us? They're our spotters. It's their job to catch us if we fall. You know, we aren't working with the gymnastics rules for this. It's a circus act," I explained, only lying a little.

"It's even riskier than what you did with your pairs partners or in cheerleading," Dad said. "Why don't you at least have mats?"

"Oh, you see that when we have a really high launch, one of the guys is there with a thick cushion for our landing. We just can't cover the whole stage in the prep time we're given. We can't use a sprung floor, so we use a springboard. It can be moved in and out quickly," I explained.

"Do you need an old engineer around to help with the setup and design? I could be persuaded to vacation in Las Vegas for a while," Dad said.

"Dad, you know I'd always welcome you here," I said. "I don't know if there would be enough of a challenge for you to engineer the show. So far, it's just a few mats and a couple of platforms."

"But you got the vote? You're moving to the next level?" Mom asked.

"Yeah. It was cool, Mom. I've never had so many people standing and cheering for something I did like this before. All four judges said 'yes.' The next round is in three or four weeks, depending on how many people get eliminated during the auditions. There are hundreds of acts auditioning."

"I want to know exactly when it is so I can get tickets," Mom said firmly.

"Are you sure you want to see it live?" I asked.

"If my son breaks his neck, I want to be with him," Dad said.

Gee, thanks.

"Now tell us about this cute little girl who's your partner. The titles said 'Sydnie and Paul.'" Mom said.

"Yeah. She's cute, but she's no little girl. She's just two years younger than I am. We met at the academy in Florida and had a chance to work together there a little. We became good friends, but her women's group was on a very different path than I was, so they left the academy for a school in Montreal the second year I was there."

"A women's group?" Dad asked. "You mean one of those trios we saw performing when you were with Tara?"

"Yes. They competed and then toured and performed all over the world. They won a couple of World Championships. They were on their way here to train for the same audition Sydnie and I took. They were in an auto accident between LA and here and one of the girls, Lena, was killed. She was really a... She was..." I struggled a little as the pain of losing Lena washed over me again. "We were really close at one time. But... anyway... the base, Eva, was also hurt and felt she needed to retire, which left Sydnie with no support. I mean, she and Eva still live together. They're married, but Eva isn't going to perform. When I saw Sydnie in the gym it was like a compulsion to ask her to perform with me. I think she's a real star. We really work well together."

"Yes, you do. Remember, Sydnie and Eva will be welcome here, too, if you all want to come to visit."

"Thanks, Mom. I'm afraid we won't be going anyplace as long as we're in this competition. We've got our work cut out for us."

"Good luck, son."

Sydnie and I were in the gym early Monday morning and started stretching and working out. Jon and Steffan were our spotters and when they got in, they immediately started rolling out mats on the hardwood and marking out the stage dimensions. Nicole came in with a sheaf of papers and directions regarding what equipment we'd need to start with besides our platform and springboard.

"I've cancelled all your massage and coaching for the duration," she told me. It had been pretty limited over the past three weeks. I'd still massage Eva and Sydnie whenever they needed it, though. "The show is covering your expenses while you prepare the next performance. But that doesn't include a salary. I'm putting you both on a scholarship that will put enough in your pockets to pay the rent and food for the next month. This is as important to the gym as it is to the revue."

"That's very generous of you, Nicole. We won't let you down," I said.

"I've been certain of that since the first day I met you. And you, Sydnie. A flyer like you could join about any act in Vegas. Are you sure you want to go through with this?"

"Oh, yes. There is nothing any act in town could offer me that could compete with what I have here," Sydnie said.

"Then let's start by going over a critique of your performance on Saturday. Staff! Let's review."

Apparently, everyone who worked at the gym had been at the event Saturday and took notes. They ranged from Jon and Steffan needing to either disappear or take part, to suggestions for another more difficult throw. Some liked our use of the full stage and some felt it diluted the performance. There was something we could take away from nearly every comment, though.

"Okay. I see our guest has arrived. Staff can go about your work. This is the acrobatics director for the New Trop Revue, Tara White."

My head snapped up and I looked straight into the eyes of my former lover. It was like being punched in the gut. Sydnie saw my reaction and realized at once who this was. She grabbed my arm and squeezed.

"Tara," I choked.

"Long time, Paul. You're looking great."

"You, too."

In fact, Tara looked incredible. I noted that she had left a pair of walking canes by the front desk and walked across the floor unassisted. She was just so damned beautiful. It broke my heart all over again.

Sydnie jumped up and moved beside Nicole, who had a puzzled look on her face.

"If you two need a minute, we can take a break," Sydnie said, pulling at Nicole.

"No. It's not necessary," Tara said. "I'm on a tight schedule and just wanted to stop by today to congratulate you on the performance Saturday. You really kicked it up a notch. I was impressed."

"Paul is a wonderful base. I'd be flat on my face if he wasn't so steady," Sydnie said.

"I hear you. Let's just sit down a minute and I'll go over a couple of notes. I've looked over the list of acrobatic acts that made it to the live auditions over the next three weeks. I actually reviewed a couple of the acts myself and invited them to audition. Seeing your names pop up was a real surprise. Sydnie, I heard about the accident and I'm so sorry for you. I'm familiar with what that can do to you and I know the pain never goes completely away. I'm so glad you found Paul."

"He's a rock," Sydnie said.

"Paul, you've made quite a name for yourself over the past few years. You can't expect the judges to have known who you are. They aren't gymnastics professionals. But you impressed them."

"Thanks. I don't really know what they are looking for," I said. "We just followed Nicole's advice and it worked."

"Nicole is a fantastic coach and you're lucky to have found her," Tara said. "As to what the judges are looking for, they want a balance of acts that will play for a year or more together. Unlike some of the talent shows you may have seen, this isn't a contest to arrive at the one best talent among the hundreds we're auditioning. As good as your act is, you couldn't survive doing ninety minutes of it."

"I'll say," I said.

"For the show, you'll probably have to put together about ten minutes of a dedicated act—maybe twice during a show. In addition to that, the troupe will interact with the other performers and may do a stunt or two that is not in their principal routine. We have a rough guideline regarding how many acts of what kind are needed for the revue. The final selection will include the mix for the production."

"So, what does it take to be selected?" Sydnie asked.

"Audience plays a huge part in it all. The judges are looking for audience pleasers. But the audience is voting for their favorites; *they* aren't trying to create a revue. Left to their own devices, the audience might choose six singers which would make for a boring revue. So, the judges are looking for balance among the acts, excitement, and a secret sauce."

"A what?"

"I'm not being facetious. The secret sauce is that something that no one has seen before. The something that takes their breath away. They want people who see the finale at home in Pittsburgh to start thinking they need a vacation in Las Vegas so they can see the show live. It is very subjective," Tara said.

"So, are you going to be coaching us now?" Sydnie asked.

"No, not as such. You have a great coach in Nicole. She has a lot of experience with acrobatics in Las Vegas shows and in touring shows, which this might lead to as well. What I'll be doing is more general. I'll make some suggestions about the overall performance, but not usually about the specific elements. For example: You showed a great use of the full stage Saturday. In putting together the revue, the director might decide he needs to reserve a large part of the stage for setup of the next act and want you to perform in a more limited space. So, now that you've shown us the broad performance, you might want to show us a narrow version. How many tricks can you do in a smaller space? Say, a space that can be lit by four spotlights rather than all the lights in the theatre."

"I get it. I hope you'll be sharing more with us, though. I have a limitless respect for your opinion—and for you," I said.

There. I'd said something that maybe would let Tara know how I still felt about her. I knew nothing about her current situation. She was still Tara White, but lots of people get married and don't change their names. She could have kids, or have discovered she preferred girls. Or have just fallen completely out of love with me.

"Among the things I'll be coordinating with you is the kind of support you'll need. For example, what would be the best backdrop to use? The best lighting and music? The best costuming? How many people do we need to provide besides your props spotters and coach in order to make you successful? What can you do to show that you could integrate into the show in more ways than your one act? Do you need to show more dance moves? You can't even imagine the number of factors that will go into the judges' final decisions."

"Where should we start?" Sydnie asked.

"Work with Nicole. Each time you appear on that stage, you need to up the bar, not only for yourselves, but for everyone else competing for this slot. More breathtaking, more dangerous, more beautiful. Now, you also need to understand that I will be working with all the other acrobatic acts that pass the first audition. In fact, I'm meeting with a group that performed last night later today, before they fly home to New York to prepare for their next performance. I'll be giving them the same advice and service to make their next performance better. What I personally want will not make a lot of difference in the selection. I'll direct the acrobatics in the revue, not choose who the cast is."

"Thank you, Tara," Nicole said. "I believe we have our orders. When will we see you again?"

"I'll plan on spending most of next Monday with you if you have built your plan for the next performance. I'll let you know if there are things I think will or won't sell well and talk about the next steps to the live selection," Tara said. "Sydnie and Paul, you look great together. You have great chemistry. I'm looking forward to what comes next. See you next Monday."

With that, she turned and walked back to the front desk, picked up her walking canes and left. No hugs. No kisses. No I love you and I've missed you so much. None of the things I was feeling.

WE WENT STRAIGHT to work with Nicole to determine what we could do that would be more spectacular than what we already did. The full floor passes were out, so our spectacular entrance wasn't going to be the same.

"Dance!" Nicole said. "We'll start with a nice slow

dance, maybe to something soft and jazzy that gets wound up a little in the middle. Let's try some moves."

We started moving where we were told. Neither of us were professional dancers, but dance had been a significant portion of Sydnie's performances. I picked it up pretty quickly, though it might have been easier if we'd actually had music.

"Now, when you spin out under Paul's hand, the normal would be to spin back and have him wrap you up. We'll change that up. This is where your sweet moment will explode. Paul, as she spins out, stretch your left leg toward her and lean away until you are at maximum extension. Sydnie, don't spin all the way in. Half a turn and walk right up Paul's leg and torso until you are on his shoulder."

It took a couple of tries, just to get the mechanics down, let alone moving smoothly into the pose.

"I don't think I've ever seen a dance move like that!" Sydnie exclaimed.

"That's because most dancers aren't acrobats. Now that you are perched up there, what do we do with you?"

And that was how our practice session went. We worked on mats while we were learning new moves. Jon and Steffan were attentive and managed to keep us from getting injured. I was sure ready for my ice bath after that practice.

"I love it. Nicole, you're brilliant as always," Tara exclaimed on Monday when she visited us again.

"We just need music and a theme," Nicole said.

"And something just a little more daring in the acrobatics. The dance is superb, but we need to up the thrill level."

We talked for a while and brainstormed a few ideas for music. We'd all heard something different in our heads when we were practicing.

"How about a romantic rooftop setting," Tara said. "The backdrop would be a nighttime cityscape low, fading into a dark night and a million stars in the sky. We can disguise your platforms as vents and air conditioner things that you'd find on a rooftop."

"And a big moon," Nicole said. Tara looked at her and both women shouted at once.

"Moondance!"

"When Paul throws Sydnie for the first time, she tries to reach for the moon. Every so often in the routine, maybe with the chorus, we should have her reach again, getting higher and higher each time."

"There might be a limit to how high I can throw her," I said.

"Not if we use the springboard," Nicole said. "Throw her and let her land on the board to launch again. You just need to catch her when she comes down."

We seemed to have the routine, music, and theme. Now we just needed to make it perfect. The next few weeks of practice were brutal.

Nor was the routine the only thing we worked on. Nicole and Tara kept trying out new moves on us, even if we decided we couldn't have them ready for the next round. We got our assigned performance date and I let Mom and Dad know. They promised they would be there and we should get tickets for all five of them.

I wondered why Sydnie never spoke of or called her family. Trust Mikey to jump in where I was too polite to go.

"What does your family think of all this?" Mikey asked during one of our calls when Sydnie was listening in. "They must be as excited as we are."

"Oh, I don't see or talk to my family too often," Sydnie said. "They're still in New Zealand. If we make the final cut, I'll ask them to come for the finale. We only talk about once a month when we can coordinate our time and schedule."

"That must be terribly hard on you. How long have you been apart?" Mikey asked.

"I moved to the US alone when I was fourteen—eleven years ago. Oh, my mother came with me, but as soon as I was settled at the academy, she went back to New Zealand and my four brothers."

"That must have been really difficult," I said.

"I was a little wild," Sydnie laughed. "I guess that's when I started giving out friendly kisses. It was amazing how quickly I made friends. I'd only been there a year when Eva, Lena, and I decided to start working as a team."

"And some friendly kisses became a lot friendlier!" Eva laughed.

"Friendly kisses?" Mikey asked.

"You'll find out," Sydnie giggled.

My sister was going to have an experience!

We met my family at the hotel the day before our performance. Mikey found out quickly what a friendly kiss was in Sydnie's parlance. Eva was with us, too, and Mom just wrapped both girls in her arms. Eva's family was in Canada, where they'd moved after immigrating to the US. They found a warmer welcome in Canada, they said. They planned to come to Vegas for the finale if we made it that far.

"You have a new family in the U.S.," Mom declared. "If we had known who Paul was hanging out with in Florida, we would have adopted you then. Please, always feel you can come home to us, even if you and Paul aren't working together."

"You might not want to go in December, though," I laughed. "It's cold."

"You won't have to worry about that much longer," Dad said. "We've found a nice little place in Sedona, Arizona. As soon as the house sells, we're moving."

That sparked a lot of questions and discussion of the relative merits of the two places. We kind of all decided right then and there that we'd meet in Sedona for Christmas if we could.

The next day, of course, we were focused on the performance. Eva was with my family at a VIP table. She'd watched our audition on the internet and decided she wanted to be closer this time.

It was great to have our families in the audience to watch us. I always felt I did better when the family was present. History might not have borne that out, but I felt better when they were there.

Of course, this was an audience selection competition (with caveats). The judges asked us questions after our performance and complimented us on raising the bar even higher. They encouraged everyone to vote for us, but the results would not be available immediately. The show was taped for broadcast starting in a month. Just prior to the beginning of the broadcasts, they would run a compilation of the winning auditions.

We would find out who was moving on from this performance when Tara called us on Monday. In the meantime, there was nothing to do but enjoy a relaxing day with our family.

"Uncle Paul! Throw me!" PJ exclaimed when we met for Sunday brunch. I picked the tyke up and tossed her in the air and caught her. "Again! Again!"

"Monster," Mikey said. "I've already enrolled her in a toddler tumbling class. If she goes further than that, I'm sending her to live with you!"

"I can think of worse things," I laughed. "I managed to survive living with her mother!" Mikey slugged me in the shoulder.

We settled in for the buffet champagne brunch, laughed, reviewed the performance from the night before, and eventually my family left for the airport.

Sydnie and Eva left me and I headed back to my little bachelor pad. I'd never gotten around to getting a larger place.

25

GETTING IT STRAIGHT

I WAS WATCHING TELEVISION Sunday evening when my phone played an old familiar tune. I think I stared at it until it was near to disconnecting before I forced myself to answer.

"Hello."

"Paul! It's wonderful," Tara said. "I've just received the list from the weekend shows and you made the cut. You'll be going to the live broadcast semi-finals in three months. The judges loved the range you showed between your audition and last night. But the audience just went wild for you. You were the top vote-getter from the weekend."

"That's wonderful, Tara. Thank you for calling!"

"I couldn't wait for tomorrow. I'm so excited to work with you on the next level for the semi-finals. The judges want you to take it up a notch again, of course, but there is a new element in the next show. In addition to your performance as a duo, they want to see you work with another group. It's all about seeing if you can integrate into a full show or if you are strictly a one-act combo."

"What do they want us to do?"

358

"It seems that they think you could do something with the trampoline act. Have you worked on the trampolines?"

"Yes, a little. I'm afraid I haven't gotten very far. They really want us to do a trampoline act with guys who have been doing it for years?" I asked.

"It's all about creating the ensemble," Tara said. "Personally, I don't think the trampoline act will make the final cut. What they want to see is if you can work with a group. Every position in the revue has its specialty, but is also part of the greater ensemble. It's a ninety-minute show and they don't want to have eighteen five-minute performances by eighteen different groups. There will be acts that might feature one group, but involve nearly everyone around them."

"I guess I can see the sense in that. How soon do we need to start working with the trampoline people?" I asked.

"Not for another month yet. That should give you time to train on the trampoline with Nicole before you even meet up with the others. I'll be telling them much the same thing. Their part of the act will be how well they can back you and Sydnie up. I'll probably have them shadow your spotters, for example. Is there a way you can integrate the spotters a little more?"

"Sydnie and I worked with her other two partners when I auditioned at GAC. They were our spotters, and even though the focus was on what Sydnie and I could do, we had them in similar costumes and they tumbled and posed next to us."

"That's what I'm talking about!" Tara said. "We can cover the details when I come to the gym tomorrow."

"Thank you, Tara. I can't believe you called my phone to give me the news in advance."

"Well, I don't have Sydnie's numb… Oh, my God! I'm so sorry, Paul. Please tell Sydnie I just called to give you *both* the news. I didn't mean to invade your privacy. I'll see you tomorrow. *Both* of you. Really. I didn't mean to make it awkward. Goodnight, Paul. See you."

"Goodnight, Tara." I think she'd hung up before I got the words out. "I love you," I whispered.

I thought about it for a minute but figured it would be awkward tomorrow if I didn't call Sydnie tonight and let her know.

SYDNIE AND I were both dragging a little in the morning when we got to the gym. We stretched and got warmed up as we continued our talk from the night before. We'd spent three hours on the phone brainstorming with Eva. What the hell were we going to do on a trampoline?

Sydnie gave me a hug when we got together, but we were both too tired for a friendly kiss.

"I suppose if we have just the flat trampoline, we can treat it like the sprung floor," Sydnie suggested as we stretched.

"Except that when you bounce on the sprung floor, the rest of it stays stable," I said. "When a person bounces on the trampoline, the whole surface gives. We've spent all this time disciplining ourselves to work on the hardwood. I'd never be in position to catch you."

"It worries me," she said. "We did trampoline at the academy, but it was just an exercise, not for our show."

"Well, with a month before we need to integrate with the other group, we should at least get comfortable with the tramp. What do you think we should be doing for the next performance of our act?" I asked.

"Eva suggested the rola bola."

We paused our warm-up and just stood there talking for a while.

"It's a good thing we've got three months to prepare," I said. "I'm okay on it now, but I've never tried to work with another person on me while I balanced on it."

"I don't know how I'd mount you on it. I think I'd have to climb. I don't think you could launch me or that I could spring to you. Hmm. Maybe. I foresee a lot of work for Jon and Steffan in this act. I don't want to break any bones—or my neck."

"What are you two talking about so intently that you aren't warming up?" Nicole asked, approaching us.

"Oh! Tara called last night and said we'd made it to the next round with high marks. I guess we're not sup-posed to let that out, though. The semi-finalists won't be announced until the end of the current round of auditions is aired starting in a month or so. I still don't know the exact schedule."

"She *called* you on Sunday night?" Nicole asked.

"Mine was the only direct phone she had, but Sydnie and I were up half the night afterward. Tara said she'd be coming here this morning, but not to expect her before ten."

"That's very unusual," Nicole said. "Paul, do you have a history with Tara?"

I figured she meant our history as lovers, but I wasn't going to go into that.

"Oh. Uh… I partnered with Tara after her accident to do an exhibition at the 2024 Nationals to show how far she'd been able to recover after her accident. She was great to work with."

"Ah. I see. Well, let's get the staff together and get their critique of your performance Saturday before they hear Tara's. Don't say a word about being selected."

We got the whole team together again and listened to what they had to say. Jon and Steffan, of course, had a unique perspective, having been on stage and up close to us. They identified a couple of missteps that the audience probably hadn't been aware of.

"Yes, I almost overshot the platform on the last attempt to grab the moon," Sydnie laughed. "It was such a relief to see you standing below to catch me if I lost my balance any further."

"I liked the addition of dance to your routine," one of the other staff said. I guess they'd all gone to watch the show. "I didn't like it being the focus, though. I felt your acrobatics were lost or overshadowed in the dance routine. It should be more obvious that you are acrobats who dance rather than dancers who tumble a bit."

"I think the danger level wasn't perceived as highly as your audition piece," another offered. "I know some of the things you did were pretty risky, but they need to *look* riskier. Even having to stop and get your balance before a move would let people know you are straining all your muscles to do this act."

"I'd have to second that," Nicole said. "The things you did were dangerous and risky and exciting, but they weren't thrilling. That relates more to the showmanship than to the actual tricks. We need to work on making it look more thrilling, even if it is a simpler move."

It was ten by the time the staff was through with their critiques and we'd learned a lot about the perception. Not only had they all been at the show, they'd sat in different sections, so we got a well-rounded view of the act. When Tara walked in, using her canes, our meeting broke up and she joined just the five of us.

"Well, the big news, if you haven't heard yet, is that you are moving on to the semi-finals. I called Paul last night to tell him when I got the news. Sydnie, I'm so sorry I didn't call you, but I didn't have your number. Maybe we can correct that now, since we'll be working more closely in the next three months preparing for the semis," Tara began. "The word that you are moving on is to be closely held, by the way. The fewer people who know, the better."

"How much more closely will you be involved?" Nicole asked.

"I don't want to take any of your responsibilities as a coach," Tara began. "My position with the company is as the artistic director of acrobatics. So, I'll ask you for things and if they are possible, you'll work on getting Paul and Sydnie ready to perform them."

We all nodded our understanding.

"So, let's go over the comments from the judges. They say only a few words after the performance, but they write up a pretty extensive report after the show."

"Who are these judges, anyway?" I asked. "I'm sure I don't recognize any of them."

"No. You aren't likely to. Sam Michaels is the president of The New Trop. He has utterly no talent at all, but he has the money. Money talks. Lee Remy is the managing director of the Revue. His responsibility is the overall theme, composition, and look of the show. If you just go around to shows in Vegas, you'll find different themes. Water shows, ribald sexy shows, music shows, Old West shows, magic shows, and just about any theme you might imagine. He will give the framework to the artistic directors and will coordinate with the technical director and designer."

"Does *he* have talent?" Sydnie asked snidely.

"Actually, yes. He has directed several hit shows and has worked with some of the top artists in Las Vegas.

He was a dancer on Broadway at the start of his career. And he's my boss," Tara said. "Ariel Deneuve is a performer in one of the top revue shows in Vegas. She had a minor accident this year and got pregnant. She performed as long as she could, but it coincidentally allowed her to take the gig of judging this competition. In the words of the movie *Sister Act*, she is not a showgirl; she's a headliner."

Another of my mother's favorite movies. I was reminded of Tara's and my first date and our common taste in old movies. It made me a little wistful and I almost missed the last judge.

"You would probably know Donna Kapelle, but you might not recognize her by sight. She plays Delilah in the television western drama, *Gold Rush*. She has a long list of acting credits on stage, film, and TV. She's known for having a keen eye for talent and has started several careers for young performers."

"So, we have three months to put together a new act," Nicole said. "Do you have some ideas?"

"Yes, but before we get to the artistic part, we should take care of business. If you don't have one yet, you need an agent. It will not be long before you'll need to negotiate your contracts. Nicole, you probably have better contacts in that department than I do."

Nicole nodded.

"For the next three months, you will all five be put on a probationary contract that will give you a living wage while you are expected to all be working full-time on your next performance," Tara continued. "That wage is set in the rules of the competition and is non-negotiable. Believe me, I think you will like the terms. It is, however, your opportunity to back out if you wish. Finally, as I mentioned to Paul last night, you will be working with another act for the semi-finals. This is in addition to your next dedicated performance. This is to show the judges and audience that you can work as part of an ensemble."

"Is everyone required to do that?" Nicole asked.

"Yes. And it will be much harder for some of them. I feel especially bad for magicians. They will need to work with another aspect of the show in order to move on. They might be performing by making a dancer disappear or some such."

"I think I'd rather have been working with dancers than with a trampoline group," Sydnie said.

"A what?" Nicole exploded.

That got us into what needed to happen in preparation for the semi-finals. It was going to be a brutal three months. Thank goodness, we had a stipend that provided a living wage. We also had a stack of information regarding agent responsibilities to the performer and to the show, union information that was not needed until we were actually cast, and a list of names and responsibilities of the dozens of people supporting the performances. We'd have a lot to work on.

Tara said goodbye after lunch and was gone before I could pull her aside to talk to her.

"WHAT ARE YOU going to do, Paul?" Sydnie asked. "We see her every week and you hardly speak to her. You must be dying inside."

"I don't know what to do. She keeps her distance and never gets into anything personal. I don't think she wants to get close to me," I answered.

"You don't see what I see," she responded. "I see her aching to get close to you, but afraid you'll reject her. I can't imagine going through what she must go through every day, coaching acrobats in moves she once did but can't do anymore. She must think all anyone sees is her canes. She doesn't even use them all the time."

"She was always a little self-conscious about them. I'm surprised to see her use them as much as she does. Her legs are fine as long as she doesn't stress them. When they get tired is when she needs support."

"See, you know her better than she knows herself," Sydnie persisted. "You have to talk to her."

"How can I talk to her when she won't stop to talk?"

"Good grief, Paul! Use your phone! She called you on a Sunday night. You must have her number. Call it!"

That might have been obvious to some, but I almost never made *calls* on my cell phone. I considered texting her first, but she'd just either not respond or would text back not to call. I guessed it would be better if I just called. But what would I say?

I looked up every reference to Tara White I could find on the internet to see if she was in a relationship. There were a few pictures of some guy or another escorting her to big gymnastic events, but never even a name. We'd been working together for five months and would be performing in the semi-finals in just a couple of weeks.

I finally just bit the bullet and called her Thursday evening.

"Paul? Are you okay? You aren't injured, are you? Is Sydnie all right?"

"We're fine, Tara. I just wanted to talk for a bit. Preparations for this event have really taken a toll on all of us, but we're tremendously excited to perform week after next."

"Oh, good. That's a relief," she sighed. "Well, what's on your mind?"

You, I thought. *Isn't it obvious?*

"Oh, we were just talking about how well we seem to be integrating with the tramp team. You don't think they'd want us to just join that team and not do our own act, do you?"

"Not a chance. It's your individual act they're interested in. The team event is just to show you are able to work well with others. Your new act is going to kill," Tara said enthusiastically.

"I'm glad you think so. As long as it doesn't kill us. We've worked hard to perfect it."

"Relax and enjoy the time. It's your moment to shine."

"Would you like to go out tomorrow night, Tara?" I blurted out. "Dinner? A show?"

"Paul! You know that's not a good idea. What's gotten into you?"

"I still love you, Tara. I miss you so much!"

"Well, that doesn't do a lot of good now, does it?"

"Why not? Is it too late for you? Do I not mean anything to you anymore?"

"You're with Sydnie! What kind of woman would I be to step between you? I'm not a cheater and won't put up with one. Even if not, I wouldn't do anything that might cause you to break up when you are at the doorstep of success!" Tara practically shouted. I jumped in before she could hang up.

"Tara! I'm not *with* Sydnie! I'm not with anyone. Sydnie is married. To a very nice woman and close friend of mine. I'd never do anything to hurt either of them."

"But... I saw her kiss you!"

"You saw Madison kiss me once, too. Is that what this is all about?"

"It looked a lot more passionate than Madison's kiss."

"Sydnie expresses her excitement with 'friendly kisses.' Her idea of friendly is pretty intense. We kiss once, maybe in a month or two. I'm surprised she hasn't planted one on you yet. She about blew my sister's socks off."

"Wait! You aren't... Really... You aren't living with Sydnie... or dating her... or making love with her... or anything?"

"Sydnie is a wonderful friend. Eva is a wonderful friend. Not only that, Sydnie is a fantastic acrobatics partner. But we aren't lovers."

"But you're so connected in your acts. The fire and passion that you have. The way you look at each other." Tara was panting out the words.

"You told me eight years ago I needed to establish a stronger connection with my acrobatics partner and I needed to show fire and emotion. Gosh, coach! I'm just doing what you said," I laughed.

"I've been miserable working with you for five months and never having a minute alone with you to really catch up. I saw you with Sydnie and thought you were a perfect couple. I didn't want to spoil anything for you."

"Let me ask you again, Tara. Would you like to go out tomorrow night? At least to dinner so we can sit and talk for a while and really catch up with each other's lives?"

"I... Yes. I'd like that."

"Text me your address and I'll pick you up at seven. I'd say six, but we don't usually quit practicing before then."

"Seven will be fine. I'm looking forward to it already."

"So am I!"

I was pretty worthless during practice on Friday. I even face-planted once. Not fun when you aren't working with mats. Stef felt terrible about not getting under me, but I rather took him by surprise.

"What's wrong?" Sydnie asked when we took a break after my fall.

"It's not wrong! I don't think. I'm going out with Tara tonight," I breathed.

"That's wonderful!" she said grabbing me to hug me tightly. "I just don't know why it has taken you so long!"

"She thought we were married. Or at least that we were involved with each other," I said.

"What? What could give her that idea?"

"Our connection and emotion in the act," I said. "And a friendly kiss she once observed."

"Oh, my God! She thought that meant we were together? Like that? I'm so sorry," Sydnie said.

"Don't be sorry. You know I *do* love you, just as I love Eva. You're pretty much my best friends in the world, and I feel incredibly connected with you. You're a wonderful partner."

"When Eva became my girlfriend—Gosh! I was fifteen!—it was a bit of a shock to Lena. By then, we had enough experience to know what it took to perform as a team, though. To watch us, you'd have thought all three of us were lovers. Eva and I both loved Lena intensely, but not as lovers. The same was true of her. We miss her so much! Just the other night, Eva said that you and I worked so well together, it was almost like watching Lena and me."

"I'd give up all this if Lena and Eva could still be performing with you," I said.

"No offense, but so would I. Paul, when we work together, I do feel a little like Lena is with us—maybe in you. But when I look at you and you catch me in the air, I think, this is my best friend and my partner and my safety net. Now, let's do this thing again and try not to knock your teeth out."

We headed back to the floor and I mounted the rola bola. This time, I maintained my balance as Sydnie flew from the springboard to my shoulders. To my knowledge, no other duo had ever performed a flying mount on the rola bola. This definitely upped our risk factor. Stef hung nearby to make sure I didn't fall again and I reminded him that the number one priority was to protect Sydnie. Regardless, his assistance wasn't needed as we did the move flawlessly.

Of course, just mounting my shoulders while I was on the rola bola wasn't enough. As soon as I was steady with her up, she put her hands on my head and pressed herself into a handstand. That was pretty exciting, but from there, she lifted one hand so she was doing a one-handed stand on my head while she did a couple different poses like she would have in acro-gym competition.

Being centered on my head was easier to maintain my balance than what came next. I raised my hand and Sydnie transferred from my head to my hand as she did an incredible Mexican arch as I counter-balanced her on the board.

If that didn't make people stand up and cheer, I wasn't sure if anything would.

We worked on our portion of the trampoline act next. When the trampolines were in use, there was one on either side of the stage at an angle. The acrobats often flew between them. In the middle was a flat tramp. It was different than what you might have in your back yard. First, it was rectangular instead of a circle, and second, it had a lot more spring to it. It wasn't unusual to find an acrobat turning flips twenty feet in the air.

Sydnie and I had just a small part in the combined routine. We jumped from a platform onto side-by-side springboards. That propelled us into the air far enough we could both do a double and land together on the tramp. We did a lot of side-by-side moves, then we altered our synchronization so Sydnie was in the air while I bounced on the tramp. We did a flying mount, so Sydnie landed on my shoulders as I was going up and she was coming down. We had a launch into a flip that might have exceeded the twenty feet we were supposed to stay below, and I caught Sydnie as she landed for our dismount. It was a pretty good bit and the other guys would be flying past us from one end tramp to the other.

"You need to go home and get ready for your date!" Sydnie yelled at me about five-thirty.

"I need ten minutes in the ice before I do that," I said. "I'm picking her up at seven."

"Don't get in a situation of having to rush!" I was instructed.

"Yes, Mom," I laughed.

"And have fun!"

I got to the therapy room and eased into the ice. That hurt, but it would feel better later. I got a shower and dressed.

As it turned out, I was in my car sitting outside Tara's fancy house at ten till.

26
LOVE OF MY LIFE

"I HOPE YOU DON'T think this is too downscale for our date," I said when we arrived at an Italian chain restaurant in Henderson. "I just wanted someplace quiet enough to talk and not be distracted."

"It's perfect," she said. "You know I love pasta."

"I think I can stand a meal of rich sauces and carbs," I laughed. "Besides, I tell myself I come here for the great salad."

"I can't believe we're out together," Tara sighed "I was so certain you were with Sydnie and I was determined not to mess it up. I figured I had lost my opportunity."

"I'm glad you think being with me is an opportunity. I had no idea if you were in a relationship either. At least none of your social media profiles listed a significant other."

"No. There hasn't been one in a long time. I admit, I tried. There was always something missing. I think... well, maybe you were the only one who never really seemed to recognize my disability. Even though I get along pretty well, my legs are skinny and marked from the braces I wear. I'm never in a skirt because it's ugly."

"I learned to know you as a partner on the mats. There was no room for a disability there. And I've always thought you were the most beautiful woman I ever met."

"It seems so long ago. Didn't you ever find someone who could... um... be with you?" Tara asked.

"I thought I had once. I stayed in Bulgaria for a year and a half because of a woman. It turned out that we both had higher commitments to our goals than to each other. She was an entrepreneur with a rising tech company, and I still thought I could make the Olympic team. It came down to either her quitting her job or me giving up on the Olympics. Neither of us could give in. Then I failed to make the team anyway."

"You should have made it. The committee really damaged their reputation among the gymnasts by making the decision they did. It's threatened to blow up like the whole women's world did back in 2016. Even the athletes who were chosen made statements that the selection hadn't been fair. And the kid they decided to put on the team because you were too old, didn't perform as well under the Olympic spotlight."

"I don't wish them any ill-will. I feel happier doing these circus routines with Sydnie than I ever felt doing gymnastics. Isn't that weird? I always thought I *needed* to be a gymnast in order to be me," I said.

We took a minute to dig into our salads and munch a breadstick. After all the preparation and excitement over finally going out, I wasn't sure where to take the conversation.

"I spent five years at the university in California," Tara finally said. "I had some good students. But I just didn't find a fit for me as a person. Every time I took a student team to a competition, I kept thinking of what it would have been like if I was competing. It just made me too sad."

"Is that what prompted you to move to Las Vegas?" I asked.

"Yes, in a way. One of my teams came here to perform in a show. It was a short contract, but I came with them and coached them through their act. When they decided to go on tour, I decided to stay. One of the directors who had seen me coaching them approached me about doing the art direction for the New Trop acrobatics. I was ready for the change and signed on."

"So, this is the second year of the show?"

"Yes," Tara said. "The first year of National Talent Search didn't yield as good a selection of acts as this year did. I guess that's been typical of just about every talent type show in the past fifty years. The real talent doesn't show up until the second year. Lee will probably hold one or two acts over from last year, but he really wants a whole new show."

"Well, a year working wouldn't be a bad thing," I sighed. "I suppose they'll replace everyone again next year."

"Don't count on it. The intent behind the Talent Search is to find one or two new acts for the main show. Sam's plan is to get a touring company together as well. He's even got an option on a Broadway theatre for a run in New York."

"Wow! I didn't know shows like a revue did tours."

"It's all about driving audience. Sam wants the New Trop Revue to be a driving force for national entertainment. He hired Lee to make it happen."

"That's a lot of pressure."

"I'm thankful *that* isn't my job," Tara laughed.

Our entrees arrived and we had to spend several minutes just enjoying the food and commenting on how sinful it was to be eating so many calories. I didn't really worry about that too much. I probably burned three times the calories each day that a normal person does. Maybe more. I just tried to have really healthy intake.

Tara had definitely put on a few pounds since I'd last seen her. I was sure I could still pick her up and toss her into a handstand, but I could see a slightly more womanly shape. Not that she'd had a doubtful shape when we were dating. I still remembered being slapped by Penny for grabbing her boobs and not having realized it. I'd known it every time I touched Tara.

Wow! What a woman!

"You know, when I went to the academy, they auditioned me immediately for pairs or group acro-gym," I said, thinking about having worked with Tara. "They never pushed it, but they always let me know it was an open avenue. Maybe I should have gone straight into that like Sydnie, Eva, and Lena did."

"Don't shortchange your gymnastic training, Paul. You were... *are* a fantastic gymnast. If you weren't so skilled and confident in your gymnastic abilities, you would never be able to do the kind of acrobatic tricks we've been asking of you. And Sydnie is able to shine because she's confident in your ability and in your commitment to never let her fall. You can't imagine how much that means to a flyer."

"I started toying with the circus tricks while I was still committed to gymnastics. Karov encouraged it while I was in Bulgaria. He felt circus acrobatics were basically what you would get if you didn't have all the rules governing the sport of gymnastics. Everyone would be trying to do a two-and-a-half with a one-and-a-half out.

Even if it killed some of them, others would relish the challenge," I said.

"You have common sense the bulk of athletes don't have," Tara insisted. "You know to work in a gym and to have spotters and instructors when you are learning new acts. You know, by the way, that either you'll need to truly integrate Stef and Jon into your act or you'll need to work without spotters when you hit the stage bigtime."

"That's a little frightening. The question is, 'Will Stef and Jon want to make a career move as spotters and setup men?' I don't know what that would pay, but they're both talented acrobats in their own regard."

"Your agent will take care of that. You do have an agent now, don't you?"

"Yeah. He signed both Sydnie and me as an act. I'm not sure how he's handling Stef and Jon," I said. "Did you know we've already received offers from other shows? One scout even offered a place with a team in China!"

"I should have warned you about that. The New Trop is footing the bill for this entire competition, and they will try to tie up everyone before the finale. Your contract, that pays you while you're training, has a stipulation that you will not accept any offers from other sources as long as you are competing in this one," Tara said. "Of course, if your agent found a fantastic deal that you couldn't pass up, you could withdraw from the competition and leave."

"I'm not going to do that again. I'm not going to leave you to follow a hollow dream without you. I wanted to marry you then and I should have followed you to California when you left," I declared.

"Shh. It's too soon to make declarations. I've never stopped loving you, but I don't know if I could still say that if we'd gotten married and moved to California together. I'd guess we'd have had a couple of good years, a few bad, and we'd be divorced by now instead of dating."

"Are we dating now, Tara?"

"Isn't this a date, Paul?"

"Yes. Yes, it is."

Neither of us were willing to end our date and go home. Of course, I wondered if Tara and I would make love later tonight, but like it had been eight years before, I was not going to push things. I shouldn't have mentioned marriage already, but being with Tara unlocked all the feelings I'd hidden away when we broke up. I was still very much in love.

We decided to order dessert and coffee as we continued to talk. Every so often, one of us would reach across the table and touch the other's hand. The touches became longer and longer, until we had scooted our chairs closer together and just held hands.

"Honey, as much as I've been looking forward to this, we should take it slow. Especially, during this time when you are in competition and I'm your mentor. Do you think you'll be able to accept me as a coach and director if you win it all?" she whispered.

"I've never had a problem taking direction from you."

"Well, then. We can date, but we shouldn't... um... you know. Not for now."

"We can date, but not have sex," I laughed. "Sounds familiar."

"I know. I know." Tara shook her hands in front of her and bounced in her chair a little. "I'm just so worried about how things will go. Can we do that again?"

Tara's voice went up a notch thinking of the painful time we denied ourselves to each other until after the exhibition. But she was right. We'd been dating for months before we made love in Minneapolis. This was our first date in eight years.

"As long as there's still a chance of kissing," I said. "Tara, I've waited eight years. I'll wait as long as it takes."

"I don't know if I can compete with Sydnie's friendly kisses."

"It's not a competition. All I want is you."

In fact, even if it *was* a competition, Tara would have won, as I found out later that evening.

"WELL? HOW DID it go? Did you spend the weekend together?" Sydnie asked when we met Monday morning.

"Sydnie! No! We had a really good time and I took her home. She had a commitment on Saturday, but we went to brunch Sunday morning. Then we went out to drive through the Valley of Fire. It was really nice."

"But you didn't...?"

"It was our first and second date. It's going to take us a while to get back to where we were."

"But?"

"But we're dating," I said, grinning.

"Yay! I want to kiss you, but I don't want to jinx things. Throw me in the air and catch me instead!"

Sydnie dropped into position for a cannonball. I launched her and she did a tuck salto, coming down into my arms. She glanced left and right and planted a kiss on my lips. It wasn't as deep as Sydnie's friendly kisses were prone to get, but it left us both giggling.

We got to work on our routine for the next show. It required all our focus.

TARA AND I went out the next weekend. At the theatre, we'd seen her nearly every day as we were starting rehearsals on stage and she was there to watch and make sure our props and background were correct. She even had some additional comments on our music and lighting.

We maintained a professional distance while working together. As perceptive as Nicole was, though, I figured she knew something was up.

Tara and I decided to see a couple of the other shows playing in Vegas. We saw one show that was entirely in, on, and over water. We even sat in the splash zone and walked out of the theatre dripping. It was a great show and had been running in Vegas for nearly thirty years. Tara explained that most of the show was the same as it had been when it first opened—before we were born!—but the actors had been replaced over time and sometimes an act was modified for the new performers, each of whom brought some unique talent to the stage.

The next night, we saw a show billed as 'The Sexiest Show in Vegas.' It had also gone through a lot of cast changes and Tara said that, according to her sources, the revue was nothing like the one that opened there years before. Not only had the cast changed, but the music was constantly updated, the routines and costumes changed, and they had cycled new acts in and out rather than keeping the same sequence and trying to get performers to fill existing slots. That was a lot more like they expected the New Trop Revue to be.

We had a great time and capped the nights off with plenty of personal time for kissing and just talking with each other.

Mom and Dad drove up from Sedona for the semi-final. They picked Mikey up at the airport. Poor little Polly was left at home with Rob to watch on TV. This was a live broadcast and the viewers on television were invited to vote via text message. The audience would also vote on their phones.

The key question on the form people filled out was a true or false statement. It said, "I would vacation in Las Vegas to see this act." T/F. The producers were focused on selecting acts that would not only get Las Vegas visitors to our show, but that would draw people to visit Vegas because of our show.

Over the past several years, sports had become the major draw to bring visitors to the city with the prospect that once people were there for a single event, they'd also go to shows, gamble, drink, and carouse. The New Trop was the first 'theme' resort to be built in several years, opting for a retro look rather than the typical glass and steel towers that had been built in the late 20th and early 21st centuries. It was decidedly for adults, as well. You didn't see a bunch of kids running around the grounds.

We didn't really get a chance to see my family before the show. We'd say hi afterward, but would get together the next morning for breakfast at an Egg Nest Restaurant. Sydnie and I were backstage with the other acts who had made it this far. Our position in the order had us working with the trampoline act early in the first act.

"Are you ready for this?" I asked.

"I'm ready. I'm so excited, I might need to kiss someone!" Sydnie said. "Don't worry. I won't embarrass you in front of your girlfriend."

"Thank you for that consideration," I laughed. "We're going to kill them tonight," I said.

The trampoline act was good. It was a little hard to keep track of what was going on because people were flying and flipping all the time. We got our forty-five seconds blending in and then returned backstage to get ready for our acrobatic act.

We didn't go on for our two-person performance—or four with Stef and Jon—until late in the second act. Tara had explained the positioning as being one of the big positives in the minds of the producers. They were saving the best for last. I hoped so.

All the week of the performance, we'd been rehearsing on the stage at the New Trop. That got us used to the scene changes and the space. The tech crew and camera crew all had to get their timing down because the show was broadcast live on Sunday evening. I was surprised at the timing, but while Saturday night shows are a huge draw in Vegas, the best television slot was Sunday evening. We still had a full house.

I felt bad for some of the magic acts. They were closeup acts, meant for an intimate environment. There were no bad seats, but a thousand-seat theatre could not be called intimate. For the live show, of course, cameras were set up all over; the audience could see a closeup view on the big screens on either side of the stage. Those might be missing in the revue that would perform as many as a dozen times a week. I just didn't think those closeup card tricks were going to survive the competition, even though they might be popular with the television audience.

Regardless, we finally got to our performance. In very much the same way that we'd costumed and used Lena and Eva when Sydnie and I did our routine in Florida, we'd costumed Stef and Jon and integrated them into the movement and tricks in our act. They never touched either Sydnie or me unless—God forbid—we fell. So, it was obvious that the act was the two of us. But they scurried around with our equipment and tumbled and posed next to us so they'd be available in the event of a catastrophe.

I honestly didn't know how we'd top this act for the finale. Our philosophy at every level of this competition was to bring the best to the stage and figure out something better for the next round. But everything went perfectly. The audience was shocked to silence when I did a handstand on the rola bola. They gasped when Sydnie started to climb up me, and cheered like maniacs when she stood on her hands on my feet.

I don't think anyone realized how incredibly dangerous this whole act was. When she went to the handstand on my hand while I balanced the board, I almost lost the thing. I managed to keep it in balance only because Sydnie didn't let the move throw her. She maintained her pose and let me worry about the balancing.

"Wow!" Donna Kapelle said when it was time for the judges' comments. "We keep asking you to raise the bar and you keep delivering! That was just wonderful! So exciting! This is definitely an act I would come to Vegas just to see. I think our television audience will agree."

"I agree and just want to watch you work," Ariel Deneuve said. "Not only do I love watching you perform, but I get so inspired! Sam, I'm going to be coming to rehearsals for the revue just to get pointers from these two."

"We might have to restrict access from the competition," Sam Michaels, president of the New Trop, laughed at her. "This is definitely an act we would be proud to have at the New Trop. I can't wait to see what you come up with for the finale."

"Well, yes," Lee Remy, the managing director of the revue, said. "Just based on the work and progress you two have shown us during this competition, it is driving other acts to up their game as well. No one wants to look bad next to Sydnie and Paul. I can say with confidence that the Revue at the New Trop will be the most thrilling and exciting show on The Strip when we open. Television audience, get on those phones now and vote for Sydnie and Paul. This is a must-see."

We got a standing ovation from the audience and finally got off-stage.

This time, Eva and Tara were waiting in the wings for us and Sydnie and I both got really friendly kisses.

"Are you sure they won't hate me?" Tara asked as we headed for breakfast with my parents and sister before Mikey's flight back to Minneapolis.

"Why on earth would they hate you. My family loves you!"

"But I left you. I broke your heart. And I'm so sorry!" she whined.

"Honey, don't even think about that. My family loves you almost as much as I do. A little hiccup in our relationship doesn't change that a bit."

"I wish it was just a little hiccup. Eight years seems like a huge belch."

"But you know what? We're getting ourselves back together. And with the prospect of a real job performing acrobatics, I feel more stable than I've ever been."

"Oh, you'll have the job. I don't get to see the final list, but I was handed the list of acceptable acrobatic acts and told to choose my favorites. I could have one aerial act and one floor act. The list they gave me had the judges' comments and preferences included. We'll hear the results of the audience voting later in the week, but this isn't one of those talent shows that just goes on audience favorites. Lee has to put together a balanced show that will be integrated and will draw a crowd. And he loves you."

"I feel bad for all the magicians," I said. "I know there are shows that are just focused on magic. They have close-up acts."

"Well, if our show was focused on magic, we'd change the setup. The screens on either side would stay and a dedicated camera crew would be hired to rehearse the magic from the correct angles and project it on the big screens. Which might still happen. But it loses something. I know what Lee is looking for is big magic. He wants something that will make people disappear, have a miraculous escape, or saw a person in half. If they can make an elephant disappear, like that guy did a few years ago, so much the better. They'd have to hire a zookeeper, too."

"That would be something to see," I chuckled. "Well, here we are. Let's go meet the parents."

"Tara!" Mikey screamed from across the little restaurant. My sister came running to hug my girlfriend and welcome her back to the family. "You *are* back with the family, aren't you?"

"Paul and I are dating again," Tara said. "I'm the artistic director of the acrobatic acts in the new show. So, I guess we'll be working together, too."

"Does that mean the results are in and Paul and Sydnie won?" Mom asked as we sat at the table.

"There will be an audience selected champion for the show," Tara said, hedging a little. "We won't know who that is until the accounting service has the final tabulation of numbers and informs the judges. But there will actually be eight or ten winning acts who will go on to the revue. I'm pretty sure that whether the audience picks them as the champions or not, Paul and Sydnie will be part of the revue."

"We bought our tickets to the finale before we left the theatre last night," Dad said. "Michelle says Rob and PJ will be able to come, too."

"It's so nice to see you again, Tara," Mom said. "We told you once and we'll tell you again, you're always welcome."

"Thank you so much, Mrs. Bradley. We're taking it slow and patching up some of the rough places we experienced before. We both hope this time we do it right."

"Part of that is having realized this is all I really want," I said. "I was off chasing rainbows, looking for a pot of gold. Or at least a medal of gold. The love of my life was here all along."

"What you are doing with Sydnie is ample justification for all the work and training you had to do," Dad said. "It's a surprise to me how you've developed all this."

"That's something else, though," I said. "I didn't think I wanted to get involved in acrobatics and circus acts. I thought it was all about winning the gold medal at the Olympics. But when I saw Sydnie in the gym and heard about what happened to her team—to Lena—it was just a compulsion in me. I *had* to become her partner. I had to lift that girl up and twirl her around on my fingers. I needed to do it for *her*. And it turns out, it was the best for me, too."

"The strongest in the pack are there to help and protect the weak," Dad said. It was like a light coming on in my mind. He'd said that when I was a 68-pound weakling. I always looked up to him as the strong protector of our pack.

"Are you happy doing the performances?" Mom asked.

"Insanely!"

"You certainly upped the danger level on this performance," Mikey said. "What's next? Will you be walking through fire for the finale or will you do a combination of the acts you've done so far?"

I looked at Tara. I expected she would let me know what was expected for the finale.

"A little of both," she said. *Fire???* "We'll pick some of the favorites from the first three performances. The flying entrance across the stage comes to mind. Also, Sydnie's springboard mount to Paul's shoulders. Probably a little bit of dance. But I want to shape it into something fresh. Do you juggle, Paul?"

"Um... a little, I guess. I mean, I've taken a lot of training in most of the circus arts, so I'm not ready to juggle chainsaws, but I can keep three or four balls in the air."

"How about people?"

"What?"

"I've got an idea, but you'll have to be straight with both Sydnie and me before we can go with it. We only have a month to rehearse and it involves props and setting."

Tara started describing what she had in mind and it blew us away!

27
FINALE!

"WHEN PAUL AND I worked together years ago, I was trying to show people I could still perform. But he had to do all the lifting, carrying, throwing, and balancing in the act. He made me look great," Tara had said in our first coaching session after the semi-final. "What I want to know is if you can become a mannequin, Sydnie. The concept for this next piece is that Paul will juggle mannequins, including you. But you can't let on that you have any flexibility at all until he's discarded all the other mannequins. He will juggle you and them before you reveal that you aren't one of the dolls."

"Oh, God! I love the idea! Can you do that, Paul? I mean juggle people?" Sydnie asked.

"I think so. You're really light as a feather."

"I know that I weighed thirty pounds more than you do when Paul was throwing me around," Tara said. "But we'll need to figure out how much he can endure before he has to stop juggling and start performing acrobatics."

"I assume you have music in mind for this?" Nicole asked.

"We'll want to use live music made just for this act," Tara said. "Like you did when you were performing, Nicole. Percussion, vocal, and whatever else we think we need. The rudiments of the act will need to be plotted out before we bring in the musicians. To some extent, they'll be able to improv a little if anything goes wrong and shifts in any way."

"I like that. Now, you should all know that I was offered a position as coach for the revue," Nicole said. "I have declined. I have a business and it doesn't run itself. Once your act is perfected and you start performing in the revue, you'll have little need for a coach. Tara will be your director. Whenever you feel you need some work or want a new element, you can come here to the gym and I'll work with you."

"Gosh, Nicole. You've been a great coach. I'm sad you won't continue working with us," I said. Our agent had called us that morning to tell us she was in negotiations for our contract. Regardless of the outcome of the finale, we would be part of the New Trop Revue.

"Well, for good or ill, you aren't rid of Stef and me so easily," Jon said. "You've really integrated the two of us into the routines and we've passed the dancing audition, so when you sign your contract, we'll be joining the chorus when we aren't supporting you."

"That's wonderful," Sydnie said, laying a friendly kiss on each of our spotters.

"No offense, but you know we're kind of more into each other than... um... girls," Stef said.

"Yeah, well, I'm married to a girl. I get it," Sydnie laughed.

"Okay. Let's see what you can do. I'd suggest working on thick mats for a while before moving to the hardwood," Tara said.

We worked our buns off. I would be juggling in this act, but I'd be tossing mannequins around and Sydnie would be one of them. Our first effort was just to get Sydnie to stay stiff as I threw her around and balanced her. Then I practiced just juggling the mannequins. They weren't as heavy as Sydnie, but weighed more for their size than I expected. We received a shipment of the dummies that were about the same size as Sydnie. I realized they were child mannequins!

WE HAD FOUR weeks to prepare our new act. That included rehearsals nearly every day at the theatre, while scene designers and technicians and musicians worked on every aspect of our performance. Of course, our rehearsals in the theatre didn't last all day. There were a dozen acts to rehearse.

They were splitting things up a little. The show would begin with a master of ceremonies introducing the show and the four judges to an unreasonable amount of cheering from the audience. I think they must have big signs that flash "Cheer Now!" to everyone when they want a lot of noise. Then the MC would give a run-down of the acts and each performer would come out to do a little something. We were interviewed by the script-writers who turned our conversations into an intro for our act.

Of course, the time we had on stage was not nearly the rehearsal time we needed. Either before or after our call time on stage, we were back at the gym working with our team to make everything perfect.

We were working six days a week on the new program.

Tara's and my date time amounted to a little kiss when we saw each other at the theatre and Sunday brunch. Usually, we managed a walk or a movie. Once we went to a play, but that month we steered clear of the big shows in Vegas. We had a big show of our own to deal with.

And finally, the grand finale arrived. We took our places for the introductory run, and were the first to make an entrance.

"IN 2028, GYMNAST Paul Bradley was disqualified from the Olympics after doing a hair-raising routine on the floor," the MC announced. "He was disqualified because the routine was *too dangerous* for the Olympics. Tonight, doing that same routine, is three-time national champion, Olympics qualifier and silver medalist, and European Challenge champion in floor exercises, we introduce to you Paulllll Bradley!"

That was my cue. I bounced down the tumbling mat with a double forward with a half twist, into a single back flip, and bouncing high to do my two-and-a-half with a one-and-a-half out to land on my hands just beyond the springboard. The board wasn't for me. It was for Sydnie. I stayed solid on my hands as the MC announced my partner.

"Performing with Paul this evening is three-time national women's acrobatic group champion, and two-times world champion, Sydnie Cragg!"

By that time, Sydnie was already into her line down the track. She hit the springboard hard and went high into the air with a single layback, to land on her feet, on my feet in the air. There was a lot of applause and she jumped from my feet to the track and tumbled down it. I sprang from my hands to the track and did a series of back flips until I reached the end and jumped into the wings.

Our spotters and a couple of other techs scrambled to remove our equipment and reset the stage for the intro of the next act.

"Wrists okay?" Sydnie asked as I removed the wraps I used when I did that routine. There was no sense spraining or breaking them if I could protect against it.

"Fine. I hardly felt it. I kept wondering when you were going to land and then you were off and going down the track ahead of me!"

"I know you're stronger now than when we started working together, but you've always been dependable. Are you good for the big routine?"

"Yes, Mommy. We've got more than an hour to rest before we do our new routine. Are you ready for it?" I asked.

"I'm stoked. I just hope I can remain stiff until the reveal."

"You're fantastic. The mannequins are heavy enough that it makes switching to you less stressful. If I was going from something that weighed ten pounds to you, there might be more shock to it."

We found a quiet spot in the ready room and Sydnie curled up like a cat on my chest and went to sleep. I tried not to snore.

And there we were, at the beginning of the second act, while the crew had plenty of time to set the stage for us during intermission. It was amazing what they could do with projections behind us. They made the entire stage look like a warehouse. Boxes were piled on one side—all of which would support our weight, so we could jump on them and climb them. On the other side were a dozen mannequins, three of which were Sydnie, Steffan, and Jon. All the mannequins were dressed in variations of gymnastic uniforms and dance dresses. Their faces were all made up like dolls.

The curtain went up and I entered as our musical accompanists joined in. I was in coveralls and was pushing a broom around the floor, occasionally pausing to execute a few dance steps with my broom as daydreams filled my head.

Then the broom hit a mannequin and it started to fall. I dropped the broom and caught the mannequin in my arms to take it dancing. Of course, the more active my dance became, the more mannequins got involved. I was dancing and tossing the plastic dolls, keeping them in the air and upright. At that time, Stef and Jon became involved, grabbing mannequins and tossing them to me. I did several moves, including backflips, climbing the boxes to catch a mannequin that went high in the air, and tossing mannequins into spins and loops—catching them and balancing them on my hands.

I don't think anyone caught on when Sydnie was tossed up onto my hands. She just stayed stiff and erect like the other mannequins as I did a few throws and flips. But it was only a minute before Stef and Jon had the other mannequins organized in their rows and stripped me of my coveralls. I was wearing tight pants and was shirtless, so there were a few appreciative gasps.

Then I threw Sydnie especially high and she flipped out of her stiff mannequin pose and landed on my hands. I held her there as we did a couple of poses to let the audience know my accomplice was real and not a doll. Then we cut loose with the real acrobatic tricks, throwing her to the top level of the boxes and then catching her as she did a double pike position salto from the boxes to my hands again. Stef and Jon moved to put two springboards in position and Sydnie and I did a couple of the passes we'd done on the trampolines, bouncing from one springboard to the other and landing in the middle with her feet on my shoulders.

She posed there atop me and moved to a one-hand stand on my head. Stef and Jon moved to where they could catch us, which was an indication that we were about to do something extraordinary. With Sydnie balanced on my head, I mounted the stack of boxes. The auditorium went silent except for a weird bit of vocalese from our musicians, building to a dramatic peak. Then we jumped. We hit our springboards and did a salto out. I caught Sydnie in my arms as the audience roared to life. We stepped forward to take our bows and to acknowledge our assistants. It was a standing ovation and when I set Sydnie down to take her bow, it was the first time her feet had touched the floor.

"Sydnie and Paul, ladies and gentlemen," the MC shouted over the tumult. That just got a bigger round of applause.

"You just keep upping the level," Ariel said. "I have never seen anything like this! I can't wait to buy a ticket for the revue when it opens. I will be bouncing in my seat through your entire performance."

"Yes! I would definitely make a trip to Las Vegas just to see Sydnie and Paul," Donna said. "Congratulations on a superb performance."

"What I want to know is if we have enough insurance on these two," Sam said. "Not only because they are risking everything with their performances, but because we will be out millions in revenue if anything happens to them."

"This is what it is all about," Lee said. "I could create an entire revue around you two. In fact, I might. The setting, the integration of props and your assistants, the incredible juggling. I don't think I've ever seen someone juggle people before. Are you sure you are the only ones who are alive on that stage? When Sydnie came to life, I was sure you would have all the mannequins start performing. Amazing! Thank you."

"Thank you all," Sydnie said. "And thank you to my wonderful partner, Paul, and our assistants, Steffan and Jon."

There was more cheering as we left the stage.

THAT WASN'T ALL. There was still what the producers called 'the popularity contest.' It had nothing at all to do with whether or not we would be in the revue. In fact, we'd signed our contracts the week before. Our agent had gotten us 'star' billing and income. But this was the part when everyone was brought onto stage and the three top vote-getters from the TV audience voting were called forward. We were all told that not even the judges knew who had won the popularity contest.

"And now, that moment we've all been waiting for," the MC announced. "While every act you have seen this evening will be a part of the opening of our New Trop Revue, the television audience has voted for their favorite. The winner of this vote will receive an immediate $50,000 bonus and will receive top billing on all show advertising, billboards, and in the program. Here are the three finalist acts. First, the Great Illusion, our magician and his lovely assistant Rita. Next, that lovely and delectable mermaid in a glass, Ondine! And finally, the soon-to-be world famous acrobats, Sydnie and Paul, with their assistants, Steffan and Jon."

Everyone was clapping and it looked to me like the party had already started at the VIP tables up front. Bottles of champagne were being opened all the way around. Of course, we had to take a commercial break before the final announcement.

I thought The Great Illusion was an incredible act. He did make his lovely assistant Rita disappear. He also waved a cloth in front of her and she completely changed her wardrobe. He had big illusions that even included having Ariel join him on stage and sawing her in half. That was quite an illusion. Especially, since he used a chainsaw!

Ondine was a beautiful woman who did dance and acrobatic swimming in a giant champagne glass. For broadcast on the network, she had to keep a demure pair of seashells positioned over her breasts. I understood, however, that the actual act would be topless, as would some of the other acts in the revue.

We were back from commercial break.

"And now, the moment we've all been waiting for." The MC tore open the envelope. "Ondine!" Everyone started to applaud, but the MC wasn't finished yet. "You are not one of the final two." There were a lot of 'aww' from the audience, but I don't think any of them were too upset or surprised. Ondine exited. "The Great Illusion vs. Sydnie and Paul. Here is who the television audience has selected." Dramatic pause. "Sydnie and Paul!"

I thought we had a good chance at winning, based on the response of the live audience, but I didn't expect it to affect me in quite the same way. I'd never stood on a podium to receive a gold medal that choked me up so completely. I picked Sydnie up and swung her around as she clung tightly to me. I was tempted to toss her into the air, but I restrained myself.

We'd done it! Not only did we have a year's contract to perform in the revue with an incredible salary, but we'd just won $50,000, top billing, and the approval of the audience, both live and on television. Tara and Nicole both joined us on stage as the judges came up to congratulate the finalists and the rest of the cast. The music swelled to a crescendo as the MC encouraged people to come to Vegas to see the newest and most spectacular variety show on The Strip: The New Trop Revue, starring Sydnie and Paul!

WE WENT DOWN to the VIP tables to greet my family and Eva and all celebrated with a glass of champagne. It was well after midnight before we actually left the theatre. I noticed two security guys stayed close to us when we went down to our families' table and kept us from being totally mobbed by fans.

Eventually, we managed to get out of the theatre and on our way to our homes. I was driving Tara home as I'd often done in the past month. She was really quiet as we drove and I assumed she was as exhausted as everyone else after the intense month.

"Paul, would you like to come in for a while?" Tara said as I pulled up to her house out in Summerlin. I'd dropped her off on numerous occasions and the gate opened automatically when I pulled up. Tara had left a remote in my car. "By a while, I mean to spend the night?"

"You mean...? I mean... Are you sure?"

"Oh, God! I've been sure ever since I saw you at your audition. I just wanted to avoid distracting you from your partner and your goal. Please come in with me."

"I will. I have to tell you: I love Sydnie as my partner. I know we've talked about how much she needs to trust me. But I discovered I needed to trust her, too. She's a rock and I want to perform with her for many years. But my goal? My goal has always been to be with you, Tara. My love has never waned, even when we were parted," I said.

I carried her to her door like I had to my door years before. She unlocked her house and I entered what was slightly less than a mansion, but considerably more than what my family had lived in.

"Wow! This place is huge," I said.

"Well, the lower level is occupied by my assistant," Tara said. "I don't need the constant care that I needed when you met Jennifer and me. But Enid is my cook and housekeeper, and is usually on call if I need any other assistance."

"Usually?"

"I don't make her work 24/7," Tara laughed. "For example, once I left for the theatre today, she was off until tomorrow. She might be home; she might not. I don't ask what she does with her time off. She has family in the valley. I knew, though, that I'd have someone else to lean on tonight if I needed him. And I do need him. I love you, Paul."

"And I love you," I responded firmly. Then we got lost in a kiss long enough that I forgot I was still carrying her.

"I'll give you a tour tomorrow. For now, the bedroom is that way," she said. I carried her there.

UNDRESSING WITH TARA was like the first time. There was a sense of awe and discovery for both of us. She traced my muscles with her fingers and I caressed her with mine. I helped her out of her knee braces and held her as we stepped into the shower. I'd been working pretty hard all day and I was sure my body smelled like it. Tara pretended not to notice, and I pretended not to notice that she'd been sweating during our entire performance.

We kissed and fondled in the shower until we were nearly prunes. She had two big bath towels ready. I'd noticed my preferred brand of shampoo was in the shower with hers. On the sink, I found an electric toothbrush with my type of toothpaste sitting next to hers. It seemed she'd been preparing to have me there.

After I'd carefully and lovingly dried her with the huge fluffy towel, I carried her to the bed and pulled the spread and sheet down. I carefully put her into bed and she pulled me with her. She was still amazingly strong. I fell in with her and we began kissing with more fervent passion.

"You worked so hard tonight with Sydnie on stage. You were wonderful," Tara said. "Are you sure you have enough strength left to make love to me?"

"Oh yes. I've discovered a lot lately. I'm strong. But being strong for Sydnie doesn't leave me weak for you. I will always give my strength to you," I said.

"Then love me. Love me. Love me."

It had been a long time since I'd been with anyone—more than a year since I left Bulgaria and began preparing for the Brisbane Olympics. I was afraid I wouldn't last long enough to satisfy her. It had been at least as long for Tara, though. She'd directed the acrobatics for last year's revue, and students before that, so she had moved to Las Vegas over three years ago. She'd been alone at least that entire time.

When I kissed my way down her body, she parted

her legs and I feasted on her nectar until she'd found her first release. It was so wonderful to taste her and love her. It did nothing to relax my own condition, but Tara pulled me up to her and guided me immediately into her.

"I don't want to wait," she said. "I don't care if it's fast or slow. I know there will be more after this."

I could hardly hear her over the pounding of my pulse in my ears. This. This was all I wanted or needed forever. I moved in her and she moved to match me. It wasn't over as quickly as I feared it would be, but it wasn't more than most men last. I'd read the average coitus was only four and a half minutes. When I exploded, Tara gripped me tightly to her and I discovered we were both in tears.

"Again, love. Keep moving in me and let's do it again. I've waited so long for this."

I had, too, and my cock was showing no signs of wanting to be released from her. We slid together and rolled to a position with her on top. I held her tiny waist as she moved up and down on me, slowly bringing us again to that peak we shared as lovers.

"I love you, Tara. I love you more than the world."

"As I love you, Paul. Please, let's never part again."

"I promise."

WE SLEPT IN each other's arms and woke in the morning for another round. Then Tara pushed at me.

"Shower!" she said. "We don't have much time!"

"What?" I asked as I supported her into the shower for a quick rinse. "What are we hurrying for?" I kissed her and continued petting her under the stream of water.

"I invited your parents and sister and Sydnie and Eva over for brunch! We shouldn't actually still be making love when they get here!"

"You knew I'd still be here?"

"Paul, I knew—I prayed—you would be here forever. I bought this house for us. When I did it, it was a day-dream. I wanted it so badly, I let myself believe it was possible. And now it is. Please don't ever leave me."

"I wouldn't even dream of leaving you." I kissed her and gently dried her, helping her into her knee braces before I turned to get dressed myself. "Um... I don't have any clothes to change into. I'll have to wear what I had on last night."

"No, you won't. I didn't buy you a whole new ward-robe, but there are a couple pairs of slacks and a couple of shirts in the closet. Underwear is in that drawer. I didn't want you to have any reason to leave once you got here. We can go get your things from that little hotel room you call an apartment later. Am I being too pushy?"

"You know what? I don't mind that you thought of all this. I don't care! Everything you've suggested is some-thing I've dreamed of. I love you. Let's go make brunch and meet the family."